For Jules, my spooky muse

NEVERBORN

Tom Newton

© Copyright Tom Newton 2024

1
Circling the Drain

'Life is a prank played when you're not looking.' Stephen White stated, trying his best not to slur his speech.

The barman nodded patiently enough, but Stephen could already tell that he had not only lost the attention of the man that had been serving him drinks since five, he had also been bleating and complaining so long that the man likely hated him by this point. Regardless, lost in his own miserable narrative and putting another pound note on the bar, he continued as the barman poured another pint.

'Think about it.' Stephen jabbed a finger at the barman's back as he tossed the crumpled note into the till and retrieved eleven pence change. 'When you're young, you think you're going to live forever. All you want to do is grow up and be an adult so you can do whatever you want. You spend twenty years growing, or waiting to grow, then suddenly you're somewhere around thirty and you realise…'

Stephen paused his unheard sermon long enough to clumsily stab a cigarette between his lips and light it.

'…you realise that you've peaked, and that you're now on the downhill slope.' He went on as the barman, with the weariest of expressions, unceremoniously slammed the pint down in front of him, spilling a little froth, with the glass handle facing him. 'So, in all of this wretched short life of ours, we spend half of it waiting to grow, then the other half dying. And the bit that's been driving me mad is the uncertainty of knowing *when that transition hit*. Like, when were you in your prime? Likely, you missed it. It's like, it's the most important thing in the world, but it's all so damned vague and indeterminable that it's impossible to know. Waiting to live, then waiting to die. It all passes you by and you don't even notice. So, yeah,' he concluded with a satisfied grimace, 'life is a prank played when you're not looking, and by the time you realise that, it's too late.'

Stephen, satisfied with himself, chugged half of the pint in one smooth draw. Then he puffed on the *Regal King Size* so hard that the burning ember on the end turned into a long glowing spear. He emitted a barrage of blue smoke into the dimly lit bar, and just like a magician on the stage, by the time it cleared the barman had completely disappeared.

'Poof!' Stephen let out a snort and waved his cigarette like a magic wand. He looked around the pub, turning on the circular bar stool, his head still spinning long after the stool had stopped its rotation.

The Green Dragon had been his local since he was old enough to drink. In fact, truth be known, since *before* he was old enough. He and his mates had been getting up to drunken mischief since they were sixteen and seventeen. He must have looked old for his age. God only knew what he must look like to other people now.

There were a couple of regulars – men much older and far more drowned in drink than he – propped up against the long bar, white beards stained brown at the lips by roll-ups and best bitter, bloodshot eyes and skin like worn leather. Dock workers that in their youth would be piled into the rusty green Transit buses that left at dawn, bound for Middlesbrough. Now their arms were thin and their fingers shook, and heavy guts hung in stained shirts over their belts.

Stephen was looking into the future. Those tired old creatures at the other end of the bar represented his endgame, and the length of polished wood that separated them was like a timeline that was growing all too short.

Beyond the bar was a few steps down into the rest of the pub. A jukebox wailed so loudly at the far end that it was a wonder the kids down there could hear themselves think. Kids with big peroxide hair and stonewashed denim, white trainers on the tables, colourful shirts and loud mouths laughed and bawled and sang as if there wasn't a care nor a fear on earth that could touch them. Stephen couldn't watch for long. It made him want to weep.

He turned his attention from the kids with their colourful drinks and the jukebox from which Kylie Minogue sang about how she should be so *lucky, lucky, lucky*, and gazed out through the frosted-glass windows behind him. The cobbles were lethal in the Green Dragon Yard at this time of year, and many a drunken fool – himself most definitely included – had slipped and cracked a rib or a knee on the smooth cobblestones, frozen over by rain and plummeting temperatures so that it was more like an ice rink than a walkway.

It was ten, and he'd been drinking since five.

Beyond this quaint little yard, a reminder of better years when horses and carriages had clopped and trundled along those cobbles, was a much modernised high street, broad and long. There was a market every Saturday with sellers hollering and old ladies in headscarves elbowing each other out of the way for a bargain, a tall town hall at the centre whose clock distantly and dolefully informed him now of the time, and soon there would be his last bus home pulling in outside of the Woolworths superstore which wasn't a stone's throw from where he sat.

Stockton-on-Tees had seen better days. Stephen White remembered them. He remembered seeing The Stones and The Beatles at the Stockton Globe in the sixties, he remembered the beautiful old cars, glossy and smooth and dazzling in the summer sun. He remembered Leslie Brown's, the toyshop he would peer into as Christmas neared, his nose against the glass as he gazed into the multicoloured lights of the magical grotto within, and Essoldo of course, the old cinema house that his dad would take him to every Sunday night.

His father, Robert White, Bobby to everyone, had been a good father. He and Stephen's mother, Beryl, had given him a perfectly good childhood. They were a council estate family through and through, but not once could Stephen ever remember wanting for anything. Christmases were magical and cozy places in the dim haze of his memory, lit by red and green twinkling lights and the smell of cooking early in the morning. His school life was unremarkable. He had the usual bunch of friends in primary school, football and playing *kissy-girl-run*, sweltering summers in grey shorts and scabby knees, and all the rest. Some of those same friends moved up into secondary school with him, some moved away, but come age sixteen and nine GCSE's later, he one by one lost touch with all of them.

His dad had worked at the ICI – a huge chemical works and industrial plant that lined the horizon from one end to the other, spewing white and grey clouds of some foul smelling substance into the blue skies over their poor little town, where they produced petrol and ammonia and gasses and such. His mother had been a housewife since he could remember, but for one stint for a couple of years in a bakers on the high street. He had always preferred it when she was home. She had been his rock when his father died, like so many of those men did, from some dastardly and cruel lung disease as a result of working with chemicals, the names of which he had never known and never cared to learn.

He had stayed with his mother, he needing the familiarity of her and their home just as much as her needing the distraction from her grief through caring for him, for many years after. By the time the sixties became the seventies, with Stephen turning twenty-four and his mother approaching fifty, he was still at home. Though by then he was staying more out of guilt than for the wanting of it. He couldn't bear to leave her alone. His older brother had already left by then.

But, in the mid-seventies, Stephen had met Angela, and...

'Bloody 'ell, cheer up Whitey!' Bellowed one of the men at the other end of the bar. The others roared with laughter as Stephen was abruptly shaken from his stupor, stopped staring out glassy-eyed through the window of the pub, and snapped back to reality as he dropped his cigarette and nearly fell off his stool.

He was on that bar stool in The Green Dragon every night as soon as he finished work, until the place closed and the last bus home called. So often, in fact, that the locals had taken to nicknaming him *Whitey*, and even given him a catchphrase, which one of them had just hollered in his ear. That's what he was to them; a one-dimensional joke. A part of the furniture. A nobody.

He sneered to himself as he reached down to retrieve the cigarette, which by then had burned out, spilling ash all over his best pressed trousers. He brushed himself down as he stood, ignoring the rabble of old folk and the jukebox which now proclaimed *I think we're alone now*, and finished the other half of his pint in another single gulp. He turned and made for the door, his head swimming and his heart heavy.

Yeah, cheer up, Whitey.

The door swung closed behind him as he stepped out onto icy cobbles. The cold took his breath away, making him gasp. He blew out a plume of frozen air and he pulled his long overcoat around him. The streetlamps were hazy with frost which hung statically in the air, haloed in the glow. There were benches in the small yard, of course unoccupied in February, and to the left and right of him two alleyways. To the left was the path that took you down to the River Tees, to the right was a snaking alley that lead to the high street. He took this path, coughing as the cold caught in his throat as he went.

He was starving. Hadn't eaten since lunch. No wonder he was so drunk. He was drunk every night now. It was all he could think to do. It was all that stopped the pain. If he was numb, then he couldn't feel. If he was unconscious, then he couldn't think. He didn't want to think or feel anything outside of work, so booze was the only answer he could come up with. Work was good. Work was hard and distracting and time consuming, but as soon as five rolled around work was over, and then it was time for reality to return. The reality in which he'd lost everything. So, he would drink reality away, go home, pass out, and get up and go to work. This method had worked well for about six months, but he could tell it wouldn't work much longer.

He was on the high street now. He passed by the window of a *Wimpy* burger place, briefly considered buying something for the bus ride home, but the twist of nausea in his stomach informed him that this was far from a good suggestion. Checking the time by glancing up at the towering town hall clock, he realised that he was a little early for his bus, so he trotted across the wide road and stood outside of a *Curry's* electronics store. It was long closed and the shutters down, but a tv remained on in the window, flickering silently on the iced glass of the shopfront. Margaret Thatcher and Neil Kinnock were yelling and gesturing at one another from opposite sides of the houses of parliament. Would that bloody woman ever be out of power? His father had hated the Tories. All working classes did. It had been that way since he could remember.

Even though Stephen White was a senior editor at *The Evening Gazette,* a local paper whose offices were nearby on Brunswick Street, he had never cared much for nor shown interest in politics. At least, not in the world at large. The wide world seemed far removed from their small-town temperament, and seemed of little consequence. All he ever needed to be concerned with was the doings of the local council, crime rates, sports results, and jobs classifieds.

He'd worked in that office all his life. His first job out of school had been delivering bundles of the Gazette to local businesses on a Moped scooter. Then, with a foot in the door, he'd become an office boy – little more than a tea maker. Eventually a junior assistant, and so on until now he was among the senior editors. And there he had stayed. Nowhere else to climb. But, he had gotten comfortable with it. Perhaps too comfortable. Just like in The Green Dragon, he was now as much a part of the furniture as his well-worn desk.

He smoked as the politicians argued, until eventually the colour tv changed to coverage of the Winter Olympics, which were taking place in Canada. Great Britain and Ireland were competing, but, much like the cloak and dagger doings of the Tories, he had never much cared for, nor developed any passion for things like sport.

His focus shifting, the tv in the window became a blur and instead he found himself looking at his reflection in the glass.

Stephen was forty-four (soon to be five), tall and thin. He wore a nice enough suit and his tie cost more than he would admit to anyone, but he certainly didn't stand out. At least, not to his mind. He was happy to go unnoticed. He retained a decent head of hair, short, neat and slicked, though greying at the temples. His beard had already turned completely grey, and so these days he remained clean shaven. This would only keep him looking younger than his years for so long, he knew, but for now he was happy to keep up the pretence. He repeatedly told himself that forty-four is *not old*, but by his demeanour, the way that he dressed and carried himself, one would be forgiven for thinking him somewhere more in his fifties. He looked like his dad had. Dad in his prime at the factory, not *thin and wheezing in the sour-smelling dark bedroom* dad.

Stephen shuddered and the cigarette trembled between numb fingers.

You're circling the drain, Steve.

Cheer up, Whitey.

He crossed the road again, throwing the cigarette onto the tarmac, and stood at the bus stop. There wasn't a soul about. It was like a ghost town. The stars were crisp and clear and the cold bit hard. The air was still and seemed frozen in place around him, piercing right through his overcoat and suit jacket. Warmth seemed impossible. The bus was due, but nowhere in sight. He sighed, his mind already turning towards the bottle of whiskey in the cupboard under the sink at home. Only then could sleep come.

Home was, in keeping with the family way, a flat on a council estate about a mile outside of town. The bus would trundle along the length of Norton Road for some time, leaving town behind and passing rows of locals shops and streets crammed with houses, a large cemetery, whose gloomy grey headstones would sweep by like a solemn parade in the dark, then industrial units, a large garage advertising cheap MOT's, then his stop. Then a long (and sometimes treacherous, depending on what kids were hanging around) walk along what was locally called *The Black Path*, a backroad that lead to his estate; Tilery. It was cheap, but it was home. He lived on the corner of *Craister Court,* a tucked-away little corner of the world where working families and the unemployed raised their families. It was friendly enough, as long as you knew which parts to avoid after dark. High wooden-fenced gardens with overgrown grass, a little square of stony asphalt where the kids would play and ride their bikes until called indoors for dinner, woodchip wallpaper and electric fires, black bins put out every other Monday.

'I am fucking miserable here.' Stephen whispered without emotion. The purity of the statement startled him. Until those words flowed easily from his lips, he hadn't realised the simple truth of them. 'I hate my life here, and I am fucking miserable.'

He nodded, then let out a breath as a vast weight seemed to lift from his chest. Only pure truth can do that, he thought to himself as his bus approached, and oftentimes the purest truths are the simplest.

So Stephen carried this new truth with him onto the number 94 to Norton, and quite without self-delusion told himself that tomorrow he would change his life. Tomorrow he would make steps, however small, to escape this place and to make a new life while he still had the chance.

But first, there's the whiskey in the cupboard underneath the sink. Sleep first, change life tomorrow.

Stephen White repeated and forgot this process every night for many months, and would continue to do so for just two more nights. It would take a miracle, or a horror, to shake him from his cycle.

The bus doors hissed closed, and the vehicle rumbled away into the dark.

2
A Miracle

Stephen's desk was small and rather chipped. You couldn't really see the poor state of it, however, as it was almost always covered by a sea of stacked papers, pens and staplers, and old issues of The Gazette. Somewhere beneath it all there was an *in* tray and an *out* tray but they had been lost to time and legend. Myth told of a plaque that had his name and job title on it, but the truth behind it would never be uncovered, much like his desk.

It was a little after nine and Stephen was sitting ready, newly-ironed suit proudly worn, to meet with the editor-in-chief, Simon Matthews. He had no hangover whatsoever, despite the generous whiskey that he had enjoyed before falling asleep in front on his tv, blacking out to the tune of a late night movie followed by crackling static. Stephen didn't have hangovers anymore.

Simon Matthews was a fair enough boss if you stayed on the right side of him. Stephen had seen the wrath of Mr Matthews when someone had displeased him, and the lengths he would go to to make someone's life a professional living hell were well known in all of the offices of the building. Stephen had always kept his head down, despite his high position, had always avoided any kind of run in with the EIC, and had generally escaped his notice altogether. But that morning he had arrived at work, last night's musings and revelations wiped clean like a blank tape cassette, to the news that Matthews was popping down from the top office to have a word with him about something.

He told himself that he did not care. That he was unshaken by such news, and that there was nothing to fear. Nevertheless his blood ran cold, his stomach tightened and his mouth went bone dry. He was not accustomed to any kind of confrontation anymore. That had not been true once. Once, he had been brash and bold, strong of character, even. Now, he just wanted to blend in, to go unnoticed. He just wanted to get through the day so he could get to The Green Dragon.

Stephen's office was grey and beige, made of steel filing cabinets and ugly floral wallpaper the colour of oranges left out in the sun. Even the circular dial phone on his desk was a sickly dark green, the colour of stomach bile. He dreaded answering it, but then, it hardly ever rang.

Gordon tapped the door twice and stuck his head in to ask whether Stephen wanted him to run the article about the new nightclub they were building, or was that more of a weekend story? Also, that fatal hit-and-run on Oxbridge Avenue had finally turned up a culprit so they were running with that for the headline along with local outrage and *what can we do to stop the scourge of drink-driving* etc. There were other things too, but Stephen had drifted away during those, merely nodding and dismissively saying 'sounds good' before Gordon gave him an unenthusiastic thumbs up and left.

Perhaps he was being too pessimistic. As far as he knew his work had been satisfactory, his deadlines always met, his articles thorough and coherent. Perhaps Matthews wanted to speak to him of more responsibility, a rise further through the esteemed ranks of their humble hierarchy. That was good. It would mean more work, longer hours, a greater distraction. Perhaps work could replace the alcohol entirely. Perhaps that was the way out.

'Come off it.' He heard his own voice, strangely thin sounding in the confines of his poky little office. 'There is no way out.'

He plucked an ashtray out from underneath a pile of papers and lit a cigarette. A spill of smoke curled around the strip light that forever buzzed like a dying fly above his head. He sighed and rubbed his eyes. Then the stomach bile phone rang.

He jumped and stared at it. It rang so scarcely that the brash resonance of it sounded alien. He plucked the receiver from the harness, fumbled with the twisted and knotted curled cord, then held it to his ear.

'Evening Gazette,' he said, 'Stephen White's office.'

'Steve, it's me.'

The shock of hearing Angela's voice seemed to enter at his ear and bounce around the inside of his skull like a bullet. He swallowed dryly and gripped the receiver hard.

'Angela.' He said, recovering enough of his voice to feign civility.

'Look,' she said quickly, 'I know it's been a while, and I know I'm the last person you want to hear from...'

His voice lurched out of him before his brain could even engage.

'A while?' He replied sharply. 'You could say that, or you could say that we haven't exchanged a word since the funeral.' With that, silence and static occupied the other end of the line for some time. At least she didn't hang up. That was a first.

'I wanted you to know that the divorce papers have gone through.' Her voice had become as cold as steel and more businesslike than he had ever heard it. Angela worked for the local council, and he had heard such corporate tones before, but never directed at him. What a wonderful shield that must be to have, he mused, wondering how a heart could get so hard. 'The money is split from the house sale, the legal specifications, all of it. It's done, Steve. You'll receive the paperwork in full, the money, and all the rest shortly.'

The first thing he felt was a longing that disgusted him. Longing for her at the sound of her voice, then despising himself for allowing that feeling to surface. Then, naturally followed the rage. Rage at what had happened, rage at what she had done, rage at her leaving him after what she had done, rage at himself for lying down and accepting it. Finally came the grief, but he would not let it in. He could not allow that horror to manifest. He closed his eyes tight and held the phone with knuckles turned white and fingers turned red.

'It's a lot of money.' She said icily. 'That has to count for something.'

Stephen had been married to Angela for over ten years, and engaged to her for three years preceding it. He knew every little subtle tone and inflection of her voice, every pore on her skin, every shift in the expression of her eyes. So, it was easy for him to hear the falter in her voice as the words *count for something* sounded out with failing bravado. He shook his head gently and snorted sharply and mirthlessly.

'It counts for nothing.' He responded. 'I don't want money. I want...' but he stopped before he humiliated himself further.

The grief was still pressing upon his heart. It burned like hot coal, just sitting there in the cavity of his chest, leaning against the pulsing muscle, making every beat a painful one. Then his stomach was falling. He was getting dangerously close to thinking about what he had lost. What he and Angela had lost. If he allowed that then his stomach would keep on falling forever, dragging the rest of him down with it. They never tell you how grief never loses its power. They always tell you that time will heal. Suddenly, as if in an automatic act of self-preservation, his mind filled with an image of his barstool at The Dragon, dark and smoky and drenched in the safe burning heat of booze.

Stephen opened his eyes, and despite the tempest that raged behind his ribs he simply answered with 'thank you for letting me know' and he hung up.

He stared at the phone as if it was a snake, not daring to move in case it struck again. Eventually he relaxed – it was clear that it wasn't going to ring. He plucked the cigarette from the ashtray and resumed smoking.

That was it, then. It was over and done with. All of those years, all of that sacrifice, struggle, celebration, triumph, misery and joyous love was now flatlined. Gone, as if it never happened. Time is the most valuable currency one has to spend, and Stephen White felt that he had thrown away a fortune.

Cheer up, Whitey.

'Oh, fuck you!' He hollered in response to his own broken brain.

'Is... this a bad time?' Said Simon Matthews.

Stephen's head darted to the door, through which his boss was poking his, and stared at him for a matter of a second, which to him felt like an hour. He blinked and stammered 'oh, oh not at all, Simon! I do... I do apologise. The, ah, the phone...'

Simon Matthews smiled. It wasn't warm nor reassuring, but a smile, nonetheless.

'The ex-wife, eh?' He grinned.

'Ah, yes.' Stephen offered a weak smile in return. 'Well, she is *now*, in any case.'

'Not to worry.' Matthews said and he gently entered the small space and closed the door behind him. He stood, leaning on the glass with his hands in expensive trouser pockets. 'I've used language far worse with some of mine.'

Simon, to Stephen's knowledge, had never married. But, judging by his youth – he was clearly ten years behind him – and his good looks, he likely had a string of notches on his bedpost, and currently had a girlfriend. A young blonde creature with money and looks and fake tits. They were engaged, at least he thought they were.

'Sorry to interrupt you, mate.' He drawled in a false ever-so-friendly way. 'I know you have your deadline by six. But, I thought it was high time you and I had a little chat.'

Stephen composed himself and sat upright in the chair. He nodded calmly and said 'of course, Simon, how can I help you?' but inside his chest his heart raced and the hot coal burned.

'Look, mate. (God, how he despised people that constantly used that word) There's no way to tactfully put this, and you've always been a good editor and a good manager of the people under you, but... well, it's no secret to anyone here as to how hard things have been for you lately.'

The overhead light seemed to be buzzing louder. A great black bluebottle in death-throes.

'Mate, anyone would have understood, me especially, if you'd chosen to take a little time off after everything. But there you were, day after day, working solidly, never missing an hour of work. It's admirable, mate, but, well, I was thinking that perhaps...'

'Has my work slipped?' Stephen countered anxiously. 'I can't imagine how, if so. I've put in every bit of overtime I can to meet deadlines, I've always gotten everything to print ahead of schedule.'

Simon was holding his hands up in reassurance as he spoke. 'Your work's been exemplary.' He replied, paused, reconsidered his tack, then resumed. 'I *do* want to offer you something that'll give you a bit of a time out, true, *but* it's also an opportunity for a *great* story.'

Story? Stephen immediately wanted to state that news scoops and story pieces were the wheelhouse of the younger lads that reported to him, and certainly not the senior editor of a newspaper. The younger Stephen would have said it, but he was dead now. So, the new-and-distinctly-less-improved Stephen said nothing but 'a story? Of what kind?'

Simon dodged the question and dangled what he clearly thought was a carrot instead. To Stephen it looked more like a noose.

'Have you been out to *Yorkshire* much?' He beamed as if he was offering him a holiday to Florida. 'North Yorkshire, specifically.'

What a stupid fucking question. Teesside was bordered with Yorkshire. He'd have to have lived a pretty bloody sheltered life to not have ventured all of forty miles outside of his home town. Stephen elected not to say this, and simply nodded in response. What his boss said next staggered him.

'There's a wonderfully fun story just sitting out there. Not a front page piece by any stretch, but you'd certainly get a lower headline and a link to, say, page six. Spooky stuff! People love spooky stuff, right? Especially when it's local. Good for tourism, good for our sales.'

Stephen couldn't disguise the look of disgust on his face. 'Spooky stuff, Simon?' he replied dubiously.

'Cast your mind back,' Simon went on unabated, caught up in his little narrative, 'remember that business in Enfield back in '77? The Daily Mirror had a field day with that one, regularly reporting on it for over two years before public interest died. You should see the figures for their sales during that! The Yorkshire Post made The Black Monk of Pontefract the stuff of legend back in '66! East Drive's a tourist spot now.'

Stephen's heart sank. 'This is a fluff piece.' He surprised himself by stating outright. 'This is a job for a junior assistant at best, no, not even *that*; a freelancer buying some sheet space! This is like that nonsense werewolf article we ran a few years back.'

'It is indeed, mate!' Simon, still smiling but with a sharp look in his eye replied. 'And you should see our sales for that issue! Steve, the world's a miserable place. Strikes, unemployment, constant talk of nuclear war. People love an escape from it all, and articles like this can turn into running stories. That woman, forget her name, who claimed she saw a werewolf when camping in Dalby Forest, she made a fortune! People scoured that place for a couple of years, some said they even saw more than one! It's exciting to people mate, the unknown, and they lap it up. I was thinking that someone of your talents could go there, check it out, write us a piece while you're there, and have a little week away on the company cash while you're at it! It'd be good for you, and good for us! What do you say?' Except the way that he said it was more like a game show host – *whadayasay?*

Stephen was furious. In his head he was screaming at the young fool, lapels gripped in steel fists, spitting into his face as he hollered *I have just buried my son, and you want me to go ghost hunting!* He was slapping the shocked expression off his face and throwing him aside as he flung the door open and stormed out, calling *fuck your job, you insensitive prick!*

Outwardly, lips pressed together and white, Stephen nodded thoughtfully. The veins pulsed in his neck as he cleared his throat.

'Is this really a story, Mr Matthews,' he said in a low, even voice, 'or are you trying to trick me into having a holiday?'

Simon, still fixed with that hyena smile, held up his hands to reveal a costly pair of cufflinks that flashed in the harsh glow of the strip light. 'You'd be well paid.' He said. 'You'd have a free holiday. I'd manage your role while you're away. And get this – I've been working on a title, but creative control of course remains yours – *The Helmsley Castle Poltergeist*. Whadayathink?'

Stephen paused a while, seeming to hold his breath. Simon noted the flash of colour in his cheeks, and though his smile remained fixed, his tone changed noticeably.

'Unless you now think that work like this is *below* you?' He added.

'It's not that, Simon, it's that you know very well that I don't believe in any of this stuff.' Steve replied, shrugging, struggling. 'It's childish. And, well, as I know you're aware, I've recently suffered a bereavement...'

'Hey, mate, hey.' Simon was using his very best sympathetic tone. Must have been practicing in the mirror because it was almost believable. 'I'm sorry. I understand. I wouldn't have offered you this opportunity if I'd thought you actually believed in this stuff! *I* bloody don't! It's just a bit of fun, and it'll be great for the paper. Think of it as a holiday – yes, an enforced one for your own good – but still, a vacation and a distraction, and you get to write a daft little sizzle piece that could really take off and be a regular bit. It's win-win, mate!'

Helmsley. He'd never actually heard of it. Stephen had imagined he was going to say Whitby, with all the vampire stuff and The Barghest. Or maybe Burton Agnes Hall with its screaming skull ghost story. But still, it was clear that there was only one answer that Matthews was going to accept to this proposal, and god only knew what would become of Steve's professional life if he refused, given his bosses reputation.

'Alright.' He sighed at last. 'Alright, Simon. You've made your case. Tell me about this poltergeist yarn, then.'

3

Pack up your Troubles

66, 77, 88.

Though he was miserable with his new enforced assignment, the old cogs of his creative brain were turning. Pontefract in 66', Enfield in 77', and now this Helmsley Poltergeist in 88'. There was a good grab in that somewhere, something to catch the eye and to make the reader feel that there was something important to it, even if there wasn't. And there most certainly wasn't.

He'd pondered this as he walked from the office, on autopilot, towards the pub. He passed the cinema on the corner, now named *Cannon,* a red-brick building with clear plastic covered images of upcoming films adorning the length of it. It still smelled the same as it did in the furthest corners of his memory as he walked by; the smell of sweet popcorn, stale but appealing and mixed with the warm scent of upholstery. The marquee said they were playing a film called *Beetlejuice,* whatever that was. He turned away from it as he was swept back to the days when the building had seemed more like an exciting and magical portal to another world, another place, another time, with his dad's hand safely enveloping his. Stephen fought tears and crossed the road with greater urgency. He needed a drink more than ever.

He passed the ice-cream place on the corner of Dovecot

Street, still fighting off the memories of dad buying him a lemon top there after the show, and made it to the high street. Fleets of buses roared up and down the length of the wide open two-road market path, and he broke into a virtual run through the crowds as he passed the Woolworth's store and down the side alley that lead to his sanctuary.

He should have been relieved to be in the old cobbled enclosure of The Green Dragon Yard, with the darkened windows of the pub shining like the eyes of a welcoming friend, but instead his heart sank as a figure, that had been waiting outside on one of the benches, stood up at the sight of him hurrying closer.

'Steve.' Said his older brother, Edward. His hair was greyer than he remembered it, almost white, but curly like their dad's had been, not straight like their mother's.

'Ed.' Stephen replied as amiably as he could. There was now an obstacle between him and his medicine, and every second counted. Today had been too much, just *too* much to stand. 'What're you doing here?'

Edward White worked and lived in Middlesbrough, and had done since the seventies. He managed a bank, was well-off, and had been married since he was twenty. He and his wife – Stephen couldn't remember her name – had three kids, a mortgage, and a nice car. Edward was a runner and climber in his spare time, he did marathons and such, had regular city breaks in London and Paris, and family summer holidays in Barcelona and Florence. Worst of all, Edward was a teetotaller.

'It's about mum.' He said. 'Mind if I join you?' And he gestured to the pub. Clearly, Stephen's nightly ritual was not as sacrosanct as he had thought. His brother had known exactly where to find him, and when. It would have bothered him more, but the words *it's about mum* had sent his guts plummeting into his legs. Surely not. Not after all of the bullshit that today had thrown at him; the final death-croak of his failed marriage, the grinning gargoyle of Matthews exiling him to the arse-end of Yorkshire on a story fit only for children. Surely not now *this* news.

'No!' Stephen gasped, to which Edward stepped forward.

'No, no, she's okay.' He quickly added. 'That is, she is for now. It's about the home.'

With a shaking hand, Stephen gestured to the pub door and nodded sheepishly, letting out a huge sigh as he did.

Without intention Stephen avoided his usual stool at the bar, though it remained empty. Subconsciously perhaps, such a sacred altar should not be defiled by the presence of another. Instead, after buying drinks, they ventured left and found themselves in a snug with stained carpets, nicotine-yellow walls, and an ancient looking dartboard on the wall surrounded by the damage of many drunkenly missed shots. Stephen nursed a pint, Edward chose a lemonade.

He drank slowly and purposefully, which felt alien. Sipping the ice-cold beer, he thought he could hear his throat hissing, burning with want. Normally a pint would last him minutes. 'It's not the funding again, is it?' Stephen ventured, desperately wanting to light a cigarette but resisting it knowing of Ed's disapproval.

'No, everything is still adequately subsidised.' Came Edward's smooth, even-tempered tones, filtered through perfectly white teeth that were set into a stubbled jawline that his brother had always secretly been envious of. 'It's mum herself, in fact. The problem, I mean.'

'Oh?'

'She's gotten quite worse, quite quickly.' Ed raised the lemonade glass, noted a lipstick stain on the rim, wrinkled his nose and put it back down. 'Her behaviour, specifically, towards the staff. Lashing out, being as uncooperative as possible. Some of it they attribute to the dementia, some of it they feel is simply character.'

'Who gives a shit what they think?' Stephen snapped. 'It's their job.'

'It is,' his brother replied calmly, 'but it's also our...' he corrected himself with a voice that went sharp, '*my* job to take a role in keeping her calm and comfortable.'

The stale pub air quickly felt smothering, like a mass setting down upon Stephen's weary shoulders, growing denser by the second. The weight of the world. His breath trembled as he said 'you know exactly what I've been through this year.'

Edward drummed his fingers on the table, four of them in rapid succession. He was irritated. It was the only sign that gave it away, offered a glimpse behind his eternally-cool exterior. 'Steve, you know you have my deepest sympathies. I'm so very sorry for what you've been through...'

(Here comes the *but*)

'...and you know you have my support and help whenever you want it, god knows I've told you enough times. But (there it is) there still exists certain obligations that we both agreed and swore to one another we would carry out. We are all mum has. I've been with her at every possible opportunity through this, and things are getting bad, Steve, *really* bad. Know what I mean?'

Stephen lowered his head. The shame weighed more than the mass on his shoulders. He nodded gently. 'I know I could have visited more often, it's just with all the...'

'You haven't visited her *at all*.' Edward stated coolly. 'Not since... well, not since your loss.' When his brother couldn't find a word to say in response, he continued. 'She only remembers who I am occasionally now, and even then with not much lucidity. I daren't even mention you to her anymore.

It would be crushing to think that she's lost the memory of you. Steve, she needs to see you. And you need to see her, before...' he paused as he looked at his brother, whose head was still hanging low. The pint glass in front of him, still set on the table, was now completely empty. '...Well, you know.'

Stephen's heart felt clutched by fingers made of cold metal. He had no answer to give so he sat there, in the stark light of guilt, without defence. He had neglected many things since the death of his son. Was it intentional? Of course not. Time had become a tape spooling faster and faster, and he had lost track of it altogether. All he could do against the crippling horror, prying and scratching at the skin of his scalp to gain entry and there to fester and destroy him, was to keep busy, keep working, and keep drunk. All else, including his mother, had blurred into background material. This was not an excuse, merely a pure truth.

'I'm sorry.' He whispered.

'Steve, you don't have to be sorry, you just have to be present!' His brother retorted. 'You've completely isolated yourself, and the very things you need – family, company, a shoulder and an ear – are the things that you've avoided like the plague.'

A hand rested on Stephen's shoulder.

'Come with me, now.' Ed said. 'There's still visiting hours 'til seven. Come on, it will do us all good.'

Visiting my dying mother who doesn't know who I am, Stephen thought, *with a brother that always saw me as his lesser and an embarrassment, on the day that my divorce came through. How in hell would that do me good? How would it do any of us any good?*

'I can't I... I have to pack.' He responded at last. 'I have to go away, for a week, tomorrow. It's a work thing, it's... well, it's non-negotiable, if I want to keep my position.'

The hand was quickly withdrawn.

He despised himself for his cowardice, and for how this looked. A cop-out, a thoroughly transparent evasion. But, again, it was the truth.

'You can spare an hour.' Edward pressed. *'Come on, Steve.'*

The disgust in his voice was sour to Stephen's ears. His fists clenched tight under the table. The spit in his mouth turned acidic and bitter and his stomach turned. Blood rushed in brisk pulses in his ears. Words and words and words of explanation rolled by in front of his eyes in miserable black and grey dirty print, like a sheet from that bastard newspaper made in that hell-hole of a prison that he called his job. And away they went, never to be said.

'I can't, Ed.' His voice was gristly and sore, like one of the dockworkers. 'I can't. It's been a bad day. Bad. I can't and I'm sorry.'

A long pause before his brother said 'I'm sorry, too' and stood. Stephen kept his eyes fixed ashamedly on the ugly swirling burgundy carpet as Ed examined him. 'You, of all people, should appreciate how precious time is.' He said. 'And time is short for mum. The time you'll spend regretting this choice will feel a lot longer.' Then he turned and left.

Stephen watched him go, broad muscular shoulders working beneath a sharp suit, until he went through the door and it squealed closed.

Numb, he returned to his usual place at the bar, ordered a double whisky, downed it, and ordered another.

He considered running after Ed, getting into his sporty car and visiting his mother. Hell, he wanted to. Desperately. But this... *thing*, this monster that had grown inside him made him stay put. Keep distracted. Keep taking your medicine.

Stay asleep.

And why the hell not? We're all just queueing, aren't we? Next one into the meatgrinder. Hurtling towards the boneyard. The young kids in the corner with their colourful clothes and what they imagine to be the whole world ahead of them, the old guys at the bar with their paper-thin souls and their broken and abused bodies, and everyone in-between, they're all just queueing. So why not drink? Why not stay asleep?

Stephen had been awoken to the starkly unforgiving truth of life on the day his son died. It was a reality that he could not ignore, and it haunted his every waking second. His dreams too, he imagined, but he was so drunk whenever he slept that, blessedly, he scarcely remembered them. The truth of life – that there is no meaning to any of it, and from the moment we suck in our first breath through the film of birthing fluid as hands in blue latex lift us from the bodies of our mothers, we are *doomed*. We are gifted fleeting moments of joy, pleasure, love, even. But the rest is *the grind*. Striving, suffering, and pain. And the only reward at the end of it is to not exist at all.

Stephen downed the second double whisky and raised a finger to the barman.

The night continued in this manner until he could not see straight. His head bobbed and his eyes rolled, and all thoughts of the next day's responsibilities were wiped clean. He tried to explain to the barman that life is a prank played when you're not looking, but the man yelled something about changing a record and turned away from him. The night closed in beyond the frosted glass and the jukebox boomed into life and the overlapping voices of a packed pub became a deafening and unintelligible roar.

Of course, this was a Friday night.

He then remembered that he had to be packed and ready early tomorrow for his stupid fucking holiday in the countryside, looking for stupid fucking ghosts. He couldn't imagine what would be worse; dying and blinking out of existence, or dying and having to be a wandering spirit, forever trapped in some dull little village where stupid fucking senior editors were forced to come out and write stories about you. Stephen tried to light a cigarette but lit the wrong end, dropping it and cursing himself. A thunderstorm of laughter erupted to his right.

'Cheer up, Whitey!' They chorused.

For the first time in his life Stephen contemplated physical violence. It played like a film in his sozzled mind. He set upon the white-bearded dock worker, bringing the whisky tumbler down in an expert arc so that it met cleanly with the man's forehead. The glass smashed like in the movies, of course, badly cutting the man but not Stephen's hand. He fell to the floor screaming for mercy as Stephen White the Triumphant stood over him, and the others all scattered from their stools, barking apologies as they went. He told them (calm and cool, like Clint Eastwood) never to set foot in his place again, and they all nodded with fear-struck grey faces.

But, naturally, all Stephen did was what he always did. He ignored them and made for the door.

Tomorrow he would have to climb into his battered old Mini Metro and make for the rolling hills of North Yorkshire, but not before he promised himself that he would make steps to change his life and leave this town and all of the vile things that came with it behind. And again all of this horrible night would be wiped clean from his pickled brain next morning like a blank cassette being erased.

It would take a miracle, or a horror, to shake him from this cycle.

And, whether he realised it or not, he had already had his miracle.

Pack up your troubles in your old kit bag, Stephen slurred and sang angrily into the indifferent night sky as he made for his bus, *and smile, smile, smile.*

4

Ghost Stories

A dense wet mist was hanging over the Cleveland Hills. In the early morning light it looked postcard-perfect, with frost-encrusted tree limbs and icicle spiderwebs dripping with dew in brash dawn light, and rolling hills speckled with snow in high places. Roseberry Topping, a huge cone-shaped hill that was as close as Teesside got to a natural landmark, dominated the landscape, peaked white, with a blazing but cold sun hanging above it as sheep grazed in the fields below and crows glided between trees, swooping to the hard ground to peck for worms.

The car rolled south, moving from the A174 to a much narrower B-road, which according to the map Stephen had scoured that morning was the B1257, a straight run to his destination at only an hour's drive. The Metro, an old thing with balding tires and bodywork somewhere between bright red and rust, screamed with exertion as it worked up steep inclines and tight turns, always jamming whenever he tried to put it in third. To be fair to the old girl, his car was rarely used and so the fact that it had started that morning, in minus temperatures and after only three attempts, was a miracle.

Flung on the back seat was a solitary suitcase that contained changes of clothes, toiletries, stationery and pads, a cassette recorder, an expensive camera from the office, and a bottle of whisky wrapped in an old pillowcase. He had considered bringing his typewriter, but he didn't deem it worth the trouble. He would shorthand the story – such as it was – and type it when returning home.

Stephen had flung the suitcase into the back because he never looked into the backseat of his car, couldn't bear to, and even when he stopped he would reach blindly back to retrieve his travel bag without even a glance. The boot of the car had fused shut, likely from rust, and he'd never bothered to fix it. He didn't look back because once, and for several years, a booster seat had been there. Now there was only the indentation of one in the seat.

The morning was bright and cold, but the car was flanked on both sides by tall and imposing trees which, though leafless, were still dense enough to block most of the sun. He had to turn his headlights on a few times, so bad it was, and it made navigating such tight roads quite intimidating, especially when another vehicle came in the opposite direction and they had to crawl past one another slowly and awkwardly as branches scratched at their windows.

Still, he couldn't deny that it felt good to leave the concrete and the industrial landscape behind. It felt fresh and open there, the sky was huge and pale blue, and the rolling hills and moorlands were a welcome salve to eyes over-accustomed to strip-lighting and office walls. Begrudgingly, something in him was relieved that he had been forced to do this, though he would never admit it to Matthews.

That morning Stephen felt thin, used-up. His stomach felt tight and sour and his fingers had trembled that morning as he had plotted his journey on the map and written a couple of notes. He remembered Ed last night and their talk about mum, but nothing much after that. He had no memory of getting home at all, but he had been awoken by his alarm clock at eight and he had been in bed, and his clothes had been folded on his chair, as if he had been cared for by another. Slowly but surely, and even though he was horribly aware of it, he was slowly becoming two people, each with their own personalities and sets of memories; sober Stephen and drunk Stephen.

And one day, sooner or later, one would consume the other.

He glanced down at the cassette that was perched on the passenger seat. A blank tape with the words *Stephen Helmsley notes* written on the case in biro. He sneered down at it.

'Right then, Simon,' he said to it with venom, 'let's hear what fairytale bollocks you've got me chasing out here.'

With one hand he unclipped the case and retrieved the tape, then pushed it into the car stereo player. He pressed play and fiddled with the volume knob as his other hand fought winding roads and tight turns.

The car was filled with the harsh crackle of static, punctuated by the loud scraping and thudding of fingers too close to a microphone, before the recording device was set down upon a surface and all became an even hiss. Someone on the recording cleared their throat, sounding like someone at the end of a bad phone line, and began to speak.

'Steve, mate!' Said Simon Matthews.

'Simon, dickhead!' Stephen muttered, mimicking his simulated cheery tone and shaking his head at the twisting countryside.

'Thought it'd be easier for you to have this tape for reference than a pile of mismatched notes,' the recording continued, 'plus something to pass the time while you drive, eh?'

Stephen cranked at the handle in his door and his

window squeaked down in little increments, filling the car with fresh morning air. Then he lit a cigarette and resentfully listened to his boss.

'So, you're booked into The Black Swan Inn as you know. Four nights, all paid for. Your contact is a Mrs Wood. We've arranged for the interview to be in the hotel bar, tomorrow afternoon at one. Give you a day to collect yourself and plan it, eh? The rest is to get some nice moody pictures for the piece, give the readers a taste of the place. There's a church and yard right next door to you, and the castle is easy to find. Castle's the important bit, obviously, so focus on that more than anywhere else. That's where the carvings made by this poltergeist are supposed to be, but Mrs Wood will fill you in on all that.'

For god's sake. Stephen rolled his eyes and exhaled smoke. Carvings made by a ghost? Absolute rubbish. What, a person couldn't possibly have made them? Laughable.

'She'll talk you through her personal experiences too, and those of the locals, but it's really important that you speak to them yourself, so get any names from her you can and interview as many of them as you can. Get a few good local ghostly tales, eh?' He laughed. *Laughed.* Who the hell was that for? He was sitting in an office recording himself, alone. Wanker.

'The Inn itself,' the wanker continued, 'is a former 15th century mansion, so there's a ton of stories attached to it already. The landlord or his staff will have plenty to tell you in that regard, I'll bet. Writes itself, doesn't it? It's got stories about a jilted bride, dead by suicide, who sits by the fire. A little boy, a Victorian pickpocket that they blame for disappearing and reappearing objects behind the bar, he's been seen too. They've got a highwayman who appears right where the old stable yard used to be, and, and this is a weird one, a gigantic black cat. Fuck knows why a cat would haunt a pub, but there it is. Got a book on the place here – Yorkshire Hauntings – and there's a whole chapter on it. There's all sorts here. More ghosts in the inn, haunted marketplace, the graveyard, all the usual stories. I won't bore you with them, though they're worth asking about. But the castle is really the focus of all this.'

The compact road opened up a little then and the trees became long rows of low hedges that sped by in browns and dirty greens. The car was again drenched in winter sun and was surrounded by open fields.

'So, the castle itself is 12th century.' Simon said, clearly reading parts from a book. 'Built under the orders of Henry the First, who also founded Rievaulx Abbey, which is apparently nearby. We've got English Civil War soldiers haunting the grounds, and ah... oh, well I never.' The sound of pages turning loudly filled Stephen's car. 'Huh! Well, it says here that there was a Duke, George Villiers. Real party boy, it says here. Swung both ways. Yuck.'

Stephen sighed irritably and flicked his cigarette out of the window.

'Anyways, he was apparently having an affair with King James the First! God, they even had them back then! What's the bloody world come to!' The disgust in Simon's voice was so over the top that Stephen wondered what all the protestation was about. 'But he also liked girls, a little *too* much. Serial bloody rapist. But he got away with it every time because he was under the protection of the King. Says here that the old nursey rhyme *Georgie Porgie Pudding and Pie* is about him. *Kissed the girls and made them cry,* eh? Bet he did. Also we've got a Green Lady; a woman that's seen haunting the grounds in a sweeping emerald dress, terrifying the locals. Hmm, no one seems to know who she is, or why she's there. And also...' he laughed out loud again, distorting the recording with a painfully loud *Ha!* '...also, it says here, mate, so don't judge me, it says they have pixies!'

You could turn this car around right now, Stephen thought to himself. *You could turn this car around and head straight for The Dragon and you could spend a week there. Just tell him you went to Helmsley. Make something up. After all, that's all this Mrs Wood and the locals are doing, isn't it – making things up? Pixies. God help me.*

'Anyway,' Simon concluded, 'that's all by-the-by, but worth bearing in mind for your inquiries. The main meat of it is this poltergeist thing. This Wood lady is saying that there are messages from the other side scrawled right into the stone of the castle, and that if you scrawl in your own question and leave, the next day when you return, an answer will be scratched there for you. Pretty cool, eh? She claims that this poltergeist visited her, and others. Like, physically. Makings of a great story if you ask me, mate. This story will be up there with Enfield, you mark my words! Right, work to do. Any issues, ring the office, otherwise have a good break, and bring me back something juicy, mate! See you soon!'

After some more loud clunking and scraping, the tape went silent.

Stephen passed by a couple of garden centres and skirted a little town called Stokesley, a place he had never been but knew from the map was the last town that bordered Teesside and North Yorkshire. After that it was more open fields and endless flat rolling moorland as far as the eye could see. The tyres rumbled over slick wet tarmac that flashed with oily rainbow colours whenever the sunlight struck it. Soon the car interior had become intolerably cold and so he wound the window up again and turned on the heaters, which stank of old dust and petrol and made you wheeze if you left them on too long.

Strange how being away from your life can change perspective so quickly. Strange how merely displacing yourself from a set routine, a stringent one at that, can make you see things more clearly. You forget there's life outside of your bubble. Stephen caught glimpses of old folk chatting at the occasional bus stops that he would pass, he caught a pheasant or two dashing across the road, one in particular that he had to swerve to avoid. He caught a flash of red as he passed a low-hanging tree upon which a robin was perched. He imagined that he wouldn't have to walk far off this little road and into the countryside before he started seeing rabbits darting as birds of prey swooped for them. Life was still going on without him. There was a world beyond Teesside and his routine. The blinkers at his eyes loosened a little and he realised, or rather remembered, that he did not, in fact, have to live in Stockton-on-Tees, and that he did not have to work for The Gazette, and that he did not have to drink every moment that he was not working in order to bear the weight of simply being alive.

For one glorious shining moment, out there in the winding countryside, anything seemed possible. He'd forgotten that he had a choice. But it was only a moment.

A car, which had been tailgating him for a couple of miles, finally grew too impatient with the very limited speed that Stephen's tired old car could maintain, and overtook him on the narrow road. He slowed as they did, glad to let them pass as he was getting tired of the harassment, and he got a glimpse of a male driver with a woman next to him. They were young, perhaps thirties, wearing the usual family outing clothing – padded jackets and woolly gloves – and they had two children in the back. A young girl, younger than ten with plaited pigtails, and a boy, younger even than her with a bob of brown hair and big dark eyes and a toy dinosaur clutched in his hand.

The car passed by and sped on in front of him, and the young boy in the back turned and looked out of the back window, one little hand holding onto the headrest alongside the other that had a green t-rex squeezed beneath it. He and

Stephen locked eyes for a moment as the distance between cars grew, and just before they went out of sight around the bend the little boy raised his free hand and gave Stephen a wave.

The car was gone before Stephen's shaking hand was raised high enough to wave back.

And just like that, invasively and unexpectedly, Stephen saw his son's face in his mind's eye. He saw his bob of dark hair, a bad home cut, his large inquisitive eyes and quite out of nowhere his toothy smile, that Stephen had somehow managed to banish from memory but had now returned. His excitable little voice and now the small delicate details of a hand that had once held his.

The pain was immediate and as powerful as the tallest waves in the most turbulent of seas, and he doubled over against the wheel. The car darted left towards the passing hedges and then violently overcorrected and almost swerved into the opposite side before righting itself in the middle.

I can see the stars, daddy.

Tears filled his vision and a deep well of sorrow that was simply too much for a human body to support drove its way up from his heart. It pushed against his throat like vomit and his mouth went slack and his lip juddered as an intense upsurge of vertigo sent him reeling. He felt the blood drain from his face and from his limbs, replaced only with numbness and weakness.

Within a minute, the memory of which was lost to him, the car was parked alongside a ditch with two yellow hazard lights blinking and Stephen was hunched a few feet away in the undergrowth, puking into a little stream between pitiful cries of pain.

The moment passed and the countryside returned. The birds flew again and the sun continued to rise and the wind blew. The wailing ceased along with the nausea, and the *click-*

click-click of the hazards filled his ears. He stood, unsteadily with juddering legs, and awkwardly bundled himself back into the car. After a few moments the car pulled lazily off the grass verge and continued on its way.

Ghosts, Stephen said to himself, *I know what real ghosts are. You don't chase them. They chase you.*

And then Stephen forgot about the possibility of hope, and wished only to reach his destination so that he could unpack that suitcase and open that bottle of whisky.

5
Helm's Forest Clearing

Soon he was driving into a small market town via a narrow road named Bondgate, fringed with rows of quaint little cottages made of pale blocks that looked a little like the material used for sandstone castles. The end of the road opened up to a large market square, cobbled and spacious, with many cars parked in neat rows all around it. Obviously this was not market day, and when this area was not crammed with metal frames covered in striped tarpaulin and people screaming about the price of potatoes, this was instead a car park for the locals.

This had to be the place. He could already make out the spire of an old church peeking above the slate roof of a medieval building that looked like a pub, and he could also see, more distantly and to his left, the peak of a castle with a turreted roofline, dark and blocky against a pale blue sky. Yes, this had to be it. He hadn't noticed any road signs as he came in. The rest of his drive had been rather a distracted affair, and he had, without realising, ran a red light a mile back. Thank god no one had been crossing the road.

He slowed to a stop at a junction where a small roundabout lay, and seeing that there were no other cars waiting behind him, he took a moment to get his bearings and find a place to park. There was a little town hall with a clock in the centre of its roof, and beside it a pretty impressive gothic spire, right in the middle of the market. Made of four columns that met in a high-reaching spike, a figure sat inside it carved from white stone or marble. A grand old man in long robes looking very stately. Town founder, perhaps?

Other than that the miniature town was unremarkable, though picturesque. There were little gift shops, corner stores, pubs, all the usual trappings of small town life. But there was one building, almost tucked out of sight by the large medieval pub, that drew his eye the second he spotted it.

It was a timber-framed Tudor house, a black and white latticed thing that sat between the pub and an ancient-looking stone wall. The wall had a low iron gate, left open, that lead into what looked like a graveyard. The windows were dark and unreflective, criss-crossed in lead, and unevenly placed along the façade. It, like many buildings of the period that he had seen before in the city of York, was a sloped and misshapen structure that looked like it could lollop to one side and collapse at any moment, but somehow never did.

His eyes ran across the ancient house and its windows as black as ebony, and for a moment he was quite taken with it. *Imagine that*, he mused, *imagine living in this little corner of this little place. A peaceful life, a quiet life of fresh air and green trees and morning walks. Imagine...*

He jolted in his seat as the car that had approached behind him gave a short sharp *beep*. He looked up into his mirror and saw the bloated, purplish face of an old man with high cholesterol and low tolerance. He gave him an apologetic wave and drove on, creeping around the little roundabout and passing the pub.

He spotted the sign above the door as he passed, and was for a moment perplexed by it. It simply read THE, followed by a white circular shape painted on wood with some kind of wooden sculpture sticking out of it, then HOTEL. He felt a fool when he realised that the wooden sculpture was a black swan sitting on a little plinth.

'Oh.' He muttered as he pulled into the open carpark in front of the archaic hall. 'Well, I've arrived.'

He parked up, reached blindly into the backseat to retrieve his suitcase, closing his eyes for good measure in case he got a glimpse, and climbed out of the car, grunting with the effort and with the pains in his head and gut.

The air smelled different there, and it felt much colder. He couldn't quite place it. Perhaps he could smell the old stone or the trees that were all around. There was more green in this tiny marketplace than there was in most of his home town. But it was pleasant, and the feeling of being far removed from newspaper offices and smog-laced air was agreeable to him. He hadn't even finished turning his key in the lock of the car door before someone was speaking to him.

'Can I help you?' Said a woman behind him with an accent so thick you could cut it with a knife and spread it on your toast. All of the h's were missing and every 'I' was an 'ah'.

He turned and saw a woman a little older than him with tight grey curls and steely eyes. She was plump and wore a pinny, in her hand was a yellow cloth for dusting. He looked her up and down, then around himself, quietly annoyed. He was standing out in the street, what on earth did she mean? Before he could respond she continued 'this is a private car park for The Swan. Public parking's over yonder,' and she pointed her duster at the market.

'Oh,' he smiled politely, 'no, I'm staying here. I mean, I need to book in. Are you the...? And he gestured to the hotel.

'No.' She grunted. 'I'm the cleaner.'

Stephen knotted his eyebrows, but smiled and said 'well then, I'd better check in with the landlord. Good of you to take on such extra responsibilities beyond your current role and paygrade.'

'You what?'

'Good morning.' He said, and pushed past her to the front door.

Nosy old bitch. Seemed that the cliches about small-town folk were well founded. He imagined that everyone knew everyone's name, as well as their business, around these parts. He was hoping to go unnoticed, clearly he'd be anything but; a newspaper editor from out of town, looking for ghost stories of all things. But, he had surprised himself. The long dead Stephen had temporarily resurrected, the Stephen that was confrontational when needs be, and had a sharp sense of humour.

Immediately upon entering Stephen was struck by how old the building clearly was. Very low ceilings, wooden beams overhead that one could easily have a painful encounter with, large stone fireplaces, and portraits of feudal lords and royals with feathered caps and ruffs and lutes and such. It was warm inside – the fire already raged in the open hearth of a room that appeared to be a dining area with circular tables and dark wooden seats dressed in studded leather. Candleholders lined the walls with electric lights wired in, in place of tapers. The carpet and hanging tapestries smelled musty and slightly spiced with old incense smoke. The rest of the room was panelled in varnished wood. The heritage of the place had been maintained through restoration for sure, or perhaps they simply hadn't changed it in centuries.

There wasn't a member of staff to be seen, and he couldn't hear anyone moving about the place. The only sound was the soothing crackling and spitting of the open fire. That was a sound he hadn't heard in a good long minute. It was peaceful, reassuring almost. It was a sound he could easily sit down and listen to for hours, and in fact he could, couldn't he? He had five days there. Five days – let's see – so, one day to interview this Mrs Wood AKA She Who Makes Up Tales to Make Cash, then the other four he could spend there in the dark and serene seclusion of The Black Swan, enjoying the fire and the contents of its cellar. Sure, Matthews had charged him with interviewing the locals and scoping out the town and castle, but really, what was he to find? Made up stories, that was what. He could do that perfectly well on his own.

There was a chair by the crackling hearth, and Stephen remembered what Simon had said about the jilted bride. He took a moment to stare at the stick-wood frame as the flames danced against its varnished surface. He narrowed his eyes.

Nothing. Of course there was nothing. Stephen could have told anyone that without having to drive forty miles to a remote pub. Though he supposed he could see why this was a setting for a good ghost story or two, if one were into such things. It was old and soaked in atmosphere.

'Help you, sir?' Said a male voice from across the room in exactly the same suspicious tone as the woman outside. Stephen peered through the hazily lit room and saw a man in a tie and shirt, whose buttons were engaged in a life or death struggle against his gut, clinging on by a thread of cotton. The man had a great beard but a bald head and was likely even younger than Stephen. He was stocky but out of shape, nevertheless not the sort of man you would want to cross. Stephen had spent enough time in enough pubs to know a landlord when he saw one.

'Good morning.' He responded. 'Name's White, I work for The Evening Gazette, I believe my booking was made by my colleague? I'm staying the week…'

'You're a bit early.' The landlord interrupted gruffly. 'Room's not ready yet.'

The fire crackled alone for an awkward few moments.

'Well, um,' Stephen stammered, shaking his head gently to himself – were all village folk this rude? 'May I leave my bag here until the room is ready, and when do you think that may be?'

The landlord looked at his watch languidly. "Bout an hour.'

Another awkward silence. Stephen forced a polite smile. 'I'll come back then,' he said as he made for the door, his suitcase still in his hand. As he went back out into the bright cold day he could feel the eyes of the landlord pressing into the back of his head.

Well, this was going to be a fun trip, or rather, enforced exile.

Outside in the square it was pretty quiet. The only people, usually in groups of only two, were exclusively grey-haired. They had walking sticks, some were being pushed in wheelchairs. Others, usually old men, meandered alone with a faithful dog, trotting beside them on a lead.

'God's waiting room.' Stephen muttered to himself. Still, it was better than ending up like one of the dockworkers in The Dragon. He glanced to his left where the old Tudor house stood, and could clearly see now that the gated wall beside it encompassed a churchyard. A spire was poking above the trees in the grounds, and he could make out a standing sign with information pamphlets and such pinned to it. He wandered that way until he was standing before the old house.

There was a neat hedge, low and clipped, around the house, and a garden gate that lead to a tiny white door that anyone – except perhaps children – would have to duck to pass through. Though clearly a much older building than the others that surrounded it, it was kept in very good condition. The timber that criss-crossed the freshly painted white stone was smooth and newly stained, and the terracotta tiled roof was well maintained, with even the old chimney stack seemingly still in use. The windows were original and undamaged, but gave nothing away as to who now lived there or what the function of the structure was.

It really surprised him, startled him almost, this house. It stuck out like a sore thumb when compared to the rest of the buildings the town was comprised of. It was a moody and crooked little thing. The sort of place one might expect Shakespeare to come flouncing out of, complete with tights and quill.

He walked by the house and made for the gate to the churchyard, being careful not to swing his leather suitcase lest anyone passing hear the sloshing of the liquid within. There was a wide wooden plinth just inside that read *All Saints Church*, and below it was a notice pinned that read *8am – Holy Communion. 9.30 Parish Eucharist. Sundays at 6pm – Choral Evensong. Church open 9-5 daily.*

So, this was the church that Matthews talked about. A haunted graveyard, he said.

Beside the information about the church, there was some local history.

The name Helmsley comes from the old English 'Helm's Forest Clearing', or Elmeslac, and the town was founded in around 3000 BC. Farming communities and settlers have lived here through the Neolithic, Bronze, and Iron Ages. The ruined Norman castle is the most significant surviving medieval structure of the town, though parts of the church and former vicarage - Canons Garth - are also Medieval in origin.

Stephen glanced back at the house. Canons Garth. He had no idea what that meant. Perhaps a vicar still lived there. Best not to go knocking asking about the ghouls in his graveyard. Probably wouldn't take kindly to it.

The sky was quickly clouding over beyond the high

trees, leafless and jagged like old bones hardened with frost. The clouds were pendulous and black; either sleet or heavy snow was coming. Great. Stephen hugged his overcoat to himself and tightened his chequered scarf. All he wanted was a warm fire and a cool drink, and he didn't imagine that the kindly landlord of The Black Swan would be interested in letting him sit inside until his room was ready. Still, noon was approaching, and the bar would be open soon.

He decided to wander for a few moments in the graveyard, and stepped past the opened iron gate. The grassy and uneven ground within was a little overgrown, and the trees were tall and imposing. The chill bit harder, likely because it was so secluded from the street behind him, and the frost had hardened on the old stones and mounds without the hinderance of footfall or salt put down to make it safe.

A narrow snaking path lead to the church. A neat, clean stone structure with the usual arched stained-glass windows and four pointed spires atop the bell tower. Though a relatively small building, it loomed amongst the trees. All very moody and sombre. Words he intended to use to describe this place in the article he would write. If you *have* to do a task, may as well do a good job of it.

The gravestones were in neat rows, though the uneven soil made them stick up out of the dirt at odd angles, like old crooked and stained teeth jutting up from a crude and earthy gumline. Hmm. He'd have to remember that for the article. *You've still got it, Steve.* Evergreen shrubs and bushes were planted between them, as still as the stones they touched in this windless place.

It was eerily still in that yard, he had to admit. And though he knew, *of course* he knew that is was simply weather and setting that created such an ambiance, he still had to concede that it was, simply put, bloody creepy in there. He smiled a thin smile and scoffed a puff of wintry breath through his nostrils and into the still air. Easy to see how the collective overactive imagination of a town could make a place like that seem haunted. Perhaps he would try and get a few tales from the locals. Beef up the editorial a bit.

The first few flakes of snow began to drift down. They floated on the warmer cushion of air around him before settling, huge and feathery, upon the graves. Stephen cursed and turned back towards the gate. No way was he standing out in this weather waiting for the pub to be officially open. He'd have to go sit in the car.

He made for the gate as the snowfall increased and the sky darkened further, leaving the strange and isolated grounds behind. He passed a few oval-shaped stones and read the names as best he could on the weatherworn granite as he hurried away.

Thomas Lackney, Ann Kipp, John Knowles…

God, he needed to get warm. He half considered opening the damned whisky in the car, so desperate he was. He thought better of it when he realised that likely every eye in the market would be on the newcomer in town.

Victoria Brown, Stephen White, Andrew Bridger…

Wait.

Stephen stopped dead in his tracks. The Path was already growing indistinct and drowned in white at his feet. He frowned and turned back, stepping closer to the stones. He half laughed and said 'did that say…?'

He touched the mildew-stained stone with a finger, wiping away the grime and frost that obscured the name. Then he chortled to himself.

'Stephan,' he said, 'Stephan Whitley.' And he shook his head as he made his way out of the grounds. Silly old bugger. Imagine, eh? No, he wasn't quite ready to see his own grave just yet. Not until after a good drink, anyroad.

He closed the gate behind him, leaving the lonely headstones to their mournful silence as the darkness smothered them and the snow buried them.

6
Like the Old Stamps

The room in which Stephen would be spending the next four nights was a pleasant enough one. It was clean and comfortable, though quite small. Not that it mattered. He intended to spend most of his time downstairs rather than up.

The ceiling was low and sloped, and the nearer he stood to the little window that looked out onto the market square the more he had to duck. The window itself was at chest level. He marvelled whenever he was in buildings like these from many centuries past, at just how small human beings used to be. Imagine if one were to time travel. One might feel a little like snow white, with a great deal more than seven dwarves to contend with.

The single bed looked old but sturdy, and the walls were covered by the same wooden panelling as downstairs, making the room feel very close and insulated, which at that time of year was a blessing. The door was old and creaky, wood and slatted ironwork, and the furniture looked like the kind of drawers and cupboards that Sir Walter Raleigh might keep his telescope and britches in.

Stephen was perched on the edge of the bed in an uncomfortably fitted suit with his tie undone at the neck. The suitcase was open by his feet and the bottle of whisky was in his hand.

He felt better already.

The light coming through the window was negligible given the state of the weather outside that afternoon, but he imagined that even on the sunniest of days not much got through. The bedside lamp did a much better job of illuminating the miniature medieval chamber than a cold February day. It was a glum little space. Not likely haunted, but most certainly depressing.

It was a little after one and the day was his. He wasn't due to meet this Mrs Wood until tomorrow at this time, and so really he should have been using the time to get started on his article. Asking around the bar for tales of apparitions and spectres, getting some good photographs, all of that. But he had four nights and five days to do that, and the rest – stories of phantoms – he could likely make up himself. Who cared? Not the great unwashed readers of The Gazette, that was for sure. Besides, the point of this jaunt wasn't really the article, was it? It was an imposed holiday. And a holiday he may as well enjoy.

He took another swig from the bottle, enjoying the burn as the spicy liquid washed down his chest, erasing all memory of the recent vomiting and the horror that had caused it. His mother swept into his mind, along with the judgmental face of Ed. *The time you will spend regretting this choice will feel a lot longer.*

'I already live in regret.' Stephen said aloud to the room. 'I have a permanent season ticket.'

He unpacked his bag and laid the clothes on the bed, deciding to change into a thick cable jumper and blue jeans. They felt strange on his skin. He lived in suits generally, but given that he could feel the very cold seeping in through the old walls, he'd be more comfortable this way. He corked the whisky bottle and pulled his overcoat back on, making for the door.

The bar downstairs did not feel friendly, and he didn't mean that in some new age hippie way. The barman that had greeted him served him a beer without a word, and the three local men that had entered the pub in his absence and were now sitting at a circular table by the window, barely said more than the landlord. Mostly they drank in silence and watched the snow flurries sweep and dance to the ground outside.

Stephen found himself a table out of the way; a dimly lit alcove obscured from full view of the room. He lit a cigarette and watched the bar like a spy in a novel.

For a time no one said a word, but by the time his drink had almost gone and a crushed cigarette butt smouldered in the ashtray, one of the men piped up.

'Here on business, Mr...?' Said an older man with a thick white moustache. He didn't even look directly at Stephen when he asked, just addressed the table he sat at. It was enough to make him laugh. What the hell was with these people?

'White,' he replied pleasantly, 'and yes, you could say that. Though I'm more on a break than here for work.'

The three men at the table exchanged a glance.

'Newspaper, is it?' The moustache man went on.

My, my. Word travelled fast around town. Stephen paused, examining the man across the room with narrowed eyes before he responded.

'Evening Gazette.' He replied. 'Teesside.'

The man didn't respond to that, though he gave a subtle nod before raising his glass to his lips. One of his fellows stole a glance at Stephen, looked at the moustache man to make sure he hadn't seen him, then resumed staring at the table, hunching over his pint.

Stephen was a keen reader of people. It came with the

territory. He was good at sensing things about people even when they didn't say much, though, the more they said the more it helped. He could gauge tone of voice, mannerisms, body language and such. He'd been interviewing people all his life, and could get a feel for things quite quickly. And, despite how absurd it sounded to his own mind, the feeling he was quickly getting was that not only was he not welcome in Helmsley, but that there was likely a good reason, or reasons, for it.

These locals were not accustomed to visitors, and they had something to hide.

He decided to test the waters. After all, what did he care? He was sure as shit never coming back to this town again.

'It's a daft thing, really.' He called across the bar cheerfully. At least, he sounded it. If the men had been able to see his eyes they'd have known he was faking it. 'But my boss has got me here writing an article about ghosts.'

All three men turned their heads and looked at him. A moment of tense silence passed. Then all three of them burst in raucous laughter.

Stephen nodded along with them, smiling. 'I know, I know. Nonsense, I know. But, it's a good excuse to get some country air.'

'Come, sit.' The moustache man said as his friends calmed down, and he reached to drag a chair to their table. In an odd moment Stephen felt a little nervous, but he dismissed it and walked over to join them. He would have liked to have thought that it was again the old Stephen, bold and brash, that had emerged and made him this confident with strangers. But deep down he knew it was the whisky.

He sat down with them and, as was customary in pubs of old, he offered a cigarette to the men as a gesture of goodwill.

Only the moustache man accepted. He wore a chequered farmer's cap from under which white tufts of hair fell at all angles. His nose was large with a crooked bridge, permanently crimson and pock-marked, and his thick white moustache was waxed at the ends. His eyes were sunken but piercingly grey, and the thick eyebrows above them were strikingly black. 'Ned,' came his gravelly tones as he offered a calloused hand, 'Ned Bailey.'

Stephen gave his name and returned the handshake. He was introduced to the other two men, Dave and Sam, and it was quickly clear that the three of them were farmers, or some other sort of agricultural workers, from the way that they dressed and spoke and the rough working hands that gripped his in turn.

The tense atmosphere warmed a little then, but Stephen could still feel the landlord keenly watching them from behind the bar as he half-filled in a crossword.

Ned gave brief introductions. Said that they worked the land north of the town, sold their wares at market, and usefully that he had been drinking in The Black Swan since he was a boy. Born and bred, Dave and Sam agreed, nodding sagely. It was clear that Ned was the spokesman, and the other two were merely backup singers to his main act.

'Funny place to send someone,' Ned grunted, 'for such tomfoolery.'

Stephen couldn't have agreed more, but decided to be tactful so as not to disrespect the natives. 'Yes, it was unexpected for me as well. I'm a senior editor. My boss thought I needed a holiday and sent me here writing a claptrap piece on ghost stories in the area as an excuse. It's a stunning place though, so there are worse places to be, for sure. Do you... do you hear much about such things around here?'

May as well be bold.

Whenever Stephen asked a question, Dave and Sam automatically looked at Ned, as if they hadn't the confidence to speak without permission, much like a child does with their parent.

'No.' Ned replied flatly. 'I don't go in for such foolishness.'

The conversation was immediately killed, eulogised, and buried. Stephen, lips pursed, looked the men over with his breath held. Then he did what every Englishman worth his salt did in situations like these and talked about the weather.

'Glad I got here when I did.' He said, nodding at the window. 'Wouldn't want to be stuck out on the roads in this.'

'Aye, it's a bad one.' Ned agreed, puffing on a regal. 'Bad time of year for us folk. Hope you're here a while, they'll be no getting out 'til week's done, by looks of it.'

Stuck in a remote village, snowed in, in a pub. Worse places to be, Stephen thought.

'Well, I'm with you.' He pressed, returning to the subject. 'I don't go in for fairy stories either. But it's my job, and I've got bills to pay. Don't suppose any of you know anybody that can help me out with a few tales? Folklore and such? I'd be very grateful to get this over with, I can tell you.'

Again, Dave and Sam looked to their chief, who this time looked back at them. Saying a lot with their eyes, they were, but sadly not with their mouths.

'Well.' Dave cleared his throat uncomfortably. 'There's that funny lass that lives next door, isn't there, lads?'

Ned didn't look happy with his friend, but said nothing.

Sam added 'aye, but you don't want to get mixed up with her. She's trouble, she is. Right wrong 'un.'

Stephen's ears pricked up. 'Oh? How so?'

'Queer sort.' Ned snapped, prickly with the topic, shaking his head dismissively. 'Folk say all sorts about her, daft buggers. Truth is she's just a nutter. You know how young 'un's are. She's, you know, into *all that.*'

'Into all *what*?'

Ned didn't reply, just sighed and finished his drink. The other two were struck suddenly mute. It was as clear as crystal that they'd overstepped a mark. Stephen was equal parts amused and curious.

'Don't bother yourself.' Ned grunted, standing up now. The others took his cue and stood with him. 'Pleased to meet you, Mr White. 'Scuse us.' And they filtered out through the door and into the snow, calling their goodbyes to the landlord as they went. Stephen was left alone, abandoned on the precipice of actually having something to work with. Well, that was confounding. He still couldn't shake the feeling that they had a story to tell, but were holding back. Whether that story was supernatural or not was up for debate, but it was all very cloak and dagger, whatever the tale. He was reminded of the Transylvanian villagers, talking in hushed tones at the arrival of the young Englishman at the inn, and when asked about the mysterious Count who owned the castle on the hill they would all fall silent and exchange knowing glances, brushing off the young Englishman and letting him wander off to his death, unwarned.

Stephen smiled to himself. Well this wasn't Transylvania and, although there was a castle, it was likely not the residence of a murderous count. Though it did have a poltergeist, if the upcoming Mrs Wood was to be believed.

He walked back to the bar, draining his glass as he stepped through the jumble of tables and chairs. The fire was raging nicely nearby and he stood for a while to enjoy it. Then he looked at the old chair that sat beside it again. It looked as if it would collapse if so much as a cat tried to perch on it. A big black ghostly cat, perhaps.

'Same again, please.' He said as the landlord reluctantly left his crossword behind to serve him. Then, as he pulled another pint, Stephen went for broke. 'I read the story to do with that chair,' he gestured, 'the jilted bride? Are you familiar with it?'

The landlord shrugged as he placed the glass in front of him on the bar and took a pound note. He turned to the till and said 'pubs always have ghost stories. Brings in punters. Folk love their superstitions.' And he pointed to a horseshoe that was nailed to the wall, right side up. 'Yeah, I know it. My dad was proprietor before I. Tales get passed down, don't they? They say it's bad luck to sit in her chair. If you do, they say she'll come for you.'

'Do they know who she was?'

'Nah.' He said, still sounding uninterested. 'Just stories. Likely she never was.' And he handed Stephen his change.

Stephen took it and made to return to his table, but stopped and turned before leaving.

'Ned was talking about a girl that lives next door.' He said. 'Weird sort, he said.'

The landlord smiled, but it was not a pleasant smile. He sat back at his stool and picked up his pencil. He examined the crossword book as he said 'they're on about Penny.'

'Penny?'

'Penny Black.' He said. 'Like the old stamp.'

Stephen knitted his eyebrows and sipped his drink. 'I don't follow.'

'The old Victorian stamps.' The landlord replied, still fixed on his crossword. 'You know. Oh, never mind. Anyway, they're on about her. Penny. She's in Canons Garth next door.

Not popular round here.'

Alright. There's one for an interview already. And the name's easy to remember, that's for sure. See? You're getting work done already, and all from the comfort of an open fire and a good drink.

'Can I ask, why is that?' Stephen asked. 'Ned said she was *into all that*, whatever that means, and they didn't seem to like talking about her at all.'

The landlord sighed, started to write something, then rubbed it out with the eraser on the end of his pencil. He gave Stephen a look that he couldn't decipher the intent of, and then he said 'here's one I'm stuck on; nine down – *folkloric hag or crone*. Five letters.'

It took Stephen only a moment to answer.

'Witch.' He said.

The landlord nodded and didn't look at him again.

'Enjoy your drink, Mr White.' He said.

7

The Ecclesiastical Court

Stephen awoke with a scream.

Not a yell or a gasp, a full-blown guttural scream. His eyes, though wide and searching, found only darkness, and though he twisted and turned his head desperately in the blackness, he could find nothing to inform him of where he was.

He felt around with damp fingers turned cold, finding the corner of the bed at last, and shoved himself to the edge. His bare feet felt carpeting. The thumping of his heart filled his ears and his breaths were rapid and shallow. He fumbled around, untwisting himself from the bedsheet, which was coiled around him in knots like restraints. It must only have been seconds before his reaching hands found the bedside table and switched on the little lamp, but it felt a great deal longer.

A heavy rock made of dread sat in his chest. A sinking, terrible thing infesting his body, dragging him down into a sensation of total horror. And he had no idea why.

He was in his room. Yes, The Black Swan. He arrived yesterday. The farmers in the pub. The landlord. For a few awful moments he had completely forgotten where he was or what he was doing.

He put a hand to his head and massaged his temples. A nightmare. It must have been. But he couldn't remember it now. He tried to, but whatever had plagued his sleep and jolted him awake, screaming in the dark, was gone and forgotten the moment he opened his eyes.

'Jesus.' He whispered as he realised that he was drenched in sweat. His vest was stuck to his back, and the cold dampness on the back of his neck and forearms made him shiver. When he turned to look at the bed behind him it looked like he had been wrestling a bear in it.

A half empty bottle of whisky sat on his nightstand next to a little teacup. He glared at it, then shook his head and stood. He walked to the little window, crouching down, and tried to look outside.

It was pitch black. Was this the middle of the night? He felt completely disoriented. He plucked his watch from atop the pile of clothing on the chair and saw that it was indeed morning. In fact, it was after eleven. He frowned and let out an exasperated sigh. Then, he lifted the latch and pushed the little window open.

A thick covering of snow fell from the glass and he was greeted by a draught of ice-cold air. The window was tiny, but big enough that he could poke his face through it and look out onto the market square.

'Shit.' He quietly exclaimed as he was met by nothing but pure untouched white. Helmsley had been buried. Thick high snowdrifts carpeted absolutely everything. His car below was half entombed. The road was no longer visible. The spires of the monument in the square stuck up through a pyramid of white. The sky was sheet grey and heavy, but it was no longer snowing. It was clear though that it had fallen heavily all night. Stephen was completely snowed in. He would just have to pray that there would be no more, and that within the next four days it would melt enough for him to escape this place. If his car even started, that is.

He could see the broken towers of the castle, peaked white, peering at him over the rooftops. Against the dark grey sky it looked like something from a horror movie. Stephen hated horror movies. He glared back at the ancient thing, engaged in some kind of fruitless staring contest for a few resentful moments before a thought occurred to him and he ducked back into his room.

He rooted around in his suitcase and pulled out a flip top notebook, bound in a rubber band with a pen. He opened it and hurriedly scribbled inside *cursed chair, Ned Bailey, Sam, Dave, Canons Garth, Penny Black.* Then he laughed to himself and rolled his eyes before he wrote *Witch?*

These people were backwards. They were living in the dark ages. They were superstitious and irrational. It was clear to him that they really believed in all of this hocus-pocus to the point at which they didn't even dare talk openly about it, instead choosing sideways suspicious glances and hushed whispers. Why on earth had the landlord talked in some kind of clumsy crossword-based code? Ghosts and witches. It beggared belief. He felt like running out into the town square with a ringing bell to cry aloud *hear ye! Hear ye! You're all delusional! You're all mentally ill and you ought to give your heads a collective shake! Grow up you looneys, it's 1988, not 1588!*

Speaking of looneys, Stephen had an appointment with Mrs Wood today, with her tales of ghostly encounters and spooky graffiti on the castle wall. That was at one. He had some time to kill and he knew what he wanted to do with it. Surprisingly enough, even to himself, this time it wasn't to drink.

He plucked a fresh shirt and a forest green jumper from his case, along with some pressed trousers and a rolled towel, and he opened his door to peek out into the corridor. When he was sure there was no one around he made for the bathroom on the landing.

Soon he was shaved and dressed and his hair was slicked tightly back. He had pulled on his shoes, wishing that he had packed some footwear more suitable for deep snow. He really had to learn to watch the weather forecast on tv before making a journey.

He trotted down the stairs and made his way through the bar area. The landlord was nowhere in sight and all of the lights were off. He patted his pocket to make sure he had remembered his key, and he pulled open the door to step outside.

The snow was easily two feet thick, and as soon as he stepped into it his shoe disappeared. He grumbled as he treaded his way out, being careful not to fall, and waving his arms a little to keep balance. Wet socks here I come.

There was barely anyone around. The post office across the square looked closed, as did the little bank. The fish and chip shop that had provided Stephen with his supper last night (after an almighty amount of beer and a whisky nightcap) looked closed too. Not a light on anywhere. Clearly this town went into hibernation in conditions such as these.

His eyes danced with black spots against the unbroken and dazzling whiteness that surrounded him, making him squint up at the steel roof of the sky. It was bitterly cold; his breaths were plumes of vapour that hung in the air around him. Already his nose was numb and the bones in his hands ached. He pulled up the collar of his long overcoat and made for his destination.

Canons Garth looked even moodier and more crooked with a covering of snow dressing it. The windows were frosted white, looking like they'd been decorated with fake snow-in-a-can that people sprayed on their panes at Christmas. The terracotta roof had become milk-coloured sparkling velvet, and the thin chimney that poked out of it was spouting smoke.

Let's see if The Wicked Witch of the North is home, Stephen thought as he stepped through the gate. He *clacked* on the door using the little iron knocker screwed in there, and he waited.

No one answered. He gave it a few more clacks for good measure, and when no one came to the door he made to leave. There was smoke pouring from that chimney, though. It was very likely she was in there. Perhaps she was worried that he was carrying a torch and pitchfork. Perhaps she'd mistaken him for Matthew Hopkins.

He pulled out the notebook and pen that he'd brought with him, and wrote a short letter.

Good afternoon, my name is Stephen White. I am a senior editor with The Evening Gazette, in town to write a piece about certain supernatural happenings around Helmsley. I was told that you are knowledgeable about such things, and was wondering if you'd be so kind as to meet with me for a short interview. I am staying next door at the inn. I'll try knocking again later, but if I don't, and if you're interested, please come and find me. With thanks, Steve.

He tore the page free, folded it, and slid it through the letter box.

He tramped away through the snow, his shoes already soaked, and each step making a sharp crunching sound as the top layer froze hard in minus temperatures.

The door opened behind him.

He turned to see a young woman dressed in about the strangest way he'd ever seen. He tried not to look surprised so as not to appear rude, but her appearance in the crack of the doorway was at first startling. She was a black mass with a face as white as the snow under his feet. He'd seen punks and rockers back in the 70's, sure, but they hadn't quite looked like her.

Her hair was like a huge ebony nest, dyed black and backcombed outrageously into a flood of tangles and tresses that stuck up everywhere, stopping around her shoulders, like she'd stuck her fingers into an electrical socket. She was wearing a velvet dress that reached her bare feet with a thick belt around her middle, swathed in little chains and decorative silver charms. The dress was sleeveless but her arms were covered in black lace that looked like some kind of old-fashioned Victorian weave, and around her thin wrists were bracelets and bangles, all silver and so numerous that they took up most of her forearms.

Her face and neck were powdered completely stark white, and her black eye makeup reminded him of an Egyptian; blocky but slenderly applied, ending in points that curled up at either side. There was a silver ring in her right nostril and large hoops through her ears.

Basically this girl was in black and white. She looked like she'd stepped from an old film into the world of colour. The only colour about her whatsoever was her eyes, which were a bright and brilliant blue.

Stephen stared in shock for a moment too long before he said 'ah, good morning. I ah, I'm sorry to disturb you, might you be Penny?'

With a slender hand and black nails she held his letter up.

'This you?' She asked.

'Ah, yes. Sorry, I thought you weren't home.' He stepped back towards the door. The girl was peering through a narrow opening and looked wary, ready to slam it at any moment.

'Yeah, I'm Penny. Penelope, but people took to calling me Penny,' she said, 'and sorry Steve, but I'm not interested in being in a paper.'

She sounded local, a soft Yorkshire accent at least, and she was about as friendly as the rest of the folk he'd met so far. She couldn't have been more than twenty by the looks of her, or what he could glean through all that makeup.

'No, of course, that's absolutely fine.' He said, folding his hands and trying to appear as friendly as possible, despite her rudeness. 'Any information I can get would be helpful, and I can cite you as an anonymous source, or not include you at all. I just need a bit of help, really. The folk I've met so far haven't been particularly...'

She laughed dryly. 'Helpful?' She finished for him. 'No, they won't be, and you can search this town from end-to-end and only find the same thing. What makes you think I'm of use?'

Stephen began to answer but it was quickly clear the question was rhetorical.

'I'll *tell* you what,' she continued, 'the pissheads next door sent you, didn't they? Go and see the freak at Canons Garth? That weirdo bitch, that Halloween nutcase, that satanist pervert, that crackpot sicko? I could go on, Steve.'

Her voice was rising, and each time she said his name it was utterly condescending. Stephen felt his face flush.

'You know what, never mind!' He snapped. 'Bloody hell, it was a simple enough request. A basic *no* would have done!' and he began to stomp back down the garden path.

Bloody teenagers. Christ, he'd just about had it with this town already. To hell with it; as soon as he had done his interview with Mrs Wood he was out of there. Fuck the rest of the week; he was going home. Bunch of backwater weirdos, sheep-shaggers, coffin-dodgers and superstitious simpletons, the lot of them. Well, fuck them, fuck Helmsley, and fuck

Canons Garth, whatever the hell that even meant.

Penny broke into soft laughter behind him. It wasn't the sarcastic kind, but rather a genuine little burst of amusement. He turned his head to see black glossy lips curled into a smile, revealing white teeth.

'It means Ecclesiastical courtyard.' She said.

'*What?*'

'Canons Garth.' She explained. 'Canon means Ecclesiastical law or decree, Garth means courtyard. This was a rectory. I thought reporters were supposed to be good researchers.'

The colour that had rushed to Stephen's face quickly drained pale. His mouth was open but no words came. He shook his head slightly as his eyes widened below furrowed brows.

'I didn't...' he finally managed, '...I didn't say anything.'

Her face was quite serious again when she replied 'you did. Well, you did in a way.' She studied him for a few moments as he stood dumbstruck, looked him up and down, and then said 'interesting.'

He glanced down at himself then back up at her. 'What... what is?'

'Alright.' She said with a sigh as she decided something. 'You'd better come in. *Five minutes* though, and no more. And I want to be anonymous, got it?'

Astonished and suddenly feeling quite adrift, Stephen nodded and approached as she opened the door for him, and with a pounding heart he stepped inside and closed it.

8
The Great Big What If

Stephen followed the girl, her feet padding on flagstone floors as her jewellery jingled and chimed, down a narrow hallway. The inside of the house looked as ancient as it did out, with low-hanging beams and white plaster covering stone. It smelled old and musty, and there was an overpoweringly strong aroma of incense in the air that was something like pine forest mixed with a foreign spice. He could all but taste it. They passed a crooked staircase carpeted red with a banister that looked like it would give at the slightest pressure, and she lead him left into a room from which strange music was playing.

Thin, distant guitars and drums that echoed as if they were in a cathedral, a cold sounding synth and a man singing in a high, maniacal way.

The room was swimming in a fog of scented smoke. It was drifting from a stick in a wooden holder beside the record player from which the strange music was coming. There was a black paper sleeve propped next to the spinning vinyl that read *Bauhaus.*

The room was small and low, as he imagined all the rooms must be in a medieval house like that, and it was dimly lit. The window was chequered with lead lining and the little squares of glass that made up the pane were very old and tainted by time, letting only muted light through. The room was mainly lit by a standing brass lamp in the corner and by the flickering from a petite stone fireplace, built into a stone wall that looked like it would be better suited to a castle keep. The floor there was flagstones too but covered mostly by a traditionally patterned green rug. She motioned for him to take a seat in an armchair that looked Victorian and threadbare, with a well-worn seat and high, curved arms.

Penny dropped down onto the rug, cross legged beneath the billowing velvet of her dress and folded her hands in her lap. Stephen took out his notepad and pen and cleared his throat uncomfortably. His head was swimming. He couldn't think straight. Perhaps it was the suffocating incense, or that fact that it was very warm in this enclosed space, but he just couldn't get his head together. The house was an assault on the senses and the more he glanced around the more things he saw that made him feel that perhaps she was *indeed* a weirdo; there were decks of cards in packs, stacked neatly on the stone fire surround. Tarot cards, oracle cards. And on the wall above it there was a tapestry hanging. It was large and made of coarse black wool, and into it was stitched a large white pentagram; a five pointed star enclosed in a circle.

'Let's just get this out of the way,' Penny began, 'yes, that is my real name, and yes, I'm well aware of what a Penny Black used to be. So either my parents had a far quicker sense of humour than I gave them credit for, or they unintentionally cursed me for life due to their denseness. Don't write that down.'

'Duly noted.' Stephen said, coughing a little. 'Now, I'm...' He crushed his eyelids together and rubbed at his forehead before picking up his pen again, '... I'm interviewing a local woman this afternoon about the castle. She has claims about a poltergeist that carves things into the stone there. But what I'm *also* interested in is the town itself. I've had a bit of a primer on The Black Swan and the ghosts people say haunt it, but what I'm really looking for is personal experiences,' inside he was cringing and had to force the words out, trying to colour them with some kind of conviction, 'sightings of spirits, witnesses of supernatural events like moving objects and such. Do you...?'

Penny was smiling that impish smile again. 'You don't believe in any of this, do you?' She said.

Stephen paused, pen poised.

'Well I... I'm not sure whether I believe in this kind of thing or not.' He said to placate her, trying to be kind.

'It doesn't care.' She said with what appeared to be total conviction. 'That's the first and most important thing to understand. If you believe, it doesn't care, if you say it's all a load of shit, it doesn't care. It just *is*.'

He glanced at her with raised eyebrows. He found that to be bollocks but it made a hell of a good quote. He scribbled it down at once, omitting the word *shit* and replacing it with *nonsense*.

'And so,' he continued, 'what is it that makes you so sure? What experiences do you claim to have had to make your certainty so strong?'

'I'm a psychic medium.' She answered with a completely straight face. 'And a practicing witch. Don't write that down.'

Stephen frustratedly paused to scribble out what he'd just written. 'A witch.' He muttered. 'Okay. Sure. And how would you define that, exactly? Don't worry, I'm not writing it down.'

'Not Wicca, if that's what you're thinking.' She said, though he had no idea what that was. 'Wicca is a new practice, and a great deal fluffier than actual witchcraft.'

'So... what exactly would you call *actual witchcraft*?'

'It's an ancient practice based on natural energies, exercised by druids and shamans since before Christendom and recorded history.' She said. 'It's about becoming attuned to the magic that exists all around us, that can be manipulated and used for good, or for ill.'

Stephen paused again. He smiled politely.

'It's alright.' Penny said, seeing his face. 'It's clear you don't buy any of this. But, you asked.'

'I'm sorry,' Stephen fixed her with a look, 'I'll be honest, I don't. That sounds barmy. I respect your *right* or whatever, to believe it, but *come on*! I could never believe what you believe.'

'My beliefs don't require you to.' She answered sharply. 'You're all the same, you lot. Someone says witch and you immediately assume a satanist that sacrifices goats and turns people into toads and rides a broomstick and all that. The men that used to burn those women made that shit up as a good excuse to light the pyres.'

He was quickly making up his mind now. That thing that had happened outside; that wasn't her performing some kind of magical trick, reading his mind. He'd said it out loud without realising, or muttered it, at least.

'And you said you're a psychic? A medium?' He asked unenthusiastically.

'I channel spirits. I sense energy. I see things, feel things. They call it *gifted*, but I don't like the word.' She said, leaning back on her hands and arching her back. 'It's something that just *is*, and takes working practice to hone.' She saw his expression and was amused by it. 'You asked, I told!'

'Fine.' He replied, waving it away, though he was desperate to ask her to prove it, knowing she would give him the usual story of *it doesn't work that way*. 'Let's get onto the ghosts. Can you tell me some of the local stories about them, or things that you've experienced?'

'Well,' she sighed, 'it's hard to say exactly. I've seen and felt so many things here that it'd be too long to list... sorry, hold on, I've got to ask, why are you doing this?'

'Doing what?'

'You think this is all *barmy* so why are you writing an article about ghosts? Pretty niche subject for a reporter like you to be chasing.'

'A reporter like...' he hissed, irritated, '... I'm *not* a reporter, I'm a senior editor. And ok, well, to be frank I'm doing this because I'm here for a break and it's a fluff piece for a little page six article that no one is going to care about! I wouldn't have picked this town or this story in a million years! I'm doing it because I have to, because my boss dictated it, and all I want to do is get out of this hole and back to my life!'

She smiled and her eyes lit up as he spoke.

'That's more like it. Feel better now?' She asked. 'Life's far more fun when you're honest. Pure truths should always be spoken.'

Pure truths. A flash of memory, drowned in booze but briefly resurfacing, came back to him.

I hate my life here, and I am fucking miserable.

He shivered, but held his hands up in surrender. 'Fair enough. Well, now I've been honest. I've been chained to a task that's below me and forced out of my office, presumably because I've been making everyone uncomfortable with my misery. So yeah, gun to my head, and all that.'

The record came to an end, and Penny hopped to her feet to turn it over. She dropped the needle, turned the volume down a little, and turned to face him from near the window.

She was a strange silhouette with little shoulders and huge hair. 'They don't know what to say to you.' She said, cocking her head slightly to the side and examining him with growing interest. 'They don't want to talk to you at all, really. They can't understand what you've been through and they don't want to. It's too heavy. Oh, I can see it on you now.'

The room suddenly felt uneasy. His chest felt a little tight. He didn't like the way she was staring at him. He squirmed uncomfortably in the chair.

She just gazed in silence.

Stephen felt genuinely creeped out now, though he wouldn't outwardly show it.

'You can...' he swallowed, '...see *what* on me, exactly?'

'Your aura.' She peered harder at him, and he could see that she was rubbing her fingers in circular motions against her thumbs. 'It's barely there at all, and what's there is black. Sludgy. There's barely an ounce of good energy in you. You're poisoned.'

He made a face and shook his head. 'Look, I don't know what an aura is supposed to be, but I...'

'Huh, that's odd.' She cut across him. 'Why can I see an image of a green dragon?'

'Hey! *Hey*! That's enough!' He yelled, and stood up quickly. 'Stop that! What the hell are you doing?'

'Sorry, you're very easy to read.' She said, straightening her head. The moment that she did the uneasy feeling stopped.

It became suddenly apparent to Stephen that she had been interviewing him this whole time, and not the other way around.

'Just...' he began, calming himself and taking a breath,

'... just tell me about the ghosts so I can leave you to do... whatever the hell it is you do in here. I don't believe in this stuff and I don't want to.'

'Good for you.' Penny smirked, and resumed her position on the rug. 'I believe in *everything*. Life's a lot more interesting and exciting when you do, you should try it.'

'You believe in *everything*?'

'I believe in God.' She said. 'I believe in Satan and the angels on both sides. I believe in spirit beings, human and otherwise. I believe in the divine goddess and her horned lover. I believe in magic. I believe that the earth is a place of deep enchantment, and that there are worlds beyond it. I believe in werewolves, vampires – well, revenants – demons and deities, and everything else in-between. And best of all, I believe, I *know*, that they are all connected and are part of the same thing. I like to call it *The Great Big What If*. You should open your mind a bit more, Whitey, you never know what you might learn.'

Stephen froze. His eyes were saucers.

'What did you call me?'

She raised her eyebrows, and seemed genuinely confused by his shock.

'That's what they all call you, isn't it? Whitey? I know you hate it, but I kinda like it.'

He stayed frozen, standing in front of the chair. He'd gone a bit pale. The fire crackled and the high-voiced man sang something about *hollow hills*, but he couldn't hear any of that anymore. He was completely lost. He needed a drink. Or seven.

'Sorry, I was just proving a point. I didn't mean to freak you out. I can *help* you, you know.' She added. 'I can do that. You need some serious healing.'

'What I need,' he barked back, furious now, a fury driven by outright fear, 'is for you to answer my questions! If you're not going to do that then I'll be going!'

She rolled her eyes. 'I can give you a simple answer, a dullards answer if you'd like – Oh, I saw a glass move along the bar and smash on the floor. Oh, I saw an apparition out of the corner of my eye in the ladies toilets – or, I can give you the truth: There are many levels to it. There are earthbound spirits, intelligent beings that often don't know they've passed on. There are repeating energies - some call it stone tape theory - they're recordings, if you like, of significant events that replay over and over. There's layers. There's no science to it but it goes very deep, anyway. So yes, I see spirits in The Black Swan and everywhere else, for that matter. Not always, but often. The earth is a graveyard, Steve. To say that only certain places are haunted isn't true. *Everywhere* is haunted.'

Stephen was slowly lowering himself back into his chair as she talked. He was transfixed for a few moments before he remembered himself, and began to furiously scribble as she continued.

'But *this* little town, well.' She looked deadly serious now. 'There's something else about this town. I'm sure that, whether you're aware of it or not, you've felt something... *off* about it.'

He pause his writing to say 'everyone seems guarded. Standoffish.'

'They're frightened.' She looked around the room. 'They refuse to face the truth of this place even though they can feel it in their bones, so they go to work and they drink and they don't talk about it.'

'What are they frightened of?'

'They don't know. They just know it's not good.'

'And do you know?'

She shrugged. 'There's lots to be afraid of. And I know for sure that there's something... sour about this ground. They think it's the pub or the castle with the poltergeist, but there's more to it than that. Like I said, it's hard to explain.'

Stephen stopped writing and looked over his notes. All very interesting, but pretty vague and unintelligible. He sighed and looked over at this strange young woman.

'You alright, Whitey?' She quipped. 'Are you sure you don't believe in ghosts? 'Cos it looks like you just saw one.'

'*Please*,' he closed his eyes for a second, '*please* don't call me that.'

She laughed loudly. 'Oh, now I'm *definitely* going to call you that!' She chortled. 'You're far too easy to wind up!'

Defeated, he nodded and stood again, tucking his notebook into his coat pocket.

'I've already taken up too much of your time.' He said. 'And as I said, I'm meeting Mrs Wood soon. I'd thank you for your time, but, well,' it was his turn to give her a dry little smile, 'in all honesty I'm only more confused and to be frank, pretty *freaked out* by you, as you put it.'

'I'll take that as a compliment.' She said, smiling back, and she stood and lead him back through the ramshackle rectory to the front door.

Standing out in the bitter midday cold, he turned back one last time.

'Seriously though,' he burst out, clearly internally battling with something, 'how did you know that they call me Whitey in my home town? How did you know that my colleagues feel that way about me, and how did you know about The Green Dragon?'

She shook her head as if patiently teaching a child.

'I told you. I'm psychic.' She replied. 'Go meet Mrs Wood. She's a bit odd. I know that's rich coming from me, but she is. Be patient with her, she's been through a lot too, just like you.'

His mind reeling and his heart heavy, Stephen only had the energy left to merely nod.

'I meant what I said, though.' Penny said in closing. 'You do need some work doing on that aura, amongst other things. I'm a good healer. Offer still stands. Anyway, good luck ghost hunting, Whitey!' And she closed the door.

Stephen slowly turned and tramped back through the snow away from the house, a very different man than the one that had entered.

9
Millie

'It just doesn't make any sense.' Stephen whispered, over and over again. He muttered it under his breath like a mantra, but no enlightenment came. His nerves had been calmed by a whisky chased with a Guinness and a chain of cigarettes, but his mind wasn't quite so easy to piece back together.

He'd come back into The Swan, demanded a drink from the landlord who had informed him that the pub didn't open for another twenty minutes, and had screamed *do you want my money or not?* The landlord had relented, and his solitary lodger had greedily consumed his remedy. He watched him now, a shaken man with a grey face, stick thin and gaunt, as he raised a trembling regal to his lips and stared into space, muttering.

'I take it,' he said, 'you went calling on Penny?'

Stephen nodded.

'Well, I did try to warn you.' He said with a sigh.

'You might have been more direct.' Stephen snapped. 'Why can't anyone around here just be straight with me?'

'Not for me to say, I don't speak for them.' Came the reply.

Stephen rolled his eyes. Classic example, right there. Question dodged, vague response given.

How could he come back from this? How on earth could what have just happened, *happened*? There was a girl next door, *a child*, that had read his mind. There just wasn't any other explanation for it, and believe him, he had tried to find one. She couldn't have researched him, she had no idea he was coming on the particular day at that particular time. She couldn't have snuck a peek in his wallet for any information, he had it on him the whole time, and there wasn't much to learn from his ID cards anyway.

There was just no way she could have known those things. Whitey. Bloody *Whitey*! No one knew that name outside of the pub. And yes, The Green Dragon, she said she'd seen an image of it – an image she saw in *his head*! And more than that, she knew how the people that he knew *felt* about him, and that he was a man who had been through something traumatic. Stephen closed his eyes and lowered his head.

'I cannot allow myself to believe in this stuff. I *can't*.' He said aloud. Though in truth he was part horrified, part intrigued. What if? Just *what if*?

A cold lingering fear coiled around his chest. If this whole thing had turned out to be some kind of sick joke, a hoax concocted by that dickhead Matthews, then Stephen would honestly have been more relieved than angry about it. But no, of course it wasn't a prank. What would be the point?

'I'll say only this,' offered the landlord, stroking his ample beard, 'people don't talk about her because they say that she knows what you think, and they say she'll put a hex on you.'

An hour ago Stephen would've laughed heartily at that. Now, not so much. 'Is that like a curse?'

'Aye.' The landlord turned and walked towards the

backroom door. 'I'll say no more. I've set you up a place in the dining area for your interview, as you requested.'

'Thank you.' Stephen replied with a gentle groan. He'd almost forgotten about that. Mrs Wood was incoming, she'd be there any minute. 'I never caught your name, Mr?'

'Bill. Well, call me Billy. If you need anything just shout, you know where I am.' The landlord replied with a softening of his features. Clearly, Stephen had his sympathy, at least.

'Thank you, Billy.' Stephen said as the younger man nodded and left, and suddenly he felt a knot in his throat and for a fleeting second he wanted to cry. People, as a rule, generally weren't kind to him. A little went a long way.

He chugged on the stout and mused on the fact that he had never missed a dingy old Teesside council flat more in his life, or the smoggy skies above the high street, or the cobbled yard of The Dragon. He'd even have preferred to have been back in his office, and that was saying something.

And now here he was, about to be serenaded with yet more spooky stuff just when he'd already had his fill of it for the day. Well, he intended to keep his promise to himself; he was going to complete this interview, get as much as he could from it, take a few pictures for the piece, and then he was out of there. He planned to be back at his stool in The Green Dragon by that evening. It was pretty depressing, really, but at least things made more sense in Stockton on Tees.

It wasn't for Stephen to know just how strange the rest of his day was about to be, and it wasn't for him to know how far down the rabbit hole went. His morning, when he would later compare it to his afternoon and evening, was child's play.

The door opened behind him, ringing a little bell that hung on a spring above it. He turned on his stool and saw a woman standing in the doorway with a mackintosh and a headscarf on. She was very thin and a little shaky as she approached him, and when she smiled the deep wrinkles of her face were apparent, though her eyes looked warm and kind through the strong magnification of her square glasses. He stood and held out a hand as she reached him. 'Good afternoon, Mrs Wood?'

'Yes, that's right. You're from the newspaper?'

'The Evening Gazette, madam, yes. My name's Stephen. Please, come and sit, might I offer you a drink of some kind?'

He led her to the circular table by the window in the next room, where the fire had been freshly lit. Mrs wood had a steaming cup of tea placed on the table. Stephen left his pint at the bar. Might as well keep up the façade of professionalism.

She took off her headscarf to reveal a spongy grey perm. In the light that came through the window, reflecting brightly against the snow, he could see that she was very elderly.

'Thank you for coming, Mrs Wood,' Stephen began, pulling out his notebook and hurriedly flipping past the pages that he had written that morning, 'I won't take up much of your time.'

'Call me Millie, young lad.' She said gently and smiled. 'Take up as much of me time as you like! There's no hurrying in a place like this. Mind you, I'm seventy-nine, so time's precious, and all that,' she chuckled.

He politely returned her smile and said 'so, I understand that you've had some experiences you cannot explain,' feeling decidedly less silly saying it now, 'and then there's the castle.'

'Oh, I can explain them!' She exclaimed. 'Nothing unexplained about them! I'm being haunted by what looks like me late husband.'

Stephen paused, eyebrows raised, before writing that down. 'I see.' He said, wondering why he found the statement so darkly humorous for a second.

'It sounds dippy, I know.' She said, reading his face, 'Not long ago I would've told you to get stuffed if you'd suggested such a thing. But I've seen him, many times, since he passed.'

'And where do you see him?'

'He stands at the end of me bed every night.'

Stephen frowned, and shuffled in his chair. It didn't seem so funny now. 'And, what does he do? Does he speak to you?'

Her warm smile became a token one. 'I think... yes, I think I'd better explain things in order. I get muddled, so I'd best tell you it as it happened.'

'Of course, madam, I mean, *Millie*. Take your time.'

'Jack and I, that were his name, used to come to Helmsley every spring. Lovely market here, I mean there were back then, and we used to enjoy the walled gardens and the little theatre. We come from Northallerton, born and bred. Jack were a miner, I were a teacher when I were younger. Anyroad, we lived through the two wars. Second one claimed both me sons.'

Stephen tried to offer his condolences but she continued over him. Perhaps she was tired of hearing that, or of even thinking about it.

'Anyroad, my Jack; he worked all his life. Never thought of retiring, though I had many years ago; his pay were enough to keep us. He was taken from me, oh, twelve years ago now. Died in the mine.'

The scratching of Stephen's pen stopped. 'Your husband worked down a mine when he was in his *late sixties*?'

She laughed. 'Heaven's no! No, he were a supervisor. Getting too old for all that muck and misery. Anyroad, he were down there with a few lads in a mine near here, a lead mine in Thirsk, and it fell in on them. Six lads and my Jack, crushed.'

Stephen dry swallowed and quietly said, 'I'm very sorry to hear that.'

'Oh, *well*,' she waved it past, not engaging with the grief she must still have felt, 'it happened and that's it. Anyroad, some years after, and with the widow's pension and all, I decided to move here to this town that we'd loved so dear. Better to remember the good times, isn't it Stephen?'

A brief but powerful image spewed itself up from his subconscious. A day out in Scarborough. The beach. Angela. Their son. The sound of amusement arcades and of the sea, the smell of candyfloss and brine.

Can I ride a donkey, daddy?

Stephen jolted back slightly, his spine striking the wood of the chair. He cleared his throat as his face flushed. Seeing this, Mrs Wood paused her story.

'I apologise,' he said, his voice suddenly as frail as hers, throwing a glance at the bar where his drink still stood, 'please continue, Millie.'

A liver-spotted hand with fingers thin and dry reached over and patted his. She nodded.

'You're grieving too.' She said kindly. 'That's alright, dear. You needn't explain, Stephen.'

A moment of painfully sharp understanding passed between them. His eyes glassed over. 'Steve.' He said.

She patted his hand one more time, then continued.

'Right then, Steve. So, I came here to the place we'd loved and shared to remind me of him, and to spend the rest of me days peacefully. Nothing happened for a long while. Years, really. But then, a few month back...'

'He started visiting you?'

She huffed. 'Aye, you could say so.'

He waited while the old woman took a deep breath, sipped her tea, and composed herself.

'First time he came, I thought it were a nightmare.' She said. 'I weren't really one for nightmares, but I thought it must have been. Something so horrible couldn't have been anything else.'

Despite the fire the room felt colder.

'He were stood at the end of me bed. He said nothing, he did nothing. He just... stared at me. Didn't move, didn't breathe, didn't blink. I called out in fright as any would, but he didn't answer. Just stood and stared.'

Stephen finished writing what she had said. The skin of his neck and back tingled. Had he had this conversation yesterday he might have thought her a crazy old woman, but today he was no longer sure he could claim that with 100% certainty. 'I can certainly see how that would be a horrific thing to see.' He offered.

Her eyes locked with his. 'That weren't the part that horrified me so. It was how he looked. He were... *wrong*.'

'Wrong?'

'You know, when you hear folk talk about seeing a ghost, or whatever they call them, they always describe it same way. You know; a pale figure in white, or a glowing pretty light. Especially when it's a loved one. But my Jack... oh, no. He were anything but.'

Suddenly, the room around Stephen seemed magnified. It was like every creak of the old wood of the inn was enhanced and abrasive, even the crackling and popping of the logs on the fire making him jumpy. It felt like the moment before a terrible event, the last seconds of peace, rising to a cacophony of a disaster. He waited, his breath held.

'How can I put it?' She said, her voice lower. 'He were...

rotten. He weren't how he'd been in life, he was as he must have been when he died. He were black, grimy, like the boys down the mines. Covered in soot and slag. And he were bloody. *So bloody*; all over his filthy clothes and the hard hat he were still wearing. I could smell the mine on him, like old smoke and coal. It were in the room as real as any smell! He were standing there in the dark covered in pitch and blood and there was a stink about him too. A stink like rot, like puss or infection. And the thing I remember most about that first time were his eyes.'

Stephen had stopped writing. He sat frozen.

'His eyes were white, all but glowing in the dark.' She wasn't looking at him now, instead gazing past him and into nothing. 'And they looked straight at me, and they never moved away nor blinked. And they looked... *hateful*, Steve. Like he hated me and like he wanted to hurt me, but he couldn't move to do it.'

A sheer chill ran down Stephen's back, raising gooseflesh on his arms as he stared at this woman. There wasn't a thing about her that made him think she was lying. If someone was going to make up a ghost story, why would they make up *that*?

'What did you do?' His voice was a whisper.

She blinked and came back to herself, looking back at her interviewer. 'Well, I screamed as I said and I went for me lamp light, and the moment it was switched on he were gone. And after I'd gotten meself together I thought I must've had the most horrible dream, and that were that. But what I didn't admit to meself until later were this; though he'd gone I could still smell the mine, and the blood, and the rot. As if he were still stood there, staring at me like he hated me, only now I couldn't see him. And the smell never went, and, as I later found out, neither did he.'

Again, the thought hammered inside his head; why would she make up something like this? She would be granted a modest payment for her story, certainly, but modest was the operative word here. She certainly wasn't in it for the money.

'Why have you come to me with this, to The Gazette?' He said aloud as the thought occurred to him. 'What help do you imagine it could give you?'

The sky outside was becoming blanketed in even heavier cloud, and the room darkened further still. Millie shrugged, then sipped at her tea as casually as if she were catching up on local gossip with a friend. 'Oh, I don't know.' She replied, blowing on her steaming drink. 'I have to talk to someone about it, heaven knows no one around this town will. I suppose I hoped that someone out there would read about it, and perhaps that someone would be the kind of person that could help with this sort of thing. We haven't had a vicar in residence here for about three years now. Passed away suddenly, bless him.'

Several things occurred to Stephen at once, and he spoke in a hurry.

'Did he live in the rectory there, Canons Garth?' He asked. 'I happen to have just come from there. Surely you know the girl that lives there now, and what everyone says about her?'

She frowned. 'She moved in a few years back. Queer sort. He left her his house in his will. Folk aren't happy with it. A new cleric should be allowed to move in. A good man, with a respectable family. But she won't sell.'

His eyes widened. 'She's the *vicars daughter*?'

Millie nodded with a sharp eye aimed at his. She leaned in and said in a quiet voice 'seems sacrilegious, Doesn't it?'

Stephen was dumbstruck. He looked down at his

notepad again, his eyes roving over the words. He caught something. 'When you first introduced yourself, you said that you were being haunted by something that *looks like* your late husband.'

'Aye.' Her voice seemed hardened.

'And why did you phrase it like that?'

'Because *that thing* in my bedroom is not my Jack.' She said. 'He would never, ever seek to frighten me so, and he would never look at me with such hate. He were a good man. A gentle man. That thing in me house is neither. It's something that looks like him, but it has evil in its heart.'

The room stayed icy cold, and grew darker still. Suddenly Stephen felt like putting Helmsley in his rear view mirror for a whole new set of reasons. Millie looked him up and down, and said 'I think it's best I take you to the castle, if you'd be so good as to help me there. There's something you have to see, before you properly understand.'

10
Help, Prayer, Bound

They crunched through high wild grass and thick snow that had frozen into a crust, then over a narrow bridge that traversed the old moat of the castle, which was now a deep waterless crevasse. The largest structure remaining of the castle, amongst low stone walls and broken peaks was what he had been told was the east tower; all that was left of the original structure. It was a partially standing block, massively high, with one wall completely gone, and had all the usual hallmarks of a ruin – long, thin windows in the grey stone, a turreted roof, and a narrow and steep spiral staircase within, mostly demolished, with the trip-step that all castles had to cause a marauding enemy to stumble and fall.

It loomed against a sky that was now as dark and as grey as the stones that comprised it. The wind was wilder there, on higher ground, and all around they were surrounded by distant forests on the hills, whose trees swayed with the winter gusts, nestled in fields blanketed white.

Standing opposite the tower was a relatively newer looking building. A Mansion, built by the Manners family in the sixteenth century, who had taken over the grounds during the comparatively peaceful period following the medieval ages.

Stephen and Millie, he holding her arm to support her, trudged through the icy wet. He didn't like a woman of her age being up there. Though he had his best winter coat on with his collars turned up, the wind bit right through it and froze him to his bones, which were already aching. His face stung and his nose was numb, so god knew what it must have been like for an elderly lady like her. He, for the third time, protested that they should get her back into the warm, but she wouldn't have it, insisting that this wouldn't take long. He supposed so. He had his camera with him, hooked over his shoulder with a leather strap. He would hear her tale, get the photos, and get out of there.

Low foundational walls were the only indication that a castle had ever stood there, though for the most part they too were little more than mounds of snow, camouflaged and dangerous. One wrong step and they could be tripping or slipping over against hard rock. She guided him through it, her eyes watering against the wind, and led him towards the tower.

'Manor house on the west side.' She said with a quick gesture to it. 'And though it has it's ghost stories, it's not why we're here. The writing's yonder, inside the tower.'

She navigated the stones and the uneven ground with ease, almost pulling him along rather than the other way around. Her face was flushed and her eyes were bright. She looked strangely manic, but not in an excited way. More like an obsessive way. There was something unhealthy about it. She took him around the base of the tower, turned a corner, and there was the entrance to the ruin; a set of steps that lead down through a fractured arch.

'Careful 'ere.' She said, and together they tentatively stepped into the castle remains.

Now they were inside a relic, the stones cold and damp, green and black with moss and mould. Bitterly cold water dripped and trickled down 900 year-old brickwork, and now the sound of shoes in snow had been replaced by the crunch of gravel underfoot.

The tower interior was a ghost of the living quarters it had once been. One could make out where the levels had been, ceilings and floors, and where the stairs had once been affixed that connected them. There was a partial piece of the roof left, the rest open to the melancholy and tumultuous sky, with the arched windows only suggesting the shape they had once been, now more like open wounds. This dwelling had seen hundreds of years of war and death, evidenced by the state in which it now stood. It was, in these conditions, like a propped-up corpse. Stephen turned on the spot, his head raised to examine it, his breath spewing out like steam. He grimaced. It was an utterly morbid place. He had no taste for it, but imagined he knew a girl that did.

Millie had let go of his arm and had walked to a dark corner opposite the door they had entered through. Stephen stepped around a low spherical column of stone, central to the room, which he supposed must have been a support pillar, and joined her.

'Here, Steve.' She called.

The corner she was standing in was more enclosed than the rest of the room, sheltered partially by a jagged outcrop made of old bricks that jutted into open sky. Even in such cold, he could smell old air. Sharp and musty, a lot of the stone matted in black mould. He peered in, wishing he had brought a torch, and stepped so that he was by the old woman's side. She pointed with a finger that convulsed with cold.

He quickly adjusted his eyes and realised that this area was covered in graffiti. Not modern graffiti, made using spray cans or marker pens, but old writing, made using a knife or other chipping tool. The names and dates were fascinating. He'd never seen these kinds of scribbles before on a building so old. A great deal of them were merely initials, though even the lettering itself was beautifully carved, more like typeset than handwritten, but others were full names and dates.

'T. Boodle.' He read aloud. 'March 1885. Wow. 1630 here, but no name. W. Haselton, 1815. William Leadley, 1787. These are very impressive.'

'Aye, yes, I suppose,' she replied, 'most castles have those, if you care to look. But here, *here* is where I mean…' and she pressed her finger to a spot among the names and dates, where new engravings had been made.

There were a few words there, yes, in rows, he could make them out now. They were lighter, shallower markings in the stone, but still legible. And they were anything but beautifully carved like the others. They looked scrawled, frantic and rushed, like the scribblings of a toddler with a crayon. If he had to guess, he'd say they'd been made with a knife. A barely sharp one, at that. The words were hard to make out amongst the other more vivid markings, but he could tell that they were English words of some kind.

He squinted at them, and said 'can't see much. They're words, I suppose, but I can't quite tell. What's the story with them?'

'Here.' She said, drawing her finger up the stones to the first of the words. 'This were the first one. In the Summer, I were here and saw it. I'd been in here the week before, and no such word had been there. I thought it odd.'

'And what is the word?'

'Looks to me like it says *help*.' She replied. 'Funny word for someone to draw on a castle wall, I thought. But, I were curious after what had been happening in me house. And though I couldn't see why those things could be connected, I had an idea. I had me knitting with me in me handbag – used to carry it everywhere – and so I took out one of me needles, and I wrote a reply underneath, here.'

She pointed to a word directly beneath it. It was clearly different handwriting, even in such a primitive form. The letters were curved, rather than the sharp and chaotic shape of the *help* above it, and it said *how?*

'I hurried off, worried that someone might've seen me defacing it, feeling very foolish, and I went home. I saw Jack again a few nights after. He were just as he always was; black and bloody and hateful, and it made me think of the castle wall. So, next day, I come back, and now there's this word here, carved below mine.'

Stephen leaned closer to read the next word. It was in the same chaotic scrawl as the word *help*.

'*Prayer?*' He ventured, with narrowed eyes.

'Aye, that's it.' She said. 'Now, though I felt terrible vandalizing an old place like this, I'd brought me needle again, just in case, and I couldn't help meself. There was something going on, and I wanted to know what.'

'Don't you think that it could have been someone having a bit of fun with you?' He said, finding it better to just get to the point rather than to tread lightly. 'It's much more likely that a person did this, rather than a ghost.'

'Of course I bloody thought that!' She exclaimed. 'I'm not a simpleton, lad. But, what can I say to you? You didn't *see* Jack, or rather, that *thing* what pretended to be him. I just had a *feeling*. I just *knew*. That's all I can say to explain it.'

Stephen sighed. Once more, his logical mind was taking hold. Though Millie's story was horrific (and had, for lack of a better phrase, put the willies up him) he had to admit to himself that all he really had here was a story told by an old lady he had just met. Stephen believed in evidence. He hadn't seen a ghost or felt a presence. All he had was a tall tale and an old wall with writing scratched on it.

He put Penny to the back of his mind. He couldn't explain her yet, though he really wanted to. The most obvious explanations are usually always the truth. He just had to find a way to find that truth. She couldn't have read his mind. She just couldn't.

'You see it, there?' Millie was pointing. 'There's what I wrote next. I wrote *why*? I wanted to know why it needed prayer to help it. Now, look what it replied the *very next day* when I came back!'

That one was easier to see. Same manic writing, but carved a little deeper than the rest.

'Bound.' Stephen read aloud.

'Yes!' Millie said, satisfied. 'Clear as day, isn't it? A spirit needs help, needs me to pray for it, because it's stuck here!'

She was linking things that had no link. She was finding reason where there wasn't any. That was what the human mind did; tried to find a pattern in the chaos. *Ok, Millie Wood, I think I'm beginning to understand you now.*

'But, you can't think that this was Jack?' He asked carefully. 'You just finished telling me how sure you are that the ghost you - that the ghost you *claim* you saw - was not him, but some other thing pretending to be him.'

As she replied, Stephen was pulling his camera out of its leather holder. He popped the cap off the lens, wound the film with his thumb, and lifted it to his eye, adjusting the focus with his free hand.

'I think it's all part of the same thing.' She said excitedly. 'I think there's something *wrong* with this place. I think there's something *bad* here. Something that's... hurting the others.'

'The others?' He snapped the shutter and a bright flash filled the gloomy corner. He wound the film again.

'The other spirits.' She said. She'd hushed her voice, as if someone else could eavesdrop. In truth, the two of them were the only ones mad enough to be up there on a day like that.

Stephen rolled his eyes behind the lens. He took another photograph before lowering the device. 'That's... quite a leap.'

'I know what you must think of me.' She said. 'And there's no way I can prove it to you, but I just know it!'

'Mrs Wood, I have the pictures, now I think we should get you inside before...'

She took his arm, her watery eyes fierce, her teeth clenched behind a jutting jaw as she looked up into his face.

'If you stay here long enough.' She muttered. 'You'll know it, too. You'll *feel* it, too.'

He examined her face, and the manic look that distorted it. The only thing that Stephen *knew* and *felt* in that moment was that this was quite clearly a grieving and, let's face it, slightly bonkers old woman who was trying to make a story out of two events that had no correlation. One was that someone - not a ghost, not a monster - a *someone* was messing about with her, writing cryptic things on a castle, and the other was... well, there were any number of explanations for her ghostly visitations. She could have early dementia and not know it. She could have had a stroke. She could have any number of maladies that cause hallucinations and delusions. Simplest one; she was having recurring nightmares that were so potent she felt she was awake while having them.

This town was mad. Here he was, standing up a hill in castle ruins in the dead of winter, catching hypothermia with a pensioner and arguing about the existence of the afterlife. There was *something wrong with this place*, alright, but it wasn't ghostly miners or phantom graffiti artists.

'Mrs Wood, please don't upset yourself.' He said, putting his hand over hers. 'I believe you, and I will write your story, exactly as you've told it. I'm sure you'll get the help you need. I'm certain of it.'

Thankfully, she did not catch onto his double meaning.

She wouldn't break her gaze. She shook her head and huffed. 'I'm not mad.' She insisted. 'These things are happening to me, and they're real.'

'As I said, I believe you...'

'I'll prove it!' She snapped over him. 'I can prove it!' And she released his arm, pulling her shoulder bag around to unzip it. She rummaged around inside for a moment.

He knew exactly what came next, and he wanted no part in it. He sighed again, and shook his head as he stared down as his snow-covered shoes. 'Millie, this isn't necessary, I'm only here to write an...'

'Here!' She said, brandishing the knitting needle that he knew was coming. '*You* scratch a question in! By tomorrow you'll have an answer, I promise!'

Yeah, I'm sure I will. He thought. *Because you'll be creeping about up here in the middle of the night writing a reply, you crazy old nutjob.*

He hesitated, looking from the long white needle to her face, the back again. He glanced around the abandoned ruins, then reluctantly snatched it from her.

'Fine.' He said. 'If it means getting out of this cold. But, Mrs Wood, should I find myself with a fine for defacing public property, I shall be sending you my bill.'

She smiled triumphantly.

He turned to the stone and without a thought began to carve beneath the word *bound*. The blunt edge of the needle cut into the soft, rotten stone easily as he worked. He kept the words small and as neat as he could, so that a full sentence would fit the cramped space between the corner and the broken edge.

'There.' He said when finished. 'Does that satisfy you, Mrs Wood?'

She looked at his handiwork, then slowly nodded.

It said - *what is your name?*

'If you want proof of something,' he added, 'then you must ask the right questions, not be led by some else's narrative.'

He foresaw two outcomes, neither one useful; either when he came back the next day it would say *Jack,* meaning that this was Millie's handiwork after all, or it would say a different name entirely, meaning that someone else was screwing around. Either way, not a ghost.

And so Stephen lead Millie away from the tower and the ruins on the hill, and back towards the lights of Helmsley. The evening was already drawing in, and all he wanted now was to get to a fireside and get to a drink.

His plans to leave that day had been scuppered by Mrs Wood. He had no intention of driving home in the dark in those conditions, and the sun would be set within the hour. He would instead leave first thing in the morning, once he had checked the castle wall again. He expected to find nothing, truth be told. Who'd be mad enough to go up to that lonely old place in the middle of the night? Not Mrs Wood, he hoped.

The two figures crossed the little bridge over the moat again as fresh snow began to drift down, dancing in the strong wind, leaving the propped-up corpse of the castle to rot in the frozen dark.

11
White Lace and Bile

With early evening came more snow. It fell softly beyond the pale windows of the pub. Ghostly white shapes were spinning by the blurry and distorted glass, and all beyond them was black. The sun barely bothered coming up in February, and even when it did, for seven hours at most, it was suffocated behind sheets of low cloud. The winter was a long tunnel with no lights, and England was only three-quarters of the way through it. Stephen was starting to wonder whether he'd be able to leave this ridiculous little town in three days. At this rate, he'd be stuck there until spring.

The blackboard on the wall behind the bar proudly informed the clientele that the soup of the day was scotch broth, and that meals (pork or beef) were served until 7 but he didn't imagine that anyone would be ordering. There was never anyone in The Black Swan. The three gentlemen that he had conversed with - albeit awkwardly - the day before, had not returned. He wondered if it was because he was staying there. They didn't exactly look the sort who only met for a drink once a week, more like the ones who were there at every possible opportunity. The ones who worked and drank and nothing more.

Just like Stephen.

It wasn't much of a leap to deduce that they were giving

him a wide berth.

Since parting ways with the eccentric Mrs Wood after their little tea and vandalism excursion, Stephen had made straight for the pub where he intended to write a large part of his article in shorthand (which he was now doing at the bar) alongside drinking himself into oblivion (which he was now hard at work at, though getting himself into the desired state was becoming more and more difficult).

The article came easy. After all, it wasn't exactly a deep political piece or a report on a complex financial crisis. He was quite pleased with it so far. He'd managed to keep the tone light and playful but spooky in the right places, and had peppered it with a tone that said we *know this is drivel,* you *know this is drivel, but it's just a bit of fun.* It was a fine line that he took pride in navigating.

To his right was the dreaded cursed chair. It glistened, reflecting the turning flames of the fireside it sat beside on old glossy varnish. He glanced at it then went back to his scribbling. Next to his notepad was a crumpled pile of notes and pennies on the bar and three empty pint glasses, along with two empty shot glasses and an ashtray. The barman, Billy, was nowhere to be seen. The pub was empty. Other than the cracking of the flames and the ticking of a clock somewhere nearby, Stephen had no other company.

He paused to light a Regal. As he held a match to the end, illuminating himself in orange for a moment in the shadowy establishment, he glanced at the chair again.

His eyes, bloodshot and more yellowed than he would care to admit when he would glance into a mirror, narrowed at it. He tried to picture a woman sitting there. A lonely ghost or a spooky cat or something.

Nope. All he could see was a chair.

He smiled and snorted a little laugh, shaking his head

gently. He felt a fool. For a few moments there he had actually entertained the crazy notion that Penny Black could read his mind, and that the things she said she believed in could be true. For a second he had even bought into Millie's story, with her vivid descriptions of her dead husband staring at her every night. He supposed, feeling quite satisfied with himself, that it was easy to see why a less logical mind could be drawn in and fooled into believing such things in a place like that. Old places were eerie and atmospheric. It was all a bit of fun, but to take such things seriously in the twentieth century was laughable.

Stephen was struck then, as tipsy as he was becoming, by a thought. He laughed to himself again. Then he stood, taking his notebook and his cigarette, and unceremoniously plopped himself down in the cursed seat.

It was even warmer by the fire. A real cosy spot. He settled into the old wood, feeling the heated timber pressing into his legs and back, and enjoying the creaking and popping of it. Very comfy indeed.

'Sorry about this, love.' He said aloud to the air. 'But if it helps I'm writing a nice story about you. Sorry about your wedding, and all that. But, take it from me – marriage is severely overrated.' Then he went back to his writing, flicking his cigarette ash into the dancing heat beside him.

Fuck superstition. There he was, unharmed and uncursed. It was a chair by a fire; a collection of wood, nails and glue. There was no magic. There was no ghost.

The wind was picking up outside, driving the snow down harder and rattling at the windows. It *whoo*'ed and whistled around the old stones of the walls and over the rooftop above him, but within he was warm and snug, his head swimming pleasurably. He felt at peace, in fact. More at peace than he had remembered feeling in a while.

Soon he had stopped writing and his pen was resting

against the pad, propped in a slackened hand. Soon, he was letting his mind drift as he looked around the ancient room. For just a moment he didn't miss home. He didn't miss his job. He didn't miss his life at all. Any thoughts of his now ex-wife and of what they had lost had blissfully fled. Just for a delicious and beautiful moment, Stephen White didn't have a care in the world.

He dropped his cigarette butt into the flames and relaxed against the comfortably-curved chairback. Wasn't so bad here after all. Stephen always enjoyed being safe and warm when such wild and freezing weather assaulted the moors and streets outside. He thought about the cold and barren trees on the hills all around, and what it must be like to be out there in that moment, barely able to breathe against the wind and ice. He thought about the castle battlements being hammered by the elements in the pitch darkness, and what it must have been like to have been a soldier standing guard there, on the night watch, with his extremities turning blue and exhaustion torturing his frozen limbs under the weight of all that chain mail.

Penny had said that Stephen needed *some serious healing*, whatever new age nonsense that was, but from where he was sitting he was healing very nicely, *thank you*. Nevertheless, he was sure that he would pay her another visit. Not for healing of course, but to get a little more story out of her. The vicar's daughter. The black sheep of the family, clearly, who had inherited his house, much to the chagrin of the locals. A self-confessed witch who believed in all manner of weird things, including that Helmsley was home to some dangerous and nasty spirits. And where was her mother? Why did she, a girl who can't have been more than twenty, live alone in that house? How could he not include something as juicy as that in his article? No, there was more digging to do there.

He was glad then that he had a few more days left in this

little armpit of North Yorkshire. There was a bigger story to draw from it, with the suspicious natives and the strange girl and the mad old lady, and he intended to find out what.

That'd show him – that grinning fool Matthews – that'd show him what good reporting was; he'd been sent on a fluff piece only to return with an insightful and polished article. Ha! Yeah, his face would soon drop when Stephen's work was the talk of the office, and everyone would realise how undervalued he had been, and that he...

Stephen froze.

Ordinarily, upon hearing a sound like the one that he had most definitely just heard at his ear, a person would leap to their feet and give out a yell, at the very least. More likely a scream or a curse. But Stephen did not. He found that he could do absolutely nothing, in fact.

He just froze. His entire thought process ceased. His eyes stared unblinkingly ahead, his breath was caught in his gullet and held itself there as his entire body went as rigid as the wood beneath him.

The fire continued to pop and growl, the wind continued to dash over the stonework outside, but none of these things could explain the sound that he had just heard, close by, in his right ear. The fire was to his left, and the landlord was not in the room. *No one else* was in the room.

So who had just said, with the soft delicacy of a lover's whisper, the word *throat*?

The quiet of the room was getting louder. Everything becoming amplified, just like it had when he had been sitting in the dining section with Millie Wood. Like the hiss of a tape recording being slowly turned up.

Stephen's heart made up for the stillness in the rest of his body by hammering, after a palpitation that felt more like a heart attack, at a speed he had rarely experienced before. The tips of his fingers and toes, despite the heat of the room, turned so cold that he may as well have had them submerged in the snow outside. He blinked now, only once, and tried to swallow with a tongue and mouth that had gone as dry as the surface of his skin.

He slowly found movement and began to turn his head. He looked right, to the source of the voice. There was a stone arch there, and beyond it two steps down to another section of the bar. There, it was as well-lit as the rest of the pub, and there was clearly no one present.

Still, remarkably, he stayed in the chair. But now he leant forwards, his fingers clasped onto the wooden arms with white knuckles and grey fingernails, and he craned his neck further still so that he could look through the arch fully.

Nothing. The pub was deserted from end to end. The landlord was not in the bar, nor was he in the little back room behind it. Even if there had been someone there, the bar and the seating through the arch was a fair distance away. What he had heard was right beside him. Someone had whispered into his ear.

'Okay.' He said aloud. 'Alright.'

He slowly started to stand. Why he moved like a film being played in slow motion he couldn't say. Some part of him that he didn't understand was telling him to. As if a sudden movement or loud noise would trigger... something, like trying to sneak out of a baby's bedroom once you've finally gotten them to sleep.

No, *no*! We're *not* using that simile. We're not going there, Steve.

He was cold all over now. His stomach had gone tight and he had performed the fastest sobering-up in all of his drunken career. His heartbeat was so rapid that stabbing pains were recurringly flashing in his chest. He was walking towards the bar, though he didn't really know why. The door that led up the stairs to the inn's rooms was at the far end of it, where anyone in their right mind would be running at that moment.

He placed his hands on the lacquered wood, hooked one foot onto the brass rail that ran below it, and with some of the best acting he had ever accomplished he called in a casual tone 'Billy? You there?'

The hiss of the tape was still growing louder. Stephen kept the muscles of his face relaxed, even let a little counterfeit smile sit there, and gently cleared his throat again before he called 'hello? Service?'

A creeping nausea was working its way up from his stomach, a slick black thing, sour and cold, making its way past his screaming heart and into his throat.

Throat. Throat. Why had he heard that word? A *th* sound followed by a flat vowel *ro* followed by a crisp *t*. A northern accent. A woman's whisper.

He had even felt breath tickle his ear.

'Bill!' His voice was driven out now, desperate and demanding. 'Billy!'

No one answered. Stephen stared at the upturned bottles of spirits in their holders, all lined up against the wall. And the packets of crisps and nuts, and the beermats that were pinned up there, and the stacked pint glasses and the ashtrays, and the clock that ticked louder and louder in the centre of the wall.

Suddenly the deafening silence, the hiss, fell dead.

And the chair behind him creaked.

He stopped his act. His face fell. His eyes widened again, still fixed on the clock. His stomach was falling now, out of his body and down into his legs. The open space behind him suddenly felt like an open door. Winter touched the back of his neck, triggering gooseflesh and an electric shiver that started there before rushing down his back and along his forearms. He felt the hairs stand on end along the length of them. He leant forwards against the bar, the strength stolen from his legs.

I cannot, and will not, turn around.

He tried to call the landlords name again, but all that came out of his mouth was a little rush of air. He blinked again, realising as water dripped down his cheeks that he had let his eyes go dry and sore. Suddenly his bladder felt painfully full, and worse, weak. He had to do something. He was going to piss his trousers right there in the middle of a pub. The door to his room was to his left. He could run. He could reach it and he wouldn't have to turn back to look at the chair by the fire to see what had caused that creak. He could hide in his room until morning. There was plenty of whiskey up there. He could drink and stay awake until morning, and then he could come down and everything would be normal, and he would laugh at himself for being such a tit, and he would understand then that he had just been hearing things, and that the strange events of his day had taken their toll on him, and that he had spooked himself and imagined the whole thing.

He pushed away from the bar, but found that he could not run. Nevertheless, he managed to start walking. The fire was behind him. It was just crackling like a fire should. The chair was silent. Never mind that the creak had sounded like a weight settling upon it. Never mind that it sounded like someone sitting down. What mattered was that it was silent now. It was just a normal chair now.

Normal, yes. Everything was normal.

He stopped.

Shit. *Shit.* His notepad and pen. They were back there.

He couldn't remember where. Had he dropped them? They were in his hand when he'd heard her voice.

No, Stephen. Stop that. It was not a *her* and it was *not* a voice.

Damn. If he left them there then they could be lost. That was some of his best work. Someone could wander in and pinch it, or the landlord could come in later and accidentally sweep it up when he cleaned. He could have just abandoned it and written it out again later, but Stephen knew very well that he would have forgotten most of it by tomorrow, and with each passing day that he drank he would remember less and less.

He couldn't leave it behind.

'Okay.' He said aloud again. 'Alright, fine. I'm going to go pick up my things, and then I am going to bed.'

So, Stephen slowly turned around. He cleared his throat casually, gave his hands a little shake, and he turned gradually back towards the fire. All that he was about to see, he was certain, was an empty chair and a lovely blazing fire, and a notepad and pen lying on the flagstone floor. Because this was the normal, everyday world. And only normal things happened in the normal, everyday world.

But instead, Stephen turned around to see the woman that was sitting in the chair. The woman that was looking at him through a white veil that was draped over her head. A woman as solid and as real as anyone. A woman whose white lace veil was stained yellow and green at the mouth, and the stain was encrusted and dried and ran down the length of her silk wedding dress. Her hands were on the arms of the chair and her fingers were thin and long, and they were far too long to be ordinary. And they were grey, and the thin veins at the surface of her skin were black threads. And the woman had dark straggles of hair that wormed their way down from under her veil and over her shoulders, and her hair was moving. Why was it moving? Why did it glisten like that? Lice. Her hair was thick and crawling with lice, scurrying from her scalp and down the length of the ropes of hair, stark and greasy against the white of the wedding dress, and they dropped off the ends and into her lap and scuttled away. And then there was the stink. A smell, brief but sharp, of rot. Of spoiled meat and turned milk, and of some kind of chemical, perhaps sulphur or something similar. It overpowered his nostrils, and then the next second it was gone. And the woman was sitting in the chair he had just occupied, and the woman didn't move, and the woman didn't breathe, and the woman was dead.

And then it was just a chair by the fire. It was empty and clean and polished, and there were no lice and no vomit-stained dress and there wasn't a dead woman sitting there looking at him. The room wasn't cold anymore and there weren't any unordinary sounds. It was just a cosy pub fireplace and this was again the normal, everyday world.

All of this had happened inside of a second.

Then Stephen *did* run. He ran without breathing, he ran without thought, he ran without hesitation. He did not reach his bedroom however, because his first port of call was the bathroom on the first floor, where he collapsed onto his knees and began to throw his guts up and into the toilet, and as the ropes of alcohol-stinking bile poured from his lips his bladder gave up its battle and a widening dark stain grew around his crotch and began to pool on the tiled floor.

Stephen blacked out then, falling from the porcelain bowl and onto his side, his knees drawn up, and his eyes rolled white, while outside the snow continued to fall and the wind continued to gust.

12
Ying and Yang

The second time that Stephen knocked on the door of Canons Garth it was not the polite *clack clack clack* of the little iron knocker set in the centre. This time it was a pounding that meant business. This time it resembled more the sound of someone either trying to knock the door down or hammering in a series of particularly stubborn nails with a mallet.

Penny answered the door a great deal faster than she had the first time. This time her hair was not a great black straggly nest but rather it was smooth and straight, for an odd moment reminding Stephen of the look of a vinyl record in the sun. Her face was as white as it had been though, and her makeup as dark. A long loose jumper was today's choice of clothing from a wardrobe he was sure must have only contained black items, and beneath it was a knee-length skirt. Her feet were bare but she was wearing tights of a criss-crossed pattern, and when her hands poked out from beneath the overly-long sleeves of the jumper her fingernails were black too. She gaped from the doorway at the man standing there, who looked far removed from the man she had opened the door to yesterday.

He was as white as she was without the need of makeup. His eyes were rimmed red and the circles in the flesh beneath them were sickly and dark. His hair, once slicked and obsessively neat, was sticking up at all angles with strands falling down and poking at his eyebrows. He was no longer wearing the jumper and jeans, but instead a grey suit which looked unsuitable attire for a man standing in snow which was now at shin height. He was trembling, but by the looks of him it wasn't due to the cold.

'I need your help.' His voice sounded like he was sitting on top of a washing machine on a spin cycle. 'Im... I'm sorry about hammering on...'

'Yeah, I can see that, Whitey.' She replied with shock still set in her eyes, and by way of invitation she opened the door wide and stepped back.

It was his turn to walk down the narrow stone-floored hallway with the girl now behind him, the smell of incense and the warmth actually pleasing to him this time, and though he took in all the usual sights – the drapes everywhere, the pentagram, the candles and the tarot cards – his mind wasn't really registering them. His mind was on the notebook.

At around three am he had woken up on the floor of the bathroom. No one had discovered him, which was no surprise because no one else was staying at The Black Swan, and the landlord had no business to go upstairs while someone was in residence. So, he had awoken with the pain in his hip, arm, and shoulder almost rivalling the pounding pain in his head. He must have been laying there, soaked in cold piss and with vomit all over his clothes, on that hard floor for something like six hours. He had cleaned up as best he could with toilet rolls, and had staggered back to his room where he had removed his clothes and stuffed them into a plastic bag, intending to dump them into the nearest bin rather than keep them to wash. During this he had remembered his notepad.

It was still downstairs. All of his work. It was still by the fireside on the floor, in front of that chair. Why this really mattered to him anymore, he couldn't say. It shouldn't have. The best guess he could make was that it was the only practical thing to do that he could grasp onto, and Christ knew he needed something practical, and ordinary, and sane, to perform.

But it was three am, meaning that the bar would be closed, and the fire would be out, as would be the lights. It was dark downstairs, and silent.

No fucking way was he venturing down there. Not for all the wines and spirits in The Green Dragon.

So he had stayed in his room, without much sleep of course, until dawn, and this was the key thing; he knew with absolute certainty that he had not brought the notepad up to his room. He had... *seen* what he had *seen* and he had fled. Notepad unretrieved. And then, when in his room, the notepad had not been there. One hundred percent, it had not been there.

So how the *fuck*, after he had dozed for a maybe fifteen minutes sitting upright, had his notebook and pen appeared at his bedside? And not only that, how had they appeared standing perfectly upright on the table? Balanced flawlessly, the pen on its flat end, and the notebook a perfect little pyramid, just sitting there looking at him. If he recalled correctly, he had let out a scream and batted them away, sending them slapping and clattering against the wall.

There were only two real possibilities left in Stephen's addled mind. Either the landlord was fucking with him, or a ghost was. And up until last night, he had been more certain than anything else in the world that *ghosts were not real*. Now, he was certain of absolutely nothing.

If what he had seen last night had been real, then absolutely everything that he had ever held to be true and false, real and unreal, was now destroyed. If the woman in the chair was real, then what else was real? What did that mean to him too, a living human on planet earth? Is there a god? Is there a devil? Is there a heaven and hell, an afterlife? Did the morality of his life and the quality of his soul actually matter, and would it be judged upon his death? Did *everything* actually have meaning? Was there a grand design, a literal *meaning of life*?

The doors had been blown open and Stephen White did not want to even look at those doors, let alone walk through them.

He wanted to believe that Billy had been messing with him, with regard to the notepad at least. But he couldn't fool himself. He knew fine and well that his door had been locked, and locked all night once he had staggered back in. His notebook and pen had, what, *materialised* while he slept? As for the woman, that *thing*, that horror in the chair? He couldn't explain that away. What, had the landlord spiked his drink so that he hallucinated? Who would even do that, and what on earth for? Besides, the horrible image of her had appeared for no more than a second. Drugs don't do that.

No matter which way he desperately tried to reason it out, Stephen could no longer look away from the truth.

Last night he had seen a ghost.

Why else would he be back here, in this strange old house, with this even stranger young woman? Who else could he have gone to with a problem like this? If she was as true as she said she was, she was THE only person qualified to help.

Once again he was sitting in the curved Victorian armchair, and once again Penny was sitting, in fact kneeling, on the large carpet. This time the curtains were drawn, and the room swam in hazy scented smoke that drifted in layers lit by several lamps around the room, and this time a woman was singing as the record turned beneath the needle, and she said *we are entranced, spellbound.*

Penny waited patiently as Stephen took a few shaky breaths.

'I don't know who else to talk to.' He said. 'I don't know what to... I don't know how to process what's happened to me. I don't even know if it was real.'

She just nodded, and with a kinder tone than he had heard her use before, she softly said 'tell me what you saw.'

He described the evening as best he could, from his interview with Mrs Wood to the castle writing to the chair beside the fire in the pub. He missed out the part where he pissed his pants and passed out. Might as well cling tight to the very last shred of his dignity. He had to pause now and again when his throat went completely dry, making him gag and cough and repeatedly apologise for doing so. At one point Penny dashed out and brought him back a hot drink. It was dark and milkless and when he sipped it it was powerfully bitter. He screwed his face up, to which she gently laughed and told him that it was green tea, a herbal remedy. He managed to retain enough of his character to tell her that it tasted like dishwater, to which she laughed louder.

Nothing that he related to her seemed to surprise her in the least. When he was done (and glad to be so) she just nodded and remarked that 'no one forgets their first time.'

He sipped his tea again and with a grimace replied 'that's all you've got to say? You're telling me that this happens to everyone here? I mean, really, like, *really*... I know you believe in this stuff, but I don't! But then... I saw it!'

'No, not everyone.' She said, a white face glowing in the near dark. 'Very few *see* something. People experience things, supernatural things, quite often, but they don't realise they have, or they don't want to admit it and rationalise it in any way they can. You heard a voice and saw an apparition. Seems you've got a bit of the gift yourself.'

'A gift,' he echoed, 'yeah, ok. Happy fucking birthday to me. Well, I don't want that kind of gift. This is mad. This is a bloody joke, this is. *Me*, of all people. I've never believed in anything other than what I can see and touch and have evidence for. What am I supposed to do with this?'

She looked like she was mulling something over for a beat. Instead of answering his question, she said 'I can tell you what I'm beginning to think is going on here, and I can show you some things – your precious *evidence* – to back it up, but it's way past your job description.'

'How's that?'

'Well, you've been sent here to write a tat article about local spookiness, and this goes a lot deeper than that, to say the least. Also, there's a warning, too.'

Such ominous prose would have made him laugh yesterday. Today, he merely leaned forward and listened intently.

'That world, beyond the veil, the one that we hardly ever see,' she said, 'the things that live there are happy to go unnoticed. They prefer it. But, if you start looking, prodding at it, it prods back. It looks back. Once you get into this stuff, you can't really get out.'

Stephen sat back again, very slowly.

'But,' she added, 'given your encounter last night, it looks to me like its *already* looking. Which is interesting.'

'Not the word I'd use.'

Interesting. That was what she'd said the day they had met, after she had looked him up and down. He referenced this and asked her what she had meant.

'Psychics are beacons.' She explained. 'You can see it shining out of them. I can, anyway. The day we met I could see something of a beacon in you. Today just confirms it. I could easily read you, and that just confirms it further.'

He sipped at his tea again. He didn't grimace this time.

'They're all scared stiff of you.' He said. 'In the pub, there. They all think you can read their minds and hex them.' She rolled her eyes and laughed lightly, to which he countered 'but you can, can't you? You read my mind at the door, and when I was sitting here last.'

'I get... vibes. I could see your aura, or what's left of the rotten thing. I get imagery, feelings, information. I can't just read your mind like I'm reading a book. And besides, my point is that you were very easy to read because you transmit it all, whether you mean to or not. You're a...'

'Beacon.' He finished. 'Yeah, I got that. Whoopee for me.'

Penny stood and turned to a chest of drawers behind her. The candle flames set upon it wobbled and danced as she opened a stiff old drawer. She pulled out a pile of papers and handed them to him, taking his tea away. He leafed through them, holding them at arm's length in the poor light, examining them with poor eyes. He needed glasses, but had never visited an optician. He would look too much like his dad.

They were newspaper clippings. Local stuff mostly, and a national. And they were all – as he was so fond of classifying them – fluff pieces. Spooky local tales and interviews and such. He unfolded each of them and read the little headlines and glanced at the photos.

'There are over twenty stories there,' she said as she, unusually, started to sip at his tea, 'all in this town, all in the last three years.'

The papers they had been taken from were either local, or independently published. There was only one tabloid piece, and that was from a very well-known purveyor of garbage and sensationalist bullshit, *The Daily Sun*. They weren't very well written, and it was clear to Stephen that they were the sorts of tales that would be dismissed outright as media tat, if indeed they were read at all.

'Three years,' he remarked with eyebrows raised.

'Pretty condensed amount of activity, isn't it?' She nodded. 'I told you there was something wrong with this place, and that everyone could sense it in some way or another...'

Stephen's mind flashed back to yesterday afternoon, when Millie had said something very similar.

'...and as far as I can tell, that *something wrong* started three years ago. I mean, this place was always haunted, *everywhere* is haunted in some capacity or another, but three years ago, something new happened.'

'What?'

'I don't know. I don't know what caused it, or triggered it, but I know it has something to do with my dad.'

His eyes shot up from the articles and fixed on her. 'The vicar?'

'Well, we've been doing our homework.' She smiled. 'Yeah. My father was rector here. His name was Everett. He'd been dead only days before these sightings began. And worse than sightings, besides...' She padded over to him and leaned in, her patchouli oil scent so potent it made his eyes dry out, and she took the papers from him. She located one, and handed it back.

'Someone *died?*' He gasped, reading the headline. 'No way, surely! No way a ghost *killed* someone!'

Penny smiled patiently. 'Yesterday you didn't believe in the supernatural.' She said. 'Today, you know you're wrong. This is just the beginning for you. Imagine what you'll know tomorrow.'

Stephen tried to find an argument, tried to find a way to dispute her, but he came up blank. She handed the rest of the papers back to him.

'Just read them.' She said. 'And read them with an open mind. An open mind is the only thing that's going to get you through this. I mean, it's clear, don't you think, that this was predestination?'

'Pre... what was it?' He said, distractedly looking through the cuttings.

'Predestination, Whitey!' She said with a little excitement. 'Means this was meant to be, you being here, now, meeting me, with all of this going on in town.'

He looked up. 'How the hell did you arrive at that?'

'You can see spirits too, even though you didn't believe. That's rare! I've been trying to find an answer to this since I moved in here, and now the fates have dropped another psychic in my lap! A reluctant one, but still! You want a good story, and I've *got* a good story! We're ying and yang. We're on opposite spectrums, but we're looking for the same thing!' She was getting more excitable now. 'God's sake, Whitey, can't you see it? Look at our *names*!' She punctuated her little thrilled outburst with a single clap.

He sighed and shrugged. 'Our names?'

She laughed boisterously then. 'Black and White!' She pointed to herself then at him. 'What are the chances! Ying and yang! Light and dark! Oh, this is *too* cool!'

His hands collapsed onto his lap and he gave her a withering look. 'Oh, *come on!*' He said. 'They're just names. Not everything has meaning, you know!'

'Yes it bloody does!' She was giddy. 'Absolutely *everything* does! There are absolutely *no such things as coincidences*! You'll learn that too! We're on a set path now, and all we can do is walk it. Isn't that exciting?'

He didn't need to reply. His face said it all. This just amused her further.

'Just read them!' She said. 'I'm gonna go get changed and then we're going out!' And she dashed out of the room. He heard her thumping up the stairs, followed by the muffled sound of chaos as cupboards were flung open and drawers were wrenched and slammed.

Dizzy, scared, and completely adrift, Stephen had his first thought that morning of a drink, and then he picked up the articles and began to read them.

13

Fluff Pieces

The Town Crier

Oct 21st, 1985

Ghoul's Out!

One needn't go to cinemas to catch the upcoming hair-raising offering from Ivan Reitman, the sequel to the smash hit movie 'Ghostbusters', one needs only to look closer to home for a terrifying tale of the supernatural. The pleasant and rolling moors of Yorkshire might not seem the sort of place you might expect a modern day ghost story to play out, but young Sallie Briggs, 9, would claim otherwise. The sleepy village of Helmsley, N Yorks, is a mysterious but beautiful corner of *God's Own County*, and now has a new claim to fame as one that not only has a haunting, but a haunted school! "He was a caretaker." Little Sallie explains. "He was dressed in overalls and he had a rag cloth hanging out of his pocket. He was in the cupboard. I opened the supply cupboard to get paints for art class and he was in the cupboard, and he was hanging by his neck by a belt, and he was swinging backwards and forwards in the dark."

Don't fear though, folks. Sallie might have had quite a fright, but the imagination, especially of young children, can frighten them to the point of not knowing what's real. Sallie's teacher, Mr Seward, tells us that "While it's sadly true that the school's caretaker, a Mr Gibbon I believe, did indeed take his own life on the grounds many years ago – the late fifties I think – tales get around the children. They do like to scare one another, and themselves, with stories of a haunted cupboard. I can assure you that all we keep in there are brushes, paints, and coloured card!"

Continued on page 4...

The Helmsley Herald

July 8th, 1986

Who is the Notorious Woman in Green?

Those with the rather eccentric interest in the supernatural; researchers and self-proclaimed 'investigators', have descended upon Helmsley castle this week following a report by Mr J. Swinson of Paddock Close, in which he claims to have seen the legendary 'Green Lady' of Helmsley. Locals will know the tales told us as children – stories of a mysterious woman in an emerald dress, seen haunting the moorland and grounds of the ancient tower, have been recounted by folk young and old for years. Mr Swinson tells that "I saw her, walking just like anyone would, and her feet were even flattening the grass! I thought she was a real person in fancy dress until she walked straight through the castle wall, right before my eyes! And I swore I saw blood. It was running down her neck!" But who, if indeed anyone, was this spectral woman? Local historian Kelly Swift thinks she may have the answer.

"My team uncovered some records that went back as far as the sixteenth century." She claims. "In it we found some brief details about a woman that briefly resided here named Mary Gysborne, the wife of a land-owning lord, who had quite the reputation for cruelty, a quick temper, and in some cases a psychotic streak resulting in bloodshed. We couldn't find many more details on precisely what she had done to earn this reputation, but we do know, thanks to the national archives in York, that she was sentenced to death in December 1566, and was beheaded the same month. All her life she was obsessed with the colour green, and wore it every day."

More on page 6...

The North Yorks Post

November 1st, 1985

Little Green Men?

Our home county is rife with ancient superstition and folklore. You only have to look at the brooding heaths and dales of our land to understand how it could inspire such reveries. Fairies, sprites and ghostly black dogs are common subjects of tales to tell around the campfire, and the tradition has been well kept from Staithes down to Leeds. But perhaps the most unusual of them tells of odd, pixie-like creatures that are reputed to haunt the castle of the sleepy hamlet of Helmsley. A bizarre incident, reported by two separate eyewitnesses on October 28th, is one to boggle the mind.

"There were four of them, I think." Says Albert Step, an elderly local man who had been walking his dog that night. "They were moving about in the long grass. Little bodies, scuttling in the dark. They were pale and their arms were long, and their heads were, like, far too big. My dog was going barmy! Had he not been on a lead I think he would have went for them! Anyroad, I walked nearer, trying to get a better look, and then they saw us coming and they screamed."

"I was on my way home from the pub," tells Charlie, 19, "and to get to my house I often take a shortcut over the hill next to the castle, and I heard this scream. It were mad. Never heard anything like it. First one, and then a few more all at the same time. It proper put the s**ts up me! I went to run, but then I saw one of them in the grass, coming down the hill towards me! It looked like a little deformed skeleton and its eyes were black! I ran straight back to the pub!"

Continued next page...

The Yorkshire Chronicle

January 14${}^{\text{th}}$, 1987

A Bride Scorned

The local watering hole of The Black Swan in Helmsley has always been famous for its warm welcome, good food, and fine beverages, but it is also known as one of the most haunted taverns in all of England. A mysterious highwayman, complete with tricorn hat, billowing cloak and brandished pistol, has been said to haunt the stables and has been seen by numerous patrons. A pickpocketing child dressed in Victorian garb, named Matthew by the bar staff, is they say responsible for items disappearing and reappearing around the pub and rooms upstairs. Lighters and matches, watches and pens, all have vanished inexplicably only to later reappear in another location. But perhaps the eeriest tale The Black Swan can offer is that of The Jilted Bride. A beautiful young woman whose name we may never know, was said to have been left at the altar by the man that had stolen her heart and promised her his. They say that he was having an illicit affair with the girl's sister throughout their courtship, and when the wedding day came he instead opted to run away with the sister, leaving the helpless girl abandoned and heartbroken. In her grief she took her own life, and is said to haunt the bar area, her spirit trapped there and bound to the chair which sits by the fireside there to this very day. But, perhaps the most disturbing aspect of this tale was her method of suicide. She bought a bottle of acid from the local apothecary, sat down by the fireside in full view of the men gathered there, and drank it.

More ghostly legends on page 3

The Daily Sun

March 1st, 1986

Tragic Death of Local Church Secretary Prompts Inquiries after Bizarre Claim

A woman was found dead earlier this week in the North Yorkshire town of Helmsley, prompting an investigation. Edith Blessed, 68, was found early morning by the groundsman, who had investigated after discovering that the doors of the Church of All Saints, the parish place of worship, had been left open overnight.

Her body was bizarrely sprawled on the altar of the church when he discovered her, but the keeper, named G. Mills, made a bizarre claim about her passing that has now prompted an official investigation.

"There were someone with her," he claims, "someone was on top of her, like he were smothering her. A black shape, it was. It were broad daylight, but I couldn't make out any detail, it were just a big black shape. Too big to be a man, I thought! And then it were gone! Just like that, it disappeared!"

Many have dismissed the outlandish claim outright as Mrs Blessed, who had been secretary there for many years, was in declining health. Nevertheless local police are looking into it.

Continued overleaf...

There were many more, but Stephen couldn't go on.

14

Reaching and Hungry and Black

Penny's demeanour changed drastically when she was outside. Stephen caught the transformation as soon as she turned her key in the lock of Cannons Garth. Within the house she had been exuberant and confident, sassy and quick, but outside, where they now walked side by side, she had completely withdrawn.

Even the way she dressed was altered, at least to an extent. She was covered up in layers – jumper, scarf, thick wool overcoat with the collars turned up, gloves covering the black nails. She wore skintight jeans and big black boots that looked more suited to a dockworker than a young woman. Her hair was silky and worn down so that it spilled past her pale features and onto her shoulders like blinkers dyed ebony. She was a stark little raven when set against the white ground. She walked stiffly with little steps and her head was down. Walking beside him she looked like a teenager that had been made to have a day out with dad, and wasn't too happy about it.

There were more people milling about than Stephen had seen before, which was surprising given the result of last night's snowfall; now it must have been three feet deep in places, and very difficult to heave through. As they had passed by Stephen's car he had regarded it with despair. There was no way it was going to start in cold like that, even if he *was* able to dig it out. It now looked more like someone had constructed a snowcar for their snowman than like a real vehicle.

They walked past little groups of gossiping pensioners, blue-rinses and lavender stinking rain-macs all round, who all ceased their chattering as they approached, eyeing Penny ruefully, then whispering once they had passed. They went by dog walkers and a postman, a bobby on the beat and a man that was heaving sacks from a van into the butcher's shop on the corner. Every single one of them gawked. Some even sneered a little. One *tsk*'ed and blew out thin breath. They all looked disgusted by the girl he was walking with, and it infuriated him.

Yesterday he saw a weird girl with a bad attitude and a head full of new age nonsense. Today he saw a girl who was just... different, and had been ostracised by her community for it. Bloody churchy folk with sharp, judgemental, conservative eyes. God forbid anyone be *young* in this town.

They were walking through the market square, devoid of stalls and instead filled with parked cars, and Penny was pointing out the local places like an underpaid tour guide.

'Post Office there.' She muttered with a flick of a gesture. 'The Wainwrights have been there twenty years. Corner shop there, old bob runs it, he's alright. That's the bank, but it's only open three days a week. Royal Oak pub on the corner there. The spire in the centre is the Feversham Monument. He was a landowner, a baron. He was an MP for East Riding, did lots to support the poor and stuff. Well liked. Up there is Bridge Street,' she pointed at a narrow avenue left of the square before plunging her hand back into her coat pocket, 'there's some clothes shops up there. Might want to get yourself something a bit more suitable. You'll be going home with hypothermia otherwise.'

Stephen became aware of a feeling of exposure suddenly. He bristled with it, and when he looked around he saw that there were people standing everywhere, at some distance, stopped in their tracks. Some in little groups, most alone. And all of them were fixed in the snow and staring openly at the pair. Stephen shook his head.

'Don't bother yourself, Whitey.' She said quietly, head still down. 'I'm used to it. I don't go out much.'

'Fucking unbelievable.' He hissed, before turning and loudly calling 'can I help you with something?'

The little gatherings muttered to one another, some laughed, then turned away to go about their business. The solitary ones shook their heads and exchanged knowing glances across the distance before skulking off. He heard a deep Yorkshire drawl somewhere far away shout 'ought to be bloody ashamed!'

Once they had finished their circuit of the square and what little shops and attractions it had, they started the make their way, without either stating intention, towards The Black Swan. Penny added that the main attraction of the town was in summer, when it played host to hordes of motorbike enthusiasts who would roar through in droves on Harleys and Triumphs. Ice creams on the stone steps, beers on the terrace, all that shit. As they neared the pub, which the mere sight of gave Stephen a tickle of dread in his already sore stomach, he saw an opportunity to find out more.

'Well, it seems like you know plenty about me,' he said, 'with, y'know, the way I *transmit* or whatever you called it, but I don't know much about you. I interviewed Millie, Mrs Wood I mean, yesterday, and she said...'

'That no one approves of me keeping the house, by any chance?' Penny cut in. 'Yeah, it's not exactly a secret.'

'It must be hard, was all I was going to say. You lost your father, and he laid this responsibility on you of a house, a vicarage no less, and you have to stay here with all these... *people*... giving you a hard time.'

'Obviously it is.' She replied, in a tone that said *what's your point?*

'Don't you have any other family to help you out?' He ventured. 'Your mother not around, or siblings? I mean, you're only, what, twenty at most?'

She stopped walking and he took another step before realising it, turning back. Penny looked somehow amused and offended all at once.

'I'm twenty-seven.' She said. 'But I'll take that as a compliment, I guess.'

'Oh. Um, sorry.' His grey face flushed pink for the first time that day, and then they carried on.

'My mother died six years ago, if you must know,' her tone had turned sharp, 'in an accident. I have two sisters, both younger. One lives in Sussex, the other works abroad. She's in marketing.' She rolled her eyes. 'Don't get many letters. Think she's in Spain, but she moves around a lot. Anything else?'

'Well,' Stephen was all but sweating beneath his coat now, 'I, ah, I just thought; wouldn't it be easier for you to sell? I mean, in the sense that it'd free you of this awful environment and financially you'd be...'

'You know,' she snapped, looking deflated 'I was really getting all excited then. The fates have given us a task. A chance for me to get to the bottom of some stuff that's been bamboozling me for years, and all you want to talk about is house sales and family issues! How old are *you*, anyway? Fifty going on seventy?'

Stephen had forgotten how it was to fight with a woman. He was quickly remembering though. He was quickly remembering how bad he was at confrontation, as well. Or at least, nowadays he was. Once, he'd been strong. He'd been able to defend himself, to stand his ground when it mattered. Now he'd become a shade. A shadow. An empty vessel that was just in the shape of Stephen White, with nothing left inside. His embarrassment turned to anger so quickly it even took him by surprise.

'I'm forty-four!' He retorted. 'That might look old to you, but then I don't walk around with theatre makeup slapped all over my face! And if I look older and act older than my years it's because I've had more than my fair share of shit that you can't imagine, and...' the wind went out of him and he dropped his head. 'Jesus, I sound like my dad. I sound like one of these wankers.' He gestured to the street. 'Sorry. I don't know what's going on with me.'

She studied him for a beat. Her bright blue eyes seemed to be scanning him from behind narrowed lids decorated with long lashes. She sighed.

'Well, that makes two of us.' She said. 'That offer of a healing is still open. If you're brave enough. Anyway, I thought you asked for my help, not my life story. Shall we go in?'

Billy looked up from his crossword. Oh, great. What the hell was he doing hanging about with *her*? His eyes went left and right. No one in yet. Thank god. If one of his regulars came in here and saw her, they'd be over in The Feathers or The Royal Oak quick as a flash, and likely not come in again. What was she doing here anyway? He'd seen her out and about once or twice over the years, but he'd never seen her in a pub, let alone *his*. God, look at her. If her father were still around, God rest him, he'd be broken hearted. Heaven's sake, now she's sat down! Right in the middle of the bloody lounge, as well!

'Morning, Bill,' Stephen said as he approached the bar. 'Hope you don't mind. It's an interview, for the article. Pint of Tetley's. And a Famous Grouse, while you're at it.'

Billy obeyed. He knew someone lost to drink on sight,

so an order of that kind this early didn't come as a shock. He said nothing in response as he pulled the pint.

'I mean,' Stephen backtracked, seeing his discomfort, 'I could go upstairs if you think...'

'Mate,' he said, putting the whisky down and watching him shoot it before reaching for his pint, 'I wouldn't recommend that.' His voice went quiet. 'People talk. Here's fine, but... be quick? I'm sure you understand why.'

Stephen gave him a nod as he lifted the cold glass and made to move. 'Gotcha.'

They sat central to the room in a spot close to a long window. The air was warm and dusty and it smelled of stone. Close by, to his right, was the fireplace and that chair. He hadn't looked at it when they had walked in and he wouldn't look at it now. He just stared at Penny. The fear in his glazed eyes was plain to see. She, having refused a drink, even a soft one, settled into her chair and slowly closed her eyes. Long black lashes sharply defined against powder-white skin.

Bill stood and went out via the little backroom door. Probably to give them privacy, but most likely because he didn't approve.

'So,' Stephen said cautiously, 'what do you... think? Do you... sense anything?' He still felt pretty silly being party to such things and using such language, but after last night it didn't seem to matter as much.

'I did the moment we stepped in.' She replied. 'Just gimmie a minute.'

Silence for a few moments. He didn't like the silence anymore. When it was this quiet you could hear even the slightest sound, and in this room he didn't want to hear any of them. Least of all the creak of a chair when sat upon. The image of a face, obscured by a white veil and spattered with acidic vomit, flashed behind his eyes. He turned his head as if struck, and rubbed at his sore sockets with two fingers.

'I'm sorry I shouted.' He said quietly. 'And about the theatre makeup thing.'

'Shh.'

After more waiting – the girl was as still as a statue, what was going on in there, anything? – Stephen lit a regal. The pint glass on the table was empty when he glanced down at it. Didn't even remember drinking it. That happened a lot. He smoked the cigarette almost down to the orange filter, letting a thin stream of smoke exhale past his lips, and when he looked at Penny she was looking back. He started.

'Oh.' He said. 'Hi. Welcome back.'

'If you're not going to take this seriously...' she said, her hands flat on the table with long, splayed fingers.

'I am. Believe me, I am.' He said, and stubbed out the cigarette. 'Sorry about that.'

'Stop apologising for everything, it's irritating.' She said. 'Anyway, it's as clear as day that there's layers in here, lots of historical energy, which is hardly shocking given this house's age. There are a *lot* of dead people in these walls. This main thoroughfare,' she gestured, 'is like bloody King's Cross.'

Stephen looked around. He saw nothing, but it felt different after she had said that. Perhaps it was simply because he was starting to believe her. Hard to disbelieve anything after last night. 'You can *see* them?'

She shook her head. 'For most people, mediums included, you get images in your head, or words, or smells or sounds. It's rare for most to physically *see* an apparition, you lucky boy.' She said this without humour, and was going to speak again but her breath caught and she lowered her head as if listening, her eyes on the old, worn floor. 'There's a great deal of suffering here.' She whispered. He didn't like the way she whispered. It was fast and breathy and thin, like the voice of something unearthly in a horror film. 'It's so sad and cold, and there's sorrow that's so deep it's fathomless. It looks like a sheet of old paper, filled with thousands of words, and all the words are unspoken regrets and disappointments and heartbreaks, and all the edges of the paper are burnt black and still glowing with embers, and that is the resentfulness and anger, the fury of helplessness. Oh, there she is.'

He leant forward. 'The... bride?' He glanced at the empty chair now, as if merely mentioning her could conjure her somehow.

Penny reached up, still staring at the ground, and the fingers and thumb of one hand pressed against her throat. She let out a long, slow breath. 'Bloody hell, you poor girl, you silly girl.'

So, the article he had read was true. His stomach, upon which the cold beer was already sitting uncomfortably, flipped. Suddenly he felt quite sick. Imagine it. Imagine that first swallow, feeling it start to liquefy the skin on your lips and tongue. That acrid, burning, dissolving liquid going in, and down it goes, and it's already too late. How painful it must have been was unknowable, and impossible to even guess at. She must have suffered one of the most horrendous deaths imaginable, and it would not have been quick. Jesus in heaven, why would anyone choose to end their own life that way?

Penny started to cry. Stephen was jolted from his horrible thoughts as he noticed. He leaned in, examining her worriedly. She wasn't screwed-up-face-and-wailing crying, she was just staring as she had been, but now tears were dripping down her white cheeks, and around the ice-blue of her eyes a line of scarlet was forming.

'Are you ok?'

She nodded and sniffed a wet sniff. 'Ignore it. Can't help it. Urgh. Hate crying. It's just the energy of her sorrow, it's so strong. Oh, oh!' She went stiffly upright in her hair so quickly that it made a dull squeak on the stones, and she looked straight at him now. 'I got an image, I saw her! Oh wow, cool!' She pulled out a tissue and dabbed her nose.

He tried to catch onto her enthusiasm and reflect it, but failed. He was too lost and dazed by it all. 'Oh, really? Like, *really*?'

'Yeah, she was beautiful, she was *so* young, too! Gods, you forget how young they used to wed back then.'

'Back *when*?'

'Seventeen-ninety-eight.' She replied without hesitation.

Stephen's eyebrows went high. 'That precise?' He blurted out. 'How can you be so sure that...'

'Shh!' She said. Then a long pause. 'She's coming forward.'

She closed her eyes as a chill ran over him. He looked around again. Same pub, still empty. But was it colder, or was it psychosomatic? A trickle ran down his back as cold as water that had dripped from a rooftop's edge and down his shirt. He shuddered once and rubbed his hands together. He watched and waited.

'She's gotta be about fifteen. He was her first love. Annabelle? Yeah, I think so. *No*, no. Maybe Annabella, or Isabelle or Isabella... Long dark hair, eyes too, she was a beauty. Oh, she lost her heart *big* time. And he did leave, but it wasn't on the wedding day. She wasn't jilted at the altar. It was... it was before that. He left her *before* the wedding day. She chose... oh, this is fucked up, she chose to die in the dress she never got to wear that day. She went to the shop and picked it up on the same day that she bought the acid. No, not bought – stole. She was *not* well. She was not a well girl. That's why he left.'

She said all of this quickly and almost without breath, like a continuous stream of consciousness. It continued.

'Her parents weren't well either. This place...' she swallowed, 'this place made them sick. It makes them sick, the fragile ones. It preys on them. The ground has gone bad. The ground has gone *bad*. Something terrible here, yes. Something reaching and hungry and black. And she can't get out. She still can't get out. And the suffering goes on, and the bad ground likes it.'

She opened her eyes again, calm, still and focused. Her chin was jutted out, though, and her bottom lip too, a little.

'Fucking hell, Whitey.' She said, her voice thick.

He just stared, mouth slightly open, eyes searching her.

'She wasn't exactly trying to kill herself.' She said. 'It was the... it was the baby. He knocked her up and ran, and she thought – *god*, she was poorly – she thought she could burn it out...' her voice whispered away into a breath.

Heavy silence sat between them. Stephen's stomach was a solid rock.

'I should have come in here before.' She said. 'I always hated pubs, this one especially. It's a good thing you found me and led me to this.'

'Why?' He asked in a way that suggested he didn't really want to hear the answer.

'Because I think... no - she was trying to tell me, I'm *sure* - that the thing you saw last night wasn't her. The Bride, I mean. It was something else, something bad. Just like with Millie's husband.'

Stephen wasn't imagining it. The room was definitely colder.

15

The First Step

'...awfully close to channelling,' Penny was saying as they walked, 'almost tipped. Hate it. Worst feeling ever. Glad I could close things up without it.'

Stephen was smoking and walking, staring straight down, watching each of his (now ruined) shoes disappearing into the snow and slush one after the other. He didn't care that his ankles were ice cold and that the water had seeped down into his socks, and he didn't care that the temperature had dropped so low that his face was numb and his nose stung. He was thinking about how small the life he had left behind seemed because of all this. He was thinking that he was entering territory that scared him so much - not that he'd dare admit such a thing to a person younger than him, god forbid - that he wanted to defrost his ancient car and get it on the road. He wanted to run, to leave Helmsley behind and never think about it again.

But it felt too late. It was really starting to feel, to coin one of Penny's weird words, predestined.

But why?

He realised she was still talking and he looked up as he sucked on the orange filter. 'Sorry, what?'

She rolled her eyes, as she so often did and much to his

irritation, and said 'have you been listening at all?'

'Of course not, and can you blame me?' He responded as they reached her house and stopped. 'I've just had a hell of a night, and had my head blown open. Can't even begin to process any of this. Not you, not this town, not what I saw last night, none of it. How can I just... go home now? How can I act as if everything's normal?'

'You can't, and you shouldn't try.' She said, her voice still infused with fire. 'You've woken up! You've opened a part of yourself that's been asleep. To pretend it didn't happen now would be to choose sleep, to stay dull, uninteresting, mindless, like all these second-rate dullards around here. You're special, embrace it! This is just the start!'

He couldn't even start to take a compliment. He shook his head but didn't reply. He knew there was nothing special about him. Nothing interesting. Nothing unique. His life was done. He said that to himself without pretension. It just was. It was done. He'd lost the life he'd built and he was done, not because he chose it, but because he knew that he didn't have the energy, nor the aspiration, to start over again. Now he was just waiting it out. That had been the plan, hadn't it? Drink and work and drink and work until...

'Shit.' He said aloud.

'It is certainly not shit!' She answered. 'It's true, you miserable old trout! All you have to do is...'

'No, no.' He dropped the cigarette butt into the snow as he raised his hand. 'I just realised....'

He suddenly saw it all so clearly. His plan, subconscious or not, was to hide until he died.

Drink every night, work every day, dodge his family, dodge friendships, most certainly dodge social situations that would encourage meeting women, dodge everything and stay asleep until he died. Died either from cancer because of the cigs, liver failure or heart attack because of the drink, any would do. Then he would be free because he wouldn't exist. He'd be gone. None-existent. Then he couldn't think, or feel pain anymore, or anything at all.

Except, now he knew that wasn't true, didn't he?

Now, it mattered. Now, everything had a meaning unknown to him, and even when he died – he *really was* starting to believe – that wasn't the end of it.

He felt like he was standing at the edge of a wide and deep void, and behind him there was a wall. There was only one way to go, one step to take, and it was the most frightening step on earth.

Penny was watching him patiently. She shot an uncomfortable glance at the townspeople milling about, not watching them outright but most certainly keeping an eye on them.

He snapped out of his stupor and he looked her straight in the eyes, which she wasn't used to and was no big fan of, and he said 'you said that you can help me, that I need a *cleansing*, was it?'

'Yeah, for bloody starters.' She replied.

'Okay,' he said, staring into those large blue eyes but in reality staring past them and into a yawning void, 'well, you're right, I do need help, and I think you're the only one that can do it. So why don't we go in and do this cleansing, before I lose my mind completely?'

He followed her in as the church bell nearby loudly proclaimed that it was 12.30, closing the door of Canon's Garth on a grey and aggressively cold afternoon. Three men stood on the steps of The Feathers, watching them across the white distance. A tall man in a cap and a big white moustache watched the pair go into the rectory, and his heavy black eyebrows knitted together above narrow eyes. The two men at his side looked from the house to their leader. He traded looks with them, they exchanged some hushed words, then they nodded before filing back into the pub.

Something had to be done.

Inside, Penny was lighting a fire in the little hearth. The old vicarage was as cold within as it was outside. The walls were bare stone merely painted in many places, and seemed to radiate cold through from the outside with the efficiency of a larder. The curtains were wide open, and muted crisscrossed white light came through, illuminating the hanging pentagram and the extinguished candles around it, the stacks of cards with odd depictions of swords and goblets and dancing skeletons on them, and the dusty old record player upon which a stationary vinyl sat whose label read *The Cure*.

Stephen was back in his curved armchair, his coat slung over the back of it. His legs bobbed nervously as he watched her stoke the growing flames.

'You said something about channelling.' He said, his throat dry and screaming for drink. 'What's that, exactly?'

'Letting a spirit so close that it can speak through me.' She replied, her back still to him. 'I hate it. Don't do it unless I really have to. Horrible feeling.'

'Like... possession?' His voice was drier.

'No.' She said, turning and standing to face him. 'Possession is rare, dangerous, and it isn't a choice made by the individual. It's a violation. Channelling is allowing them to speak using your voice, for a time. It's a mutually beneficial agreement between the medium and spirit.'

Stephen listened to the fire and the sound of his shoes scratching against the stone as his legs juddered. The girl in black smiled and said 'it's okay to be freaked out. I'm used to it, is all. I get why you're not.'

'Did she, the bride I mean, Isabella or Anabella or whatever, did she try and do that?'

She nodded. 'She wanted to. Without my permission she can't, and I didn't give it. It's…'

'Horrible.' Stephen finished. 'What does it feel like?'

'Remember when you're at school,' she said, hugging her arms around herself, still in her winter coat, 'and you tip back on the chair you're sitting in, so that you're balancing on the two back legs?'

'Yeah.'

'Well, there's like this… tipping point, isn't there, when if you tip too far back you lose balance and then you fall? Remember that moment when you lose balance and control, the panic of it?'

'Most definitely.'

'Feels like that.' She said. 'Except the panic moment keeps on going and you feel like you're falling forever. It's happened to me before. By the time I'd come back to myself I was on the floor, there was blood on my lower lip and the people there were staring at me, horrified and screaming. I couldn't remember a thing. I'll have to tell you about that sometime.'

Stephen swallowed with a click. 'That won't be necessary.' He replied.

She laughed but it was a gentle one and kind in nature and she removed her coat, throwing it over the old chest of drawers by the door.

'There's a few things I need to prep for this,' she said, 'and you need a drink.' She saw his face light up and added 'not *that* sort of drink, Whitey. *Man*, you need working on. You need something to cleanse your body as well as your spirit.'

'Making potions?' He glumly shot back. 'Made from the children you lure in with your gingerbread house?'

'Herbal tea, dickhead.' Again, this sounded oddly good natured, like the tone of a close friend. 'We'll talk about the alcoholism later.'

He raised his eyebrows. 'That obvious, huh?'

She made for the hallway that lead to the kitchen, calling over her shoulder 'it couldn't be more obvious if it was written on your t-shirt. One step at a time, Whitey. It's like an domino effect – fix one broken part, and the rest naturally follow. I'll see you right.'

Those last words were far more comforting to him that he could admit to himself in that moment, but the relief of surrendering himself to the will and to the care of another was something he *did* know he felt. It was a feeling he hadn't enjoyed in a long, long time, so he decided to let himself bask in it for these moments. And just like that, as easily as deciding what clothes to wear, or what to eat, or where to shop, he relinquished control of himself and his entire life, and gave it to Penny Black. A girl he'd known less than two days. Was crazy enough to make sense. Made a hell of a lot more sense than his life so far. Hell, why not? He could let it all go for an hour or two, couldn't he? And just for once, it wasn't drink he was yielding to.

This was his third day in town. Tomorrow was his last, then the following morning he would be bound for Stockton with a handful of messy notes, a head full of horror, and a smirking boss waiting for him along with a desk in a little sterile room without windows. Did he even want that anymore? And if not, what *did* he want? The article, which seemed worthless now, had enough content to be done. Once back behind his typewriter he could easily hammer out a piece, and he had enough pictures too. But that, quite suddenly, had stopped being the point of this. Now there was a bigger picture, a picture so big that he could no longer see the edges of it, nor fathom the detail.

Penny re-entered with a wooden container in her hands about the size of a shoebox, it was shiny, lacquered, and had an odd design on the lid made from inlaid copper or bronze – a circular moon edged by two other moons that were crescents. She placed it on the floor and moved to close the curtains. All was dark, save for the shimmering firelight, until she began to light candles all around the room with a long taper. In that setting it was quite a remarkable transformation to Stephen's eyes; they'd gone from sitting in a living room in the 1980's to sitting in a medieval chamber some four hundred years before. The way the fire looked against the ancient stone, for some reason, made his skin goose up. His temples pulsed rapidly. His throat burned. A hot drink – more of that bitter green tea – was pressed into his hand, and this time he drank it quickly and without complaint.

She told him to take his shoes off and he obeyed gladly, putting them down by the fire to dry them. She told him socks too, which reluctantly he also did, dropping them over his shoes like great grey slugs. He was becoming increasingly uncomfortable. What next, trousers? What culty black magic was this? Was it really like those Hammer movies, with Christopher Lee saying black mass and waving a dagger over a naked sacrifice while a figure with a goat's head looked approvingly on?

She knelt by his feet and opened the box. He couldn't see what the contents were from his angle. She took out something that looked like a very thick white cigar, bound with twine, that contained very pale dried white leaves of some kind.

'This is called *smudging*,' she said, 'it's a very old burning rite.'

'You're gonna set fire to me? I'd go up like a distillery.'

'Shush, Whitey.' She flashed him a look like a white ghoul in the dark. 'This, if you cooperate, will cleanse your aura. Also, I'd like to take a look at aligning your chakras.'

Stephen cupped both of his hands over his crotch.

'Will you *please* take this seriously?' Her pleasant tone disappeared. 'This isn't like some medical procedure where you just sit back and let the surgeon do the work. This requires your participation, and if there's any doubt whatsoever in your mind then it won't work. You have to *want* to be healed, and submit to it. You have to believe.'

She then took a clamshell from the box that had been painted so that it looked like a rudimentary bowl, and with it a long black feather. He decided not to speak further to ask their purpose, even though he had no idea of what was about to be done to him. She laid the objects on the rug beside her and then said 'open your hands.'

He did so, and into each of his palms she pressed two stones. He tried to examine them in the dim light.

'Quartz and Selenite.' She said. 'Cleansing crystals. Close your fists, and hold them until I tell you otherwise.'

He silently obeyed, though the humour of the moment wasn't lost on him. A few days back he'd have thrown them across the room in disgust. Now, and it was really rather thrilling to believe it, he realised he knew nothing anymore and had no right to judge a thing. Life really knew how to take a sharp left when you least expected it.

'Now.' She said, and stood to face him. She was pretty

short without those big black boots, but no less intimidating to him. 'I want you to close your eyes, and when you do I want you to try, *really* try, to picture your intentions. I want you to see the outcome of this cleansing in your mind's eye. See yourself not as a man in a suit, made of bones and skin and all the rest, but as a being. A thing of light. See yourself coated in something black, something smothering and sticky that's coating you like tar. Then, as the ritual goes on, I want you to picture yourself growing brighter, and brighter, and as you do I want you to picture the black coating start to burn and peel away. Picture it falling from you in pieces, bit by bit.'

'Isn't that just... using my imagination?' Stephen asked, though his tone was more respectful.

'Same diff.' She said. 'Intention and visualisation are things of magic. People have just forgotten. You can do magic, Whitey, all you have to do is visualise and believe, and the rest will physically happen.'

'But... I'm sorry, but... isn't that just self-improvement?' He pressed on. 'Like, isn't that just wanting your life to be better, and imaging what it'd be like, and then doing it?'

She smiled and winked. 'What do you think magic is?'

'Then what's the point in all this stuff?' He gestured with a closed fist at the items on the floor.

'That's *my* job.' She said. 'I'm the witch and these are the tools, but without you their effects won't last. True change has to happen within. You have to open yourself to the possibility, and open yourself to my work. You don't need to understand something to accept it. Faith, Steve. It's all about faith.'

He paused, uncertain. His bloodshot eyes searched her face but he couldn't find any words.

'Look where you came from,' she said softly, 'and now look at where you are. Last night you saw a spirit being, and it was trying to tell you something. They've noticed you now, or *it* has, and there's no going back. You were meant to be sent here, you were meant to see it, you were meant to meet me, and this cleansing was meant to happen. You're following a predetermined path. You have been this whole time and you didn't know it, but now you do.'

'Where does the path lead?' His voice was quivering.

She answered him with one of her now trademark grins and said 'Wanna find out?'

Suddenly he felt a wave of emotion that he wasn't prepared for. His eyes turned glassy and he felt ashamed because of it. His throat felt thick. It was as if he'd been sleeping on a fast moving rollercoaster somehow, and had now awoken to find himself spiralling on a ride that he hadn't remembered boarding.

'I'm frightened.' He whispered.

She seemed pleased with that and she nodded. 'Perfect place to start.' She said. 'And I swear to you that by the end of this you won't be. Quite the opposite. Told you - I'll see you right, Whitey.' She reached up and gently patted his chest over his heart. 'It all begins with a first step, and that's the most frightening part. After that,' she laughed softly, 'well, you'll see. Ready?'

Stephen fought tears and nodded.

And the ritual began.

16

Purging

His eyes were closed.

In a vast black space stood a being in the shape of a man. It was coated in glistening black tar. It shouldn't have been glistening because there was no light source, but Stephen wasn't too good at envisaging things, and it was the best he could do.

Beneath the black tar there were cracks of light, like bright networks of veins all over the body that hummed with light from beneath the dark crust. But the black goo was stuck fast and had hardened and would not move. The figure of light couldn't breathe. The figure of light hadn't drawn a breath of air for a very long time.

Stephen could smell something burning. It was sweet, but so strong it was acrid, and when it drifted by his face, which was periodical, he wanted to gag and cough. He could hear a voice too.

'Air, fire, earth and water.'

He tried to do what she had said. He tried make the light glow brighter, tried to make the light burn stronger to peel away the black covering.

It didn't work.

'Body, mind, spirit, magic.' The voice said. 'Be cleansed, be purified, be freed.'

The black coating hardened further. He could almost feel it on his own skin. It hardened like a mould setting. It suffocated his pores and tightened around his muscles, it pressed around his chest like a tight band and wrapped around his neck, squeezing his throat. *You will not breathe. You will never breathe again. You don't deserve to. You don't deserve light because you are not a creature of light and you never were. You are exactly where you belong; in the dark and of the dark. This isn't going to work because you don't want it to. Not really. You're worthless, and deep down you know that can't change. You need a drink, don't you? You want to sleep, don't you?*

Stephen's closed eyes screwed tighter. He jerked his head. He felt surrounded by smoke. He felt like he was burning on a pyre, only without the heat or the pain. He took a breath that was short and tried not to cough.

'Mother, Goddess, divinity, light.' The voice said.

'Cheer up, Whitey!' Called the chorus of drunks at The Green Dragon.

'The time you'll spend regretting this choice will feel a lot longer.' Said Edward, with a look of barely-disguised hatred on his face.

'Think of it as a holiday, mate!' Said Simon Matthews, like a grinning Cheshire cat wearing expensive cufflinks.

'Throat.' Said the dead woman in the chair, speaking with cold lips behind an acid-stained veil.

Stephen felt a wave of something wash over him. It wasn't anger, no, but it had all of the energy of it. It had all of the will of fury, and it had it in spades. He stopped thinking and instead elected to *feel*. He let it wash over him and he directed the feeling with intention and he let it grow, in spite of the voices, in spite of himself, and in spite of the black tar.

He listened for her words and he accepted the smoke that consumed him, and then the strangest thing happened.

The smoke, the burning stuff around him… it stopped flowing over his skin and instead it felt like it was flowing *through* him! Quite suddenly it seemed that he had stopped being a solid object and had instead become… glass, maybe? A glass statue of himself. But the statue was hollow and smoke found its way in, and through, and filled him like a goblet is filled, and it exited the cup again. And then it flowed through him instead of just around him, and he could feel it inside of himself like light, and he could taste it, and he could breathe it.

Stephen inhaled sharply.

A voice said 'Good.'

And the being of light beneath the dark crust began to shine more brightly.

'Breathe in the light,' said the voice, 'and breathe out the blackness. Spew it out. It's poison. You don't need it. Breathe in the light, breathe out the dark. In through the nose, out through the mouth.'

Stephen obeyed and the being grew brighter, and then the cracks of light that looked like veins began to grow. Pieces, small strips of the black tar peeled away on the lower calves of the being.

You haven't had a cigarette in ages. God, a cig would be good. Imagine a whiskey right now. Clear up that hot throat of yours. You can run, you know. Not too late. You can get away from this weird girl with her mumbo-jumbo and you can get in the car. You'd be in The Dragon by five. You miss it, don't you? You even miss the warmth of the bus ride home. You even miss your little flat, don't you? A dump of a life in a dump of a house in a dump of a town. You miss it because you know you belong there and it's all you're worthy of. This won't help you. Nothing can help you because deep down you don't want help. And that's right. You know your place. This is all just smoke and mirrors and when it's over nothing will have changed, and that's okay. Then you can go home, where you belong. You can go back to sleep.

'It's a lot of money.' Angela said coldly. 'That has to count for something.' Her icy features looked sharp and unforgiving. Her lips were thin and grimacing. Her eyes regarded him like she was looking at an animal dying in pain; half sympathy, half revulsion.

'Life is a prank played when you're not looking.' Stephen appeared now, and he was looking at himself. His eyes were red and puffy bags hung beneath them, his stubble was silvery and there was a dried trace of the sauce from his sandwich earlier staining them. His teeth were yellowing and he was sneering in such a self-satisfied way that wanted to slap the look right off him. He was waving a cigarette about and it stunk, and on the crotch of his trousers there was dried piss. He could smell it.

He didn't see himself. He saw the town drunk. The town loser who'd lost everything, that everyone knew about and whispered about and watched out of the corner of their collective eyes with pity and disgust.

Dear god, was that what he was?

Yes, it is what you are. But soon you'll be dead and you'll be glad of that won't you? Have another drink? Have another cig?

The light grew dimmer again. The tar dried again and tightened harder around his flesh.

'Fight, Steve.' Said the voice, and then it resumed chanting again 'air, earth, fire and water. Mother, Goddess, divinity, light.'

No, there is more to it all. He said to himself. *There is more than the office and the deadlines, and the town hall clock and the bus ride home and the whisky and the sleep and the divorce and that I LOST MY BOY!*

The darkness seemed to retract. It flexed, somehow. Grew and shrank. Trembled against a flashpoint. The light didn't just grow now, it erupted.

From beneath the black crust the veins ignited again, only this time they blazed with the light of a sun, throwing off heat and shafts of light akin to those one would see breaking through clouds after a storm.

Oh God! My Boy! Stephen screamed without sound into the black void. *Why did it take my boy? How fucking dare you! How fucking dare you take my son! He was pure, he was beautiful, he was all that mattered and it took him away!*

'Body, mind, spirit, magic.' The voice repeated. 'Be cleansed, be purified, be freed.' And then it added, even more softly 'you're doing *so* good. Remember; breathe. Breathe in the light, breathe out the dark.'

I was supposed to be his dad! The silent being screamed in the void, and Stephen saw that when it screamed there was something coming out of its mouth, and that the substance was black and thick like the tar that covered it. It was puking out the black matter as it silently roared with a voice it hadn't used in years. *I was supposed to be his dad! I was supposed to see him grow! I was supposed to see him become a man and it took it all from me! We should have been at the park on Sundays, we should have been playing on the weekends, I should have been reading him his stories! Oh, Jesus Christ he loved it when I read to him! I wasn't done reading to him yet! I wasn't done holding him yet! I wasn't done loving him yet! I was his dad and he was my boy and that was my world and it took it away! Oh, god help me! Please god, bring him back and help me!*

The being exploded. A white flash that for a moment

completely nullified the dark with a soundless explosion. The being at the centre threw its head back and opened its arms wide. The white light didn't just burn away the black crust, it simply vaporized it and turned it to dust, and then it burned away the void itself. There was no void anymore. There was no being anymore. There was only light. And for the first time in years, the being took its first breath of clean, pure air in a desperate gasp.

And then Stephen fell. He fell through the smoke just as the smoke flowed through him, and he collapsed onto something hard, and he began to wail.

When he opened his eyes he was on his knees. The rug was course and the stone beneath it was hard and cold against his elbows. He was bent forwards on his knees, leaning on his elbows with his hands covering his head like someone waiting for a bomb to go off. He sobbed hard into the ground, his back heaved and his interlaced fingers trembled.

He felt her hand gently press onto his back.

He sobbed and wailed until his voice no longer sounded like his own, and the hand resting on his back meant the world to him. Without it he didn't know what he would do, or where he would go. It was the only thing anchoring him to the earth.

After some time, could have been minutes, could have been longer, he started to calm. His hysterics had subsided, though the tears kept coming. He silently wept, still on his knees and curled up like an animal in defensive posture. Penny only spoke once.

'What was his name?' She asked in a whisper.

'Samuel.' Came the reply, muffled by the carpet.

The girl in black leaned over and held the broken man. She rested her cheek against his back, bobbing up and down with each lurching breath he took, and she wrapped her arms around his middle. She stared sadly past him and into the light of a candle, and she waited it out.

17

Twelve Across

After the phone had rang thirteen times, Stephen gave up.

The hand that held the receiver trembled and every so often spasmed, making his arm jolt and tense again to steady it. Aftershocks, following the great quake. His whole body felt like it was vibrating. Not in his bones, nothing so deep, but it was all over the surface of his skin. A tingling, throbbing sensation that remained ever present all over his frame. It felt warm, vibrant almost. His face was grey but the eyes set into it were somehow brighter, sharp and focused as he stared through the glass of the telephone box and out at the snowy square.

Emotionally he felt spent. He had cried it all out, at least for now, and was for the moment savouring the feeling of freedom the strange ritual had afforded him. He felt like a man that had been carrying a massive weight across his back and had finally put it down, though the aching in his muscles, in his very marrow, told him that he had been carrying it for a very long time. He felt physically lighter for it, as if he had lost weight, and the feeling was blissful.

He put the receiver down and opened the red painted door. Penny turned in the snow. The day behind her had brightened. There were even blue patches breaking through the low white cloud above them. The snow remained deep and frozen hard, but it was clear that no more would fall.

'No answer.' He said to her, then he faltered a little as his leg buckled. Penny made a quick move to catch him but he held up his hand. 'No, it's ok. I'm ok. Christ, what did you do to me in there?'

'Me? Nothing.' She replied, watching him carefully. 'I just held the door open for you. That was all your work.'

The afternoon was moving at a pace. Soon it would be dark. Stephen looked from her to The Black Swan over the road. And for the first time in his memory he didn't think about a drink when he looked at it.

'Millie said she would meet me again today, to go back to the castle.' He said. 'She must be out. Guess I should try again later, but it's going to be dark soon and I'm not wandering about up there in the dark. Not now.'

'I could go with you.' She said at his side, but he shook his head.

'No, you've done more than enough.' And then he said 'thank you' and the words felt weird in his mouth. He didn't say, nor have cause to say thank you to many people, at least not sincerely, he realised.

She watched him for a beat as he stared at the ancient inn.

'It's clear as crystal you don't want to go back in there.' She said.

Without hesitation he replied 'I don't want to see that thing again. Or any of the other *things* that might be in there. And... also I...'

He couldn't say it. They stood wordlessly for a few moments as a car rumbled by on newly-salted tarmac. Penny smiled beside him.

'Here's an offer for you,' she said, 'and believe me, if you knew me well you'd realise what an offer this is, Whitey.'

He looked at her and as he did he reached for the pack of Regal king size in his pocket, but his hand stopped just short, hovered there, then lowered again.

Penny took a deep uncomfortable breath, then spoke her offer quickly on the exhale.

'Why don't we go get your stuff from your room and put it in my house?' She said hurriedly. 'It's only two more nights, right? No point you being in that place with... *her*... and, well... instead of being around that bar why don't you come for a cup of tea instead? I'm no cook, but I can knock up something to eat for you, I'm sure. When did you last eat?'

'Can't remember.' He shrugged.

Penny shuffled on her feet awkwardly for a few more seconds, looking down at her boots. 'So, what do you think?' She said to them.

'I've imposed on you enough.' He said. 'You don't even know me. What if I was secretly a serial killer or, y'know, *worse.*'

She laughed suddenly. 'Believe me, I'd know.' She said. 'And bloody hell, Whitey, it isn't *that* kind of offer. Yeuch. No offense. Alright, look, I'm pretty at shit at subtlety...'

'You don't say.'

She shook her head, smiling wryly, and continued. '... I'm pretty shit at subtlety so I'll just say it. You need to be away from the drink, and you're too scared to stay in that place. I don't blame you either; nearly every brick of that thing is haunted. With me you'd be sober and safe. I'd be keeping you away from *spirits of all kinds*.' She gave a little laugh at her own pun but Stephen didn't respond in kind. 'So, there's the offer. Just say yes or no and do it quick, the countdown is on.'

'Yes.' He replied almost before she'd finished speaking, surprising both of them.

Billy looked up, startled, from his crossword as the middle-aged alcoholic and the freak from next door entered. His expression went from *alright Steve, what'll it be* to *oh, god, not you again* in a second.

His eyes narrowed cautiously as he said 'afternoon' and stood to approach the pumps.

'Alright, Billy,' Stephen said as he arrived, 'nothing for me yet, mate. Just stopped in to get some stuff from my room. Still busy with the interviews and such. How's tricks?'

Billy paused. The newspaper guy looked... different somehow, but he couldn't tell how. 'Can't complain.' His tone was less than warm. 'Better than some.'

'Oh?' Stephen said, and once again he reached for his cigarettes, stopped, and lowered his hand back into his trouser pocket.

'Aye.' The barman replied, sighing and dumping his ample frame back into his chair by the till. 'Take it you haven't heard?'

'Heard what?' Penny said. Bold for her, Stephen thought. She stepped out from behind him and stood at the bar.

Billy lowered his eyes. Couldn't look at her. Stephen wanted to laugh suddenly. *Don't want no trouble here, ma'am. Don't turn me into a toad, miss.* But when he looked instead at Stephen his eyes looked somehow both sad and suspicious all at once.

'Mrs Wood,' he said, 'old Millicent, the lady you met yesterday? Passed away in the night.'

Stunned silence reigned. Stephen felt his new friend stiffen at his side.

'Oh, bloody hell!' He gasped. 'Why, I was just...' he gestured to the phone box through the window, '... I was trying to get ahold of her to... Oh, Bill, I'm very sorry. Oh hell, I can't believe...'

He'd turned his head to Penny as he was speaking, and the look she was giving him cut his words dead. A strange moment passed between them. He couldn't have said how, but he knew exactly what the look was telling him. A new chill danced down his spine and he frowned. He turned back to Billy.

'My deepest condolences. I will, of course, not include her story in my piece.' He said with a new professional tone. 'Is there anything I can do?'

What Bill said next wasn't exactly hostile, but it wasn't exactly friendly either. The best Stephen could glean from it was that it was a request, and a pleading one at that.

'Nothing the likes of you can do.' He said, looking down at his crossword book and picking up his pencil. 'The folk here will see to her and the arrangements. Your last day tomorrow, isn't it? Well, you take care of your business and we'll take care of ours. If you need anything before you're done, let me know. Otherwise, I'll say good day, sir.'

It was the most restrained *finish up your business and fuck off* that Stephen had ever heard.

Billy didn't look up from his crossword as the newspaper guy and the freak creaked their way across the pub after a fumbled apology, and he didn't look up when they both filed through the door that lead upstairs to the tenant's rooms, but as soon as they were gone and he could hear their footsteps on the boards of the first floor he reached over and picked up a little black phone with a long, curling cord. He dialled and waited, still studying twelve across. After two rings someone answered.

'Eyup.' He said. 'They're here. Well, you said to tell you... well, I'm not sure. Said he's getting some stuff for interviews or summat. Yeah, well, what do you want me to do? You're not paying me to do *that*. Best guess, I'd say they're going to Canons Garth. Heard him say something about the castle as well. Think that's what he said anyways, could just about hear him.' He paused a while and listened. 'Look mate, I want no part in that.' He shook his head. 'What you do with him is your business, not mine. I've told you what I've told you and that's it. He's bound to be back in here drinking before the day's out, I'm sure. So, there you go. He'll be gone after the morrow anyroad, so why...' Billy looked up, startled by the voice on the line. 'Alright, alright, fine. I know. I know it's got to be done, but like I said, I want no part... *alright* mate, calm yourself. I'd better go, they're coming back down. I'll find out what I can. Oh, before you go; twelve across – *Group scheme, agenda,* ten letters.'

He laughed dryly when the voice told him the answer.

When the pair came back downstairs the landlord was gone, and as ever the pub was devoid of customers. That was good. He didn't want any of them to see the packed suitcase in his hand. They left the bar quickly and made a hurried journey through the snow before disappearing into the old rectory. The street outside was quiet. The square was too. More good news. Didn't want the locals gossiping about the old man sneaking into the young woman's house with his luggage, god knew she had enough rumours surrounding her already, and unlike Stephen she was stuck there to face the judgemental stares and abusive language they'd hurl because of it.

Penny didn't have a couch, just the curved armchair. There were spare rooms upstairs, sure, but most of them didn't have furniture. A lot of it had gone to her sisters when their father had died. The upstairs rooms that did have furniture had no beds, and acted more like storage areas for unused tables, bookshelves, desks, and neatly stacked boxes of old keepsakes and clothing. The house looked like it was in a permanent state of half-moved in, half-moved out. It reflected very well, Stephen mused, the state that he was starting to suspect Penny existed in; not fitting in, not even in her own home, not quite staying, not quite leaving either. A self-imposed limbo.

So, why did she stay?

He had a lot of questions for her, and after everything they had already been through in such a short time, and with the fact that he was now a guest in her home, he felt a little more confident in asking them. He would, soon. He was sure, too, that she had questions for him. They'd only just touched on the subject of Samuel, and he knew that sooner or later he'd have to discuss it, he supposed. It'd be a first for him. Since his son's death he hadn't discussed it with anyone at all. How weird it should be a stranger that he disclosed it to. Or perhaps, how ideal. Either way he was dreading it, but now wasn't the time. Penny had other ideas.

'We need to find out what happened to poor old Millie.' She was saying as she pulled a record from her collection that was stacked untidily against the side of the fireplace. He watched her, as ever from the chair, as she put it on the player and gently placed the needle down.

'Well,' he ventured, 'she was seventy-nine. I don't think it would be too much of a leap to conclude that...'

Penny help up a black-tipped finger and he fell silent. More of her bizarre music – at least, bizarre to his ears –began to play. Electronic drums and fuzzy guitars, a man with a deep, warbling voice accompanied by a woman harmonising him; *The Sisters of Mercy*, the sleeve read. Didn't sound like nuns to him.

'Don't suppose you've got any Beatles?' He muttered, to which she gave him a withering look.

'Millie was elderly, and she was frail, yeah.' Penny said, dropping her coat onto the floor before dropping herself onto it. She began pulling her giant black boots off. 'But *come on*, Whitey.'

He'd seen the look she'd given him in the pub, and while it was true that the look insinuated something that chilled him, he couldn't get behind it.

'You don't seriously think that someone...'

'No,' she snapped, 'not *someone*.'

He shook his head. 'Ghosts don't kill people, Penny.'

'No,' she tossed her shed boots into the corner, 'not as far as we know. But something does, clearly. Remember the newspaper clipping about the church secretary, Edith?' He started to protest but she spoke over him. 'I told you when we met that there was something wrong with this place, and Millie, she was trying to tell you that there was something rotten here. Hungry and reaching and black? Something that's hurting *the others*? And, what, she just happens to die the day she speaks to you? It all fits, Steve. It all fits with what I've been suspecting.'

'Which is?'

'That there's something *bad* here. Something that's beyond spirits and repeating energies. Something with a mind and a will. It all started when my dad went. Three years ago, he died, and it's been getting worse ever since. That's why our meeting was no chance. That's why we've been set on a path.'

She was shaking his head, utterly lost. 'What are you talking about? A path to do what?'

She looked at him as if it was obvious. 'To stop it. Brew?' She made for the kitchen.

He was seriously contemplating a cigarette now. He sneered. He had seen and felt things beyond comprehension, yes. He couldn't deny that, but he quite suddenly felt that he was playing part in a young girl's delusions again. Ghosts were one thing, but a murderous *something worse* was something else.

'Well, I left home in a rush and forgot my proton pack, so...' he called through.

A kettle began to boil as she called back, the old kind that whistled when ready.

'What happened to surrendering yourself to my will? What happened to the bigger picture, so big that, how did you put it, so big that you can't see the edges nor the detail?'

Stephen scowled. He hadn't said those things out loud. 'I do wish you'd stop doing that without my consent. That's invasive, that is. If there were laws about such things you'd be in violation of more than one!'

She laughed. 'You transmitted it and I heard it. Same as talking. Can't arrest someone for hearing someone speak, officer Whitey!'

He sat silent and stared up at the pentagram. Beside it he noticed a circular shape, smaller, ceramic, and hanging by a hook on the wall. It looked like a wheel. Around the wheel were written words he didn't know; *Imbolc, Ostara, Beltane* and more. Inside the wheel were colourful depictions of the seasons of the year, winter through summer.

'The pagan wheel of the year.' She called. 'Old words for the seasons and the accompanying celebrations and rites. I'm making sandwiches. I'm vegetarian so I hope you like cheese and salad.'

'Stop reading my mind!'

'Stop being psychic!' She laughed again. 'Right, so here's

the plan. Tea and sandwiches first. Then the castle; let's see if you got a reply from our poltergeist. Then... have you ever taken part in an Ouija session?'

Long pause. 'No.'

'Cool.' The sound of a knife on a chopping board. 'What about a Psychomanteum?'

'Obviously not!' He shouted, then muttered to himself 'that's not even a real word.'

'Well then, you're gonna have a very interesting night!' She sounded delighted again, her enthusiasm returning. 'And it is a bloody real word! Oh, and somewhere in there you're gonna go and buy new threads, and you're gonna shower too. You look and smell like a homeless drunk.'

'None taken.' He called back.

Penny returned with plates of sandwiches and hot tea, and together they ate and drank in silence as The Sisters of Mercy sang that this was *no time to cry*, and Stephen wondered how on earth he had found himself in this alternate reality where people read minds, ghosts appeared before your very eyes, and kindly old ladies were murdered by *something worse*.

He was never going to get through this without a drink.

18
Turning Point

Two hours later Stephen was well fed, newly clothed, and standing up on the castle hill.

The sun was getting low in the sky. The clouds were gone and the orange light was dazzling, making a freezing cold day appear warm and cosy as it ignited on the old stones of the tower and coloured the hard ice and snowdrifts that were turning slowly to slush. He squinted against it as he crunched his way towards the looming corpse of the fortification, with its exposed ribs and hollow wounds for windows. His new clothes felt alien and ill fitting – winter boots, new jeans and a thick cord jumper beneath his overcoat – and the colour had returned to his face. The DTs had started though, as he had known they would. Usually they began late in the afternoon, but when he was at home he would know that he'd soon cure his withdrawals with a visit to The Dragon. Now there was no pub in his future, and that made his symptoms all the worse.

A sickly grey headache was worming its way through his temples and wrapping itself around his eyes. His heart was palpitating like a caged bird fluttering in his chest, and he felt unusually hot.

But all of that was forgotten as he reached the east tower.

He made his way down the steps, slipping once and catching himself as a gloved hand grabbed at a jagged outcrop of bricks, and he stumbled awkwardly onto the gravel floor. The light was dying by the time he reached Millie's wall, but the sunset lit the words up like a spotlight on a stage.

There was the jagged lettering, close to the edge of the broken wall, amongst the ancient graffiti. *Help. How? Prayer. Why? Bound.* And then, beneath their discourse, Stephen's words – *What is your name?*

There was a reply beneath it. That was clear before he'd even reached it. It was clear because the response to Stephen's question was scrawled in much larger lettering than the others. It was in the same chaotic scribble as the rest, no doubt, but it looked even more manic, and the lines had been cut deeper into the stone than the other words.

The wind had been whistling through the keep as he had stepped through it. There had been crows too, a whole murder of them perched on the battlements, cawing in that abrasive, shrill way, echoing around the cold, open grounds. Those things all fell silent as he read the words.

His breath caught. His temples pulsed with dull pain. The ground beneath him started to tip, as if the earth had loosened itself from its natural orbit. He felt like he would soon begin to slide across the wet shining pebbles and loose his balance and fall, and keep falling without end.

'It's not possible.' He said it out loud, his voice distorted by the kind of vibrato one would expect from an opera singer. His heart sped and jolted, stopped and started erratically, thumping up into his throat and burning past his ears. His head prickled with feverish heat.

His knees went loose and he staggered backwards, slamming his back against the drenched blocks of the tower wall. Had his eyes been any wider, they might have popped out and rolled down his cheeks, which had now returned to grey.

Still, he managed to maintain the presence of mind to

unsheathe his camera, which he now held to one bulging eye with hands he could no longer control. He pressed them hard against the device, steadying them enough for a matter of seconds to snap several pictures. The interior of the tower flashed white, one, two, three, before returning to darkness.

The orange light went pale as he stared, and dimmed. Then, as the sun was strangled out by the sharp branches of distant and dead trees, the castle fell into night.

'Whitey?' She said, pausing at the steps. The girl was almost invisible in the darkness, save for a face as white as a bleached skull. Her hair was a fine black river, her slender form was enveloped in a long black coat which brushed the toes of her big black boots. Black lips turned down, eyes framed in thick black lines that looked all the more vivid as they watched him, then read the words he was gaping at, shining her torch along the letters of the psychotic engraving. 'What does *that* mean?'

Stephen's lips juddered as they tried to form words. His breath hissed past them without engaging vocal chords.

It was happening again. The silence was growing louder. The air pressure was changing. The stillness was becoming suffocating. Someone was turning up the hiss of the blank tape until it was unbearable.

The reply was carved with hate. He couldn't think of another way to put it. It was cut, stabbed even, into the stone with a mocking, hateful, spiteful rage, and the words broke his heart in two.

I can see the stars, daddy.

He was shaking his head, his eyes never leaving the writing. He began to back away, scraping his back along the wall on legs that could no longer support his weight. He bumped into Penny as he went and she braced herself against him. White hands with glossy nails reached up to hold his shoulders and prop him upright. Eventually she managed to turn him, pulling his gaze from the words and forcing him to look at her.

At first he wasn't looking at her at all, just staring over the top of her head into the fading light where the sun had been. She gave his shoulders a gentle shake.

'Steve!'

His eyes snapped back, sharp and haunted, and looked into hers.

'I have to get out of here.' His voice was suddenly solid and steely. He took her arms in a grip that hurt her – and frightened her - for a second, and moved them away before he stomped off, crunching through the gravel and breaking into a sprint as he reached the stairs.

'Hey! Hang on!' She started after him. 'Whitey, what does that *mean*?'

They were making for the bridge that went over the dry moat. Stephen was running like a drunk, zig-zagging and almost falling forwards. Penny was catching him up, carefully dashing over the stones and low walls encased in ice. 'Wait up!' She called. 'Whitey! *What the fuck*?' Her last words were coloured with real fear.

'This was all a mistake! All of it!' His voice was a howl in the echoing black. 'I should never have come here! What the fuck was I thinking! I'm going home, and I'm going home right now!'

He hammered across the wooden bridge and disappeared around the curved hill, back towards the town square. Penny broke into a run as she reached the cobbles.

'The hell you are!' She yelled, her boots clopping through puddles. 'Whatever it is, we can work it out! If you run now you're doing *exactly what it wants*!'

'Well then it's what we *both* want!' He shrieked, turning a corner into the town. Darkened shop windows flashed by. An elderly couple had to part and duck into a doorway as he passed, gasping and tutting at him. Stephen was heading for his car.

It was still enveloped in white, a glistening mould of a car that sparkled with colour beneath the streetlight above it. He reached it, far ahead of her now. She turned to call 'sorry' to the old couple he'd nearly knocked over before she turned back and yelled 'Wait for me!'

When she finally caught him up he was swiping madly at the roof of his car with the sleeve of his coat, sending waves and chunks of encrusted ice through the air that flashed white in the streetlight before thumping into the dark ground. He clawed with black-gloved fingers at his windscreen, throwing the snow aside and scraping at the thick layer of transparent ice beneath.

Breathless, Penny thumped him in the arm.

'Hey! *Dick*! Calm down for a second and talk to me!' She hissed, trying to keep her voice down as she glanced at the lit windows of the pub. 'Stop it! Stop for a second!'

He turned on her then, spinning on the spot and fixing her with a look that truly unnerved her. For a second he didn't look like Stephen, and she realised that this was a man she really didn't know. She took a step back.

'Was it you?' He jabbed a finger at her face.

'Was *what* me?' Her eyes were wide and searching his.

'Did you, y'know,' he gestured frantically before putting his other hand to his temple, 'did you get in my head again? Did you read my mind and did you write those *fucking words* on the wall?' His voice broke.

She looked disgusted, her black lip curled into a sneer.

'Of course not! How could you even think... tell me what they mean!'

He calmed then, panting for breath and glaring at her with eyes like fire. He brushed his soaking forearms and shook them uselessly. His gloves were soaked now too. He peeled them off and shoved them into his pocket, then from the same pocket he pulled out a key.

Moments passed. He just glared at her and held the key. She stared back, equally as mute.

'This place is dangerous, and poisonous, and anyone that stays here must be fucking *mad*.' He spat. 'And whatever this... *thing* is that's wrong with this town, it... it can get in your head. That's why Millie saw her husband, but said it wasn't really him. That's why the bride by the fireplace wasn't really the girl you... talked to, or whatever you do. There's something rotten here, and it knows what's in your head.'

'Stephen. I know that. I told you that.' She leant in. '*Tell me what the words mean.*'

He looked her up and down bitterly. He caught his breath finally and took in a deep swallow of air before letting out a long sigh. He looked down at the key between his fingers.

'They were my son's last words.' He virtually whispered.

He turned away from her, not wanting her to see his face distort. He enclosed himself in shadow, away from the light above them, his eyes tightly squeezed. From the darkness he spoke again in a voice as weak as water.

'No one could possibly know that. I was the only one present when my son passed away.'

Seeing the bride by the fire was proof enough of ghosts to Stephen, but this, *this* was proof of so much more. So much that he dared not contemplate it. There is *something*, ever present, and it knows you, and it can get inside your mind, and it does not do it with good intention. The words were written mockingly. This *something* was cruel.

'I can't stay here.' He said, stepping back from the light. 'You can't expect me to. Not after this. This is too much for me, it's too big for me. I'm a middle-aged drunk with a simple life and a simple job. I didn't sign up for this.'

Penny examined him, head cocked, hands in pockets.

'If you were alone in this you'd be right.' She replied. 'But you're *not* alone in this. I won't stop you if you really want to go, but something tells me it's just fear that's making you run, and I believe you're braver than you think. Bravery is fearing something and facing it anyway. There's a reason we've been brought together, and I believe that reason is for us to get to the bottom of this and stop it. I've always known I have to stop it, but I've never known how.'

He snorted. 'Then what good am I? You're the medium, or witch, or whatever. I'm just a bloke with with a wrecked life and a shitty car. I'm nothing.'

That felt like one of his pure truths. The fact that it did broke his heart.

They stood in tense silence. Penny wouldn't stop staring at him. He couldn't hold her gaze for long.

'You're the closest thing I've had to a friend in years.' She said quietly.

He physically started and a hand went up to press on his stomach, but he was shaking his head. 'You don't know me. We only met three days ago.'

'So?' Was the entirety of her reasoning. 'It's still true. You've noticed, I'm sure, that there's very few people in this town under the age of sixty? Anyone born here, with any sense, gets out as soon as they're able.'

'So why didn't you?'

'Already told you.' She stepped forward. 'There's been something paranormal going on here since my dad died. I feel a responsibility to find out what it is. That's why I stay. And I believe that you coming here is part of the answer.'

The alcohol withdrawals were worsening. Stephen had to fold his arms and press his hands into his chest to keep them still. 'What is it you think I can do? Other than, y'know, freaking out and crying every five minutes and drinking myself unconscious.'

'I don't know yet!' She snapped. 'But if you go now then I'm never going to find out, and I'll likely turn into one of these coffin-dodgers you see every day in the square! I'll go to my own grave never knowing what happened to dad, or why his death sparked this situation!'

Stephen stiffened as she spoke, then he stepped forward too. 'What do you mean, *what happened to dad?* You don't know how he died?'

The stare-off continued for a few seconds, but for each lonely soul it felt like a great deal longer.

'I'll do you a deal.' She said at length. 'Come back inside and we'll share stories. I'll tell you mine if you tell me yours. Maybe... I don't know, maybe that's how it needs to start. Then, maybe we can start to figure out why we've been brought together. Then, if you're still sure of it, you can leave, tonight. But, if you're not sure...'

'I need a bloody drink.'

She smirked now. 'Well you can't, can you? If you did then you couldn't drive, and you'd be stuck here another night.'

Stephen broke his stare now and gazed off, around the square. The night had set in. The icy cobbles were shimmering under the streetlamps and from the light cast by pub windows. The parked cars were black and cold, like coffins made of metal and glass. No sound for miles. Not even a breeze. Not even a bird called. Clouds, so static they looked painted, hung against the bitter starry sky. He looked down at his boots, defeated, and said 'shit.'

Penny moved to stand beside him, and with her hand still in her pocket she offered him her elbow. After a few moments of very clear internal struggle, Stephen relented and hooked his hand through her arm.

'Fine.' He said. 'One hour. We'll talk. But after that, if I'm not happy, I'm gone.'

'Deal.' She said with obvious relief.

So together they turned away from his car and back towards Canons Garth, only to see the monstrosity that had been standing beside them, watching.

19
Millie (Reprise)

Penny's arm tightened fast against her side, trapping and crushing his hand against her ribs. He gasped long and high and made to pull away, to run, but she held him there. She said nothing but her intention was clear. Do *not* move.

He was staring at *it*. She was staring at it too. They were both seeing it at the same time and in the same moment. No possibility of hallucination here. No chance of it being a nightmare now. Nothing but the plain and simple fact that the two of them were looking at a ghost. And then it spoke.

First it kills you, then it keeps you.

A voice without breath. A voice without tone or timbre. A voice without flesh or blood or sinew or vocal chords, nor air to active them. A soundless thing that was loud. An impossibility standing before them and speaking, against every ordinary thing that the world had ever made, against everything that was supposed to be factual and imaginary, against *sanity itself*, there it stood, and it spoke to them.

Its hair was matted and grey and streaked with dark slime. It smelled coppery and sour. Blood, not quite congealed, not quite clotted. A thick substance that slicked its hair to its head, and ran in lazy streams down the side of its ruined face.

It had skin like grey leather; a thin membrane, dry like

old paper and lined so deep it looked like cuts. The skin and the lean layer of cold flesh beneath it hugged tightly to a skull from which small watery eyes, white and without pupils, pierced through the gloom and looked at the pair. It was looking at them. Somehow, straight at them.

It spoke again, soundlessly and yet so loud that it hurt Stephen. Not his ears, no, it wasn't that; it was hurting his *head*. The words pressed against the centre of his forehead and it hurt with each word, syllable, and consonant, like an invisible finger was jabbing at him. The thing spoke using its mouth, a mouth that was dark, wet with the same black slime as its head, and toothless. Yet the words didn't seem to be coming from that horrible mouth, the words just *were*.

FIRST IT KILLS YOU, THEN IT KEEPS YOU! It shrieked at them.

Penny was shaking, perhaps even more so than Stephen was, as she held him fast. And now he was digging his fingers into her forearm as he held it so hard he was worried he'd break it.

It was wearing an old floral nightdress and a slip, ugly pink and orange. Faded, like it had been worn for many years, and just like the dead thing that wore it, it was stained black with thickening blood. And then that smell; sulphur like old eggs, and the sharp stink of urine that reminded Stephen suddenly of the ammonia stench of a cat litter tray.

It moved, at least, it *must* have moved because now it was standing further away from them, and it was no longer facing them but facing sideways towards the town square. He hadn't seen it move as such, but there was the suggestion somewhere in-between that it had. Like frames in a stop-motion animation or a badly-made photo flipbook, it jumped between positions. Stephen looked down at thin feet, grey and bare and covered with black broken veins, and toes with unclipped yellow nails that he now realised didn't leave any tracks in the snow.

'Her head.' Penny hissed so quietly it might have just been the breeze, and he looked and he saw what she meant. The thing was standing side-on and they could see, even though it stood some distance from them now, that the blood it was covered in was from an appalling head wound. So appalling that he could see, beneath the matted hair that glistened black under the streetlight, a shattered fragment of skull and beneath that, deeper in the cavity and shrivelled, its dried out brain.

Stephen wanted to scream but he couldn't allow it. If he did he wasn't sure he'd be able to stop. Instead he drew in a thin wavering breath, and managed to say a single word to Penny, even as the nausea pressed against his throat and his head swam so badly he thought he would go over, dragging the poor girl down with him.

'Millie.'

The apparition lifted an arm that was no more than bone from which loose old skin hung, and with a finger crooked and swollen from arthritis, it pointed away from Canons Garth and towards the graveyard gate beside it.

And then it was gone.

The air pressure changed, and Stephen's ears popped as if he was at high altitude. The pain in his forehead became a dull numbness instead. The stench was gone. The horror of it – a skeletal and rotting thing reeking of old blood and butchers' meat and piss – was gone. Now they were just in a normal street on a normal night, but things could never be normal again.

Penny's grip loosened. The silence rang hard in their muffled ears. Stephen managed to blink his bulging eyes and he looked down at his feet.

'So,' he managed at length, 'does this make us *both* lucky now?'

'Wow,' she even managed a laugh, though it was mirthless.

Stephen let out a laugh too, dry and short. What else was there to do?

It soon died down when the weight of what they had just seen pressed down on them. That had been Millie, and Millie was dead. And Millie had come to tell them something; that she had most certainly not died of natural causes, and that there really was a *something worse,* that...

'Kills you then keeps you.' Penny whispered, making Stephen look up from his boots.

'Yeah,' he replied softly, 'she was right all along. Something here is preying on people, and when they're dead it… hurts them somehow. Keeps them.'

Penny let out a long thin exhalation. 'Poor lady.' She said. 'The effort it must have taken her to come forward and do that. The fight she must have had against…'

'We need to know what this thing is.' Stephen said after she'd failed to finish her thought. 'We need to get inside and we need to talk. I think you're right. I think that's how this has to start.'

She nodded and said 'yeah,' shortly followed by another, more mystified 'wow.'

They both stood, still side by side, still linking arms and staring at the spot the apparition had been for more moments.

'Can you move?' He said as he stared.

'Not yet.' She replied. 'Let's give ourselves a minute.'

Eventually they had made their way inside. It was a slow and reluctant act, as if the pair were heading for the gallows. As Penny had shakily pushed her key into the lock of her door, Stephen hadn't been able to stop himself glancing repeatedly at the spot the entity – no, Millie. It had been Millie Wood – had been standing, terrified that she'd appear again. A strange thing; he was almost disappointed that she didn't. Morbid curiosity, or unhealthy fascination, perhaps.

I can see ghosts, and ghosts are real, he thought as he followed his new friend down her hallway, *and I'm not mad, and I'm in a whole new world now where everything means something and there's so much more to this life than I ever dreamed possible.*

'She was pointing at the graveyard.' He said as they entered the living room and Penny went about thrusting the curtains closed. 'She was telling us where this thing is.'

'I know,' she replied as she switched the standing brass lamp on and began lighting candles, 'but I don't think she was pointing at the graves. She was pointing at the church.'

Rather boldly for him, Stephen didn't politely sit down in his usual chair as he had so many times before. This time he remained standing and moved to examine the decks of tarot cards on the mantlepiece. 'What makes you so sure?' He said.

'Well,' she brushed past him in the small room and made for the record player, 'since we're going to be sharing stories, I think I'd better go first, to answer that. Please don't take those cards out of the box. If you touch them you'll contaminate their energy and they'll need cleansing.'

He obeyed, placing the cards down gently. 'Is this something to do with your dad?'

She pulled a record from a card sleeve and blew on it

before placing it on the turntable. Soon the ringing silence of the room was blessedly filled with sound, albeit at a low level. This time it was a band he actually knew. The bass-heavy beat and synthesisers of Depeche Mode's *Never Let Me Down Again* kicked in. He wondered if Penny's constant need for background music was because of her passion for it, or for some other reason.

'Already said it was,' she said over Dave Gahan's crooning, 'I just don't know what. What I do know is that it has something to do with the church. Follow me.'

He followed her into her kitchen, which was nowhere near as small as he imagined it would be. It was at least equal in size to her lounge, and was neatly tiled above the surface of the countertops, above which it became the same whitewashed stone and oak beams as the rest of the house. The floor was even polished flagstones, and there was a little latticed window cut into the thick wall beside her oven. She filled a steel kettle with water from an antique looking porcelain basin and placed it on the gas hob, lighting it with a *click, click, click*. 'Over here.' She said as she moved to the window. 'Look.'

He did, and beyond the smoky glass he could make out the graveyard. The back of Canons Garth was not only adjacent to the churchyard, it was part of it. The ground beneath his feet was in the cemetery itself. He looked out at a stretch of grass populated by the dark solemn shapes of headstones, and at the snaking path beyond them – the same path he had walked along on his day of arrival. Far to the right he could see the church, or rather the silhouette of it, bulky and looming, with a sharp tall spire poking at the stars.

'You must get some... trouble here,' he said, 'of the supernatural kind, I mean, living in a graveyard like this.'

'Well, ordinarily I would say, and I've always said, that the last place you'll ever find a spirit is in a graveyard.' She responded. 'The ones that don't move on after their passing, they usually cling to the place they died, or to somewhere dear to them, or to somewhere they have unfinished business, good or bad. But in this case, well, I'm not so sure. But no, I don't have that kind of trouble here. This house is protected. I bless it and make a barrier of it almost every day.'

He paused for a beat, then said 'have you been inside the church, since your father's passing, I mean?'

She shook her head. Then she withdrew and made for the lounge again.

'I need to shower and meditate. It won't take long.' She said as she went. 'Make us both a brew, would you? Then we'll get to work.'

He did as she instructed and soon there were two steaming mugs of tea – not herbal this time, blessedly, as he'd managed to find regular teabags – on the kitchen counter. He glanced at his watch and found that only ten minutes had passed, though it had felt a lot longer. Then he noticed that the kitchen had a back door, and, putting his hand to the pack of Regals in his pocket, he made for it.

A big iron key was sitting in the lock, which he turned with considerable effort. Clearly this door was never used, or at least it hadn't been in years. When he pulled it open the crack that followed made him pause with shock, thinking that he'd broken something. As it turned out everything was fine; the swollen wood of the door had moulded itself tightly into the frame over the years, and the crack was simply the parts separating.

Outside was a small garden which was completely overgrown, as far as he could tell from the light of the kitchen. There were bushes that had gone completely wild, though it was obvious that once they'd held a neatly pruned shape, there was a lawn which was now easily at knee-height, though the grass was soggy, brown and dead from the frost and the snow, and a little stone wall encircled it all. Past that, there was the graveyard. It was difficult to see in the gloom, but it was there. He could feel the stillness of it. The damp silence of it.

There was a lit cigarette between his lips. He didn't remember performing the action, but there it was. He dragged on it thoughtfully and stared out at the stones and at the hulking black shape of the church, half expecting – was he hoping? – and half-dreading to see another apparition. No such thing happened, but as he dropped the cigarette onto the back step and crushed it beneath his boot, he had to admit to himself that he was a little disappointed.

He paused to examine the All Saints Church a moment longer, running his eyes over the angular, ominous quality of it, and over the tall stained-glass windows, presently colourless and almost sinister because of it.

Churches were supposed to be holy places, sanctuaries, right? They were supposed to be places where evil dared not go, the last shelter from the wickedness of the world for those that sought solace. God's house. Sacred ground, and all that. Yet *this* church, the one that Millie's ghost had pointed to as she'd said those chilling words, was the same place that a woman had been found dead, and where a groundskeeper had claimed he saw a black mass smothering the poor lady.

Had the answers Penny had been looking for been right under her nose the whole time? Was that building home to anything *but* God?

He closed the door on it, glad to do so, and when he turned around Penny was standing in the kitchen. He started, having not heard her enter, but mainly because he at first thought it wasn't Penny at all.

Her makeup was gone. Her stark white face had been replaced by the smooth skin of a young woman, flushed pink from hot water. Her eyes looked somehow smaller, and he quickly realised that it was because her blocky black makeup was gone, wiping away the illusion that her eyes were unnaturally large. Her lips looked thinner too, and they were red now, and her eyebrows were thin, and in fact very pretty now that they weren't covered by angular black oblong-shapes with spiked tips. Her hair remained ebony of course, so black that it looked bluish in certain lights. She had changed into a pair of black jeans and a baggy T-shirt with the logo and name of a band – *The Chameleons* – that he didn't know. She patted towards him on bare feet.

'I've had a thought, Whitey.' She said, the characteristically spirited tone of her voice gone, replaced by a grim seriousness. She approached him slowly and carefully, examining him again in that head-cocked way that she had the day they met. 'If I'm right about this, then it all makes sense.'

Stephen's weary old heart was already clutched by adrenalin-laced fear, it seemed to be its default state now, so her words didn't conjure any more nervousness than he already felt. The young woman was standing uncomfortably close to him now. He found he couldn't hold her gaze for long and his eyes darted around the room uneasily. 'I'm all ears.' He muttered, swallowing dryly.

'You saw our poor tragic bride when you were alone, yeah?' She said, pausing her train of thought to interject with 'take your coat off.'

'I was,' he replied, doing as she asked with a whole new fear tickling at him, 'I was completely alone.'

She took the coat and threw it onto the kitchen worktop and said 'but this time, tonight, when we saw Millie, we were together. Roll up your sleeves.'

He pulled the sleeves of his jumper up, exposing his thin wrists and forearms. 'What's this about?'

'You know I was saying that we're ying and yang? That we're, quite literally, black and white? And that there's a predestination to all of this?' She was raising her hands.

'Yeah?' He said with wide, sharp eyes full of equal wonder and dread.

'Well,' she said, 'here's the thing. I suspect that somehow we're two halves of a whole, two pieces in a bigger puzzle. I feel like I've known you a long time, even though we only met three days ago, and I think that, even if you won't admit it, you feel that way too.'

'Penny,' he made to back away but in response she stepped forward, maintaining the closeness, 'what're you getting at? I don't see...'

'Think about it, Steve. Hold your hands out, palm up.' He did so, frozen now and staring. 'What was different about your second spirit sighting, apart from the fact that we saw it together?'

He paused, searching her face. Then the answer came as easily as breathing, and something in him knew it was right.

'We were touching.' He said. 'I was holding your arm.'

'Yup.' She said, a touch of a smile tugging her lip. 'Now, check this out.' And she reached up with both of her hands and grabbed his wrists, and in turn his hands wrapped around hers, and then Stephen White's life changed forever.

20
Symbiosis Pt 1

He didn't know what love was until he met his son. We all have our ideas of love in the first couple of decades of our lives, like your first love; you never forget that person as long as you live. The person that just comes into your life and turns it upside down, changes you on a cellular level, blows your mind, breaks your heart, it's all too much when you're that young. Then there are the loves that come after. The ones where you're a little wiser, a little more clearheaded and careful. Guarded, perhaps. The ones where you may buy a house together, maybe even marry. But still, underneath it all you can't help but feel, no matter the assurances of your feelings or those of your partner, a little niggling uncertainty that *this isn't quite it*. That there's a place, deep down inside you, that doesn't feel satisfied. You're still not whole.

And then you have a child, and then you know what love is, and then you're whole.

He did. He knew it when he first held him in the delivery room. He knew it when he looked down at this tiny, *god, so tiny*, little human being that was made of his flesh and of his blood, and the bones inside him were made of the same material as his, and there was a tiny heart beating and a tiny brain, perfectly made and waiting to begin its journey of learning and growth. Visceral love. Primal. The only genuine love he had ever felt.

He understood his place, finally. Only this love could finally show him that. He had a job to do, he had a real meaning and purpose in his life for the very first time, and it was to dedicate himself to the nurturing of this new life until he was no longer on this earth to do so. It was so simple, yet so complex. His path was set and his heart was full.

More and more often, as his son grew and baby formula became fruit pastes and soft pasta, and as nappies became training pads became pants, and as shaky first steps were taken, he would find himself wondering whether Angela felt the same way.

He had fallen in love with Angela when they were in their twenties. She was a fierce woman, but he liked that. Fierce in her character and in her appetites, career-driven, strong, a zero-bullshit type. She had a hell of a sharp sense of humour and boy, could she drink. They had years of fun and debauchery, travelled the country, rented a house, made friends, all that good stuff. But when Samuel was born... well, did things change, or did she simply stay the same while he changed?

He spent way more time with Sam than she did. He would read to him – that was his favourite thing to do with daddy – drive him for days out, drop him off at nursey then school, and he would be on his hands and knees on the living-room rug most days playing with marbles, plastic soldiers, and colouring books with the boy when all that Angela seemed to do was watch. She would stand in the doorway, smiling, sure, but never really engaging. Every night there was a drink in her hand. Then the nights became afternoons too, and those afternoons started to become earlier. He worked for the Gazette, Sam went to school, and she drank. All of those career aspirations slowly dissipated after she gave birth. He offered to be a stay-at-home dad so she could chase whatever dream she wanted, she declined. Whatever he suggested, she declined.

Samuels' favourite colour was blue. His favourite show was Scooby Doo. His favourite place was the beach. His dark hair was always messy and when his little angelic voice sounded his R's were W's. Sam wanted to be an astronaut more than anything else in the world. He bought Sam a picture book about space when he was very small, and the obsession started there. The kid had more toy spaceships, rockets and space stations than any kid at school. By the time he was six he had a little library of books about planets, moons, solar systems, Apollo missions, rovers, and spacecrafts. His wallpaper was patterned with suns and stars and his nightlight was a globe made to look like a full moon.

Sam's knees were always scuffed, his eyes always wide and inquisitive, his little hands always trying to take things apart to see how they worked, his little mouth never stopped working. *Daddy, why is the sky bwue? Daddy, why are my veins bwue but my bwood is wed? Daddy, how do fish bweathe?*

As his relationship with Sam deepened, his relationship with Angela faded.

She would find arguments. She would make sure there was a fight, any way that she could. If there was no drama to be found then she would make some herself. He would know it as soon as he got home from the office. He would see the look in her bleary eyes, the half-smirk on her face and the alcohol-scented cloud around her, and his heart would sink. No matter what he did, it was never enough. No matter how much he worked, no matter how much time and affection he poured into the family home, it was never seen as sufficient.

Things worsened quickly. Soon, he started drinking too. Then he started fighting back.

At first he was merely defending himself. Why shouldn't he have? How much should a man have to put up with before he snaps? How many slaps across the face, how many cruel belittling words, how many dodged dinner plates and cups before it becomes reasonable to respond? But after a while it became a game. After a while it became nothing more than a petty battle of one-upmanship. Digs here and there. Every sentence carried a double meaning. Everything a trap. Everything passive aggressive, then just outright aggressive as the building pressure of the games finally became too much and turned to screaming, slapping, and broken vases.

By the time Sam was seven Angela and her husband downright hated one another, but neither would leave. Neither one would *give in*, as if there was a prize to be won for who could hurt the other most without walking away from the marriage. In the end it was purely toxic, he just as bad as her, and in total stalemate. And the most beautiful little boy with the purest of souls had to sit there and watch it all. A little creature made of light and only seven years of age had to see and hear things that no child should. Sam would not see eight.

Angela started going out at night. He should have been furious about it, after all he was certain that he knew what was going on there. But in truth he was relieved. The house was peaceful again and life became simple. It was just him and his boy, singing and playing and reading stories and dreaming about sailing through the stars. Some nights Angela didn't come home at all.

Then, in the late spring of nineteen eighty-seven, Stephen White lost everything.

We dread the phone call, don't we? Your kid is at school and suddenly the phone rings halfway through the day and all at once your nerves are set on edge. It's the same as the three AM phone call, or the policeman knocking on your door. The dread hits you so hard you almost fall. Stephen would, in those moments of invasive thoughts one can't help but have sometimes, entertain such horrid notions. Dreadful scenarios where the phone rings and the person at the other end has a voice full of horror as they say *I'm very sorry, Mr White, but...* He would shake such vile thoughts away as soon as they intervened, assured that such things were so far-fetched as to be impossible; Sam was healthy, strong, and safe. He had a good school, good friends, and a secure network around him. To think that anything untoward could happen to him was daft. Pure fantasy.

But one day his phone did ring. He was in his office editing a piece for page two and the stomach bile green phone rang. This was hardly unusual, his phone rang a lot back then. But this time he just... *knew.* This time it was different and for several rings he just stared at it, his hand frozen in his lap. Something in him knew, he would later reflect, that this call was the turning point. This was the call that would destroy him.

Eventually of course he did pick it up, and the headteacher of Newtown Primary School explained to Stephen in a sombre voice that there had been an incident. Sam had collapsed while in P.E, playing football on the school field. The ambulance was on route.

What? What? Did he break his leg, or his arm or something? Was he struck by another boy? Did he have a bad fall? *What do you mean, collapsed?*

The teacher said that he must get there right away and that he didn't know the cause of the incident, and before any more could be said Stephen had dropped the receiver and had ran out of the office, leaving the handset bobbing up and down on a curled cord as a thin electronic voice said *hello? Mr White? Hello?*

He didn't remember the drive to the school at all. It was a wonder he wasn't in a crash though, as he arrived so quickly it seemed impossible. He did remember the headmasters' face though, and the look the secretary gave him. That was one of the things he remembered most. There is nothing quite as horrifying as someone telling you that you're about to enter hell with nothing more than a look. Suddenly you're not part of normal life anymore. Suddenly you're on the flip side, where the bad things happen. The things you only read about in papers or see on the news. They're in their safe little lives, healthy and happy and normal, and you're out in the cold. All with a look.

He remembered them telling him that the ambulance had already left, and then he remembered the run from the hospital carpark to the reception desk. That was all. The details in-between were again completely gone.

The rest is just fragments. But the fragments were burned into his mind with crystal clear clarity. The fragments were moments that he would remember every day for the rest of his life. The worst moments that a human being can endure, or not endure in his case, were the ones that would stalk his every waking moment, and every dream, torturing mercilessly and without end.

He remembered the receptionist calling through, and the doctor that came. He remembered the way the doctor spoke in a hushed tone like they were sharing a secret, and the way the doctor touched his arm to gently lead him into a corridor. He remembered the look on his face too. That *practised* look and tone of voice. One that he'd no doubt had to use many times. The *I'm very sorry* look. The patient explanation. The lowering of the head. The squeeze on his shoulder.

Hypertrophic cardiomyopathy. He remembered those two words clearest of all.

His son had a heart defect. They hadn't detected anything wrong when he was born, and he seemed to be healthy and strong. He had, the doctor said, likely been in heart failure for some time and had not known it.

The doctor guided him to a chair in the corridor and he gestured to someone. A nurse then appeared with a glass of water. Stephen couldn't feel his legs. He couldn't look at the doctor, or the nurse, or the glass of water she held out to him. He just started at the doctors' blue tie and white shirt beneath his lab coat. Blue. Sam loves blue.

He asked the doctor if his son was dead. The doctor told him that his son was unconscious, and that his son wasn't going to wake up.

He is not suffering, the doctor said, *and he will not have known what happened, Mr White. You must know that.*

Then Stephen was in a hospital room and he was looking at Sam. He was looking at tubes and wires and monitors and listening to strange erratic beeping noises and hissing sounds like hydraulics and a low even buzz that for some reason was horrific.

Sam was asleep. He just looked asleep. There was even colour in his face. His little chest was bare and there were wires attached to his little ribs by sticky circular pads. His little chest was moving.

Sam was alive. They were wrong, he was alive. Look at him! He's just asleep, that's all. He's breathing for god's sake! No. No, he's going to be fine. He just had a fall and he's just sleeping and soon he'll wake up and he'll ask to go home and he'll want to press all the buttons to see what they do and he'll be carried home and they'll be so relived in the car and so happy, and wait until we tell your mother about this! And then he'll have a bubble bath and he'll be in his favourite Buck Rodgers pyjamas and he'll be in bed with his nightlight and daddy will be reading him a story just like always, and everything, *everything*, will be alright.

A nurse was there. She'd been sitting beside the bed, and she stood and gently walked to him. She told Stephen to sit with his son.

He did, and he reached over and took Sam's hand. There was a device clipped onto his little forefinger and there was a little light on the side of it that was flashing red. His hand was stained with colourful marks from felt tip pens. Sam's hand was warm. He was alive! The doctor must be wrong because look at him! He squeezed his hand and said his name, and he leaned over and put his palm to his little round forehead. He said his name again, he told him that daddy is here, my darling. And when he did his son made a noise.

It's truly remarkable how the human brain protects itself. It will do anything, believe *anything*, no matter how improbable, to delude itself into believing that everything will be alright. Stephen's brain was telling him that his son was warm, breathing, and alive, and now he had made a noise. He was going to pull through, he was going to speak! He was one of those miracle cases you read about, where death seemed certain but the patient pulled through! He could write about it in an article and share the joy and elation their family basked in with the whole town!

Stephen held his son in his arms, being careful not to move him or the many wires and tubes, and he kissed his son on the head and he again said that daddy is here, and that he could wake up now, and then his son spoke some words. His eyes did not open, and he spoke with the slurred quality of one in a dream.

I'm fwying, daddy. I can fwy.

And Stephen broke into tears and laughed and kissed him again and said wow, you can fly, can you? Well, fly back home to me then! And then Little Samuel White spoke again.

I can see the stars, daddy.

And as the words went the breath went with them, short and thin, and Stephen felt some kind of great relaxation sweep across the little body he held, and as Sam fell silent the machines around him flew into a rage. An alarm sounded high and rapid, and another sound – the worst sound – ran beneath it; where there was once erratic beeping, now there was only a long drawn out tone. A flat, empty tone.

He remembered the door bursting open and a flurry of white coats and skirts as they forcefully moved Stephen aside and crowded around the little bed with the little boy in it. Then he could remember no more.

He remembered the pain though. And the horror, too. They remained. And remained to this day. Stephen thought that he had lost everything, but there was a little more to lose.

Angela came, eventually. In a taxi.

The school had called the house initially but no one had answered. Thank Christ the school had his office number too. The reason she hadn't answered wasn't because she was not at home, she hadn't answered for another reason.

Sometime after his son had died, he didn't know how long, it didn't matter anymore, Stephen had called home. It took several attempts but eventually she answered. She slurred and rasped down the phone at him after he couldn't speak for a few moments. *Spit it out! What do you want?*

He told her.

He heard a heavy clunk – the receiver hitting the floor – and he was pretty sure he heard her running, it sounded like that, at least. What he was certain he heard though, was a man's voice. A man whose voice he couldn't quite make out, saying something like *Annie, what's happened?*

Stephen hung up.

21
Symbiosis Pt 2

Her mother died the day after her twenty-first birthday.

The juxtaposition between one day of total contented excitement and another day of total horror left Penelope with a sense of whiplash that never really left her. On Friday she was surrounded by family; her father, Everett, the local parish priest, her mother, Patricia, a primary school teacher, and her two sisters. On Saturday the family fell apart.

She was thrown a merry little party (family only. No friends, naturally, she had none) at their home beside the church. They made a real fuss of her whether she liked it or not. Even her two sisters, Emily, nineteen, and Mary, sixteen, were kind to her that day. On strict instruction, she was sure. Dad once famously said that God had given him a lifelong trial in blessing him with only daughters, and a trial they were.

Penelope found it an amusing scene when she imagined it from an outside perspective. There they were, the classic countryside Christian family in their Sunday best – pastel coloured jumpers and pleated skirts, hair in braids and clean, makeup-less faces smiling politely – and then there was Penelope with her messy black bob of hair and her punky T-shirt ripped at the neck with her tartan skirt and big boots. Literal black sheep if ever there was one.

But, when the sisters weren't at each other's throats, it

was a happy home. Her father was a kind and patient man, and her mother was a gas. Everyone always said that Penelope got her wicked sense of humour from her. Most days the house would be filled with cackling laughter, and it was nearly always Penelope and her mum. Emily and Mary were more like their father; reserved, respectable, and obsessed with order and propriety.

They all went to church, of course. It couldn't have been any other way. The head of the local parish could hardly be giving Sunday sermon without his family sitting front row, now could he? Penelope liked the church, actually, and she enjoyed the songs and the stained glass and the old stone, and the peaceful tranquillity of sustaining faith in such elegant, holy surroundings. Penelope believed in God, just not quite the God that the catholic faith offered. God presented himself in physical form as Jesus Christ of Galilee, and if she knew her bible (and believe her, she did, cover to cover) then the God she knew told his followers to find him in the open fields and on the high planes and by the running waters of a stream or the crashing of the ocean waves. He didn't mention cold medieval stone rooms, and he didn't mention people attending them out of obligation and social standing, half-heartedly muttering songs without any conviction. *Her* Christ was a beautiful man who believed only in love, tolerance, and freedom, who brought a message of safety and reassurance. Through me you will have salvation. How that became a fear-filled warning of eternal hellfire should one put a foot wrong, she had no idea. But still, she liked the candles.

The only thing she didn't like about church was being forced to wear sensible shoes and a long skirt, complete with a white blouse one would expect an Edwardian to wear. Her father tolerated her dyeing her once brown hair black, but insisted that it be combed neatly back in a little ponytail, and as for the makeup, forget it.

Anyway, after the party she and her parents played cards and ate cake (her mother was a shark at cards, she never knew her lose a single round, whatever the game) while her sisters were content to sit on their long sofa beneath the window, weaving together friendship bracelets from colourful threads of wool and talking in excited little whispers about boys. Yeuch.

They thought Penelope never saw the little looks of disgust they gave her whenever she and her mother would laugh raucously while their father looked on approvingly, but she caught every single one. And more than that, she knew what they thought, too.

From a very young age her gifts became apparent to her, but she never let on. She never went to her father with it, and certainly not her siblings, but one day when she had been ten she had told her mother, and her mother never said a word of it to the family.

She could hear what they said inside their heads as if they were saying it out loud. Not all of the time, but sometimes. The worst part was their dreams. She would hear the nonsense that spouted out of their collective brains as they dreamt, and it often kept her awake. *Very* interesting, some of it. As she grew she learned to switch it off when she wanted to, and switch it back on when she was feeling curious. In a house full of girls there were a lot of secrets, but not to her. Her mother knew that much, but Penelope never told her about the dead people.

When she was a child Penelope was terrified on a daily basis, but she never told mum. She thought there was something wrong with her, and if she told her mother what was wrong with her then she'd be taken away. The men in white coats, the ones who took away the looneys and locked them in a room with bars on the windows, they'd come and whisk her off and she'd never eat cake or play cards or laugh with her mother ever again. Because, almost daily, she'd see the dead people.

Not in front of her eyes, but inside of her head. They'd come forward and they'd show her things and tell her things that she didn't like. They'd always be looking for something or someone, or they'd always be showing her how they died (those were the worst ones) and asking her for help, but she didn't know how she *could* help. Eventually, with age and practise, she learned to turn that off too. She rarely turned it back on.

There were other times too, when the dead people intruded. Didn't matter if she switched it on or not. Her dad or her mother would come bursting into her bedroom in the middle of the night to answer Penelope's horrified screams, only to be reassured by her that she'd had a nightmare. Penelope had a lot of "nightmares". Once assured by the little girl with the pale face and the wide eyes they'd plod off back to bed, completely unaware of the dead man with plague sores all over his face, or the dead little boy with the cleft palate, whose chest was crushed and still bore the marks of a carriage wheel.

She didn't know whether it was possible to have a nervous breakdown at the age of ten, but if it was then she'd certainly suffered one. Before she got things under control her mother had taken her to the doctors on multiple occasions, fearing that these night terrors were a condition of the brain, but it all came to nothing. It was only when Penelope told her about her gift, her ability to hear people's thoughts, that her mother stopped the appointments. She said that it would be alright. Just switch it off. Keep it switched off. The older you get, the easier it will be. Then, one day, you won't even have to try and it will stay gone.

In the many years of her mothers' silence on the subject that followed, Penelope wondered whether her mother had learned to switch hers off too.

The day of the party passed. The next day her mother had to go to Pickering to visit their grandmother Elsie. The weather was icy that November. A real cold snap had hit, sleet and hard rain. The temperatures had been in the minuses overnight, so the pavements were frozen over, and Grandma Elsie had trouble getting about. Penelope's mother and father shared a car, so mum had taken it that day to help Grandma do her shopping.

She left early, around eight thirty. It was barely dawn.

Penelope could never quite remember her mother's last words to her that morning before she left. There were things like *don't forget you promised to help your dad today with the church* and *ask your sisters if there's anything they need from town before I go*, but she could never quite, in the years that followed, remember her last words to her. She was standing by the door, keys in hand, looking as beautiful as she always did and smiling, and she had said... what?

Stars.

What?

Oh yes, there it is. Now she remembers, and here, in this strange place of recollection, a recollection she feels that she's sharing with someone else, she can see her mother at the door and speaking her final words to her.

'Ee, heavens!' She said. 'It's still dark out! I can see the stars, sweetheart!'

And then she was gone. And soon after, she was *gone*.

They later found out that the cause of the accident had been a big white transit van that had lost control coming the other way down the A170. There was a dip about a mile out of town and water had pooled there overnight and frozen, a regular ice-rink in the middle of the road. The van was carrying tons of supplies for the grocers, and was, as it turned out, overloaded to the point where the back doors had to be tied together to keep them closed. Anyway, the berk had been speeding when he went over the ice-rink, and he'd slid sideways along the two-way road, just as Penelope's mother had been coming over the bank the other way. The side of his van must have filled her windscreen completely before she struck it. The van crushed the car completely, and, just for good measure, pushed her Ford Fiesta straight into a tree on the opposite side of the road, flattening it entirely. Patricia Black had died instantly.

The strangest thing was that Penelope couldn't remember getting the news. Couldn't even remember who it was that had told her that her mother was dead. She remembered her sisters' frantic screams and their inconsolable hysteria, she remembered her fathers' silence and his sorrowful daily routines too, but she never saw him cry. Not even when he conducted her funeral in front of his girls and a church with aisles so packed that people had to stand in the nave did he cry. He was never the same after that.

Penelope wept often, and always privately. But when the day of the funeral came and went her tears ended, because the next day she saw her mum.

She came to her in the early hours of the morning, just as the sun was beginning to rise over the graveyard outside her window. At first Penelope thought she was a trick of the light as the dancing dust, caught in the shaft of warm auburn light coming through her pane, seemed to form itself into the shape of a woman.

Penelope sat up in bed, staring with wide eyes, but she wasn't afraid. Quite the opposite, in fact; all she felt was love. Soon the dust had arranged itself into the familiar features of her mother; kind eyes, soft smile, and hair that seemed to be twirling in a breeze that Penelope couldn't feel. And she had felt her speak to her too, in that special way that only Penelope could hear, and she had said not to be afraid, and that we go on after, and that everything is going to be alright. Her last words were that they would see each other again one day, and that she loved her, and then it was just dust caught in the light of the rising sun, and nothing more.

It was on that day that Penelope decided to hone her gifts and to become a student of all faiths and spiritual practices, to open herself up to the unknown rather than shy away from it.

As the years passed her father continued to respect her privacy and her individuality, though they never discussed her beliefs and practices together. He didn't gently urge her to change the way she dressed and wore makeup anymore either, as he had before his wife's passing. He simply let her be. His only request was that she continue to attend church and to pray with him to sustain her faith, which she was glad to do. She never told him about her mother's visitation because she felt that such a notion would deeply disturb him, and force him to face questions about the nature of his beliefs that he wouldn't want to ask himself. So, she left him in peace.

By the time Penelope was twenty-four her sisters had both moved away to attend university. They would visit during the holidays, and would both go on to lucrative careers in the respective cities they had studied in. Emily even went abroad to do an apprenticeship for a big energy company. Now it was just her and dad, working together to keep the house and garden in good order, and overseeing the renovation of the church.

It was an ancient building, and so often required maintenance. Currently the exterior was covered in scaffolding and tarpaulin, and burly blokes in high visibility gear and hardhats were moving about the place yelling things at each other and carrying equipment back and forth from white vans. Her dad couldn't leave them to it, though. He always liked to get involved. The church was his pride and joy, so he would often be wearing a hardhat and overalls himself, with paint all over his fingers and dust all over his face.

They were knocking through a very old interior wall on the southern side of the transept that was no longer safe. It housed a medieval chapel, a tiny room that had once held a little row of pews and an altar for the virgin Mary, or so the old floor plans had said. Now it was a sealed-off space that hadn't been used in years, hidden behind great velvet drapes and quietly rotting for decades. But as time had gone on, the wall – already in bad repair when Everett had first taken position there – was in danger of coming down, and it had to be demolished and replaced.

Penelope saw an opportunity to help and she was fascinated by hidden rooms, so on this particular day she was wearing a hardhat too and was wielding a large rubber mallet that she could hardly lift, much to the protestations of her father and the amusement of the workmen.

Still, Everett allowed it, under his strict supervision of course, and together they began swiping at the old rotten stones with their tools, sending bricks and dust and debris tumbling into the dark space beyond. She even caught him laughing as they did it. Dad wasn't one for laughing, and it was a delight to see some light in his eyes for the first time in three years. As they worked, demolishing a seven foot wall brick by brick, he even said that they should continue work on the room, perhaps even restore it rather than seal it up again. A project for the two of them. It could be a little chapel once again, as it had been when Richard the First ruled the country. She asked him how long this room had been sealed off and he said he didn't know, only that it had been this way since he took residence, and that had been before she was born.

The air inside that little chapel was sour and sharp. It stank of mould and wet rot. When they finally took down the wall, and as the workmen came and went with their barrows to clear the rubble, Penelope didn't really want to go inside. The air was wet and black and when she did finally go inside, at the insistence of her dad, she could feel it somehow soaking into her overalls and hair. When she touched her face there was some kind of residue there, slick and grimy. Her dad shone a torch and they were astounded to discover that there were still medieval illustrations painted on the walls – a long red serpentine dragon to represent Satan, a tortured but serene Christ, and monks and saints of all kinds – and the altar still remained, little more now than a great sandstone block with steps.

It was very, very cold in that room. Despite the warm day outside it was like a freezer in there. Hardly odd, given that it had been in the dark for potentially hundreds of years, but to Penelope it just felt... off. She shivered as a trickle of electrically-charged ice dropped down her back, and she backed away. She understood energies by this point, and she knew that some were benevolent, and some were not.

Anyway, the room soon warmed up and was quickly filled with spotlights and the feeling passed, and her dad, satisfied with their day's work and their discovery of this *beautiful little sanctuary* as he had put it, said to Penelope that he was parched and hungry. *Why don't we go and get sandwiches and tea together?* A special moment. He usually always ate alone.

So they left to do so, a new bond forming between them as the excitement of a new project to work on together grew. This, of course, wasn't to be. And the tea and sandwiches would be Everetts' last meal.

The next day her dad had gone back into the church at first light, before the workmen would arrive, to get started on some painting. Penelope couldn't join him that day as she had her own work to attend to; she had taken on a part time job at the local antique shop on Bridge Street. It was just after ten when one of those workmen burst into the shop to tell her that they'd just found her dad, collapsed and unconscious on the floor in front of the altar. The ambulance came and went, Penelope going with it. Many hours later, when she returned home alone, Penelope was an orphan.

The cause of death was inconclusive. He was a healthy strong man for his age and he looked after himself. Never so much as drank. But the hospital just couldn't find a reason for his death.

And so she was now tasked with telling her sisters that they too were now parentless. It did not go well. The only real moment Penelope recalled about those horrendous phone conversations was the moment that Emily had screeched *why weren't you with him* at her.

They visited for the funeral, and she rarely ever saw them after that.

The biggest surprise came a few weeks later when the solicitor phoned. Only a month before his death, while they had been working on the church together, her father had drawn up a will and he had left the house to her to do with as she wanted. He said he hoped that she would sell it in order to get herself set up. A surprisingly large amount of money, for their modest income, came with the house. Penelope didn't want any of it. She just wanted her dad back.

Reeling from these things, and only after another few days had passed, it all began.

People started whispering in the pub about things they had seen, but surely could *not* have seen. Strange things started happening around town. Strange sounds, bizarre sightings, and then the deaths started. That year they lost a number of the elderly residents of the town, which were mostly dismissed as age and disease, as any rational person would agree. But Penelope suspected otherwise. Then poor old Edith Blessed was found dead in the very same church. Were these old folk dying of natural causes, or was something else responsible? Was something scaring them to death? Or worse?

Penny couldn't let the house go. It meant too much to her. It contained everything that had once been her life. It was all she had left of her family. Even when the new priest moved to town to take over All Saints, she wouldn't surrender the rectory. The communal outcry about it was deafening.

So Penny Black obscured herself away with her house and her money, worked on her craft, and mourned alone. She never set foot inside the church again.

The feeling got worse, too. The feeling that something was wrong with the very ground beneath her feet. The feeling that the town was growing darker and darker, even as summer heated the concrete and the tarmac and the town buzzed with tourists, there was the feeling that the light and the warmth never quite penetrated. Nothing ever felt quite as normal as it should. The locals became paranoid as the paranormal sightings and the strange deaths spread.

One day she would figure out what was going on, and why it hadn't started until her father's death, but she knew then just as she knows now, that it couldn't be done alone.

Black and White.

Ying and Yang.

Balance.

22

The Psychomanteum

Their hands parted.

Stephen jolted and physically stumbled back away from the girl. She didn't move, just stared with her hands still held out in the same position. He didn't stop his retreat until his back thumped against the back door of the kitchen, where he then slid until he was resting against the countertop beside it for support. He was shaking like a dog left out in the cold. A quivering hand was clapped over his mouth and his eyes were red.

'Well,' Penny whispered, 'that was really something.'

He shook his head quickly as he quaked, his eyes like saucers as he hissed from behind his hand 'who the hell *are* you?'

'An orphan.' She said, taking a deep, quivering breath. 'A child without a father. Now tell me. Who are you?'

'A father without a child.' He said immediately without wanting to, his voice muffled behind a cold sweaty palm.

'Symbiosis.' Penny said. 'Two halves of a whole. When we're joined we're complete, and, apparently, pretty bloody powerful.' He was still shaking his head but she pressed on. 'This proves it; we were destined to meet, here, now, in this place. Our souls are made of the same... *stuff*. There's far too many synchronicities. Didn't you see them in our joining?'

As if he hadn't heard her he ignored her question and spoke in a rush.

'I saw your life!' He spat. 'How is that possible? How the *fuck* did I just experience your life? I felt what you felt! I was *you!*'

She nodded patiently. 'Yeah, and the same happened for me. I saw your life and your losses. I was inside your skin. Did you hear what I said? Did you see the synchronicities?'

'What the hell is a...'

'The ignorant call it coincidence.' She said a little more impatiently. 'Catch up Whitey, you're gonna need to. They call them coincidences and as I said, I don't believe in them. Think about it. Your son's last words to you, my mother's last words to me; they were virtually the same! I lost my parents, you lost your son!' She started pacing the kitchen. He just stared as if she was another ghost. 'We showed one another details of our past that even we'd forgotten! And what you helped me remember... oh, wow! The church! It all makes sense! Wait...'

She stopped pacing and turned back to him. Her head was cocked again and her eyes were narrowed.

'I'm here to help you and you're here to help me.' She said, calm again. 'I heal your pain, you heal mine. I give you spiritual and emotional help to free you from your trauma, and you help me do the same by showing me the connection between my father's death and the trigger that started all this evil.'

'I don't know what you're talking about.' He said. 'What trigger? What did I do to help?'

'I haven't thought about the days leading to dad's death in years.' She replied. 'It's like... it's like they were wiped away, erased from my brain. But you just brought it all back! *You,*

Steve! You're the only one that can help me end this, and in doing it you can help me get away from this house and this place. You're the key! And *I'm* the key to you changing your life! You need to forgive yourself, Steve! You need to let go of your self-contempt and your anger and you need to free yourself, and I can help you do that!'

'Penny, you're babbling. I don't...'

'Quick!' She cried suddenly, her eyes perfect circles. She thrust a finger at him and said 'after the count of three I want you to tell me your birthday!'

His fear of her slid momentarily away to be replaced by irritation. 'Did you go upstairs to do drugs or something? What's that got to do with it?'

'Just do it, *please*!' She said. 'You'll see. Ok? One, two, three.'

Then, as he spoke, Penny did too. And in perfect unison they said exactly the same thing.

'April the first.'

The kitchen tap dripped alone in a void ringing with breathless silence. Outside, snow began to fall.

'Cosmic twins.' Penny whispered with wonder in her eyes and a wide smile. 'There's no such thing as coincidences, Whitey. Come on! We've got work to do!'

She pulled him through the house by the hand. His head was spinning like a top. He had just experienced what it was like to be someone else. He had just undergone the most profound connection with another human being that he had ever felt. Even as her slim fingers grasped his and pulled him out of the living room and into the hallway, yanking him up the stairs towards her room, he could feel something happening inside him because of the physical contact. He *knew* her as if she was his own child, or his own sibling or something like that, but it felt deeper still. He surrendered himself to it, to her, again. There was nothing else to do. He had inadvertently boarded a rollercoaster and strapped himself in. All that there was left to do now was see where the ride went. Nothing he knew before this mattered anymore, nothing he believed before this was true. Keep your arms inside the ride at all times.

She pulled him into her bedroom and closed the door and as she released his hand the profound sensation stopped and he felt alone again in the saddest way. Her room was an odd amalgam of a child's bedroom and a teenager's; there was wallpaper that looked antiquated and pretty, something to do with flowers, but it was mostly covered by posters and photographs. Large glossy prints of bands, *gothic rock* bands he would later be informed, adorned almost every inch of it. In-between those were photographs. Pictures of Penny as a little girl with her dad, Everett. Her mother and her sisters on a picnic. Her dad standing proudly alone in his chasuble, stole, and white collar in front of his church with a bible clasped between his hands, smiling at the camera. These were people that Stephen now knew intimately even though they'd never met.

He turned in the near darkness of her room. It smelt strongly of patchouli here and of a thousand other incense aromas once burned in censers, long gone but absorbed into the fabrics of the room. The bed was black with a velvet throw. The curtains were heavy dark drapes.

'Sit here.' She said and guided him to a stool at a dressing table with an oval mirror standing on top of it. Click, click, click went a lighter, and now there was a solitary white candle in a silver holder standing on the wood, reflecting in the glass in front of Stephen's face. He stared back at his own features in the glass and saw a man much older than his years with yellowed eyes and deep lines, made all the more intense by the light of the candle. Penny turned off her bedside lamp and now the single flame was the only source of light in the room. His face in the mirror was a detached head surrounded by complete blackness. The flame danced with each breath he took.

'This is a Psychomanteum.' She whispered excitedly behind him. 'Scrying. This is how we see the dead, or visions, or messages. It's an open portal for a medium.'

'I'm not a medium.'

'You are now, Whitey.'

The room was cold, far from the warmth of the little fireplace in the downstairs chamber. It was so quiet he could hear the snow coming down, something like sleet, on the tiled roof above the low ceiling.

'What do I do?'

'We do it together.' She replied, and now her face appeared beside his in the gloom. Two pale masks in the dark, looking very much like the famous Greek muses one sees in a theatre, one grinning with delight, the other despairing. 'We need some answers. We need to know what we're dealing with. If we open ourselves up to this portal, then maybe we can see for ourselves.'

'What makes you so sure it'll do that?'

She shrugged. 'Logic doesn't apply here. Only intention, will, and magic. I'll show you how, it's pretty simple really. All you need to do is stare into the glass and keep focused on your own face. That's all. Don't think. Don't daydream. Just empty your head and focus on your face, and allow whatever comes to come.'

That sounded potentially terrifying. He swallowed and took in an uneven breath, and then he stared. It was uncomfortable at first, this studying of one's features so closely. He tried not to look at the young face beside his, and decided to simply stare into his own eyes.

The snow fell. The wind rattled at the glass. The house creaked and cracked around him like old bones settling as they broke down in a grave.

Stephen became too aware of his own breathing and suddenly he felt very constricted. He was trying too hard to breathe evenly and in doing so he wasn't concentrating on *not* concentrating.

'This is harder than I thought.' He whispered.

'You're new at this, be kind to yourself.' She answered. 'Let it all go. Let your grief go, let your fear go. You're safe with me. Whatever you see, know that it cannot hurt you. It can't do anything to you at all. This is scrying, not communing. You're merely an observer.

More time passed and his breathing fell back into his subconscious. His heart, earlier an erratic and screaming thing rolling around in his chest in the throes of withdrawals, now ebbed as peacefully as a tide. His eyes started to play tricks on him, but he knew that it wasn't magic. It was the low light and the eyes being fixed on one spot. He'd done it before as a kid. His face started to distort in his peripheral vision, becoming a pale featureless blob, and his eyes seemed to undulate as if detached from his head.

'Nothing's happening.' He whispered.

She hushed him softly, and then he felt both of her hands reach over his shoulders, her body pressed against his back, warm and comforting like an embrace, then her hands came down and closed over his hands which were laying in his lap. Her cheek pressed to his cheek, and together they stared.

'You showed me the missing detail when we joined,' she whispered, her lips moving against his skin, 'you showed me the memory that this place, this *thing*, made sure I'd forget.'

He kept staring into his own eyes. A strange heat was growing in his chest, and then in this throat, and then there was a strange pressure building in the centre of his forehead. A warm energy had worked its way through his core to his brow, and now it throbbed there. What was this?

'Your chakras.' Penny answered him. 'Aligned perfectly and working with mine. We're two cogs in a machine much bigger than the both of us.'

The feeling strengthened. The darkness around them grew darker while the light of the flame on their faces grew brighter. The peace though, was something he hadn't expected. The sensation of complete serene stillness felt more powerful than anything actual action could accomplish. Was this meditation? No wonder people raved about it.

'What did you forget?' He breathed so quietly that it didn't even disturb the flame.

'The connection between my father and this thing that haunts Helmsley.' She said into his ear. 'He was the one that let it out. The day that I helped him break down the wall to the old chapel in his church. He couldn't have known it, but I should have. Probably why it made sure I'd forget it.'

'There was something... *in* there?'

She nodded. Her hair ticked his cheek. 'Something was imprisoned there. Someone trapped something in that holy chapel and then walled it in. Me and my dad let it out and then it killed him. Then it went out into the town and slowly but surely it started taking hold.'

His mind whirled. 'First it kills you, then it keeps you.'

'Exactly.' She said. 'So, what is it? And why was it contained in a church?'

They stared at their own faces in the dark mirror for

what felt like a contained eternity. Stephen didn't know it but their breaths had synchronised in the silence. Soon after their heartbeats matched up. The strange energy, hot and steady, pulsed between them through their joined hands. The pressure in his forehead increased.

Then he saw something.

His face, already featureless and watery, faded away into nothingness and was replaced by what looked at first like grey water. It was textured and muddy and swirling like a deep puddle in concrete with a grey sky overhead. Soon the image began to solidify and the swirling slowly steadied like disturbed water settling after a boot had splashed through it, and then Stephen realised that he wasn't looking at grey water. He was looking at stone. Bricks. Ancient bricks made of cold grey rock. It filled the mirror and his mind and he could smell mould and dust. Something was behind the bricks. Something was angry.

'Are you seeing...'

'Yes.'

Between the bricks, where mortar should have been, there was light now seeping through. Dim at first, breaking through the rough stonework, then becoming brighter and brighter. An unnatural light. Nothing that he recognised as organic at all – not sunlight, not the stars or the moon or a fire, not electric light or even anything bioluminescent. This light was otherworldly. This was a light that human eyes could not usually see.

The thing behind the wall was angry, and as the anger intensified the light grew. The bricks began to move. They jiggled in their fixings as if a great wind was behind them. Dust and mortar and gravel began to sieve through the cracks as the great heavy blocks began to work themselves free.

Was the light... *shining out the mirror now* or was he

imagining it? He began to squint against the white ghostly blaze shining through - yes, it *really was* shining through the glass from the other side - but he wouldn't look away.

The light grew and the mirror radiated, and now his eyes were beginning to hurt but he wouldn't close them. The light felt like it was burning into the soft tissues of them, straight into his very skull. The light penetrated him. The light knew him. The light hated him.

'Penny.' He said her name as a thin needle of fear spiked his chest.

'It can't hurt you.' She said as her hands pressed down harder over his. 'It can't do anything to you. Don't let go, not yet.'

The stone blocks were virtually dancing now and pale sand was pouring out from between them. The light broke through in thin shafts like lasers. Stephen blinked once as a hot pain shot through his retinas, his eyes watering now, but he kept them fixed. He didn't want to see what was behind the wall. He didn't want to see the source of the light. The angry thing. The spiteful thing. But he had to keep looking.

And then, just as the light reached a level that felt like it could permanently damage him, the bricks gave way.

And the mirror exploded.

A flash and a detonation. An explosion from behind – within – the mirror. It banged with the short sharp intensity of a firework going off. Penny let out a scream and released him. Stephen threw himself back, throwing his forearm over his eyes. Then he felt the glass.

Like a hail of thin bullets the mirror burst into a thousand daggers that showered the two of them. He felt a keen pain, slim and hot, glide across his cheekbone. He felt a thousand needles thudding against his raised forearm, into the thick jumper he wore, and then the stool went past tipping point beneath him and he tumbled back. His spine connected heavily with carpet as he let out a yelp, and he felt and heard Penny strike the floorboards too, followed by a sound of rolling, of limbs and joints striking furniture. She cried out again as the bright but terrible music of broken glass showering down on wood and plaster walls rang out.

Then it was silent and still and there was no more light. The candle was gone.

Stephen lay on his back in the pitch darkness, his arm still over his face, his breath held in his chest. Warmth was spreading across the left side of his face, the part that wasn't covered by his arm. The warmth was filling his ear now. His arm was stinging but he didn't dare move it.

Somewhere in the dark a girl started to cry.

'Penny?' He said, muffled behind a wool sleeve. 'Penny? Are you ok? What *was that*?'

The girl sniffed and wept quietly in the black, and then she spoke.

'I saw it.'

23
The Custodian

It was almost three in the morning by the time Stephen and Penny were standing in the kitchen tending to their wounds. He'd lost all track of time by this point. He had no idea how long he'd been in this damned little town, and he had no idea how much longer he was supposed to stay. Such details didn't seem important anymore. He couldn't possibly just go back to his regular life now. How on earth could he? What, was he supposed to pack his bags come morning and go back to Stockton, and his office, and The Dragon, and his miserable little flat and just pretend that these things hadn't happened? It just wasn't feasible. But if that was so, then what was he supposed to do now?

Penny had composed herself away from prying eyes. After they'd fled her bedroom she'd disappeared into the bathroom for some time, leaving Stephen to stagger downstairs. By the time she reappeared she was once again in full gothic regalia and makeup. More like armour to her than an aesthetic choice, he now realised. She had grazes on her forearm and a pretty nasty cut on the outside edge of her right hand, but nothing more. Stephen had come off worse.

A long thin slash, neat and shallow but extremely sore, ran from his cheekbone almost all the way to his ear. Too shallow to need stitches but too deep a cut to easily heal. Had that shard of glass been an inch higher it would have gone straight into his eye, and he had a horribly certain belief that this had been the intention. His thick cable jumper had protected him from the worst of the damage. All along the length of his forearm were tiny slithers like clear darts, embedded in the wool. One by one he'd picked them free and dropped them into the sink. The worst he had was a couple of scratches and nicks on the surface of his skin. It could have been much worse.

Penny was pressing cotton balls soaked with TCP against his wound. Each time she touched the slit his cheek was set fire anew and he winced, drawing a sharp breath through his teeth.

'Keep still.' She said sullenly. 'You'll be fine. You'll have a scar though, for a while at least.'

'Great.' He said sulkily. 'Can't wait to explain this one to the boys in the office,' but once again the thought hit him that he couldn't possible go back there. But what else was there to do, become a hobo?

'Just tell them you were in a fight.'

He snorted. 'Trust me, they'd never believe *that*.'

There was more than an elephant in the room. It was more like a great woolly mammoth. But for now neither of them were willing to acknowledge it.

'You tired?' He ventured. 'It's almost three.'

'If you're asking whether I'm going back into that bedroom tonight then the answer is no.' She answered as she fixed a long plaster in place along the length of his cheek. 'I've cleaned you up best I can. There's a little dried blood in your ear though.'

He studied her face for a beat before he said 'I take it that what just happened doesn't normally happen when you're scrying?'

She let out a short laugh but didn't smile. He took that

as his answer.

'It tried to hurt us.' He said, still staring into her face though her eyes remained averted. 'It tried to kill us.' She just shook her head.

'It tried to *scare* us. That was a warning. It didn't know we'd be able to see it and it was furious to have been discovered.'

'What does it want?'

She shrugged but added 'I think it already has what it wants; a feeding ground. People have accidents here all the time, people die suddenly - usually the elderly, but who knows how much we still don't know - and I think we both know now that they're not accidents or medical emergencies. It can make things happen. It doesn't want anyone to leave this place. Not ever. When you die here I think you stay, and I think that's what sustains it somehow.'

'You got all of that from an image of a brick wall and an exploding mirror?'

'I get a lot more than simply seeing things. I'm very well versed in this stuff.' She looked at him now, her ice-blue eyes sharp and frightened. 'I felt it. It's made of spite and fury and it has no end. I saw it.'

Finally they'd come to it.

He didn't want to ask. Eventually he tried to but the words caught in his throat.

'It isn't human.' She said at length. 'It never was.'

A throb of dull pain worked through the chambers of his heart and sped away from it, into his shoulder and down the length of his left arm. The pain coupled with the dread to create a jet of adrenalin that made him start and then briskly dash away from her towards the back door, which he then flung open. There was a cigarette between his lips within a second and a shaking flame was raised to the end of it.

Snow was falling in the gloom. The headstones were white again. The air was bitingly cold but still. Stephen glared at the shape of the church in the distance as he smoked.

'Someone trapped it in there.' He gestured with his cigarette. 'Why? And *how*?'

She didn't answer him, so instead he pressed her further on her first statement. 'If it was never human then what is it?'

'Why the fuck do you think I have all the answers?' She snapped. 'All I know is that it's an elemental, and before you ask me to explain what that is, please understand that just because I practice spiritualism it doesn't mean that I have a thorough and working encyclopedia of every paranormal entity ever conceived. An elemental is a blanket term. It just means that there is an entity, an apparition, a being, whatever you want to call it, that was never born, never lived, and never died, it just *is*.'

He smoked in silence without turning around. She stared at his back. As if to remind them of what they were facing the bell in the church tower chimed three long mournful notes. If he didn't know better he'd swear they sounded ominous, like some kind of warning.

'So, what do we do?' Stephen said to the night air.

There it was. The big question. The worst question one can ask when faced with something so huge. Course, there was actually a simple answer, he knew that. Run. Just leave. Run away, never look back, never return. Simple as that. But there was also option B – try and stop it. Try and stop an immense, unknowable, immaterial but immeasurably strong *thing* that has evil intent and endless power. Stephen preferred option A. If this wasn't so mind-blowingly frightening he'd laugh.

'Well,' she said after an agonising pause, 'I think I'd better put the kettle on.'

He laughed bitterly. 'That's the British way, eh?'

'Then,' she continued over him, 'I think the only obvious step to take is to find out more. We can't face something we have no understanding of, so we need to get some understanding. One step at a time.'

'And how do we do that, *get some understanding*, exactly?'

He swore he could hear her smile. What a bizarrely dark little moment this was.

'The only people who truly know what this thing is are its victims.' She said. 'They either saw it or felt it in life, and in their last moments they truly *knew it*. Now that they're dead, they're *with* it.'

He didn't want to ask her how that could help them understand this entity because he already knew the answer, and as that answer neared he felt that a path had been solidly set now, and there was no escape from it. In truth, he felt doomed.

'We contact one of them.' Came the words he was expecting. 'Now, here, tonight. We find one of them and we bring them forward, and we find out what this thing is and whether we can stop it.'

The silence pressed down so hard it felt like it had actual weight. He felt sick. Cold water filled his mouth and his stomach twisted. Quite suddenly the strength seemed to wash out of his body and his limbs felt as heavy as iron.

'Channelling?' Was the only question he had left as he threw half a cigarette away.

She nodded as the witching hour began.

***

She led him from the house. They moved through the falling snow, the air bitingly cold and highlighting the pain in Stephen's cheek with a sharp throb, and approached the church. For a heart-stopping moment he thought she was going to lead him straight inside, but to his huge relief she merely followed the path around it to reach the far side of the yard.

Other than the sound of their boots crunching through the drifts it was silent. So very still that it pressed down with an eerie pressure upon his ears. White flakes settled and stung on his face, slowly melting and soaking him, his hair already drenched. Every light in every house all around was out. The world was asleep. Only the two of them walked at this hour. Though, perhaps not entirely alone.

He felt colder still as his flesh goosed and his back tingled. He looked around anxiously. Had they ever been alone here? Was something always watching, ever present?

They moved deeper into the gloom, into a place that the streetlights didn't reach, and now a white spotlight appeared with a click. Penny shone the torch over the stones.

These were ancient. So old, in fact, that they no longer had names carved into the sandstone, nor dates, nor any identifying marks at all. Time and weather had worn everything away. The bones beneath their feet – if they were even bones anymore – belonged to those so long dead that they'd been forgotten entirely.

Beneath a crooked old tree, dried and twisted, and beside the outer wall of the cemetery, a single stone stood alone. She aimed the torch at it and the spotlight bounced as she gestured.

'There.'

It wasn't much to look at. Where once a simple square block of sandstone had stood, now there was only a shard. The top piece had long broken off, and all that remained was a misshapen base. The surface was eroded and uneven, any words long gone. One would have to look twice to even realise it had ever been a headstone.

He grimaced at it. 'Who was it?'

'My dad was a keen keeper of records,' she said as she approached the grave and squatted down in black jeans, 'and when we were renovating he brought me over here to show me this. According to his research, *this* is the oldest grave in the yard. This was the first hole dug.' She reached out and placed her hand on the rough surface of it, ran her fingers over the contours of the thick stone. 'Do you know about custodians?'

'Take a wild guess.'

'According to ancient belief, the first person to be buried in a new graveyard is bound to be its caretaker.' She retrieved her hand and brushed off the wet grime. 'The first soul interred is the custodian.'

'And what does the custodian do, exactly?' He said in the darkness behind her. 'Trim the hedges, host coffee mornings, things like that?'

Without missing a beat she replied 'I know you're hurting. You're hurting just like I am. Reliving the loss of your son must have torn you apart, and I imagine it still is now that you've walked through that nightmare again. Certainly true for me. I also know that you try and use humour to hide it. You pretend you don't take things seriously so that maybe one day you'll believe it. Thing is though, it doesn't work, and it never did.'

After a long pause, filled with his wordless anger, he said 'so, what, I should take it seriously? I should let the grief consume me?'

'I also know you're frightened, and so am I.' She went on. 'But my point is that there's a time and place. This isn't the time for taking the piss. This is a time for sincerity, and more importantly, respect.'

The wind blew the flakes into little spinning cyclones around them. An owl hooted distantly. The moment hung heavily in the air as his anger subsided and was replaced. He walked over and squatted down beside her.

'I apologise.' He said.

She just kept examining the stone. She lay the torch down on the icy soil so that the light stayed fixed on it. The she closed her eyes and began to breath evenly and deeply. He watched her quietly, his fingers steepled below his chin. After a few breaths he interrupted her.

'I was thinking,' he ventured, 'and there's no one more qualified to answer this than you, I was thinking... what if it *was* Samuel?'

She frowned but didn't open her eyes. 'Hm?'

'The carving. The words on the castle wall.' He repositioned himself on already aching knees. 'My son passed over, but what if... you know... what if he was trying to...'

'It's never a kid.' She replied. 'Children don't stay.'

'But the words...' he struggled, '... *those* words. I know we thought that this *thing*, this entity was mocking us with them, but what if...'

'Whitey,' she said more patiently, 'it's *never* a kid. Anyone who says they've seen the spirit of a child or contacted one is either lying or has been duped. These beings, they're tricksters. Malicious ones at that. And what better way to torture someone than to have them believe that their deceased child is with them? No. I'm sorry Whitey, but no. Your son is on the other side. He's at peace. Children don't stay.'

She let him sit with it for a while. She'd been in this world so long she'd forgotten what it must be like for someone new to it. She knew he was weeping again in complete silence, as he had several times since their strange joining, and she patiently waited it out.

'If it helps, and I hope it does,' she added, 'you *will* see him again one day. Don't forget that.'

From behind her closed eyes she felt him quickly look up at her. It hadn't occurred to him. 'Oh...' he stammered, '... oh my god. I hadn't...'

She smiled. 'For all that scares you about this, don't forget the comfort of it too. One day I'll be with dad, one day you'll be with Sam. Our fathers, mothers, ancestors; they're all waiting. I don't know what's on the other side, but I know that we go on. Most importantly, we go on *together*.'

A very long period of silence. He only broke it to whisper 'thank you' in a fractured voice. She nodded, then resumed her breathing.

No one had been in this burial ground longer than the custodian. He didn't need to ask why she had chosen this tomb. If this spirit had been watching over this place for centuries, then there was none more eligible to answer her questions. It occurred to him then that he was about to speak to the dead through this young girl, and he wasn't in the least bit prepared for it. Who was coming? What would they be like?

'Osmund Jourdemayne.' Penny whispered in response to his thoughts. 'Buried in the thirteenth century. I can almost see him. I think he's coming forward.'

24

Naefreboren

A high pitched tone filled his ears. Like tinnitus, it rang high and pressed on his eardrums uncomfortably. The air pressure had changed. It felt more condensed, thicker and now harder to breathe. Stephen shuffled so that he was further away from Penny, leaning on one knee and watching her carefully. If she went all *Exorcist* on him he was ready to jump to his feet and run for it. Run back to The Black Swan.

If he thought about the taste of cold beer or the beautiful heat of a warm whiskey one more time he was going to scream. Throughout all of this his brain had still somehow remained fixated on booze. He couldn't do this. He couldn't be sober. When this was over, one way or another, he knew that without Penny his resolve would be none-existent and the first thing he would do would be to drink himself unconscious.

She broke his obsessive train of thought by speaking in that strange way she did when doing her spooky stuff; talking low and quickly in a weird tumble of rapid speech.

'Very, very old. Very, very wise. Very, very angry.' She repeated the three phrases over and over until it started to really unnerve him, then suddenly she stopped.

'I can't understand his words.' She turned her head for a second towards him, but her eyes stayed closed. 'Old English, maybe. Don't know. Could be an old European language. But he's here. He's speaking. He's showing me things.'

'What things?' He looked around himself, relieved to see nothing there but snow and stones.

'A bright sun.' She replied. 'An unspoiled sky. A much younger world. The air was sweeter, the winds were pure and cleansing. The meat was good, the bounty of food that was harvested from the ground was untainted and exquisite. We have corrupted this world, he says. We've poisoned the sky and infected the soil.'

'We?' Stephen huffed. He despised the collective *we*. As if the everyday man was somehow responsible for the huge choices that governments made. There was no *we*. Just everyday folk surviving while those in power take their money and ravage the world with it. He resisted the urge to go off on one of his rants, instead simply saying 'well he might think so, but the dark ages weren't exactly a utopia. War, disease, and a life expectancy of forty aren't my idea of...'

'This land... Elmeslac... I caught that word. Helmsley. He's trying to tell me it was a good land. A safe place. But then the ground turned... sour.'

Stephen touched the pocket of his jacket with a hand trembling with DT's, feeling the cigarette box there before lowering it again.

'They woke it up. It was sleeping. It was older than the stars, but it was slumbering. It... they disturbed it, and it came up... up? I think so, yes, up? It was below them. It was in the ground and they awoke it. Then the ground went sour.'

'Did he see it?' Stephen leaned in. 'What was it? What is it?'

She shook her head, annoyed, as if trying to listen to something. Her hands came up and her fingers rested on her forehead as her eyelids squeezed hard. 'He's... he wants to speak...'

Her hands dropped. She fell completely silent and still. Her head lowered until her chin touched her chest.

Tipping point. The chair falling backwards. Going under.

Stephen drew back again. He didn't dare do so much as breathe. He eyed her warily. Stretched moments passed.

Then Penny Black spoke. Except it wasn't her voice. It was a deep whisper. A voice impossible for her slender throat to produce. It had the gravel of a male voice of advanced years. It had the quality of a thick neck, an Adam's apple, and some kind of speech impediment. It spoke one word at first. Over and over.

'Naefreboren.' It rumbled. 'Naefreboren.'

The ancient dead were speaking through this young girl, right in front of his eyes, and all Stephen could do was stare in disbelief.

'Uf fram hellia.' Came the guttural growl from young lips painted black. 'Etan ure sawol, se naefreboren.'

Stephen didn't know old English. Didn't even know how it sounded when spoken up until this moment. But the similarity to the modern spoken word was clear. If he was right, he had the basic gist of what it was saying. He forced his voice out now, which at first sounded only in a dry whisper.

'Up from hell?' He asked it. 'Eat? Eaten? Your soul... *eating your soul?*'

Penny, and the thing that was using her to speak, remained still and said nothing. Her head was still resting on her chest and rose and fell rhythmically with it, as if she was asleep sitting up.

'How do we stop it?' Stephen shuffled closer on his

knees in the soaking snow.

She took a sharp breath and the deep voice said 'thou cunnan. Tis naefreboren. Undeadlic.'

Cunnan. Can't? *You* can't, maybe? Undeadlic? Like, *undead*? Or perhaps, *undying*. As in, immortal? He couldn't figure out the other word it kept saying. Naefreboren.

Then he realised it was two words put together as he said it aloud.

'Nae. Well, nae is *no*, right? Naefre. Never? Boren…'

Born. That was what Penny had said. Something never born, never dying.

'Neverborn?' He hissed.

The thing puppeteering his young friend nodded her head, repeating 'uf fram hellia.'

Then suddenly she seemed to stiffen and to struggle, as if something deep beneath her skin was wrestling with something else. Her head went up and then back, her spine arched, and her hands reached out with tendons as taut as ropes. She took a huge gasp of surprise and her voice broke through, letting out a long moan of apparent pain. He realised that he could hear the voice of the spirit too, underlying hers. Two voices coming from one throat in unison. A horrible harmony of a young woman in distress and the rumbling sigh of a man long dead spewing out into the graveyard as her physical body wrestled with something he couldn't see.

'Penny!' He exclaimed, forgetting his fear in his shock, reaching out for her and grabbing her by the shoulders. She was like ice to touch. Even through her clothes he could feel it. Her eyes were rolling in her head. Foamy spittle was running from her mouth and mucus from her nostril. She kept making a sound like her throat was closing up, and then after a few frightening seconds of strangled silence her throat was open again and she gasped for air, and it kept repeating.

Something had her. Something was throttling her.

He shook her and yelled 'Penny? Penny! Let her go! Let go of her! Why are you doing this to her?'

Wait. Was it this spirit, Osmond something-or-other, or was it something else?

He slapped her lightly on the cheek and shook her again. 'Penny! Come on, girl! Wake up!'

The spirit spoke in a wet gurgling roar, and Penny's voice screeched in unity with it.

'Clysan se porte! Clysan se porte!' It repeated, each phrase louder than the last until it was screaming. A delirious, fervent mantra that went on and on until Stephen couldn't stand it and wanted to drop her and clamp his hands over his ears.

'Stop it!' He hollered over the pandemonium. 'Just stop it! Enough now!'

The words it spoke stopped being words and instead became a long and deafening shriek. Her mouth was a gaping black chasm, her scream like the final agonised cry of one fatally wounded. Her body was thrust away from him, as if pulled or shoved by an invisible force as strong as a bus, and it took him completely by surprise. He went off-balance as she twisted out of his arms and slammed down into the snow covered grass, and he fell with her.

Then, just as suddenly as the violence had begun, everything went quiet.

He rolled in the ice from his back to his front, his elbows holding him up as he looked for her in the dark. The torch had been kicked and had rolled away, the white beam was a spotlight in the soil now, catching the falling flakes. He clambered to his knees and made his way toward the black shape sprawled in the snow.

He called her name again as he reached her, grabbing her by the shoulders and hauling her up again. She was a ragdoll in his arms, thin and limp. Her clothes were soaked and her makeup was a mess of black smears across patchy white foundation. Her mouth hung slack, her eyes still rolled up. He gently shook her, panicking now.

Where was the nearest hospital? Was there even a hospital anywhere near this fucking dead-end town? He clumsily felt for a pulse, put his ear to her opened mouth to listen or feel for breath.

She was alive, breathing rapidly as if she'd been running, and she was still so very cold beneath his hands that it was a wonder she wasn't shaking and shivering like someone with hypothermia. But she was still. Far too still.

He was going to have to carry her. He had to get her back into the house and warmth. If he stayed out here with her in this state too long then it could become very serious indeed.

She groaned like someone being disturbed from deep sleep as he hoisted her up. One arm hooked beneath her knees, the other under her back. She weighed less than he imagined, but the strain on his already tired body was immediate. The air was knocked out of him as he struggled to his feet on knees that knocked together. His heart, racing, sent an electric shock of pain across his chest that tapered down his arms, but he paid it no mind.

Like some monster from an old hammer movie he staggered like a laboratory creature, carrying the young woman draped in flowing ragged black velvet, lurching through the stones and making for the light of the old Tudor rectory. At this point he had completely separated from reality, and from his sanity. This was a waking nightmare, while being so outrageously unreal it verged on farce.

'You should...' he gasped, '...have let me... get in my car... you stupid girl!'

She was trying to speak in response as he reached the back door of Canons Garth, her eyes moving rapidly beneath her lids. It was, at least, her voice now. Her voice alone. The old spirit was gone.

'Clysan se porte.' She was slurring, fighting to speak through semi-consciousness as he brought her inside, turning to kick the door closed behind them. Whi... *Whitey*. Clysan se porte. Close.... Close the portal.'

25
Breaking Point

So, in the space of a couple of days Mr Stephen White of Craister Court, Stockton, had gone from being a senior editor at a newspaper with a small flat, an estranged wife, a deceased son, and a mother soon to follow while in the care of a hypercritical older brother with a superiority complex, to a *ghosthunter* who had physically seen two ghosts with his own eyes, been attacked by a haunted mirror, undergone a spiritual cleansing, and had now communed with a six-hundred year-old dead *custodian* that was channelled by a young goth/witch/psychic who claimed to be his cosmic twin, who was then attacked by what he now suspected was the *something worse* they were looking for in the first place.

He couldn't quite figure out, nevertheless, which was worse. As average weeks went, this had certainly been quite the eventful one. These thoughts passed through his painfully sober mind without the slightest hint of humour, as he saw to his patient in the living room of her creepy old vicarage.

There is still half a bottle of whiskey in your room above the pub, the addict portion of his brain reminded him for the umpteenth time, *and you still have your key. It'll be dawn soon. You could see to Penny, then leave her rest while you sneak back in, take your medicine, and sleep in a simple bed in a simple room, far away from this lunacy. And think of the sleep you could have; drunk and dreamless. Let's face it, it's the only way you're ever going to be able to sleep again after all this.*

He screwed his eyes shut as he knelt by the chair. He'd gotten the fire going and had wrapped the young woman in a blanket. She seemed to be sleeping, though by her groans and twitches she was clearly wrapped just as much in a nightmare as a woolly throw. His clothes were damp and dirty, his feet frozen in soaking socks, his head throbbing with pain and his stomach cramping with hunger. The damned shakes remained too.

Did he dare do it? Did he dare leave her alone, especially in *this* house where this entity – what had she called it, elementary, ele... oh, never mind – had attacked them with broken glass? Were they safe *anywhere* now?

'Bollocks.' He whispered to himself. He knew the answer already.

He stood up and studied her for a beat longer, wincing as his stomach cramped again. Well, they *were* safe here, weren't they? Penny had said that this house was protected. So what if he... what if...

What if you go and get the whiskey right now, and dash back here with it? She'd be none the wiser. Come on Steve, it'd only take a matter of minutes. It's right next door! You can fix yourself in moments with a good drink. Haven't you earned it? Go on. Go and get your drink and then come back, and you can sleep right there on the rug in front of the fire. You can keep an eye on her, and you can fix yourself right up in one fell swoop.

He knew it was the wrong thing to do, but try telling his legs that; they were already taking him down the corridor to the front door of Canons Garth, and his hands were already reaching for the latch, clicking it up so that the door would remain unlocked while he rushed to The Black Swan. And then he was out in the sub-zero chill of pre-dawn, and it was still snowing. God, would it ever stop? Was even the *weather* normal here, or was it, just like the ghosts and the locals, under the influence of this *neverborn* thing too? Maybe it was trying to keep them there; cutting of all means of escape.

His feet moved through soft, freshly-lain snow as he fumbled in the pockets of his overcoat for the set of keys that, blessedly, tomorrow he would hand back to Billy behind the bar. When he reached the side door of the pub he stopped.

The lead-lined panes of glass were distorted by bulls-eye motifs, and all beyond them was black. The interior of the pub beyond may as well have been a black hole. What was in that darkness within? Was *she* there again, waiting for his return, perched in her chair by the silent fireplace, cold and dead and soaked in dried bloody vomit, watching him from behind her bridal veil?

Come on, man. Are you brave or not? Look what else you've dealt with since *her*.

His key had slid into the lock, and he was about to turn it. Salvation was in sight. Yes, yes, he knew what alcoholism really was; slow suicide. But tonight he didn't care. When things were normal again, *yes*, when life was normal again, *then* he could focus on getting off the booze. But not tonight. Not during all this.

A voice stopped him from turning the key fully in the brass aperture.

'Took your *sweet bloody time* leaving the Garth, Mr White.' Said a voice behind him, familiar enough to fire his brain, but indistinct enough for him to be taken completely off guard.

He didn't have time to contemplate this though. The heavy blow to the back of his neck swept such thoughts, and everything else, away.

***

Penny opened her eyes with a gasp.

What was that? Why did she just feel like something had been snatched from her? She sat up in the near darkness, lit only by orange flickering flames, and looked around the room. She was in her house. How had she gotten...

She'd been with Osmond. He'd been speaking in her head, slow and sluggish, like the words had crawled up from the deep cold earth like vines, stinking of old rot and clay-thick soil, wrapping themselves around her and pushing their way into her skull. The words were ancient and tired, yet timeless and humming with power, and she'd spoken them for him. She'd all but seen him; a deformed man, hulking and broad, with eyes like black coals. Thin lips and jutting teeth. Greasy hair stuck to his face. At the same time he hadn't appeared as a man at all, more like some ancient old tree, like a rotten and diseased oak, dried up but still somehow standing. And then....

Then something had intervened. Yeah, that was it. Something had come forward and grabbed her, and grabbed Osmond, and it had shaken Osmond out of her head. She had been deep under. She had been in full communion with the dead, past the veil and deep in the other, and that was how this thing – this neverborn thing – had been able to interfere. Penny reached up and touched her throat. No pain there. No evidence of an attack. But attack her it had. It hadn't been her flesh that she felt was threatened. It had been her soul.

'Whitey?' Her voice rang cold in the dark. No answer.

Something had been snatched away just now. It had woken her from her stupor. A connection had been severed, and it wasn't her connection to the dead.

She unwrapped herself from the blanket and stood, letting it drop onto the wooden boards. She was warm now but her clothes were soaked and dripping onto her boots. She called his name again, and again there was no answer. He wasn't in the house, but worse than that, she couldn't *feel* him.

'Shit.' She muttered. 'You've fled, haven't you? It got too scary and you split.'

She had so much to tell him, though! She knew so much more now! Osmond had made it clear.

She started to wander from room to room, just to be certain. She even dared to venture back into her bedroom where the broken mirror still lay on its back and where the stool was upturned and where there were spots of blood on the floor. She changed her clothes in there and hurriedly fixed her face, all the while never taking her eyes off the mirror.

Pulling her woolly black overcoat back on, she had hurried down the stairs and back into the lounge. Maybe she could still catch him. That car of his was scrapyard fodder, he'd said so himself. Maybe he couldn't get it started in the snow and she could catch him. She turned and opened the heavy drapes that covered the diamond-latticed shapes of her front window and peered outside.

It was still dark. No idea what time it was. And... wait. Who is *that*, standing...

There was a shape, a person shaped-shape, standing just beyond her gate in the cold night, and it was looking straight at her. She jumped. She had been so busy looking out into the market square, blanketed in snow, that in the murky light she hadn't seen it at first. It certainly saw her, though.

Its eyes were white. It was standing crookedly. It was as still as a photograph.

A cold wash ran from the back of her head down to the base of her back, and goosebumps rose down the length of both her arms. Her shoulders juddered with a shiver. She took a step back from the window as a twist of fear pulled her heart down into her belly. That was when she saw the others.

There were more of them. Were her eyes merely adjusting to the darkness out there, or were these figures just *appearing* one by one?

Black shapes. People, materialising in the street. Silhouettes. Walking shadows. Blacker than black, they were, and even though the streetlamps were still on, not a bit of the light they cast could touch these creatures.

They all had white eyes, but though those eyes were without pupils she knew beyond doubt that they were all watching her. Men and women, children too. Tall, short, thin, bulky. Crooked, some of them, malformed. They just kept on appearing until the market square was crowded. All staring straight at Canons Garth. All staring straight at *her*.

We see you.

'Oh, you've noticed me now, have you?' She said aloud, swallowing dryly, her words assured but her voice wobbling. She backed further away from the window. She had half a mind to go to the back door and check there too, but she just couldn't find the courage to do it.

She knew what she'd find if she did.

'What, so I'm surrounded now?' Came the same trembling voice, desperately trying to sound fearless. 'Is that supposed to scare me? If you know me then you know that this house is protected, and I am too. There's no way you're getting in here, you sludgy old bastards!'

Her bravado trailed off as she realised that they didn't want to.

From her bedroom upstairs, the room she had been in only moments ago, a great thud sounded. It shook the floorboards once. Her head shot up. Her shivering stopped. Her lungs tightened like a knot and held her breath there.

Another thud. A great, weighty sound. An elephant foot. A boulder being dropped. Then another, further across the room upstairs. Towards her bedroom door up there.

Something was in her room. Something was walking towards the bedroom door.

She lowered her head and looked back out through the window. The dead filled the square outside. Watching. Waiting for something.

She heard her bedroom door open upstairs. A long creak. Then another bulky thud as something stepped onto her landing.

Her entire body washed with gooseflesh. Electricity tingled in her fingertips and toes. The strength was stolen from her legs. This was impossible. This just shouldn't be. She had cast more protections over this house over the years than she could count, performed more cleansings here than most. A hundred blessings and rituals flew threw her frantic mind, and dozens of tools that she could use, but she couldn't get her head straight. Besides, it was too late now.

The *thing*. The *something worse*. The Neverborn, or some part of it, was in her house.

It was the growl that finally snapped her from her frozen terror and made her move. Something growled at the top of the old rickety staircase in the hall. Something huge was at the top of her stairs in the dark. It growled low, long and deep. It sounded like something between a restless bear and, more horribly, it had a human quality to it as well. The sound echoed, perfectly audibly and not inside her head, through the house. The living room door that lead into the hallway was beside her and it was ajar.

The entities outside were keeping her in the house. Keeping her in with something unearthly, and it was coming for her.

She closed her eyes and began speaking blessings and benedictions, old words with old magic, phrases and rites she'd known and used countless times. The thud that struck the first step at the top of her stairs rattled her concentration and she stopped. She was too scared to think straight.

She turned and ran into her kitchen.

'Ghosts can't hurt you.' She kept repeating. 'Ghosts *can't* hurt you. Keep your head. They're trying to scare you. They're trying to stop you going any further with this. They're... they're... *fuck*!' Her teeth were clenched and tears sprung into her eyes. 'Okay. Okay. Come on, calm down. Just run out the back door. Keep your eyes closed. They're gonna be outside too, of course they are, but they can't hurt you. Just get out of here and get to Steve. Come on, lass. You can do it.'

The light in there should have helped matters, but it didn't. Bright sterile light filled the kitchen from the fluorescent strip overhead, but she felt no safer for it. She glared at the back door. Was she really going to do this; run out of the house and into an ancient graveyard full of ghosts? Better than staying in *here*. At least with ghosts she knew what to expect - with this thing that was in her house, she had no idea what it could do.

If you start looking, prodding at it? It prods back. It looks back, she'd said to Stephen. At the time she had no idea how right she was.

She paused and listened. The thudding, the footsteps,

had stopped.

The silence rang loud in her ears, broken only by the pulsing and rushing of blood in her head. She held her breath, poised at the door, her fingers mid-air and close to the handle, and she listened hard.

Then the footsteps came again, only this time they were fast, and louder, and angrier. Something was thundering down her stairs at full pelt, coming for her.

She screamed then, tore the kitchen door open and sprinted out into the darkness, shrieking the name of her only friend as she went.

***

Stephen opened his eyes.

Did he hear someone scream just then? Was someone saying his name?

Wait.

Was he unconscious? Sleeping? What the hell happened?

'Blacked out on us there, lad.' A deep Yorkshire tone. 'Welcome back.'

Oh. Right. Now he remembered.

As his senses returned so did the pain. The explosion in his side that became a vein-like network of burning strings in his ribs had not faded. Nor had the blow to his stomach, which now felt like he'd somehow swallowed a large heavy rock that was sitting there. His once simple withdrawals headache had now enhanced to a feeling akin to having one's skull split, or so he imagined. The pain wasn't throbbing anymore, now it was just a constant scream of agony that encased his head, particularly his temples.

Strangely lucid in his thinking, he reasoned out the following things; concussion, broken rib or *ribs*, and maybe a stomach bleed though perhaps not quite as serious. Severe bruising, at least.

The base of his neck felt twice as large as it should, and there was a keener, sharper pain at his cheekbone. Oh, yes, the cut. The cut from the shard of glass. Perhaps it had opened again when something – a fist? Some kind of wooden tool? – had thumped him there.

He'd expected to find himself in a room but no, he was outside. He was laying in the snow. His clothes, coat and thick jumper, were so soaked it had saturated all the way through to his skin. Even half-conscious he was shivering uncontrollably. A quick cognitive check of his body told him that nothing else but his rib was broken, at least as far as he could tell.

The snow had stopped. The sky was still that ever-grey sheet overhead, but it was lightening. It was dawn.

'Right, Mr White, shall we go through it one more time?' Said Ned Bailey, smiling amiably behind his thick moustache, his big black eyebrows raised. He talked to Stephen as if he was pleasantly addressing a friend. 'Or perhaps have you got the message now?'

New territory, this. Stephen had never so much as had a pub scrap, let alone a beating like this. He'd never known if he was a brave man. Only situations like these could tell you. He'd been what others had described as brave when he'd stood by his sons casket and read aloud from a tearstained sheet of paper that trembled in his hand, but there was a different kind of bravery required now. Did he possess such a quality?

Ned's two cronies appeared in his line of sight. Sam and Dave, was it? They looked more frightened than Stephen did. They looked down at him and then glanced nervously all around. Keeping watch, he supposed.

'Alright lads.' Stephen greeted them, tasting blood as he drew breath. 'Mind if I get up out of this snow?' And he made to sit up.

Ned put a mud-caked boot firmly on his chest and pushed him back down with a short, sharp stamp. The bomb in Stephen's side detonated again and he screamed.

'Right, boys.' Ned sighed. 'Looks like he's not quite got it yet. One more time then.'

Stamp. Something cracked. Stephen couldn't draw breath enough to scream again. Blood flushed into his face and his eyes bulged out of their sockets as his side burned like acid.

'You're leaving, Mr White.' Ned said calmly, still in that friendly Yorkshire drawl. 'You're leaving this moment. You're getting in your car over there and you're never coming back. You're never seeing or contacting that bitch at Canons Garth ever again. You're going to forget everything you saw here. You're not writing an article. You've never even been to Helmsley. Clear enough?'

Stamp.

Stomach bile, burning and putrid, spewed up into Stephen's mouth and he spat it out sideways with a gurgling cry.

'Do that, and you'll be just fine.' Ned went on, throwing a glance at his comrades. '*Don't* do that, and... well. If you don't do as you're told like a good lad, then we're gonna have to put you in me van, and then we're gonna have to take a little drive down to me farm.'

Dave chirped up. '*Ned.* We've got to *go.*'

Ned fixed him with a bloodshot stare so intense that he didn't speak again, instead choosing to study his shoes.

'Got a nice storage room.' Ned said in a calm whisper, leaning down, his smiling face leering over Stephen. His boot pressed harder with his weight. Stephen choked. 'Could hang you up in there and open you up like a heifer at slaughter. Feed you to me pigs.'

Well, as tests of bravery went this was really up there. So, was Stephen a brave man?

Turns out, no.

Stephen nodded frantically, shielding his face with a bloodied hand that shook so violently it looked like he was waving.

'Message received.' He croaked. 'Got it. I'm gone.'

The boot was lifted. Stephen broke into barking, bubbling coughs and curled up, foetal in the icy slush.

Ned held out a helping hand. 'Got your keys on you?'

He heaved Stephen to his feet. His legs shook and he nearly fell twice. Ned caught him and supported him as if he had just rescued him from an assailant. Stephen retched and bile came up again. He bent double in Ned's grasp and spat again.

'There, there, lad.' Ned said, friendly and relaxed. 'You'll be alright, lad. I'll walk you to your car.'

Stephen was behind the wheel. He was alone. He glanced at his rearview and saw the three men standing there like bouncers guarding a club entrance, arms folded. It took four attempts to get his key into the ignition, and it took far more attempts to get the old girl started, but sure enough, the cold engine somehow managed to fire.

Ned gave him a little wave.

Caked in dirt, soaked to his skin, bloodied and bruised, Stephen pressed the accelerator and the car slowly began to rumble over the hardened snow and ice, and as the sun began to rise over the town he turned the corner and left Helmsley, the scream of the old engine of his Metro fading into the distance.

'Gone, is he?' Said Bill.

Ned turned and smiled at the landlord of The Black Swan. He'd stepped out of the pub in a duffle coat, a little Jack Russell on the lead he held.

'Morning, mate. Aye, he's off.'

'That's good.' Bill replied. 'For the best, really… but, what if he, you know, *tells* folk? What if he comes back?'

Ned snorted a little derisive snort.

'Come now, Billy. You know they never come back. In fact, poor Mr White won't be going anywhere ever again.'

26

The Weirdo and the Normie

A pale, broken man piloted a rusty red car along a country road now illuminated by the rising sun. The day was bright but frozen. The snow clouds were finally gone, but it would be a long time before the dense snowdrifts on either side of the tarmac thawed. The black asphalt glittered as the sunbeams struck it, still frozen and dangerous to navigate. The man drove on autopilot.

A deep purple bruise was forming under his left eye. The slash along his cheek was freshly swollen too, a thick slit of black encrusted blood now, and his face was half painted red. His shirt was bloody and soaked from the ice, his coat too, and he now discovered as he pressed the clutch and brake in turn that he had lost a shoe. His side burned and spasmed now and again as he drove, a white-hot ember jammed between his ribs, and he could feel the swelling growing there and in his stomach. Every part of him ached and stung.

Regardless of all this, Stephen simply drove, blank-faced and wide-eyed.

Chewed up and spat out, he passively thought, *and going home*.

It didn't matter that his clothes were in his suitcase at Penny's place. It didn't matter that his notes and his work had been left too. He didn't even seem to care, at least not in this moment, that the expensive camera (property of The Evening

Gazette, Brunswick Street, Stockton) had been left behind too.

After driving for about ten minutes, Stephen saw a sign for Rievaulx Abbey. Someone had mentioned once that it was nearby, he couldn't remember who. Soon he had pulled over into a layby beside the historic site. He looked over an expanse of grassy land brushed white at the tall ruined peaks of a crumbling abbey, stark and grey against the vivid blue morning sky. He glanced around, making sure there was no one about, and only then did he allow himself the shameful act of breaking down into sobbing tears.

He'd never been beaten up in his life. The shock was overwhelming, but the initial numbness was starting to dissolve away, and beneath it was raw emotion. He could have been killed. That could have been it for him. He remembered the dull blow to the back of his neck that had felt oddly wooden, like a rolling pin or something, and he remembered every single punch he had taken afterwards, after he had blacked out for a few moments. Ned's henchmen were holding his arms, and their manure-stinking, ale-supping leader had driven a set of knuckles (wrapped in something, he remembered, maybe a dishcloth or rag) at full force into the soft flesh of his lower belly. Another went into his ribs, and then another one with so much force that even Ned gave a grunt of exertion. That was the one, he believed, that cracked a rib. He'd been bent double at that point, naturally, and was so winded he couldn't take a breath. His head was hanging low as the men held him in place, so Ned had decided that it was a good opportunity to land a couple more blows. A crunch and a deep thud as a fist arced through the air and split his cheek back open, snapping his head sideways, and then another blow to his chin. He hadn't lost any teeth, but a couple of them certainly moved differently when he tongued them in a mouth that tasted metallic.

His hands gripped the steering wheel at ten and two, his

head pressed between them against the leather, and he sobbed.

Stephen White was done. Done with ghosts, done with Penny Black, done with trauma and mourning, and most of all, done with Helmsley. He was going home. He was going to his flat, cleaning himself up, and then he was going to The Green Dragon.

What day is it? Was I supposed to leave today, or was it tomorrow? I have absolutely no clue where I am in the week. That place. That fucking place, it does something to you. It clouds your brain, it turns you around. It drains *you somehow.*

First it kills you, then it keeps you.

He rummaged around in the glove box and found a packet of tissues. He wiped at his eyes, mopped his face, and blew his nose. When he looked down at the paper it was scarlet. His eyes were drawn to the left, to an object laying on the passenger seat. A blank cassette case, upon which was written *Stephen Helmsley notes* in the obnoxious handwriting of the obnoxious prick-of-a-boss that had sent him on this hellish journey in the first place. He grabbed it so ferociously that the plastic cracked, wound his window down, and threw it with force out onto the gravel with a cry of pain as his ribs reminded him of his ordeal. Then he reached into his pocket, retrieved a cigarette from a battered box and lit it, drawing hungrily upon the filter.

He exhaled a torrent of blue-tinged smoke as he said 'I'm sorry, Penny. I'm really so sorry. I'm not the man for the job. God, girl. I hope you get out of there and never look back.'

Jesus, what if those men went after her next? His eyes widened. He hadn't thought of that. *But no. Surely not. They're scared of her, scared of what she might do to them. But, but what if they* do? *If anything happens to her then it's on your head, Steve!*

His knuckles turned white as they gripped the wheel harder. The engine ticked over. He stared at the old abbey ruins.

'I can't!' He explained with fresh tears to the ancient structure. 'If I go back then I'll get worse than a beating, I'll be dead! I'm so sorry Penny but you're on your own! If you've got any sense you'll get the hell out of there, too! You should have done it years ago!'

'Yeah, well. Hindsight is always twenty-twenty, Whitey.'

Stephen screamed aloud like a starlet in a B-movie being attacked by a giant radioactive spider. He twisted around to see Penny, climbing up onto the backseat from the footwell. She settled into the chair, a mess of smeared makeup and rat-tailed hair, and said 'morning.'

He was purple-faced and mute for a few moments, and then the river broke through the dam.

'What the fuck are you doing in my car? *How* the hell did you get in my car? What the fuck happened to you? What the hell is going on?'

She was full of her usual bluster, but as she spoke Stephen could see in her eyes that she was genuinely frightened, and that she had been crying.

'Well, let's see.' She replied, squinting out at the bright sun as she looked around. 'For one, your car wasn't locked. So, either you forgot to lock it when you first arrived or someone has broken into it since. No signs of forced entry, mind you, so it's probably just you. As for the why; I was hiding in your footwell because last night, while you were... wherever you were... I had a vision of a huge crowd of the dead, all standing in the street, all watching me. They wanted me to know that they knew what I was up to, and that they were onto me. Also, they wanted to keep me in the house because that *thing* was in there with me, and it was coming for me, so I ran. Nowhere else I could have gone. I happened to try your door and it was open so I hid and waited for morning. Anyway, I think the more pressing question is *what the fuck happened to you?'*

Realising how he must have looked, Stephen turned around again so that he was facing the windscreen. He looked at Penny in the rear view mirror.

'Hell of a coincidence.' He muttered. 'I get beaten half to death and thrown out of town, and you just happen to be hiding in my footwell.'

'No such thing, Whitey, I keep telling you. And what do you mean *beaten half to death?* Who did this?'

Stephen flicked the cigarette out of his window and stared over at the abbey again.

'I was grabbed at the door of The Black Swan,' he said, realising his confession too late and wincing as he continued on, 'I was... well, I was going to get a drink. Sue me. So, I was grabbed by Ned Bailey and his two lapdogs, dragged around the back and given a broken rib and a black eye. Told me never to come back and never talk about what I'd seen, which at least proves something.'

She was quiet. Eventually she said, softer, kinder, 'I'm really sorry, Whitey. *Bastards.* Do you need a hospital or something?'

He just shook his head.

She sniffed, wiping at one eye smeared with black paint. 'What does it prove?' She added at length.

'That they know what's going on in that town. That they're in on it. That they don't like outsiders poking about, especially ones that befriend the local *weirdo.'*

'A weirdo, eh? I'll take that, and gladly. And did you just admit that we're friends?'

'You can't stay here.' Stephen sighed, ignoring her. 'I'm

bound for home, or next time they'll do more than tenderise me, and that isn't paranoia; they said as much. You need to get home, and if I were you I'd pack up and sell up as soon as humanly possible.'

'No.'

'*What?*'

'No, I said. This just proves that we're close to an answer. Just proves that we've got it scared and it's trying to defend itself.' She smiled at him in the mirror as she explained what had happened at Canons Garth, adding at the end 'pretty mad, eh?'

He just gaped back at her. 'Seriously? You really mean it was literally *in your house?* What did you see?'

'Don't know. It's a trickster. Didn't stick around long enough to find out.' She said. 'It got its wish - it had me running and screaming like a normie. But I didn't need to see it, anyways. I felt it. And what it felt like was... hard to describe to you.'

'What, a *normie* like me?'

She laughed loudly in the confined space. 'Yeah, like you, sure!' She teased, then she paused, her eyes searching. 'It felt like cold, black evil. Call that cheesy if you want, but it did. Remorseless, malicious, and darker than dark. Just hungry, and greedy, and restless, and most of all it was angry, spitefully angry.'

'And you still think there's some way *you* can stop something like that?'

'No. Not me. Not alone.'

He sighed, trying to keep himself calm. He failed.

'Penny,' he barked, 'you need to get out of this car, go back to your house, and sell the fucking thing! Get away from all of this! It's dangerous and it's getting pretty bloody serious now! I'm going home, alright? I'm going home and back to my life, such as it is, and you should do the same. I can't do this anymore! I'm a middle-aged newspaper editor with a drink problem and that's all I can be! I'm not what you think I am! Psychics and witchcraft and ghosts and a town under the influence of a *Neverborn*, whatever the fuck that even is; it's all beyond me! I'm not who you need, and no, *we're not friends*, Penny! We're strangers! Cosmic twins and connections and all of that, it makes no sense to me and I don't want it to! I want no part in any of it!'

She shook her head. A black mop dancing in the mirror. 'No. You don't mean that. You're scared.'

He was bellowing at her now. 'Yes! Yes I am and so should you be, you stupid little girl! Christ's sake! If you keep on with this you'll end up dead and so will I! So, no thanks, I'm not interested in embroiling myself in this shit any longer at the risk of my own life! I don't want to help you, and I won't! There! Ok? I *refuse* to help you, because what you want me to help you do is impossible! Get out of Helmsley, Penelope! Save yourself before you get in so far over your head you can't get out again!'

Penny was looking down at her knees.

'I came here for a break!' He broke into bitter laughter. 'A fucking break! A stupid little article! And what do I get? You! You treat me like I owe you something! You treat me like some sort of apprentice that needs teaching! I'm not fucking interested, Penny! Get it? *No* is my answer! Can you wrap your dumb little head around that? Pull your head out of the clouds and get real! No, I won't help! Now *get out of my car* and let me go!'

He couldn't look at her in the mirror anymore and dropped his eyes. White sparks danced in front of them and he felt a wave of sickening dizziness wash over him. When he lifted a little corner of his shirt to look at his side, it was black. Resounding silence pressed on the two of them. He knew he'd gone too far. Course he had. She didn't deserve it, but he just couldn't take it anymore. If this is what it took to shake her out of her delusions and ultimately save her, then it had to be this way.

'Samuel didn't speak his last words to you.' She said suddenly.

He turned in his seat. His pupils were small and sharp.

'Wha... *what?*'

'In the hospital room.' She said to her knees, flashing a glance up at him. 'When I saw what happened. You said he spoke to you, but he didn't.'

His face flushed bright pink, but his voice stayed low. 'What the fuck are you talking about, Penny?'

'You were gifted before you met me, Stephen.' Strange hearing her call him by his actual name. 'You're a natural psychic, you just didn't know it. You don't remember the hospital room as well as you think you do, but I saw what really happened. He was in a coma when you arrived. People in comas don't talk in their sleep.'

The car engine idled noisily. Stephen glared at her.

'Samuel was already gone.' She said. 'He was travelling. He had already passed when you were holding his hand. He was trying to tell you that he was free, that he could fly. That he could... see the stars. You communed with him.'

Stephen turned away and his shoulders hunched.

'I didn't do this to you.' She continued. 'You were already gifted. And whatever you say, I still know that we were destined to meet, and that the purpose of that meeting is to put a stop to the demon that's infected my town. I'll go. Ok. I'll go, but you have to hear this first. I know what's going on now. I know *everything*. And I know how to stop it.'

But just then, the sun went out.

Darkness consumed the car, and then they both heard a loud boom followed by the sound of metal screeching, screaming against concrete, and a low rumble that grew louder and louder.

Stephen spun in his seat as Penny cried out. A tanker. A huge eight-wheeled behemoth was tearing towards them, bent at an angle, carrying petrol, and completely out of control.

The following seconds were slow motion, just like in one of the old westerns that his dad would take him to see at the picture house on a Sunday afternoon, where the hero would leap and roll and reach for his gun. Stephen's hand went for the door, his abdomen screaming at him as he tumbled out and landed hard on the muddy verge. He was scrabbling to his feet, sliding in frost covered filth as Penny fell into his line of sight and onto her back. They locked eyes on the ground and the movie reduced from slow-motion to a complete stop. Frozen eyes, fixed together. Reaching hands. Open mouths hollering in the bizarre silence.

Her hand found his.

He wrenched her to her feet and then the frozen moment in time became slow motion became speed, and they were running for their lives. Feet pounding at dirt as the roar and the screeching and the ground-shaking rumble grew so loud it pressed on their ears. And then there was heat and sparks and the most horrifying sound Stephen had ever heard. A bomb went off. Solid steel ripping like paper, glass exploding, thick rubber tyres detonating one by one, the terrible shriek of metal meeting metal, and blistering heat at their backs.

Then they weren't running anymore, they were flying.

27
A Choice

Beep.

Stephen's eyes felt like they were coated with thick Vaseline when he opened them. He blinked, screwing his eyes shut and opening them wide, but everything was ill-defined and smudged. He was in a bed, he could see that much. A bed in a cold, sparse room. The walls were an offensive pastel green, his bedsheets were white.

Beep.

He raised a hand – a hand that felt as heavy as lead – to wipe at his eyes, and he saw that there was something sticking out of the back of it, between his knuckles and his wrist. There was a needle there, deep in his flesh, and a long tube ran from it, down the length of his arm and across the sheets. A cannula. He rubbed at his eyes with the base of his thumb, wiping away crust and sticky discharge. He'd had conjunctivitis as a boy, and it felt a little like that. His hand moved down his face now and he could see a lot better, and when his hand reached his chin he found a good thick amount of stubble there, verging on a thin beard.

Beep.

A hospital room, a private one at that. Small and clean, reeking of antiseptic and the distant smell of hospital food. He was in a silver-railed bed. Beside him there was an IV drip, a bag of clear liquid hanging on a metal stand. He was wearing a set of pyjamas that weren't his, open at his chest, and there were two circular sticky pads above each nipple with wires trailing from them. The machine beside him beeped again. He tried to turn his head on the pillow to look at it but the blinding shock of pain that went from one temple to the other stopped him. He screwed his eyes shut and groaned.

He tried to speak, but when he drew breath his side contracted and pressed tight against his internal organs like he was crushed in a giant vice. He looked down at his body, gently pulling the sheet aside with his cannula hand, and saw that the right side of his torso was black with bruises, purple and yellow and swollen. Then he saw something on the sheets he recognised; a single black box with a red button that had a black curling cord running from it. He picked it up and pressed it at once.

Further exploring his face, he found that the long cut across his cheekbone had been stitched, and that the flesh around his left eye was inflamed, though he could see through it perfectly well. He looked around the room. Nothing much there. A stack of bedpans. A portable television on a table. A window to his right with the blinds half-drawn. Outside it was light. Rain was falling. There was a door to his left, closed, and beside it there was a simple chair.

His suitcase was standing on it.

Everything came back pretty quickly then. The beating he'd taken. The car. Penny. The tanker. Jesus, the tanker!

As Stephen was trying to sit himself up and failing against the wall of pain that pushed him back down, the door opened and a nurse came in.

'Mr White,' she said, a young thing with light hair tied into a severe bun, 'you're back with us.'

She clopped across the room in shiny black shoes and checked the machine beside him. Then she walked to the foot of his bed and retrieved a clipboard with a paper form clipped to it. She scribbled something on it with a pencil.

'Gave us cause for concern for a while there, Mr White. How are you feeling?'

His mouth was bone dry, his tongue felt too big, and it hurt to breathe, but he managed to say 'spectacular' as the nurse examined him. She shone a little torch back and forth into each of his eyes, then she repeated it. She felt the glands in his neck, examined his torso, and looked over his stitches.

'Good.' She said.

'Good that I feel spectacular, or…?'

She smiled and said in a pleasant but practiced tone 'good that you seem to be recovering, Mr White.'

'What's the damage?'

She put the clipboard back onto his bedframe after scribbling more things down, and said 'Severe bruising to your abdomen, but nothing broken; a hairline fracture, at worst. A little internal bleeding which had us concerned but now seems to be healing adequately, a nasty laceration to your face – you'll have a scar to boast about – and a concussion. The concussion was our primary concern, but please be assured that with proper rest and time, you will be on the road to recovery.'

He tried to speak but his throat burned. The nurse moved to his bedside, out of sight, and he heard liquid being poured. Her thin fingers slid between the pillow and the back of his head, and with the gentlest pressure she lifted his head forward. He groaned behind lips pressed together. She brought a glass of water to them and they parted. He sipped at it and his throat all but hissed like hot metal going into a water bucket, then he sipped again, eager to guzzle it, but she took the glass away again and lowered his head, adding 'little and often, Mr White, at first.'

'The room's spinning.' He groaned.

'You're on a lot of medication. An unfortunate side-effect.' She answered. 'It's best at first to keep your pain manageable while you heal.'

'I don't... I don't remember coming here. I don't remember how I... where's Penny?'

'Penny?' The nurse said, walking to the blinds and pulling them up. Light rain pattered at the glass. 'Ah, you mean your daughter, of course.'

Daughter? Oh, right. Makes sense. Visiting rights.

'Oh thank god, is she alright?' He croaked.

'She is, Mr White. You and your daughter are incredibly lucky to be alive.'

He glanced at his suitcase again. 'Did she bring my things here? I'm... having trouble remembering everything that happened.'

The nurse walked across and lightly sat on the end of his bed.

'She did, after she was examined too. She got off extremely lightly. Nothing but a few cuts and nasty bruises, Mr White...'

'Stephen.'

'Very well, Stephen. Please be assured that your daughter is unharmed, and in good health. Now, do you know where you are?'

'Hospital, but I don't know which one.'

'York General.' She said. 'That's alright, Stephen, it can take a while to readjust. Do you remember how you acquired your injuries?'

He paused. Answer carefully, Steve.

'The petrol tanker.' He said. 'I remember running as it came towards my car, but nothing else.'

'You were lucky that the accident occurred early morning.' She said. 'The staff at Rievaulx Abbey Visitor's Centre were just arriving for the day when the crash took place. They called the emergency services immediately. I can't say precisely what happened, Stephen, but from their accounts a tanker was heading north when it allegedly had a tyre blow out. The driver lost control and was headed straight for your car. You got out just in time, and luckily you were far away enough to escape any real harm from the blast radius when the vehicles collided.'

'It... *exploded?*'

She nodded sadly. 'Huge. It could be seen for miles. The driver died on impact, I'm very sorry to report. As I said, you and your daughter are extremely lucky.'

He swallowed dryly, blinking.

That wasn't an accident. It tried to kill you both. Don't try to reason it out and apply your logic. There's no comfort in that anymore and you know it. Penny was right. You got too close to it and it tried to kill you. It can make things happen. They couldn't kill you in Helmsley. Too noticeable. Too obvious. It'd bring more people with questions, it'd bring the police, it'd be disastrous for them. But a road traffic accident? Nice and neat. That means it isn't just in Helmsley. That means it can get you anywhere. And now a man, just a bloody lorry driver doing his job, is dead.

'Where's P... where's my daughter?'

'She visits every day.' The nurse replied. 'It's a little while until visiting hours but I'm certain she'll be along. Hail from Helmsley, don't you? Beautiful little town.'

Yeah? Get to know it.

'She brought your case in a few days ago.' The nurse went on. 'Off on a little holiday, were you? I'm very sorry that it was ended by such a horrible accident.'

Stephen squinted up at her. '*Days* ago? How long have I been here?'

The nurse paused, but answered him straight. 'You were brought in by ambulance five days ago. Your daughter was discharged that evening, and you were brought to intensive care. You were unconscious for the first forty-eight hours, then you would come around in fits and starts. We kept you carefully anaesthetised then for a couple of days. It's best that way, Stephen, to keep you from moving your head. An injury to the skull like yours is a serious thing. You've been in and out for days. Today is the first time you've really become alert and spoken to us.'

Panic struck his already stricken gut as he realised that his office would have no idea what had happened to him. He almost forgot himself to ask her whether The Evening Gazette in Stockton had been contacted, but that'd blow the cover that Penny had put in place.

He could lose his job. He tried to care but failed.

'Now, Stephen, there's something else we need to discuss.' She leaned in. 'The doctor will be doing his rounds soon, and he will discuss with you what I'm about to tell you, but it seems imprudent of me not to discuss it with you before he arrives, since you're clearly lucid and are entitled to all information when it comes to your health.'

'Hit me.' He said, reminding himself of Penny.

'When carrying out your examination and treatment, we discovered something else.'

Cancer. Big, huge letters in his head, filling the screen,

obliterating all else. Six vile letters making a horrific word. Stephen said nothing.

'What would you say your average intake of alcohol is per week?' She asked.

'I... ah... I never really figured out units.' He stammered a reply. 'It's a lot, I can tell you that.'

She nodded. 'You have an enlarged liver. It's working overtime, and has been for a good while. Also your blood pressure is very high.'

'Yeah, well it's been quite a week.' He said, sighing with something like relief. 'I thought you were going to say the big C or something worse.'

'Make no mistake, Stephen, this can be just as serious.' She said sternly. 'You *must* control your drinking. Already it's taken its toll. You can reverse these effects with abstinence and healthy living, but it will take time. If you continue on this course then your current blood pressure can lead to all sorts of things; heart attack, stroke, kidney disease. You're young enough for your organs to recover from this if you take the right action, and of course when the doctor arrives you'll be given medication to help treat it. Do you understand?'

He understood alright. Those pains in his chest, and the ones down his arms. It had happened more than once this week. The massive headaches too. But goddamn it what was he supposed to do? Sip water, run on a treadmill? He was past all that. He'd almost laughed out loud when the nurse had said *young enough*. He was a beaten up old man with his life behind him. He was...

... beginning to no longer believe these things he told himself. Huh. That surprised him. He was just about to launch into another of his internal monologues about how doomed everyone is, how nothing matters, how what he'd lost had erased any hope of hope, but the words barely managed to form in his mind. They fell away. All he could think about was Penny. All he could think about was his cleansing, his... release? Was that the word? His liberation from his own self-made prison.

Magic.

Just like that, change seemed possible.

'Clever little witch.' He said with raised eyebrows and half a smile.

'I beg your pardon?'

'Oh,' he blinked, his eyes returning to the young nurse, 'nothing. Sorry. Lost in thought for a moment there.'

'Please carefully consider what I've told you.' She said, standing, 'the doctor will be along shortly to discuss things more in depth. We might even see about getting you something to eat. I'll let you rest now, Stephen.'

Stephen called a very genuine *thank you* as she left and closed the door behind her.

The room was still. A serene, enclosed silence. The hospital noises – carts clattering by, people walking or running this way and that, the sound of telephones ringing and people talking and yelling – seemed so far away as to be inconsequential. It was just Stephen and his thoughts.

Well, Steve. Here we are at the bottom. Mentally drained, emotionally spent, and physically broken. What would Penny call this? The end of the line, or an opportunity? An opportunity, of course. An opportunity to reset. To start over. To begin again. Recovery can be as traumatic as birth, and at the end of it, if you do it right, you can be born again - so to speak. And it's just a choice. That bit's easy. So, we make a choice, start at the bottom, and work our way up. What do you want to be, Whitey? What do you want to do?

He already knew. He knew from the moment he opened

his eyes.

It seemed like a miracle but it was true. Stephen White no longer wanted to die. He knew too much now. He knew that his son went on without him, but that he would see him again. His dad, too. He knew that there was a power in the world, beyond it, beneath it, that he had never known but was starting to. He knew that life mattered, that life had a predestined course, and all one needed to do was understand it, acknowledge it, and surrender oneself to it. Did he now feel... hope? Not yet. But perhaps, just *perhaps* he felt ready to *receive* hope. The Stephen from before all of this would have watched that tanker coming and not have moved a muscle. Just a minute more and it would have been over. But he'd fled. He'd fled because he had something now, something to fight on for. Penny. And himself too. Perhaps he wasn't done yet. Perhaps he really was ready to *live*.

The doctor came and went, giving him the same sermon the nurse had. He despised a telling off, he always had, right from school. Even though these people were right – he was drinking himself to death, which had been the plan, hadn't it? – he was still glaring at them resentfully from the bed. But once they'd left he thought long and deep about it. His plan had been working, sure. He was killing himself, staying asleep until it was all over. Slow suicide. But now... now it all sounded empty. It all sounded like a man sitting in a pub named The Green Dragon that everyone laughed at and dismissed outright. A local drunk that Stephen didn't recognise anymore. Here at the bottom, the Place of the Reset, he wasn't sure he was that man any longer. He could choose not to be.

At around two o' clock, after he had eaten a small meal of steak and potatoes which to most would have been pigswill but to Stephen was a banquet fit for the gods, there was a knock on the door of his room.

In came his little saviour, dressed in what was for her a modest black dress and boots. Her hair was the same big black nest it had been when they'd met, her face as white as Helmsley snow, her eyes framed in black. She paused in the doorway and smiled an uncertain smile. 'Hi.' Her voice was small and hesitant.

Stephen smiled back, which seemed to surprise her, and his eyes brimmed with tears, which surprised her more.

He opened his arms wide in the bed, and she ran to him.

28

A Phone Call

Ring tone.

Click.

'Hello, Evening Gazette, Managing Editor Matthews speaking.'

Nothing but a hiss at the end of the line for a while.

'Hello? Evening Gazette? Anyone there?'

A deep calm voice. 'Good morning, Matthew.'

A confused pause. Sudden recognition.

'Stephen? Stephen, is that *you*?'

'Yes, Matthew, it's me.'

'Mate! *Maaaate*! We... I... where the heck have you been, buddy? It's been weeks! What happened? We've been so worried about you here! All the boys in the office have been... we were going to call the police, but...'

'I'll stop you there, Matthew. No need to stammer your way through more lies.'

Silence, followed by the sound of readjustment. Simon spoke in a new, harder way.

'Beg pardon mate, but what's that supposed to mean? I send you off on a four day mini-break at my own expense to write me a story and you disappear for *weeks*. So excuse me, mate, but *I'll* stop *you* there and ask for an explanation.'

'I'm not your mate, you stuck-up little shit.' Flabbergasted silence, so he continued. 'See, I remember things a lot more clearly now. I've been in what I suppose you'd call therapy. A new friend, a good friend, has been helping me with it. Lots of sessions. Lots of discoveries. Suppose I should thank you for that. If you hadn't sent me off to Helmsley I'd never have met her. Anyway, back to the point. I'm sober now. Sober, clean, and thinking more clearly than I have in years. So now that the booze has gone it's all come back.'

'I... won't be spoken to like this. Who the fuck do you think you...'

'The day my son died you were fucking my wife.'

Hiss. The crackling broadcast of movement and a dry swallow.

'You'd wait until I got to work, leave the office for an hour at lunch, and fuck my wife.' Stephen listened calmly. 'Nothing to say? Alright, I'll do the talking. Suppose I should thank you again, for ridding me of her. She's a poison. Gets into your system, see? She makes you like *her*. Before you know it you're constantly angry, constantly drunk, and you've forgotten who you used to be before. I needn't tell you that though, you've probably learned that yourself.'

'You're fucking fired, Stephen.'

'You sent me to Helmsley on a stupid story you dug up to get me out of the way. You wanted me gone so you could spend some quality time with Angela. And no, I'm not fired, because I quit. Just got back from the bank. The divorce settlement and house sale really paid off. I'll be fine for a good while. So, thanks once more for that.'

Heavy breathing at the other end. Absolute fury. 'Are you done? Can I get back to work now?'

'Not yet, no. You might want to hear the next bit. Got a surprise for you. And I've got a question for you.'

Quaking breath. No verbal answer but he didn't hang up, so he took that as one.

'Question first, then. And before I ask it, please, Simon, *please* don't bother lying to me. Don't bother pretending that what I ask sounds crazy, and that I need my head examining etcetera, etcetera. Just answer me. Call it a parting gift.'

'I've got things to do, dickhead. Just get on with it.'

'Did you know about Helmsley?'

'Did I know fucking *what* about Helmsley?'

'I think you know. I think you know exactly what was waiting for me, and that was why you sent me there. Did you try to get me *killed*, mate?'

A hard, angry laugh. 'Are you fucking *insane*? What the hell are you…'

'Ah, ah, ah.' Stephen chastised. 'I told you not to bother with all of that. Let's just skip to the answer, shall we? Did you know? And, now I think of it, if you *did* know, then how?'

After more silence three beeps sounded. Stephen slotted another ten pence piece into the payphone. He could wait. He had all the time in the world.

'You can't stop it.' Matthews said, and now it was Stephen's turn to be stunned into silence. 'I was there. I was there last year. I saw things too. It… did things to me. It hurt me. I nearly didn't come back. But I did, and when I did I swore to myself that I'd never speak about it ever again, not even *think* about it ever again.'

A woman spoke. It was barely audible. Simon couldn't make out what she was saying. What he *did* hear was Stephen put his hand over the receiver, and in a muffled voice say 'you were right' to whoever was there. He released his hand again and said 'well, I appreciate your honesty. First time for everything, isn't there?'

'What... what are you going to do?' Suddenly Simon Matthews, Mr young, confident, and wealthy, sounded like a six year old.

'Well,' Stephen said, still with a perfectly calm and reasonable tone, 'I have a little more healing to do. Still not quite back on form, but I'm doing well. Then, I have something that I need to do. Something very important. I might come back from it, I might not. But if I do...'

Simon swallowed again.

'... then I might just find my way back to Stockton-on-Tees. Not to the offices, mind you. I don't work there anymore, after all. No, I might pay a personal visit. I know where you live, Mr Matthews.'

'Is that supposed to scare me?'

'It should.'

A false laugh. 'Are you threatening me, Steve?'

'Yes. Directly.'

The woman, faint and crackling on the other end, laughed.

'Right, I think we're done here,' Stephen said, 'oh! Silly me. One more thing. Wouldn't want to forget your surprise.'

'I'm calling the police after this, Steve. You're in such deep shit. I'll fucking bury you, you arrogant old bastard. I'll have you done for harassment and making death threats.'

'Might wanna hold off on that, Simon. Don't you want to know what your surprise is?'

'Oh, get *fucked*.'

'Before I called you, I called your fiancée. Samantha.'

Dead silence now.

'Told her everything. Seems she didn't know about Angela – the fact you're still seeing her, I mean – and she wasn't too happy. Not too happy at all. But that isn't the best part.'

Distantly, a faint voice trembled, 'Oh, oh my god...'

'The best part, *mate*, is that I called Angela too. Told her that I know everything. I'm suing her for infidelity and divorce under false basis. Also told her that you have a fiancée. She didn't know that either. Can you imagine? Anyway, I've given her Samantha's number so I'm sure they've been having quite the chat while we've been talking. I imagine your phone will be ringing again very shortly. Got to go, old chap. Good luck. I think you'll need it. And don't forget, *mate*. If I come back, I'll be seeing you soon.'

'You son of a...'

Click.

Dial tone.

29

Keep Your head, and Hold My Hand

'No, that's not accurate. It can't *get you anywhere*.' Penny said as the 31X from York to Helmsley turned a sharp corner, shoving its passengers against the grimy rows of windows, the old bus engine struggling against the winding country road, 'we weren't far from town when the "accident" happened. This thing, neverborn, demon, whatever, it only has a sphere of influence so wide.'

'Osmond told you this?' Stephen said, wincing and holding his side as the bus jolted. His swollen eye was just a dark mark now, and the stitches in his cheek had been removed. Beneath his suit – black pinstripe with a waistcoat, a black shirt undone at the collar – were fresh bandages holding his abdomen tightly together to prevent twisting.

'*Showed* me, yes.' The goth girl replied, leaning in and keeping her voice low. 'He spoke to you through me, but he *showed* me far more. Those guys from the pub that beat you, Ned, Sam and Dave? They killed Millie Wood, and others before her. All elderly folk, or people in poor health, are up for grabs. They make them look like accidents; a fall or a drowning in a bath, and people don't think twice about any foul play. Remember Millie's ghost? That horrible head wound? I looked into it. They said she had a bad fall in her kitchen and her head hit a countertop corner. Yeah, right. And it's not just Ned and his guys doing this, there are others too. This entity, its influence is strongest in the centre of the town, and people like them, *men* like them, are the most susceptible to it.'

Stephen nodded. 'Like you said when you were communing with the bride back in the pub – it preys on the fragile ones, makes them sick.'

'Yup. And you can bet the barman, Bill was it? You can bet he's in on it too. There's eyes everywhere in that town, remember the market square with everyone watching us? Their eyes are *its* eyes.'

It had been close to five weeks since Stephen had been hospitalised. That morning he had finally been discharged. Penny had visited him every day as he healed. When she visited she taught him things – meditation, visualisation, simple prayer, even a basic spell or two. Touching, in his elementary way, the divine. The Great Big What if. And he had completely opened himself up to it, surrendered himself to it. He accepted that things were happening as they were always meant to happen, and he allowed himself to be carried down that river. He'd never felt so free in his life. He hadn't touched a drink nor a cigarette in over a month. A very different Stephen White had left the hospital; clean shaven, sharply dressed, and bright-eyed.

The headaches remained but the doctors said that the danger was gone. His ribs would heal fine too, provided he was careful.

'I just don't get it.' He said. 'Why? Why is it making these guys commit murder? Just for the sheer evil fun of it?'

She shook her great black nest, her large hoop earrings jingled. 'Remember what Millie said? First it kills you then it keeps you. I think it needs souls. She was right all along. This thing is using their souls to sustain itself somehow. The apparitions we've seen, The Bride and Millie, not to mention the ghosts that everyone else has seen over the years – the caretaker and the green lady from those newspaper clippings – those are tortured souls, souls being held by this neverborn, feeding it. When it can't scare someone to death it instead uses people like Ned Bailey to do the job for them, and then it eats well. Been doing this for centuries.'

'And it gets inside your head in other ways too.' Stephen sighed. 'It knew my son's last words.'

'That's how it breaks you down. It was trying to get to you, too. Remember your cleansing? Remember what was going on in your head?'

Those things that he had heard and assumed was his own self sabotage and depression talking - *you don't deserve light because you are not a creature of light and you never were. You're worthless, and deep down you know that can't change. You need a drink, don't you? You want to sleep, don't you?* That had been *it*. It had gotten into his head, exploiting him, wearing him down. Good god, what might have happened if he'd stayed longer, if he'd not met Penny?

He shivered.

'Lucky you've got me.' She said, one corner of her lips forming a smile. 'Witchy warrior, me.' And she held up two fists covered in silver rings in a pseudo boxing stance.

Outside the thick snow had become slush had become flooding. Rain had been falling for a week, only stopping recently, so where had once been a blanket of white there was now only deep pools of muddy-brown water, drenched asphalt, and saturated grasslands. The sun was a grey orb in a covered and ashen sky.

'So, did your custodian show you how it was stopped? Who put it in the church?' Stephen said, watching the moody sky darken beyond the bus window.

'That's the craziest bit.' She said. 'It wasn't trapped in the church. Not exactly.'

His eyebrows knitted together. 'You've lost me. I thought that you released it when you and your dad renovated the place.'

'Nope.' She sounded almost giddy. 'Oh, it's too wild! Get this, Whitey; the church is where it's tethered.'

'*Tethered*?'

'What an act of heresy, eh? What a blasphemous thing!'

'Penny, you're doing it again. Chill out, and start from the beginning.'

'Sorry, pops. Okay. So.' She breathed excitedly. 'Think about what the custodian said. Clysan de porte. Close the portal.'

Stephen's eyed widened. 'The portal is *in the church*?'

'Bingo.' She grinned. 'That church is *not* holy ground, and it hasn't been for a long, long time. Someone, some time in ancient history, summoned a *bloody demon*, right in the middle of a church!'

'What the hell for?'

'A middle finger to god?' She ventured. 'The ultimate sacrilege? The last place anyone would suspect dark magic going on would be in god's house. I wish I could find out who, and how. *Insane*, right?'

'So, it's tethered to a portal?'

'Yeah. Don't think of a dimensional portal as some great swirling black hole like in the movies. It's something we can't see. I could feel it, though. Likely, you would too. I mean, *now* you would. It's an invisible doorway but it's a powerful one! Osmond showed me that this being is tethered to this gateway, so while it can have dominion over the town it can't leave it. It's trapped in my home town! Helmsley is quite literally cursed.'

The ground turned sour. Uf fram hellia. Up from hell.

They fell silent into contemplation of this for a while. The sky outside grew darker, even though it was still morning. The lights inside the bus flickered on. Stifling heat pumped through the vents at the base of their seats from the engine, but the two of them felt very cold indeed.

'So there are thousands, if not *millions* of... souls, ghosts, whatever, trapped there, under the heel of this neverborn.' Stephen said. 'And people are dying. Real people with real lives are being sacrificed to this thing.'

'That's about the size of it, yeah.'

Maybe his concussion was worse than he thought, because anything resembling normal life had gone the way of the Dodo. Or, perhaps, Stephen was just seeing the real world in its *entirety* now, rather than the world that ungifted people saw, or as Penny would bluntly put it; normies.

'So how do we stop it?'

Penny's eyes were shining, twinkling with passion. Her smile was wider than he'd ever seen it. These things thrilled her. These things did not thrill Stephen. He raised his eyebrows and shook his head, saying 'you're bloody loving this, aren't you?'

'What I am loving, Mr White, is two-fold.' She replied. 'For one, I'm loving seeing this new you, open minded, spiritually awake, and ready to rock. I'm also loving the fact that I've spent years of my life trying to find the answers to all of this and now I'm finally getting them, and without you it would never have been possible! And to answer your question, we've already been told how to stop it.'

'You did this on your own, Penny.' He sniffed, waving it

away. 'You're the witch, the psychic, the hoo-doo-voo-doo girl. You'd have managed perfectly well on your own without...' He paused, looked over Penny's shoulder and said in a loud voice 'are you getting all this? Would you like a notebook and pen to get it all down?'

Penny turned in time to see an elderly man jolt and look away in embarrassment. She giggled, turning back. 'When I was channelling Osmond and the neverborn attacked me, what did you do?'

'I didn't do anything, did I? Erm... I...' He paused, his eyes meeting hers. 'I grabbed you.'

'You're on fire today, Whitey. Yes. We touched. And when we did my connection to that grimy old spirit was doubled. I saw everything he was trying to tell me. The pathways were opened, wide, clean, and crystal clear. Without you, without this connection we've got, I wouldn't have learned everything I've learned.'

They were passing through Sproxton now, a tiny village with a little church steeple poking up from between tall trees. They were close. Soon they'd be back. Soon, it would all begin.

'It was sleeping, this entity.' Penny continued. 'It was...' she searched, '... dormant, I suppose. When we broke down that inner wall, my dad and me, we disturbed it. I'm a beacon, just like you. Maybe I somehow... maybe my energy piqued its interest. Whatever caused it we woke it up, just like Osmond Jourdemayne said when he talked about disturbing it when it was slumbering. *Older than the stars*, he said, *but we woke it*. Maybe it was on the other side of the portal and it came back. Maybe *a lot of things*. There might not have even been a church on this site in Jourdemayne's time, I don't know. Point is, we know how it got here, and now we know how to send it back.'

'Do we?'

'Yeah. We close the portal.'

He narrowed his eyes at her. 'That sounds far too simple,' he said, 'I take it that it's far from the case.'

'Wouldn't know,' she shrugged, 'never tried it. Don't even know how to. But come on Whitey, think about it – look what we can do together when we connect. You think it's happenstance that we met just when we're needed most? We were destined for this. So I'm not too worried about figuring this portal thing out, because why would fate guide us here only for me to fuck it up at the last hurdle? That's not the thing I'm worried about.'

He nodded thoughtfully. 'It's going to try and stop us.'

'It's going to throw *everything it has* at us.' She added, looking out of the rain-streaked glass at the now familiar streets passing by. 'It can control people to do its will, as you've already painfully found out, but don't forget that it can make things happen too. A lot of the deaths in this town weren't down to Ned and his pet morons, a lot of them were the work of this entity itself, making them look like accidents. Look what nearly happened to us, for god's sake.'

They both looked out at the soaked streets, water running down gutters and flooding the potholes in the old beaten roads. Stephen glanced at his new friend, and tried his best not to sound afraid. 'What if we bump into them again? Ned, I mean.'

'Give me some credit.' She smiled. 'I planned our return trip for today because I know for a fact that they're out working their pastures. They won't be in town drinking until tonight, usually around six. Sometimes they don't come back into town for a few days. Either way, we have plenty of time to sneak back to my place and prepare.'

He huffed. 'Me? Prepare? How am I supposed to…'

'I meant me.' She said, and her smile had dropped now. 'I'm going to need to pull together everything I've ever learned for this, and I need to reach out to my guides and meditate. I need to figure out how to find this portal and close it down for good. There's a parasite in my home, and its fed too well for too long. It needs cutting out.'

Stephen's heart fell as the familiar sight of the market square came into view outside. There was The Black Swan, Canons Garth, the crumbling heights of the castle, and the graveyard, all consumed in falling rain.

'So,' he said with a trembling breath, 'what am *I* supposed to do?'

'You just do what you do best, Whitey.' She said, standing and pressing the button in the handrail to signal the bus to stop. 'Keep your head, and hold my hand.'

30
Regret, Personified

'I just can't figure out how it got in here.' Penny said, frozen, her eyes darting quickly over the room, reminding Stephen of a scared rabbit, 'I've kept this place protected for years. How the hell was it able to get in *now*?'

Canons Garth was dark and chilly. The fire hadn't been lit in days. The curtains hung closed, gathering dust. The candles were long cold.

Penny had only been home once since Stephen's hospitalisation, to collect his suitcase for him, the rest of the time she had spent in a cheap B&B in York, close to where Stephen had been recovering. This was her first time home since a huge, nameless and deathless *something* had stomped across her bedroom and thundered down the stairs towards her, quite intentionally scaring her out of her own home. But why?

Stephen ran his eyes over the room too. The large pentagram still hung on the wall above the tarot cards and candles. Her wooden sets of drawers were closed. The chest that she kept all of her witchy tools in was unmoved. The old curved chair that he had first sat in when they'd met was in the usual place. Nothing was disturbed, nothing was missing, nothing had been tampered with.

'How does it feel,' Stephen ventured, 'to *you*, I mean?'

She took a deep breath and blew it out slowly.

'Like I'm in someone else's house.' She said this with a cold annoyance staining her voice. Standing beside him, she held out her hand as if she was a waiter carrying a tray. 'See for yourself.'

Hesitantly he reached out and took it and their hands, equally cold, dropped down beside them. The abruptness of the change was startling.

Suddenly he felt as if he was standing in a castle, or a dungeon, a thousand miles from home. It was cold, and damp, and darker than dark, and even the walls themselves felt menacing, as if they might grind across the wooden flooring towards them, crushing them bloody and flat like a hydraulic press. In every corner the darkness had become so dense it looked more like black drapes smothering everything, blinding them to whatever horrors lurked behind them. The air pressure felt different too – suddenly his ears were ringing in the oppressive stillness. He didn't hear the hissing of the blank tape slowly becoming louder like he had before, though. That was good.

'It's not here anymore.' He said. 'But it somehow... tainted this house, just by being present here. It left its mark. Any good energy, any light, has been smothered.'

'I'm impressed.' She said, giving his hand a quick-second squeeze. 'Exactly right.'

'It doesn't explain why it came in here, or how.'

'The *how* I haven't figured out yet.' She started to walk across the room, pulling him with her. 'But the *why* is clearer. It might *look* like nothing has been moved, but you better believe it's all been touched. And by touching, spoiling, tainting my house and my things, it ruined them.'

'Ruined them?'

'The cards, the smudging tools, the crystals, the herbs,

everything.' She pulled him to the kitchen door and pushed it open with a single finger as if she didn't want to have to touch it at all. 'All rendered useless. And further, it probably contaminated them to the point that, if we should try and use them, it would have an opposite effect. A *dangerous* effect, even. In short, Whitey, we're unarmed.'

Ice went down his back. 'How very strategic,' he grimaced.

They moved into the kitchen. The door, as the front door had been, was closed and locked with no signs that anyone – anyone living – had tried to get in. Somehow he could still smell his cigarettes, a stale smoky smell clinging to the room, and it made a craving bite hard in the base of his throat. His lungs ached for sweet smoke. He pushed it back down and took a deep, clean breath.

There were still two cups on the counter, half full of stale tea going mouldy, lit gloomily by the single small window set into the deep stone wall. Other than that everything looked normal, though the intense feeling of darkness remained. Something had walked in this house. Something ancient, inhuman, and evil.

She stepped further into the room, still holding his hand tight. At one point he loosened his fingers, testing whether it was okay to let go, as he didn't like this feeling at all. This insight was something he didn't want; to see beyond the seeable. But she kept his hand firmly in her fist, her interlaced fingers turning white.

'This is where I ran.' She said. 'I kept my eyes down as I went through the graves. I didn't see the ghosts, but I felt them. Ran bloody *through* them.' She tensed beside him.

Stephen sighed, looking around with little interest. He glanced at her and then slowly closed his eyes. 'I can't believe I'm the one that's going to suggest this,' he said, opening them, 'but I think we have to go upstairs.'

They exchanged a look that spoke volumes. She nodded. 'I know. I've just been avoiding it as long as I can.'

They moved deliberately slowly, back through the living room and into the narrow hallway. The air felt thicker somehow, harder to breathe, and colder still. The day was bright enough, though grey, outside, but the light didn't seem to find its way in through the windows at all. The house was too dark.

Stephen's stomach tightened and his heart jumped into a gallop, which made him doubly nervous given what the doctor had told him. He was already on his prescribed medication – pills for blood pressure as well as a blood thinner – but this fact wasn't enough to quell his worry. This'd be a hell of a time to drop dead from a heart attack or suffer a stroke.

They stared up the dark staircase.

A rickety old thing, with several steps that leant awkwardly and unevenly to this side and that. Hard to comprehend that something inhuman had walked – no, ran - down them. Goosebumps raised on his arms and the skin at the back of his neck.

Each step that took them closer to the landing at the top changed the very air around them. It was getting denser, the gloom, and the air was becoming sharply cold. Stephen's nose had turned numb and his fingers hurt. There were several rooms off the hallway containing storage boxes and unused furniture, but he knew that they were only heading for one.

Penny's room was at the end of the hall. The door was closed.

'I didn't close that.' She whispered now.

They were now moving so slowly that they looked like a bride and groom, moving at a predesignated pace. One step.

Stop. Another step. Stop.

Each step grew colder. Their proximity to her bedroom door worsened the goosebumps. His fingers tingled with static. Suddenly his breath became visible.

'You know when you said that it would try and stop us?'

'Yeah?'

'I think it already started.'

'Me too.'

They were standing in front of the door now. This was the room she'd heard this thing take its first step. This was the room it had appeared in. This was the room where they'd seen it in the mirror and it had attacked them, just like it attacked them again by trying to kill them on the road. She was reaching for the brass handle when he stopped her, pulling her back.

'Wait,' he said, 'just hold on. We're alone here. What if it tries to hurt us again?'

'I have to know how it got in.' She replied sharply, her abruptness driven by fear. 'If I can figure out how it got through my defences then it won't be able to do it again.'

They locked eyes intensely for a few seconds, neither one relaxing the painful grip their clenched hands caused. It was Stephen that blinked first.

'Fine.' He whispered. 'Together, then.'

She reached and closed her fingers around the handle, and slowly, *so* slowly, turned it as if there was someone sleeping inside that they didn't want to wake.

She pushed it open to reveal a void of complete and total darkness.

His stomach fell as he gazed from a gloomily lit

hallway into absolute black. There may as well have been an ebony curtain hanging inside the door. The darkness was impenetrable and total. Her bedroom curtain was drawn within, so it was a given that the room would be dark. But this was too dark, too smothering. It was more than shadow, it was a vacuum devoid of anything at all.

The cold was more intense within, and so silent that not even the deepest grave could be so still. They stood together, frozen at the cusp. She felt Stephen begin to shake beside her.

'I can hear the tape.' He breathed. 'It's getting louder.'

The room in front of them may have been as dark as a black hole in deep space, but there was undoubtedly something in there.

In a voice that feigned as much bluster as she could manage, it was Penny that spoke to the cold gloom first.

'Who are you?' She said. 'Name yourself.'

Silence. Morbid, endless, unforgiving silence. But the silence spoke for itself, because it felt malicious. Stephen spoke next.

'What are you doing in this house?' He said with a dry, husky throat. 'You don't belong here.'

A pressure in the centre of his forehead. A ringing in his ears. The hiss of the blank tape grew louder and louder as the volume leapt up. Then the voice. The horrendous voice of something speaking in their heads again. A croaking whisper, cracking with each word and breathless and stinking and dead. The smell hit them as it spoke, a sour, earthly stench. The smell of decay.

'Time is short for mum.' It said.

Stephen gasped, his arm tensed like pulled rope.

'The time you'll spend regretting this choice will feel a

lot longer.' It concluded. It was a jeering, vile voice. But it was not the voice of his brother.

'M... m... *mum?*' Stephen stuttered.

Footsteps now. Slow, dragging footfalls in the pitch darkness of the room. It was coming towards them.

Stephen backed away, his mouth hanging open. Penny stepped with him but her eyes were fixed on him rather than the thing in the dark. 'It's not your mum.' She said sternly. 'That is not your mother, Whitey. It's messing with you. It's trying to hurt you.'

Your mother has died, Stephen. She died alone and without you, just like you knew she would. You had the chance to see her, to comfort her. Ed tried to make you go, and you wouldn't go. You just drank and hid like the coward you are. And now it's too late. Now she's here and she hates you and she should, because you've betrayed her and let her down because it's too late.

'*Mum?*' He cried again in a broken voice.

'No! Steve! No it isn't!' Penny barked, squeezing his hand hard. 'It's using her against you. Wake up! Stay here and now, with me!'

The steps grew closer. Stumbling, shuffling, lurching. Though it should have been visible by now from the light cast into the room from the hallway, nothing could be seen.

'I forgot.' It said. The words heartbreaking but the tone wicked. 'I forgot piece after piece of myself until there was nothing left of me.'

It was her voice. His mother's voice. The voice he remembered that had comforted him and chastised him and called him in for dinner and welcomed him home from school. But the voice was corrupted. And as it spoke the stink of the grave came with it.

'Then I forgot how to speak.' It almost sang with evil

delight. 'Then I forgot how to eat and to drink and to think at all.'

Penny started to whisper at his side as they backed away.

'I bind you. I banish you. I forbid you from doing us harm. Begone from here. Go back to the shade. I bind you, I banish you.'

Her voice was drowned out as the creature in the dark grew nearer and began to screech. Nails on a blackboard. The screams of a dying child. The brutal shriek of a tortured animal.

'You left me to rot in the dark!' It cried. 'You left me in a cold bed in a cold room. I was so frightened! All I wanted was you! You left me to die! I fell into hell, and I am still falling!'

Stephen screwed his eyes shut, and now he stumbled backwards. Penny fell with him, catching herself against the wall of the hallway but refusing to let go of his hand. She continued to speak. 'I bind you, I banish you.'

Then the entity stepped into the light.

It was so painfully thin, muscles so wasted, that it shouldn't have been able to stand at all. Grey legs poked out from beneath a hospital gown, as discoloured and twisted as tree branches, and they shook under the weight of the entity as it lurched, limping towards them. The gown was pale blue and stained. Urine and sweat and spilled soup gone sour. Her arms were as thin as fingers, old skin wrapped tight around fragile bones. Her hands, claws, reached out for them from the shadows.

Her face was a skull. The eyes were sunken and gone. Lips withered away to thin strings, pulled back over teeth as yellow as egg yolk. The flesh in her cheeks had shrunken away into deep cavities, just like the circles of her sockets had. She appeared blind. Reaching. Searching.

A grey skinned skeleton with greasy grey hair. A monster in the shape of his mother. A pitiful, horrifying thing. A regret, personified.

Stephen couldn't stop the scream. No one in their right mind could. Penny's incantation rose to a yell to meet it, though.

'I bind you from doing us harm!' She hollered. 'I banish you from this place! Deprecare Deum pacis, ut conterat Satanum sub pedibus nostris!'

And then it was simply and suddenly gone. The hallway was just a hallway. The bedroom beyond was no longer a black chasm but a normal room, partially lit by the light streaming in through a thin gap in the curtains. The hissing stopped, the stench was gone, the air became warm. Now, rather than a screaming tomb, this was just a house. As fast as changing a slide in a projector, replacing the image, one thing became entirely another.

'And stay out, you skanky old bitch.' Penny added for good measure.

Stephen snatched his hand out of hers and stumbled away down the hall, away from her room. She watched him go with a frown.

'Where are you going?' She called. 'We did it! This is a result!'

'That was my mother!' He called over his shoulder. 'Not some *skanky old bitch*! My mum, she's...'

'That wasn't her!' She snapped back. 'I told you! For all you know your mother may be alive and well! It tricks you, it fucks with your mind! Don't let it scare you!'

'When I left my mother was dying,' he called, now from the stairs and he unsteadily made his way down them, 'if she's passed away while I was here... I... I have to find out. I'm going to find a phone.'

Penny heard the front door slam and then turned back to her bedroom. 'Never mind that it isn't safe to be seen out there.' She muttered sulkily. 'Idiot.'

She stepped into the mess of her bedroom and pulled the curtains open, allowing muted light to spill over the unmade bed, the dresser with makeup paraphernalia spread all over it, and carefully stepped over the shards of glass that littered the floor. She stood, hands on hips, and surveyed the space.

'How did you get into a house that was spiritually locked up tight?' She said to herself, focusing her mind and narrowing her eyes. 'Was it us? Did we do something wrong?'

She walked to the window to see if she could spot Stephen outside. If anyone saw him, if *the wrong eyes* saw him, then they could both be in far more physical danger than a simple apparition could cause. As she reached the pane something crunched beneath her boot. She looked down.

A big piece of broken glass from her mirror. An unwise scrying session, she realised now.

She reached down and carefully picked up the triangular shard, holding it up to her face. Her own eye, framed in black pointed lines, looked back at her.

Then the eye went wide.

'Mirrors!' She yelped, dropped it, and ran.

31
Believe

He was going to call Ed, but he figured that on a weekday he was certain not to be at home, so he directly called the nursing home instead.

The receptionist was pleasant and surprisingly unmatronly when he asked about his mother, Beryl White, and how she had been doing. After a pause as long as a bad winter, while the receptionist flipped through papers, she answered his query.

'White. Here she is. Yes, Mrs White is stable at present.'

'So she's alive? So she's okay?' Stephen spluttered over her. After a confused pause, she answered him.

'Yes, Mrs White is... still with us. Might I ask who you are and what this is about?'

'I'm her... I'm her son, Stephen.'

She paused again, and when she spoke again her tone had changed entirely.

'Ah, yes. Your brother, Edward, mentioned you recently. A lot of the girls here thought that Beryl had only one son until then. Do you plan on visiting? At this stage, it is rather important to...'

'I have some... business I have to attend to.' He said quickly, trying to mask his relief. 'It can't wait, unfortunately.

I hope to have it concluded as soon as humanly possible. Today, if I can. Then I'll be racing back and I'll indeed be visiting her. Does she...' he swallowed the lump in his throat, 'does she mention me, at all? Ask about me?'

The receptionist sighed.

'No, Mr White.' Was answered. 'She says little at all now, and not much that is comprehendible.'

Stephen looked out at the rain soaked streets outside the public phone box. He pressed a palm to the glass and lowered his head. 'I see.'

'You've left it too late, you see.' The receptionist said.

Stephen's head shot up. '*Excuse* me?'

'I said you've left it too late, you coward.' She repeated in the same pleasant voice she had started with. 'She spent her whole life caring for you, raising you, educating you, keeping you safe, and when things got challenging you tucked tail and abandoned her.'

His breath hissed out as his face turned pink. 'Who the hell do you think...'

'She'll die alone. She's forgotten everything else. You had your chance to comfort her, to share in your memories, and to hold her hand as she faces the horrible end of her life – and it's so very horrible, Mr White, the *worst* – and instead of stepping up and doing your duty like a good son should, like a *man* should, you ran away and shunned her. It's too late.'

'I want to speak to your superior! Right now! How dare you speak..'

'She'll die slowly. Badly. And when she's released she'll go straight to hell. Straight down into an eternity of suffering along with that cunt child of yours.'

Stephen froze solid.

'No one can save you.' She went on, speaking as if she was talking about the weather. 'No one can stop what's coming. You'll suffer, that little slut you parade about with will suffer too. You can't stop it. You can't even comprehend it. It is as old as the sun, as powerful as the heart of a quasar, it is the beginning of all things and it will be watching when they end.'

Stephen, with a quaking hand, drew the receiver from his ear and stared at the handset, his skin as grey as the concrete outside.

'You and your bitch have interfered quite enough.' The voice on the line said. 'So now it is coming for you. Enjoy the day, Whitey. Enjoy the sun. You will not see it rise again.'

His heart hammered in his throat like a machine gun as he slowly moved to hang up the phone. The strength had gone out of his arm, but he maintained enough to drop the handset back into the cradle.

Who the fuck had he just spoken to? He stared at the dial and the numbers on the device, at the grey phone and the curled cord, and tried to fathom what he had just heard. Nothing came. His mind was blown open like a bomb had gone off. Something was coming for them, and it was everywhere. It could make things happen, and now it could speak through a person like a puppet. It had eyes everywhere, ears everywhere, and as long as they remained in this town it could get to them. It was omnipresent. Like *god*. How can you fight something like that?

Knock knock knock.

Stephen jolted and a cry involuntarily leapt out of his throat. He span on the spot.

Penny was standing outside the phone box with a big white-toothed smile, stark against black lips. She pulled the door open a few inches and poked her head in.

'You scared the *shit* out of me.' He gasped, closing his eyes and pressing his hand to his chest.

'Wondered what the smell was in here.' She replied. 'Hey, listen; I've figured it out. I know how it got into my house.'

***

The afternoon drew on.

Stopping at the corner shop, they retreated back into the rectory. Penny made a black bean salad, which Stephen resisted at first – who could eat at a time like this? Not to mention that it looked to him like rabbit food – but when he finally relented he had to admit to himself that it was delicious. They set about putting her house back together, pulling back all the curtains and letting in as much light as they could, and as they did Penny had explained everything.

Mirrors.

To spirits, mirrors were a multifaceted thing. They could be used as communication tools, as something to project images onto, and most importantly…

'Doorways.' She had sighed, shaking her head. 'It's my fault. I should have remembered it sooner. We used the mirror to scry, but because of what this entity did with it I forgot to close our session down safely. I *left the door open*, so to speak. It bypassed my protections and used a back door straight into my house. And then I realised that the mirrors are the key. Think about it. Every house has mirrors. Every house in this town is filled with them. It can transport itself from place to place, house to house, through mirrors.' She held up a black plastic sack filled with broken glass. '*This* is going outside. And we need to find every mirror in this house and cover it. Even something as small as a looking glass or makeup mirror. All of it has to be covered or gotten rid of.'

Soon, every mirror in the rectory was covered by, or wrapped in, towels. Every reflective surface, mirror or not, had been covered with cloth, or at least obscured. One would think someone had recently died in the house. Stephen chose not to see this as any kind of portent.

While a band called *The Mission* performed a song ironically named *Dance on Glass* from her record player, Penny and Stephen sat together, each holding steaming cups. He was in the armchair, and she, as ever, was sitting cross-legged on the rug.

No more rain had fallen outside, but the sky remained an ominous heavy grey. People passed the window, but none of them appeared nor acted strangely. Still, Stephen couldn't shake the chilling words of the woman – if that's what she was – on the phone.

It is coming for you.

He had told Penny about the disturbing conversation he had just had. With raised eyebrows she had listened quietly. When he asked her if anything like this had ever happened to her before, she answered with 'I doubt something like this has ever happened to *anyone* before. As far as the spiritual world goes, this is off the charts.'

In silence they pondered the enormity of it.

Two people that couldn't be more different, drawn together to face off against something unknowable and eternal. What had real life *even been* before this, and how could one ever return to it? Had his whole life been designed for this one purpose? Was he, rather than a man with a normal life, options to take, roads to walk, simply nothing more than a tool, always destined to be used for this one end? At least his life had meaning, he supposed. Not many could say that.

Penny had been listening again. She answered his thoughts, staring past him into the middle-distance, steam from her tea rising past her powdered face.

'That's the terrible truth of life, isn't it?' She said dreamily. 'Everyone pretends to know what they're doing and that everything makes sense, but no one really knows what's going on, or why we're here, or what the point of it all is. We blunder from horror to horror, hoping that one day there'll be an explanation, a meaning to it all. But, to me, that's what faith is; faith is a choice. We can choose *not* to blunder blindly, we can choose to stay awake and stay present. We can choose to *believe*. We can choose to accept every fantastic and mystical thing there is with our whole hearts. We choose to trust in it, we choose to believe, and by doing so we make magic.'

He stared at her as she spoke. He examined her young face. Amidst all this horror and fear, she was the one shining light that he clung to now. She had plucked him from the bottom of the pit and shown him a completely new way of life. As terrifying as this was he had never felt more alive, and dare he say optimistic about the future.

If he had one.

'You know what, Penelope Black?' He said quietly. 'I think you might be the best thing that's ever happened to me.'

A touch of a smile reshaped her black lips.

'Ditto, Stephen White.' She said, a little embarrassedly.

They both let the moment sit. A moment of friendship and of calm. It felt final.

'So then,' he said at length, 'we're *unarmed*, as you put it, and now this thing is already focused on us – on stopping us, rather permanently at that – and we have a task ahead of us that neither one of us knows how to execute. Suppose you can guess what my question is.'

'What do we do?' She sipped at her tea and stared out through the latticed lead at a sombre day. 'The only thing left to do, I suppose. And I'm hoping that once we do it I'll get some idea of what to do next.'

'Which is?'

'I need to do the one thing I've avoided since dad died.' She replied. 'We need to get into that church.'

Stephen pulled up the sleeve of his black shirt to look at his watch.

'It closes to the public in one hour.' He said. 'Will that give us enough time?'

She sighed, and Stephen saw something rare in her expression now. She looked terribly uncertain, and perhaps even afraid. Not of entities or demons though, scared of something far more dangerous; walking back into her troubled past.

'There's no services today.' She said. 'The curate, the vicar I mean, comes in from out of town for daily mass and stuff. But the warden I've seen come and go. Perhaps he's there.'

'Warden?'

'Like a second-in-command.' She put her tea down on the hearth and stood. 'The assistant to the curate. Like a caretaker with benefits. He wears a dog collar so I'm guessing he takes care of stuff while the vicar is away. If he's there, then maybe we can...'

'Hi father,' Stephen stood too, raising an eyebrow, 'mind if you keep the church open a little longer for us tonight? Why? Oh, nothing much. We just need to close a portal to hell in order to cast a demon back through it that's been murdering and feasting on the souls of the dead for centuries.'

While he spoke, Penny walked over to her little chest that stood beside the drawers. The record had stopped now and the house had fallen quite silent. She opened it slowly and carefully, and with great hesitation reached inside and pulled something out. Stephen saw what she was doing and stopped his sarcastic diatribe. 'Should you be touching that stuff given what you just said?'

She was holding an instantly recognisable item; rosary beads. A chain of dark brown orbs that looked wooden, upon which hung two silver items – a crucifix complete with Christ in death throes, and a silver coin which upon closer inspection depicted Saint Benedict.

'This was dad's.' She said, examining it sadly. 'I suppose I was hoping that the entity couldn't...' Her brow furrowed and her eyes widened. She dropped it back into the chest and slammed it shut in an instant.

'What?' Stephen asked, stepping over to her. 'What's wrong?'

'The... ah...' her voice was dry. 'The crucifix. It was... It shouldn't be possible but it was... inverted.'

He stayed silent. Something felt fundamentally wrong all of a sudden. He felt cold.

'Something removed the cross from the clasp and put it back on upside down.' She said, grimacing down at the chest with her arms wrapped around herself.

Stephen put a hand on her little shoulder. The sun was setting quickly outside and they were standing in near darkness. 'I'm sorry.' Was all he could think to say, adding 'why would it do that? A warning?'

'An insult.' She replied quickly. 'An offence against everything that my dad stood for and believed in, and against divinity itself. It's what these creatures do. Pathetic fucker.' She reached up a hand and closed it over his, pressing it against her shoulder. 'That's it. That's enough. Come on. We've got work to do.'

He pulled in a shaking breath, looking from her to the darkness that was creeping over the town outside. 'And what am I supposed to do?'

'I just told you.' She said, patting his hand before striding towards the door. 'Choose to believe.'

32

Unclean Spirits

It was obvious from the moment they stepped outside that something was wrong.

It was dusk. The unbroken cloud was heavy and low and the rain had slowed to a cold drizzle. The gloom was smothering and absolute. There was no wind, just a stale chill that hung damply in the air around the pair. As if it needed stating Stephen said it aloud.

'The streetlights aren't on.'

The carpark was barely visible, and the market square beyond it was lost to darkness. It was so very quiet that the two of them could hear their own breath. The instinct to whisper was strong. Once again, they felt that to make any loud noise would attract the attention of... something.

There were tall streetlamps along the length of the street and all around the square, and not one of them was lit. Beside him Penny looped her arm through his, linking him tightly. They looked left to The Black Swan, then across the space at the cottages, houses and shops that surrounded them.

Not a single house had a light on.

'Power cut?' He whispered.

'More than that. Look. There's no one around.' She

hissed in the dark. 'It's only a little after four. Shops don't even close until five or so.'

Everything was closed up. Not a door open, not a car on the road, not a footstep. The local bank stood cold and bare. The town hall beside the monument in the square had empty black rectangles for eyes.

It were as if the sole inhabitants of Helmsley were Stephen and Penny.

The urge to run to the pub and knock, or to go and try the doors of the cottages, or to try and enter the corner shop nearby was powerful. The desperate need to break this spell and to reassure themselves, to prove that everything was actually real and that they were mistaken was overwhelming, because the alternative explanation was too much to take.

'How can it be doing this?' Stephen squinted into the gloom all around. 'This is impossible.'

Penny pulled her torch from the pocket of her overcoat and clicked it on, spilling a harsh white beam onto the watery pavement. 'Stay close to me.' She said. 'Don't let go.'

She turned in the direction of the graveyard gates, and as he squeezed her arm tight against his side, ignoring the stabbing pain it caused in his ribs, they slowly began to walk.

Water poured through flooded gutters overhead. The sewer grates in the kerbs beneath their feet ran with deep rushing rivers. Still the rain fell.

The gate loomed ahead. The low wall made of old pale stone was still visible, as was the sign just inside the short gate that Stephen had paused to read on his day of arrival. All else – the large graveyard beyond – was enveloped in black. Just an empty space, or perhaps more accurately a space *full of something*, lay beyond the street. The stones within, the tombs and monoliths, felt like they were waiting. They felt like they were watching in the dark.

The act of putting one foot in front of the other, of approaching the cemetery, was something that Stephen thought he'd be incapable of. But here he was, doing just that. Without Penny beside him he'd have run a mile, of course. Nevertheless he felt a strange quiet pride in that moment. Perhaps he was brave after all.

They stopped in front of the gate and Penny shone her torch inside. All was still and silent within. The headstones emerged from the melancholy shadows as her light passed over them, crooked and jumbled in the damp earth. Rows and rows of seemingly endless graves. The white circle of bright light touched the soaring wall of the old church and hovered there.

'Locked too, you think?' Stephen whispered.

'Whitey.' She ignored the question, her uncertain tones making his heart leap. 'Does it seem... I don't know... *bigger*, in there?' And to illustrate her point she made another circuit of the churchyard with her beam.

Perhaps it was the darkness, perhaps it was their minds playing tricks on them. Whatever it was, she was right. The yard looked impossibly larger inside the little walled enclosure somehow. The church seemed farther away than it normally did. It was as if there was a barrier between that graveyard and the outside world, and all inside didn't follow the laws of physics.

She gathered herself. He felt her stiffen. 'It's just trying to scare us.' She whispered. 'It doesn't want us going in, and that's a good thing.'

'How's that?'

'It means there must be a way to stop it. Why else would it try and deter us? If it was impossible it'd just let us in without resistance.'

They stood for a few moments more on the boundary. One more step would put them inside, and he felt with every fibre of his being that once they did that there was no going back.

'I guess it's time for us to connect.' She said, unlinking him and holding out her free hand.

He just stared at it as if it was as dangerous as the graveyard. Did he really want to see what was in there, what was potentially all around them? Did he really want to know what horrors were waiting, breathing down his neck right at this moment? Yet again he stood at the edge of the cliff with only a wall behind him. Nothing to do but jump. This was the only choice he ever had, anyway. It was all leading to this.

He sucked in a deep breath, closed his eyes, reached out his hand and...

... found only thin air.

There was a swoosh of air as strong as a sudden gale, the rippling and snapping of clothing in strong winds, and a feeling of a great weight soundlessly rushing between them, all within a split second.

Stephen opened his eyes.

Penny was gone.

Not a scream, nothing. Just the rushing of powerful wind followed a second later by eerie calm. Stephen was alone at the churchyard gate.

He stared in shock at the space she'd occupied. He looked down with wild eyes and saw her torch, switched off now and spinning on the ground with a plastic clatter.

'Penny?' He said with a quiet, warbling voice to the dancing object, then he looked up and into the night his voice echoed with a scream. *'Penny?'*

He grabbed the torch and switched it on, spinning on the spot, the circle of light dancing frantically across the gravestones, the church, and then back at the square.

'*Penny*! Penny?' He called again and again as his heart thundered into a gallop, sending a flash of pain across his breastbone and downward in a thin burning line towards his stomach.

His cries were only met with absolute silence. Not even a bird chirped. The animals in the distant fields were mute. The falling rain doused the tarmac indifferently.

'This can't be happening, this can't be real,' he stammered in a manic mantra, 'this can't be... *Penny*! This isn't real, it's a nightmare. Yes, a nightmare. You'll wake soon. This isn't real life, this is just...'

He stopped spinning when the beam fell on a figure some distance away.

He began to call her name again, but the breath went out of him. That wasn't Penny.

The figure was so far away that he couldn't make out any features. It stood across from him in the centre of the market square, beside the monument with the white statue. He froze, his light barely making it through the haze of drizzle to illuminate the figure, and puzzled at it.

'Hello?' He said, not even loud enough for anyone to hear so far away.

Something was immediately wrong. He couldn't figure out what it was until he had studied the woman – yes, that was definitely a woman – for a few more moments.

The monument, *Feversham* had Penny called it? It was a tall, spired thing. Easily as high as the town hall. What, twelve feet or more? So why was the woman standing next to it almost the same height?

She was... she was *too tall*. She was *too thin*. She was... *grotesque*. She wasn't, and couldn't have been, human.

Pure fear twisted in his gut as the spotlight trembled on the woman. He saw the green of her dress now. Emerald and silk, glistening in the rain. She had her hands over her face. Impossibly long thin fingers encasing her skull. Her arms were like twigs, bleached white, with painfully sharp elbows poking out below emaciated shoulders.

The strength seemed to sap from his limbs as the figure began to move. His legs doddered beneath him as he remained anchored to the spot. He saw the red now. A red streak, pouring from her neck. The arms fell by its sides, far too long, hanging far below skeletal hips encased in dirty green satin.

Somehow, Stephen had the presence of mind enough to remember an article he'd read. The Green Lady of Helmsley. Mary Gysborne.

She started to move towards him, and Stephen screamed.

***

Penny ran through the gravestones, her boots pounding at mushy soil and sodden grass.

This was impossible. This was beyond anything she'd ever experienced before.

One moment she'd been reaching for his hand, the next she'd been standing inside the graveyard, far beyond the gate and the path, holding out her hand to nothing, merely collecting water in her palm.

There was no light here.

She could make out the outlines of tall gnarled trees, and the oval tops of the old headstones. She could see the blocky oblongs of tomb chests, though she ran into them and bashed her shins where the shadows were too dense. There was no sign of the exit, and no sign of the church. This was not possible. The graveyard wasn't this large! The church was huge and impossible to miss wherever you were standing.

So she ran. She darted through an obstacle course of gravestones, weeds, mausoleums and monuments, keeping to one straight line as best she could. Beyond the trees she could make out nothing, but there *must* be a wall eventually, or even better, the gate back into town.

But no matter how far she ran she found only more grassy mud, graves, thorny wild bushes and the ancient barks of leafless trees.

She stopped, gasping for breath, her heart a steam train. She leant against the rough hide of a yew tree, soaked to the skin in a long velvet skirt now pitted with watery earth and her overcoat, which was now so saturated that it clung to her bare arms beneath. Panting, she turned this way and that, calling out the name of her friend for the hundredth time.

Her desperate tones echoed in the black expanse, fading to nothing. No voice replied.

She trembled, cold down to her bones now. Her teeth were gritted.

'You're not having it.' She hissed into the rain. 'You're not having my fear. You're not getting tears either. 'Cos the thing is, you old fucker, *you* killed my dad. So the only thing you're getting out of me is anger. All you're getting from me is banished.'

A whip of wind blew through the stones, dancing around the tree and shaking droplets from its twisted branches, and for a moment Penny could have sworn she heard a gentle laugh.

This pushed her into a stumbling walk and she left the tree behind, moving aimlessly away and into the cold darkness. Standing still seemed like a bad idea. It felt as if something could rush at her, or approach her unseen on silent feet. Mind you, moving didn't seem like such a good idea either. What if she walked straight into the arms of... something?

And where the hell were the paths? There were several of them, wide and obvious to see, she'd walked them all her life. But here there was only endless mud and lawns long uncared for. Was she even in her home town anymore? Was she even in the real world?

She stopped again in a clearing of tall grass, where the graves were either absent or unmarked, wrapped her arms against herself in a futile attempt to fend off the icy chill, and looked around. She knew what this bastard wanted her to think; that she was trapped here forever. That this was hell, or purgatory, and she was forever condemned to wander in this dark dead place forever. Well, bollocks to that. No chance mate. She was a witch, wasn't she? She had the gift, didn't she?

She closed her eyes and began to speak.

'Horned Lord, Oak King, Pan, Cernunnos, lend me your protection. Goddess of the Moon, Diana, Bridgit, Hecate, give me your guiding light. Shield me from harm, and show me the path. Bless me with your guidance. Consecrate me with your strength.'

She knelt in running water. The icy grime soaked into her knees through her tights. She pressed her hands together.

'Lord God on high, cast out this wickedness. In the name of Jesus Christ I call for your divine love to steel me in the face of evil. Let no harm come to me. Shepherd me to your light.'

The wind rose again. It whipped at her long black strands, plastering them to her face. This time the wind sounded not like a laugh, but like a growl.

'Libera me a malo.' She said, bowing her head. Then she concluded. 'So mote it be. Amen.'

The rain stopped. It didn't slow to a stop, it didn't move off with the clouds, it just stopped as quickly as someone turning off a shower. Now there was only the sounds of water running down pathways and pattering from tree branches. All else was a ghastly, still silence.

Penny opened her eyes. Her breath steamed in the dark, icy vapour hanging in the damp air like mist. She climbed to her feet, covered in mud, soaked through, with her black hair stuck to her face in rat-tail strands. Her makeup was streaked and ruined, her lips were a black smear. She looked around again, hoping that her incantations had caused some effect, revealing an exit, but she found only the same endless cemetery. The cold had become so extreme it was stinging her face. And then she heard a voice.

An abnormally high voice. A lunatic voice. A voice made of malice. And in the sing-song tones of a court jester it spoke.

Georgie Porgie pudding and pie...

Penny stiffened and her breath caught.

The voice came from all around her, all at once.

She began to walk backwards, edging away from the stones. Her head darted this way and that.

'Gods, help me.' She whispered.

The voice came again, thin and high and wickedly gleeful.

Kissed the girls and made them cry...

Penny turned and ran, and the moment that she did something gave chase. She could hear it, a *slap slap slapping* of feet pounding at wet grass and splashing through deep puddles. A high laugh, delighted and amused, followed. It kept pace easily.

Her heart burned and her limbs had gone numb. Her brain had switched from reason to pure and simple survival. She knew the stories. She knew the spirit.

Not this. Anything but this.

She tore through the night, passing stones high and low, dodging through trees, and scratching her hands on sharp-leaved foliage as she reached out into the darkness. There's got to be a way out of here. There's got to be a way to escape this thing. Her lungs burned. Her heart screamed inside her ribs.

Then the pursuing footsteps stopped all at once, and Penny's boots hammered at the dirt alone.

She made a big mistake then. She even knew it was mistake as she did it, but she had to know.

Penny looked back.

Nothing but an expanse of black, from which trees and graves peered at her. No spirits. No monsters. It was gone.

But then her mistake bore the only fruit it could. Penny wasn't looking where she was running.

Her foot collided so sharply with with an overturned headstone that it felt like her big toe broke. A hot flash of pain surged through it and up her foot, culminating in a cold tightening that wrapped around her ankle. She spun sideways, letting out a cry half of fear and half of frustration, and she hit the filthy ground so hard that it knocked the air out of her. She rolled several feet, only coming to a stop when she felt cold granite hit her back.

All was still.

She stared in shock at a starless sky. She was laying at the bottom of a shallow incline. A black marble memorial had stopped her rolling any further. She sucked in a painful and rattling gasp, winded. She sat up, completely soaked through now and covered in soil, and cursed into the clouds.

She was about to climb to her feet.

But then it was on her.

A great invisible weight slammed onto her, and her breath was knocked out again in one long wheeze. She could see nothing, but she could certainly feel it. A huge, freezing mass, pressing her down into the dirt. A horrible voice at her ear. Breathing? Perhaps that, but she felt no breath. Just the grunting, slobbering, wet rasping of quick breath. Excited breath. She screamed and began to thrash. Clawing at the air. Twisting her body in spasms beneath the crushing weight.

Hands were on her. Invisible thick fingers with cruel gnarled nails, pulling at her skirt, clawing at her tights. Forcing itself on her.

The strange and simultaneous sensation of heat and cold washed through her as fresh adrenalin took hold. She thrashed and clawed and screamed herself sore, but her hands found nothing. She tried to roll, but couldn't. She couldn't touch this thing, but it could touch her.

She heard the fabric of her tights ripping, and felt the icy night air touch her thigh.

'Get off me! Get the fuck off me!'

An unseen claw tore at the neckline of her top, trying to

rip her clothing open. The marks on her skin were already red and raised. Something vile, something as cold as a corpse was grabbing at her legs, at her crotch, squeezing her breasts, and the vile breath of arousal coursed in her ear as the impossible weight pressed down harder.

This cannot happen. This cannot happen to me.

The stink. Oh gods, she could smell it now. Hot breath that smelt like rotten eggs and the decaying roots of black teeth, an unwashed body that reeked of infection and sharp musky filth, and the sickening stench of faeces long dried into old clothes. A contaminated thing. A corrupted soul.

By all the saints, by all the angels, by all the gods old and new, give me the strength to stop this.

But then her hand found something. Something warm, and real, and alive.

Her wild eyes looked up, beyond the horror that was assaulting her.

Stephen wrapped his fingers around hers, and heaved her to her feet.

'Run!' He cried.

Suddenly she was free of it, and she found her connection to her cosmic twin again, and they ran.

The unclean spirits pursued them.

33
God is not here

Suddenly they were running through a perfectly normal graveyard. It was the right size, it was partially lit by the streetlights out beyond the gate which they could now see, and the church was at the centre, tall and black and watching.

Penny was sobbing as they dashed onto the tarmac path that snaked around the stones, stumbling and lurching from side to side, almost losing her footing and going over, but Stephen wouldn't let go, hauling her along with him.

'The gate!' He yelled. Penny didn't answer, but something behind them did.

It was a shriek that reminded Stephen horribly of a time in his youth, when he had witnessed a cat hit by a car on his way to school. The poor animal hadn't died straight away, and had lain broken in the gutter, screaming in a way he'd never heard before or since. He'd never forgotten it and it had haunted his nightmares for years. Now, this screech was all too similar.

He glanced back and saw the thing that pursued them.

The impossibly tall entity, drifting quickly through the misty haze. Repellent thin arms reaching with skeletal fingers as long and as knotted as twigs. A ragged green dress that barely clung to the emaciated form, dragging audibly with a hiss along the asphalt below.

Thin whisps of hair danced around a skull mostly bare, and wicked white eyes burned with unnatural light in the dark. The mouth was open, toothless, a black decaying tongue lolloping against its pointed chin. The neck was wide open with a bloody deep wound, the spine visible through the tattered flesh. It looked like the head could roll off the stump any moment. A famous ghost, a local legend, The Green Lady of Helmsley, right there with them – *coming* for them like a nightmare made real.

Stephen was dragging her towards the gate and the lights of the town. He couldn't run much longer. His legs had gone numb and the pain in his chest was as sharp as a knife lodged between his ribs. His lungs felt scorched, and the spit in his mouth tasted sour and bloody.

'Back... to your house...' He gasped as he ran.

Penny came back to herself at that and pulled at his hand, her fingers like steel and crushing his bones.

'No!' She yelled. 'No way! I'm not running!'

She dragged him to a stop, but still he yanked at her like a disobedient dog on a lead.

'Are you mad?' He huffed. 'We have to go! Now!'

'Keep hold of my hand Whitey!' She replied, and dragged him in an arc to face the monster that pursued them. 'Back up onto the grass!'

They stumbled onto a space of land, mostly mud now due to the rain, that was surrounded at a distance by graves. Then she dropped to one knee, almost pulling Stephen to the ground, but still she kept his hand in a vicelike grip, his fingers turning purple in hers.

She quickly grabbed a short thick twig sitting in the wet clay and dug it into the ground, then she started to turn on the spot.

'Turn with me!' She said, her eyes wild, her mannerisms feral. Stephen did as he was told, and within a few seconds she had scored a circle around them in the mud. Then she jumped to her feet again as the spirit approached and held out the branch as if it was some kind of weapon at the ghastly woman that had now reached them.

Stephen broke out in goosebumps and waves of icy shivers shook his body as the thing came close.

'We are bound in a circle of protection!' Penny screamed at it. 'Come no further and do no harm! I bind you from touching us! In the name of God, in the names of the elements, this circle is a place of light and nothing of the shadows may enter!'

They gazed up at the abomination. A thing that looked like a photograph stretched out, too thin, too long and too tall. A distortion of a thing once human. It had a look of disgust disfiguring its face. Its eyes burned with fury. The hem of the ragged dress settled on the ground around it, and Stephen realised that its feet couldn't be touching the ground. It hovered a mere foot from them, grimacing down at them with strands of filthy hair moving around as if underwater.

'Mary.' Penny said. 'I bind you from doing harm. The circle is sacred. God protects us.'

It spoke only once. What lips it had, thin and papery and dried and dead, did not move. But, it spoke.

God is not here.

The pressure in Stephen's forehead again. A vulgar whisper inside of his head. The voice made nausea twist in his guts.

'Maybe not,' Penny said, never taking her eyes from it, 'but *I* am. And I know the old ways, Mary. Go back to the veil.'

The scream it gave them sounded more pitiful than angry. More sorrowful than malicious. It was a miserable cry that turned Stephen's heart to stone. And then, without so much as a sound or a flash, the horror was gone.

The two of them gasped for breath, frozen in place for long moments. At length, she dropped what he supposed must have been some kind of makeshift wand, and she fell down again onto her knees. This time Stephen let her drag him down too, and he collapsed beside her onto one knee. He tried to retrieve his hand again but she kept it.

'Don't...' she said between gulps of air, 'don't leave... the circle yet.'

He obeyed, running his wide eyes over a perfectly normal small village graveyard, then he found the church. The black monolith stood indifferently some distance away. Above, some stars had broken through the cloud. Lights burned in the windows of outlying houses. The world appeared to be normal, for now at least.

'How did you know that would work?' He said after a while, watching her worriedly. Her head was bowed, her free hand splayed in the mud. She shook with cold in a black dress torn at the neck. Her bootlaces were undone, and the tights above them looked like they'd been shredded by cat claws.

'I didn't.' She said from beneath a mass of wet hair. 'Told you. Faith.'

He nodded to himself, looking around again to make sure they were alone. 'Are you alright?' He said.

In response she twisted in the dirt, let go of his hand, and in one moment she'd flung herself into his arms. Her head was pressed into his chest along with her balled fists. He wrapped his arms around her and rested his chin on top of her matted hair. Kneeling, filthy, and battered, they stayed there for some time, like just another sorrowful statue decorating the yard.

'Thank you,' she said, muffled, into his chest, 'for saving me.'

He jolted with one sharp laugh.

'You kidding me? Thank *you* for saving *me*!'

She didn't laugh with him and he noted this. He looked down at her and frowned, against resting his head on hers and squeezing her tight. 'Are you hurt?'

She shook her head, but added 'scratched me though. So much for *ghosts can't hurt you*. Are you okay?'

'Scared witless, but no, no damage. Don't think my poor old battered bones could take any more. What was that, that was happening to you? I heard you screaming and I ran, and you were just... thrashing about on the floor but I couldn't see...'

'Don't wanna talk about it, Whitey.' She stopped him. 'Not for a good long time. Thank god you got to me in time. That's all I'll say.'

Stephen's features darkened. He understood enough. Enough to not speak on it further and instead comfort his friend quietly. Finally catching his breath, he changed the subject.

'So, what the hell do we do now?'

She looked up into his face with red-rimmed eyes. Her makeup was virtually gone, relegated to a few smears of white and black. She felt thin and fragile in his arms, willowy and weightless, but as far as he was concerned she was as tough as iron.

'We've come this far.' She said. 'I'm not stopping now. We get inside the church, and we finish this.'

'What if it's locked?'

'This isn't a holy place, sure as shit isn't God's house, so I say we kick the fucking doors in. Okay with you?' She said, and at last there it was; that sneaky little smile had returned along with the fire in her eyes.

He nodded and then made to move, but Penny held him fast and pressed her head back down into his chest.

'Just a few more minutes.' She said quietly. 'Just want to make the most. It's been a long time since I can say I was held.'

Stephen was all too happy to oblige.

**

The outer door of the church swung open and footsteps echoed, scratching on the dry stone floor. A flutter of damp air breezed in along with the sound, caressing the leaves of a large potted plant that decorated the vestibule, along with the pamphlets that stood in a rack upon the wall.

The young cleric had his back to the strangers that had entered. Dressed in a floor-length cassock and white collar, the bearded warden was bending to turn a large key in the lock of the inner door. He turned his head slightly at the sound and cold breeze.

'I'm sorry, the church is actually closing for the day now.' He said apologetically. 'Opening hours are from nine until five, except for Sundays, in which case it is six. *Oh!* Oh, dear me.'

He had turned to see the two people that had just walked in.

A tall thin man with slicked back hair and a large scar across his cheek stood left, dressed in a black pinstripe suit which had certainly seen better days. The knees were black with mud and the once shiny shoes below them were clotted with so much filth that they may as well have been wellingtons. His coat was askew and his shirt hung open, one of the top buttons ripped out. He had deep dark circles beneath his eyes and was as pale as a paving stone. But it was the girl to the man's right that really shocked him.

She looked as if she had been assaulted. She was as soaked and shivering as a homeless mongrel, and dare he say just as thin. Her coat was hanging off her at one shoulder, and the top of the dress beneath it had been pulled and ripped. There were three angry looking scratches on the exposed skin there. The entire bottom section of the dress was drenched with muck, and he could see from her exposed shins that the tights she had once worn were now more akin to black ribbons, barely clinging on for dear life, that cascaded in strips over her ruined boots beneath. Her hair was plastered to each side of her face, and what was left of the strange girl's makeup was a disaster scrawled across her face. Her eyes were a startling blue, but the whites of them had gone quite pink from tears.

'Lord have mercy!' The young man exclaimed hurriedly. 'What's happened to you two? Should I call the police?'

The young woman's head was lowered and she made eye contact with the warden only once before looking up at the taller man. The taller man exchanged a look with her, and elected himself to answer.

'I'm terribly sorry father,' he said, 'sorry, is it father? I'm not very good at... anyway, I must apologise for our appearance. We've had quite an evening. Well, quite a week I suppose... actually come to think of it the last month has been...'

The girl nudged him.

'Ah, right, yes.' He stammered on. 'No, no, we're both fine. Well, far from fine as you can see, but there's been no attack on us. I mean an assault. I mean, no, sorry, we *haven't* been assaulted. We just... how do I put this... we just *really* need to enter the church. Tonight. It can't wait until morning.'

The young cleric stood dumbstruck. He answered eventually.

'What on earth is this about?' His tone was less friendly now. 'I would suggest you both get yourselves indoors and, I don't know, perhaps a hospital would be more in order.'

It was the tall man's turn to look to his younger counterpart for help.

'I'm very sorry for my uncle.' She said, suddenly breaking into a delightful smile and using a posher accent than Stephen had ever heard her use. 'He's quite the nervous sort. Firstly, I must apologise for our appearance and the lateness of the hour. My name is Penelope Black, and this is my uncle Stephen. My father's brother.'

The young man's countenance changed. 'Goodness me, you're Everett Black's daughter?'

'I am indeed.' She smiled. 'It's good to know that my father's name lives on in this parish. Now, I must quickly explain; you see, I met my uncle in York this afternoon, he's visiting from... Stockton, and well, wouldn't you just trust our luck, his car broke down a few miles outside of Helmsley, and we had to make the rest of the way on foot. Terrible storm out towards Thirsk, did you hear?'

The warden blinked. 'Erm, no. No, I didn't hear. We've had nothing but a bit of drizzle here.'

'Ah!' She laughed delicately. 'Just our luck again. Well, we were trapped in a right gale, and we were making our way here, suitcases and all, and I took a bad tumble right into a deep ditch out by Rievaulx, went right through a nasty thornbush and ruined my clothes. Uncle Stephen here helped pull me out.'

'Oh, I see.' The young man said pleasantly enough, though there was suspicion on his face. 'What rotten luck. But, what brings you here, tonight?'

'I've not been able to get back here for years.' She said wistfully, looking around the foyer. 'I grew up in Canons Garth just there with my dad. I helped renovate the old medieval chapel section with him. Again I apologise for the time, we meant to arrive much sooner. I am just *so* desperate to see the old place again, if only for a moment. We could visit in the morning of course, but we've been through so much to get here, and it means so much to me, that I was hoping if I might persuade you to stay open, say, fifteen minutes longer? It would mean a very great deal to my uncle and I. Then we'll be out of your hair.'

He paused with his key still in hand, examining them and struggling with himself.

'I'd be extremely grateful for just a few minutes.' Penny added. 'And would make sure to reflect it in a generous donation.'

That clinched it. He allowed them in, unlocking the inner door again and holding it open to let them both inside. He reminded them that the rules set out by the parish priest in charge were extremely strict, so he could only allow them a few minutes at best. Once they had disappeared inside after offering enthusiastic thanks, the young man stood alone.

There was a grey payphone on the inside wall of the vestibule, as there were in many churches and social areas then, and once he was sure the two had gone he gently lifted the receiver, dropped in a ten pence piece, and dialled.

He nervously craned his head through the half open

door, trying to see the pair, as the line rang. Eventually someone answered.

'They're here. The church.' He said, and hung up.

34

The Unholy Apostle

Penny entered first with Stephen close behind.

The young warden had flipped a single light switch, activating two hanging sets of bulbs which were affixed to circular iron chandeliers, hanging by long chains from the high roof. Those lights alone were poor illumination for such a large space. It was far from the bright, warm, and vibrant place of worship that she remembered. Now it was cold, gloomy, and without a heart.

She heard Stephen exclaim a quiet *wow* behind her. He was looking at a frieze painted on the facing wall of the nave, which is the first thing one sees upon entering. It depicted colourful angels painted in the traditional way with flowing robes, huge wings, and golden halos, holding a large scroll at each end. Upon the scroll was written the names of every vicar that had served the church, as well as bishops and archbishops, along with dates stretching back as far as the fourteen hundreds. The wall had several tall arched windows of stained glass, depicting Christ and his disciples and all the usual biblical figures and saints.

They turned right into the centre of the long nave, and Penny's heart flooded with feeling. She knew every stone, every slat of wood, every inch of this place as if it had been her own home, and she hadn't set foot in it for three years.

The huge bowed ceiling was made up of such densely packed wooden planks that it more resembled the inverted underside of a Viking longboat than a church roof. The floor looked equally ancient, made of thousands of neatly made mosaic tiles of red, black and white. The usual rows of pews were on either side, and in front of them the pulpit that her father had given sermons from, day after day, for years of her life. Lectern to the right, shining with polished gold in the dimness, where Penny had stood as a child and given short biblical readings to please her dad.

At the furthest end naturally there was the altar, with high candles and a huge golden cross with a stained glass tryptic depicting Christ, Mary, and his followers.

To Stephen it looked like any village church, and secretly he hated it as he was never one for churches, finding them to be morbid, miserable places. To Penny it was like seeing her father resurrected. She tried not to cry, for she hated being visibly vulnerable, and would have succeeded had she not just been through such a traumatic event.

She sniffed in the dark. Stephen kept a respectful distance and waited.

To the left of the nave, close to the altar steps, there were two huge supportive pillars, circular with ornately carved summits, which made of themselves an arch.

'It's through there.' She pointed. Her voice, even kept so low, echoed continually around the huge space.

Stephen moved to her side and peered through the dusty darkness to where she had indicated. 'The chapel you and your father discovered?'

She nodded as they walked slowly towards it, casting long gloomy shadows across sandstone from the dull chandeliers overhead, until they were leaving the light behind.

It didn't reach this secluded area. The small chapel room, the oldest part of the church, once walled in and lost to time, had now been restored into a chapel just as decorously complete as the rest of the church. The many windows, once bricked up, were now made of colourful stained glass, brand new and vivid. Where once there'd been a simple medieval stone altar there was now a tall elaborate wooden plinth with a large sculpture of Jesus hanging from a cross, surrounded by candles and crests. Above it was the old wall, just as it'd been in Penny's recollection; a huge red dragon to represent the devil, a serene Christ in white robes, and monks and saints and all the rest. The final strokes of the painting had been completed with a brush held by a hand some five hundred years dead.

It had pews of its own now, the walls were freshly painted alabaster white, there were bibles on every seat, and it looked just about as far from an evil place as one could imagine.

'Well,' Stephen remarked, standing at the edge of the room with Penny, 'it certainly doesn't look like a gateway to hell.'

Somehow he heard her roll her eyes in the dark.

'Not like the movies, already told you.' She replied. 'I can feel it though.'

'What does it feel like?'

She paused for a moment, and the heavy stillness settled on them unnervingly. He felt exposed somehow. He felt the age of the room, and the centuries of life, death and suffering that it had housed.

'It feels like...' she said, searching, '... like a grave. Like a deep grave, and just as hopeless'

'Well, couldn't that just be...' and he pointed down to the graves that made up the floor at their feet. A huge jigsaw of tombs belonging to past clerics, whose bones lay in deep dark silence far below them. Penny shook her head and offered him her hand.

'Should be interesting.' She said, wiggling her fingers once. 'And by interesting I mean we'd better brace ourselves. I've got no idea what our gift will show us in a place like this.'

'I do wish you'd stop calling it that.' He muttered in reply.

Far on the south side of the building, too far for the pair to hear, the inner church door gently closed and a key turned in the lock.

Stephen raised his hand to take hers, but paused before they touched.

'Say our connection shows us the portal, shows us… this neverborn *thing*, what are we supposed to do then? We've got no way to fight it. Look what happened the last time we got a glimpse of it.' And he pointed to his scar.

'Less questions, more action, Whitey.' She said firmly. 'Remember what I said – keep your head and hold my hand. That's your only job. I'm a believer, a medium, a witch, and more than all of that I have faith in powers far greater than me, you, or anything in this miserable little world. We have the divine on our side. Look how far we've come.'

He had no reply other than to nod resignedly.

In unison they both took a deep, preparatory breath.

Then their fingers touched.

And were immediately yanked apart again.

They both stared wide eyed at their hands, and then at one another.

'What the *fuck* was that?' Stephen immediately hissed.

She just shook her head in disbelief. Her mouth an O, her eyes crazed. She swallowed dryly and said 'okay. Okay. Wow, okay. So, maybe I was wrong. Maybe it *is* a bit like the movies.'

'Seriously though,' Stephen stammered, taking one step back, 'did you see what I just saw?'

'I did.'

The room around them suddenly shifted, ever so slightly. It felt like the solid stone stillness around them took a breath. The slow, groaning breath of something that hadn't taken air for centuries. The walls seemed to expand and contract, though they didn't physically move, and the air around them seemed to swirl in an icy rush of air. The room fell silent again.

Penny looked around them, scanning the walls and the dark corners of the ceiling. Something indistinct stirred with the sound of deep stone rumbling, yet there was no evidence that anything had moved at all.

Then it fell to stillness and silence again.

Stephen just stared at her. He didn't dare to look anywhere else. His eyes were white circles in the dark, popping from his skull. Behind her, her shadow mingled with the gritty darkness there so that she appeared to be standing in a total void.

'What was that?' He whispered so low it could have been the wind.

She shrugged in response, and as she did Stephen noticed something.

Her shadow didn't shrug.

His eyes shifted to the black silhouette behind her, and his jaw fell slowly open.

She saw his expression, made to turn, but stopped herself. Then she seemed to feel something. Something at her back. Something pressing against her. Something cold and dead.

Before either of them could speak or make a sound Penny lurched forward as if pushed hard, and with a yelp she toppled forwards. Instead of reaching forward to catch her, Stephen leapt back as something sharp and cold shot through his heart. He cried out in fear as Penny hit the stone floor, almost losing his footing and stumbling against the wall of the old chapel.

The black shadow gained form and started to shuffle past Penny and towards him.

It began to wheeze. A wet, rattling wheeze. Air being sucked painfully into ruined lungs, full of fluid. It coughed loud, audibly in the room, and it echoed with horrific resonance all around.

It was then that Stephen realised that it hadn't been a shadow at all. The figure was black because it was covered in something. It was a human form, smothered from head to toe in a viscous black fluid. If it had eyes then Stephen couldn't make them out, nor could he see any other features than the yawning chasm of its mouth. The teeth inside were black and green and decaying, and the tongue was rotten from the root, bloody and dripping. Again it drew a wheezing breath, choked, and spewed out a thick yellow gob of phlegm, marbled scarlet, with the next rattling cough.

A low scream broke from Stephen's throat, rising to a bellowing cry, and he scrambled away from the entity, backing away and unable to draw his eyes away from it. Then the stench hit him.

The thing reeked of chemicals, sharp and stinging to the eyes. It smelt like ammonia and acid, like paint stripper and petrol, like burnt plastic and molten rubber. Like...

... like the smells that would drift across the fields that he played on as a child, chemicals from the factory that his...

Dad. Stephen didn't speak the word but he mouthed it in absolute horror.

The thing advanced, retching and spewing up more foul smelling puss. Breath full of asbestos and blood clots. Hands with black melted fingers, reaching, blindly searching for him. Stephen continued to stumble away from it, half mad with panic, but he managed to find his voice again and howled 'you are *not my dad!*'

But it kept coming, and everything in Stephen told him that this thing *must not touch him.* If it touched him it would infect him. It would burn him. It would poison him.

He fully turned from the monstrosity and ran full pelt down the length of the nave, beneath the chandeliers, and towards the door.

Penny pulled herself up, swearing loudly before calling after him. She watched him running like a madman. But... what was he running from? He just kept glancing back in terror as he bolted. She called his name again and started after him. It was clear that he could see something she couldn't.

'Stop running!' She called. 'Whitey! Stop! Whatever it is, it's just trying to scare you out of here! Wait!'

But just as she reached the pulpit at the base of the altar, something materialised between her and her friend, and she stopped dead.

Every hair on her body stood on end and she rippled with static electricity.

A priest. A devil.

It was clad in a long white chasuble stained with slashes

of bright red blood. Beneath it it was dressed in a traditional black cassock that shone and glistened with gore in the half-light. The white dog collar was crimson.

Its head was a skull. Eyeless, lipless, fleshless. It grinned blankly at her above a flesh and blood body. The white bleached bone had been drenched red and was dripping all over the holy garments below. In a soaking hand it held a black bible with a silver cross on the cover, and the cross was upside down. The other hand it held up, close to its unbreathing chest, a closed fist with the thumb, forefinger, and middle finger raised. The traditional gesture that represented a teacher, of holiness. But there was nothing holy nor sacred here.

This is our fault, Penelope. It said without speaking. Her head buzzed with words as black as death. *We set it free. We woke it.*

Penny dreamt about her father most nights, and remembered his voice as clearly as if she'd heard it yesterday. This was a vile mockery of that voice. A vile mockery of the father she had admired and loved. She froze on the spot and stared the spirit down.

'How dare you stand where he stood, how dare you use his voice.' She said in a tone as sharp as glass. 'You are not welcome here, and you are not my father. Why won't you leave? Why won't you go back beyond the veil. You don't belong here.'

The intense shadows of empty sockets studied her. It kept its obscene posture like a mannequin.

I am an unholy apostle. It rattled around her brain like a frantic insect. *Sent to perform works in the name of the one that devours.*

'You're being held by it.' She countered. 'I can set you free.'

Blood started to pour from between the pages of the bible it held. It ran like a wound, pattering and soaking into the tiles around black shoes containing dead feet. The smell was coppery and sour. Still, Penny glared at the grinning skull without flinching.

We are dominion. It said. *We are pestilence and pain, abortion and disease, the rape and ruin of angels. You cannot comprehend us. But, you will join us.*

And then the entity vanished along with the stink and the blood, and Penny was left staring across the empty nave towards the door, where she could see Stephen and the men that held him.

35

Skirmish

A man with white hair and a farmer's cap was holding a pocketknife to Stephen's throat. His eyes looked black in the dim light beneath heavy eyebrows. Standing behind Stephen, he had one arm bracing him across the chest and the other pressing the blade to his throat. It flashed when it caught the chandelier light. There were two other men too. One, an overweight younger man with a round face, and the other a wiry lad with greasy hair and acne-marked skin. The two of them were holding Stephen by the arms.

'Been meanin' to catch up with you, lass.' Ned Bailey said, his voice low and threatening. Penny stepped as close and she dared and stopped, glancing once behind her to make sure that nothing else was coming.

Lost as these spirits, these boys were, and just as enslaved to the evil that diseased this place. Penny watched them and said nothing.

'If it weren't for this daft young'un,' he nodded his head at an ashamed looking Dave, the youngest of them, 'sending Mr White here your way, then we wouldn't be all in this fix. Mind you, he's paid his fee for his transgression.

Dave's thin hand was bandaged, but dirty and brown with dried blood. It was clear from a glance that his little finger was missing from the way that he was holding Stephen's arm.

'Anyroad,' Ned continued, 'that's by the by. Point is, we're in this mess now. We gave you a chance as well, Mr White, we let you off lightly and saw you out of town. Now, why would you go and come back?'

Stephen was ghastly white, and looked like he was in pain. His eyes, glassy and huge, stared only at Penny as he replied.

'We have to stop it.' He said in a thin, pained voice. 'It's making you do this. Just like it made you kill all those people.'

'But we can stop it.' Penny came in. 'Me and Stephen. *We* can stop it. You don't know what you're doing. This thing has ground you down and worn you out and now it controls you, but this *isn't you* Ned. You're not murderers. I remember you from when dad was alive. Just… just let us help; Stephen and me. We can help you. We can help everyone.'

Penny heard movement to the right of the door where the men held Stephen. She glanced, and there in the shadows was the young warden that had let them in. His hands were clasped, his head was down, his eyes were closed.

If he was indeed praying, then it wasn't to god.

'Here's what's going to happen.' Ned said. 'You, little lass, are going to come over here. Then the two of you are coming with us to the van outside. We're going for a little drive.'

The cold tickled at Penny's back. The portal. Endlessness. A void of unimaginable horror so close by she could taste it. All she had to do was close it and this would all be over. But she couldn't do it without Stephen.

She knew what she had to do. The moment that their hands had touched, just for that split second, she knew what they had to do. Because what they had seen was…

'What if we say no?' Stephen said, his voice shaking. 'What if we won't go with you? It's not like you can just...'

'We kill the both of you, right here.' Ned said. 'Then we close the church for renovations for a week, clean up our mess, and put you both in the ground. No one will question it. No one will suspect anything. No one will remember it. No one will remember *you*. This place, it makes you forget.'

Sam held out a thick, stubby hand to Penny. 'Best do as he says, eh?'

She looked from the hand, to Stephen, to Ned. The air grew heavier and colder still. The church breathed again, and an eddy of icy wind made the chandeliers sway.

'Why do you do this?' Penny ignored the hand, and started to pace back and forth over a short patch of marble. 'What's in it for you? It doesn't make sense.'

The young lad, Dave, spoke up. 'It spares us.' He simply said. 'We surrender and do as we're bid, and we're spared.'

Stephen hung by the arms in their grip and listened. He felt the tight band of Ned's wiry arm pressed across his chest like rope, and the keen cold metal of the blade lightly touching his rapidly pumping jugular. It must have been the fear that was causing the strange cold sweat he felt, that had sapped the strength from his limbs. He felt distant and dreamy, as if he was watching this happen in a movie or in his sleep. At least he'd been spared the beating this time, he supposed. Now it would just be one simple drag of a blade and he would watch a flood of claret pour from him like a fountain before blacking out very permanently. Worse ways to go, he mused. Certainly not the one he'd envisaged for himself. In his strange moment of calm he pondered how pointless this all had been. All of this magic and predestination, all this business with cosmic twins and spiritual awakening, and for what? Just to be murdered at the final hurdle? *That* was his divine destiny? More importantly, he gave up drinking for *this?*

'If you let Mr White go, *everyone* will be spared. Get it?' Penny was saying. 'We can stop it, but only together. After that you can go about your lives without, oh, I don't know, *fucking murdering people*! Everyone will be free of it!'

Stephen was limp in Ned's arms now and his vision was blurry. How strange. Was he blacking out? Regardless, he was still aware of himself enough to realise that one of the hands that held his arms was slackening. Was it Dave or Sam? Didn't matter, he supposed. Maybe whoever it was was actually listening to Penny.

It was almost comical, this. How had he drifted so far into a realm of absolute lunacy? He'd been an editor, hadn't he? He lived in a flat, he went to the pub, he watched TV, didn't he? He didn't have ghosts attacking him and divine interventions and a destiny to stop a demonic force feeding on the souls of the dead. That was Dungeons and Dragons territory, wasn't it? They were still arguing when Stephen felt the hand, the one that held his right arm, drift down the material of his shirt as if it was going limp.

It was a bandaged hand.

And then he just moved. Timid, broken little Stephen White forgot the man that he was supposed to have been and he moved. Despite the knife to his throat, despite being outnumbered, he did something that he never thought he'd ever witness himself doing.

Stephen fought.

He slipped down and threw his head back and the blade of the knife scraped his jawbone. He pushed his weight against Ned, throwing him back against the door and pinning him there, at the same time wrenching his arm free from the dirty bandaged hand of Dave, who in response tried to grab at him. Stephen grabbed Dave's arm and, like some sort of ghoulish vampire, he bared his teeth and bit as hard as he could into Dave's damaged hand. He aimed his jaws straight at the patch of dried blood on the soil-tasting bindings, and felt a crunch as his teeth closed over the freshly severed stump of his finger. Dave screamed in such a high pitch that the air seemed to vibrate. Had there been a glass it may well have splintered at the tone.

He couldn't see where the knife had gone but he took this moment of chaos to flip his head back as hard as he could, feeling the back of his head strike Ned Bailey's red and swollen nose so hard that it emitted a loud short crack. He heard the knife hit the ground with a high musical clatter.

Sam, the bigger man, did not let go of his left arm. Instead, while the other two fell back clutching their wounds, he swung Stephen around to face him with a strength that made him fear his arm would break. His other hand became a fist, rushing at Stephen's face. That was all he got the chance to see. The next moment was a flash of light and the high ringing pitch of tinnitus, and then Stephen felt as if he was floating in outer space.

Everything fell to silence for a matter of seconds before the screaming and grunting and scuffling of feet came thundering back into his ears. Stephen was on the church floor. He opened his eyes.

'Whitey, come on!' Penny screeched.

He scrabbled up onto his feet. Dave was rolling on the floor, his face in floods of agonised tears, gripping a bandaged hand that now poured with blood. Ned's neat white moustache was now red, and he held his nose with a shaking hand as bloodshot eyes glared at him. Sam, the burliest of them, was on the floor, and he wasn't moving. When Stephen looked back at Penny she was holding a large golden crucifix in two hands, which she now dropped to the tiles with a deep metallic *clang*. Then, she started to sprint away from them and back towards the small chapel. She screamed for him to follow her, and without a thought he did.

Their boots hammered at the tiles across the length of the church until he'd caught up with her. They were once again standing in the smaller renovated space with the medieval altar and paintings. The home of this supposed portal. Stephen turned back and he saw them coming.

Ned had retrieved his knife and it swung in a bloody hand as he dashed for them, his face drenched red and his eyes crazed. Beside him was Dave, brandishing the same crucifix that Penny had just dropped, his face purple with pain but his teeth gritted with fury. Back by the door, Sam began to stir.

Stephen couldn't get his breath. It felt as if an elephant was using his chest for a stool. Sweating bullets and as white as milk, he tried to say that there was no way out, but Penny was already hollering at him.

'Do you trust me?' She demanded, and she held out both her hands. The she repeated 'Do you *trust me*, Stephen?'

Dave and Ned were upon them now, and their makeshift weapons were raised.

Stephen, mute and gasping for air, just nodded. And with that Penny grabbed both of his hands in hers.

And then Ned and Dave were gone. The church was gone. Helmsley was gone. The world as they had known it was gone.

And a new world waited.

36

Neverborn

It was the heat that Stephen felt first. Before he could see anything, the smothering humidity overwhelmed his senses. His mind flashed back to his only time abroad, when he had stepped from a cool air-conditioned plane out onto the runway of an astonishingly hot Spanish afternoon. But this was different.

The air was... wet. Damp, slick and hot and suffocating. But, they were not outdoors. There was no sun here. No natural light of any kind. He could feel the very air (was it even air?) leaving a slick residue on his skin like slime, like some organic fluid, like saliva, like some kind of putrid discharge. And the smell, *dear god* the smell. It was like nothing to which he could give comparison. The best he could come up with was, whenever he breathed (was he breathing?) it smelled like what he imagined the inside of a bowel smelled like. A diseased one, at that. Sulphur. Rotten eggs. Sewers. Sickeningly sweet and bitter all at once. Was this perhaps some kind of horrible organic prison? A womb. A corpulent holding cell.

Were they *inside* something?

The fear was deeper than physical. The fear cut so

deeply that it infested his very soul, his very mind, everything that made him *him,* and he shook with it.

He could still feel Penny's hands in his, and – *oh thank you, thank you God* – the assurance it gave him was tremendous. She was the last sane thing to cling to here. The only thing left that was good. He squeezed the hands, and the hands squeezed back.

He tried to speak to her but he found that he couldn't. Things were too indistinct here for him to be able to tell, but he wasn't sure that he was breathing, or even whether he was real. It had the quality of a nightmare, where nothing made sense and the laws of physics were irrelevant. So he opened his mouth – or where he imagined his mouth must still be – and nothing came out.

Can you hear me? It was Penny's voice, but he hadn't heard it. It just *was.*

He didn't know how to respond. He opened his mouth but, again, the idea of speech seemed impossible.

Focus on me. The Penny voice said without speaking. *Think aloud. See the words in your head in the order you want to think them. Visualise.*

The oppressive warmth clung to his skin like paste. He felt smothered on all sides, but there was space here too. They weren't in a sack or a bag or a casing or some kind, they were in a space, like a room. Too hard to say for sure. Nothing was consistent.

I'm so scared. Stephen said. He saw the words, even spelled them out in his mind like words rushing by his eyes as quick as speech.

Me too. She replied.

Where are we? Jesus Christ Penny, where the hell *are we?*

I don't know. But, do you remember when we touched

earlier, just for that second? We saw the same thing, right?

The floor, or whatever it was, beneath his feet felt smooth and soft. Was he wearing shoes? Did he even have feet? This was maddening. No, this was horrible, this was... he had to get out of here. He couldn't do this. He needed air. He needed the cold. He needed to feel something.

Just keep holding my hands. She squeezed harder. *Focus on me. Tell me, what did we see?*

He was panicking, most definitely. But could he feel his heart racing? Was he tingling with nerves? Was he sweating? No.

The portal. He said. *Or... an opening? It wasn't a door, it wasn't a swirling thing like... like you said they make in the movies... it was...*

A membrane. Penny agreed. *A veil. Something made of flesh, and somehow not flesh at all. Just... something else, something we can't understand. I think our brains just did their best to process what we were looking at. Just like now. Wherever we are, whatever this is, it might not be what we perceive it to be. Whatever the truth of it is, one fact's solid; we are definitely here.*

But were they? Stephen didn't *feel* real. He felt Penny's hands, yes, but was he really feeling *skin* touching his? He didn't know. He didn't know anything anymore. His brain was firing erratically and in all directions and he couldn't compose a single rational thought. All he knew for certain was this:

He didn't feel like he was in a physical body anymore.

There was no pain. His head didn't ache. The pressure on his chest was gone along with the pain in his heart that had been streaking across his chest. His jaw didn't ache from Sam's ample fist, and he wasn't in a feverishly cold sweat anymore. He didn't feel anything at all in fact, but he knew that he was real, and himself.

Are we dead? He said. *Are we ghosts?*

Penny seemed to consider this for some time. The heat pressed on. Stephen's whole body felt coated in jelly. He squirmed uncomfortably, but he wouldn't let go of Penny. Not now, probably never again.

I think, Penny said slowly, *that our physical bodies are still in the church. I think – and this is a guess, an educated one, but still a total guess – that we're projecting. That we're travelling. These are our astral bodies. So no, we're not dead, but we're not exactly alive either.*

Stephen broke into quick, panicked speech.

What, so Ned and his cronies could be stabbing me to death right now? He exclaimed. *Sam could be stoving your head in with that gold crucifix! We could be dying right now! Or, dead even!*

Penny shrugged. Except she didn't.

Does that matter now? Was her simple reply. *We're here now. That's all that matters. We had a destiny, me and you, and I think that destiny was clearly for us to be here, now, connected. We're on the other side. I think... no I feel that this is the only place where we can really, truly do something to stop this thing. Out there, in the physical, we're powerless.*

Stephen stepped closer to her. Perhaps he could feel the soft wet floor sliding beneath his feet, perhaps it even made a sound similar to walking through a puddle on a rainy day, or perhaps his brain was just telling him that. Whatever was real or not, he drew close to Penny and felt her body there, and they held one another. The top of her head was under his chin, and her little form was pressed against his chest. She was real and she was here with him, and he surged with comfort.

We must not let go of one another. She said. *Not for one second. If we do, I feel like we'll be lost to one another and we won't find our way back. So don't let go, ok?*

Never. Came his quick reply.

A third response came then. Something outside of them. Something *most certainly not* them. It laughed. Just once; just a single sound of amusement. It sounded close, but everything sounded close in this humid, confined space.

The pair of them stiffened.

What the fuck was that? Stephen thought in words so large they eclipsed all else. *I can't see anything. Why can't I see anything? We need to be able to see at least, otherwise...*

The room, the space, whatever it was, shifted and contracted ever so slightly. The floor gave a little tremble, and the air around them gave a swirl and a rush of a hot breeze.

Just like in the church.

Well, Penny reasoned as she spoke, *we don't even have eyes to see, do we? We aren't physical things anymore. But we can touch and feel, can't we? We can hear one another, right? Because we choose to! So... so if we choose to... then why can't we...*

See! Stephen finished her sentence, followed her logic, and activated something in himself he never knew was there, all in one instant.

And then, just like that, he could see. So could Penny. The darkness evaporated and a sourceless light, soft and muted, surrounded them.

The two broke their embrace but kept their hands firmly gripped, and they looked at one another.

Penny was dressed in the same clothes that she'd been wearing before, but now they weren't ripped and muddy and askew. She wasn't wearing the corpse-like makeup that was her trademark, and her hair was straight and clean and long. There were no scratches or wounds of any kind on her that Stephen could see. And... did she look younger? A little, at least.

She smiled at Stephen brightly. He was in the pinstripe suit he'd been wearing too, but it was immaculate and pressed and clean. There was no scar on his face. He was no longer as thin and emaciated as he'd appeared before, and his skin was even, smooth, and healthier than it had ever looked. His bright eyes lit up at the sight of her, but his smile wasn't as wide. He most certainly looked younger than he had, by a great deal. His hair had not a strand of grey in it, and was thicker than she'd ever seen it. He now looked somewhere around thirty.

They studied one another in awe, but it was short lived.

They pried their eyes from one another and looked around their new environment.

This was the church. But this was not the church.

It was the same shape, same size, and had the same proportions as the building they'd been standing in, but it was nothing short of a disgusting, horrific mockery of the holy place it mimicked.

The walls were flesh. Where there should have been stone and marble there was raw meat. Uneven and organic, running with clear fluid and thin bloody trails that pooled. It had blue veins inside the skinned translucent surface, and arteries too; thick tubes that were purple and bloated, trailing like cables across the smooth wall of the flesh and then sinking deep into the muscle and white streaks of fat.

The floor beneath their boots was the same material, and where the wall met the floor there was no corners, just curves. The whole structure was made of unbroken, greasy organic matter. And again it moved.

A ripple ran across the floor, and the flesh shuddered like a mini-earthquake, then the ripple, like a wave, went up the walls in a slick roll, reaching the obscene pointed arches of the roof. Hot air rushed through the space, churning around them before settling again.

They turned together on the spot too stunned to think, let alone speak to one another, and faced the small medieval chapel.

This was different. The repulsively glossy and un-angled shape of the real-life room was still the same, but there was no plinth or steps, or anything else that the physical counterpart contained. The room contained only one thing, and no matter how much Stephen stared at it, his brain couldn't make sense of the information his eyes were feeding it.

There was a huge, roughly circular... *something* there. It wasn't set into a wall, it wasn't on the floor, it was just... there. Hovering? No, not hovering. It was in place in the air, but it was part of the air too. It was there and not there. That was the best he could do with what he was seeing.

It pulsed and surged, moved and throbbed, undulated and grew and shrank. It was huge, too. Stephen could have easily driven his car through it, though that was not a thought he liked to entertain. It seemed to be made of flesh too, or rather, like an opening in flesh. Like, as Penny had said, a membrane. A thinning of skin. An obscene breach.

This place is alive. Penny said. *It used to be something else. It used to be clean and ethereal, but then* that *opened.* And she pointed to the opening.

This is the portal. Stephen stated.

More like a wound. She added. *And something came through it, and it contaminated this realm and it made it its own. Hell spilling over.*

He swallowed nervously. Except he didn't.

Hell, like hell with a capital H? He said. *As in, the devil, and demons, and eternal suffering and all of that?*

I think it's more than that. She answered. *Remember*

what I said about The Great Big What If? All faiths, all spiritual beliefs and realities, are aspects of the same thing. The great, unknowable infiniteness of realms beyond our understanding. The divine, but also the impure. The unholy. Evil, Whitey. We're looking at evil.

They stared at it, transfixed by its hideous life and pulsing power. The room shifted again, and the hot sticky air rushed. Stephen glanced to the right of the horror they were studying and saw the arteries and veins pulse along with the portal. Black arterial blood rushed through tubing, veins stood out for a beat and stopped again. He felt sick, more repulsed than he had ever felt in his life.

This is not the dwelling place of spirits, Penny said, *at least, it shouldn't be. This is a place designed by something never human. Something else, far worse than anything any human can imagine. This... this is way bigger than I thought it'd be. I don't know. I don't know if we should be here.*

Fear and disgust ran cold through Stephen. He couldn't stand to be here anymore. He couldn't stand the heat, the stink, the flesh and veins. This stuff, whatever it was, that drifted invisible in the air and settled on your skin like warm biological mucus. He couldn't stand to look at it anymore. He closed his eyes, but they didn't seem to. No matter what he did, he had to continue to look. He could see through his own eyelids. He couldn't bear that they were standing inside some kind of great lung. Some abomination, alive, and pulsing, breathing and feeding...

Feeding? Why had that word come to him?

Stephen's eyes went like saucers and his jaw went slack. He turned his face to Penny and his eyes bore into hers with a look that was so absolutely horrified it made her start.

This isn't a realm. He said. *This isn't a place at all. It wasn't designed by anything.*

She searched his face. *What do you mean? What is it, then?*

His eyes drifted away from hers and across the malevolent architecture of this living, breathing, scornful church.

This is the Neverborn. He said. *We're inside it.*

37

The Minister and his Parishioners

A demon as infection. A parasite spewed out through a portal that lead to a place unthinkable, poisoning the territory it had sprung into. Spreading like a disease far faster and more deadly than most, and the worst of it; it did so with intelligent intention. It had spread itself, infesting every inch of everything it could touch. It had not only corrupted this place, it had *become* this place. A vast unknowable entity, eternal, powerful beyond imagination, and made entirely of pure evil.

And Stephen and Penny were standing inside it.

The ground has gone bad, the custodian had said. Neither of them had realised now literally he'd meant it. This place, realm, whatever one wants to call it, one that mirrored its real life equal, had been engulfed and contaminated by it. A being that wanted to stay, tethered as it was to this portal, this part of *itself* that was the doorway, so that it could feast. And feast it had, for centuries.

We've walked right into the lion's mouth. Penny said. *It's got us.*

Let's just go back! Let's just get out of here! Stephen shook her hands, bringing her eyes back to his. Just... do whatever it is you did to get us here and reverse it!

Those eyes were pouring with anxiety when she said *I can't. I didn't do anything. I just had a hunch.*

A hunch?

That we needed to join on this particular spot, and then... I don't bloody know, Whitey, I'm making this up as I go, just like you. I don't know how to get back.

What the hell happened to 'keep your head and hold my hand'? Stephen yelled without yelling. *What about 'trust me, I'm a witch with the divine on my side' and all that other shit you were shovelling?*

She was about to answer when something new caught her eye. Movement on the ground. Shadows.

Her eye followed the vague shapes as they began to move. They had no firm outline and they were faint but they were definitely moving. And then she realised that there was illumination here, all around them, and that they had created the illumination.

Just by wanting it, they had *created* it.

But then, before she could follow the idea further, her eyes had tracked the long shadows to their source, and she saw the ones casting them.

Stephen saw her face and then he followed the tracking of her eyes.

The spirits were coming.

They walked, a multitude in silhouette, with a faint bioluminescent light behind them through the thick, putrid air. Monsters, rotten and bloated, crooked and limping. Some were so decayed that they were little more than animate skeletons. They filled the church from wall to wall like an unholy congregation, and they were coming towards them.

Stephen started to see faces he recognised.

Millie. Old Mrs Wood was close to the front of the crowd. She stared with white, pupilless eyes, just as all of her fellows did. Clots of dried blood ran in dry riverbeds down her ruined face from the appalling wound in her head. Her brain, visible, was pulsing in the cold vessel of her skull. She was still in her gore-soaked dressing gown and her blue feet in pink slippers slapped across the moist floor. Beside her walked a man with a full beard and thinning hair, as thin as sticks in baggy work overalls. The dungarees were black and covered in thick soot, which danced in the air around him. That had to be Jack.

Others, Stephen had never seen. There were children amongst them. Girls and boys in nightdresses and little suits from a time long gone. Some had wounds which still bled; a knife wound to the heart, or slit wrists that ran red. Others were just pale blue and soaked through from a drowning, or stumbled on broken limbs from an accident. There were more adults than kids. Some skeletal and starved to death; sunken-cheeked with bulging, frightened eyes and lipless mouths, with concave stomachs and ribs poking out like blades. Others walked with their heads slumped to one side, lolloping and disconnected. Broken necks and rope burns. And then Stephen saw the bride.

She was further back but she was unmistakable.

Her veil, yellowed with time, was stained with acidic vomit at the mouth which ran in a green and black river down the length of her dress, it swished through the damp air as she walked on staggering feet. Her matted hair crawled with lice which fell to the floor all around her, just like it had in The Black Swan.

The pair watched the flock coming, and were too frozen with fear to do a thing but watch.

There was The Green Lady. Standing twice as high as the others, she towered over the group with whisps of hair dancing around a skull tight with grey skin. A rotting horror with hands like bird claws, reaching.

Penny gasped and Stephen looked to her, then he followed her eyes.

A grotesquely overweight thug was coming with the gathering, walking a little separately from them at the far left. He was dressed in an ill-fitting frockcoat, complete with frilled sleeves and stockings. A white wig, stained and askew, was dancing on the top of his bulbous head as he lurched and lumbered. His face was purple and pockmarked, his teeth were black – no, made of wood – and the smirk that housed them was as sinister in its intent as that of a crocodile. His eyes were black. Mirrorless, empty, black.

Penny shrank back, pulling Stephen with her. She never took her eyes from the horde.

Is that the one that tried to... Stephen began, *... that assaulted you?*

She nodded and said *Villiers.*

To their back was the portal room, and the disgusting swarm was shuffling towards them with the main (and only) doors behind them. There was nowhere to go. Penny pulled him towards the altar at the head of the nave. They backed towards it, making their way with extreme care up the fleshy steps that mimicked the sanctuary, their crazed eyes fixed on the ghosts.

We are not dead! Penny projected the words, but they weren't directed at Stephen. She was looking up at the roof. *We are not dead! You can't have us! You can't touch us!*

The room, or rather, the gigantic organism shaped like one, shook violently. The slick ground bobbed with fat and churning blood and the two stumbled against one another. The walls vibrated and spasmed, and the length of the church isle became a wind tunnel. A gale of hot air whistled down the nave, across the heads of the walking dead, and whirled around them like a hurricane. Stephen and Penny were thrown about, slamming into one another like marionettes, their hands still firmly locked.

She fell awkwardly, almost pulling him over with her. He guided her back to her feet as the strange convulsions of the room became still again.

Don't let go of me, no matter what it does. She said.

He pulled her close. *What was that? A response?*

Penny began to answer but then she spun on her heels, dragging him with her, and she screamed.

The horde was upon them.

So close that they could reach out with bony hands and touch them, the entire group – how many there were was impossible to tell, they seemed to somehow stretch on forever into the distance, even though they were standing in a finite room – had come to a stop at the foot of the scarlet stairs. Rows and rows of white, dead eyes stared at them.

Stephen trembled down to the marrow of his bones. Penny just glared at them. Even as terrified as she must surely have been, she stood fast against them and stared right back. With narrow eyes she looked across a sea of lifeless faces.

Speak! She demanded.

They just stared, as still as the grave.

Behind the pair was the space that should have been occupied by the altar itself. It was simply a mass of flesh and muscle, crudely square like an oblong box, with no candles nor a crucifix to speak of. They backed away together until their spines were pressing against it. Stephen felt the damp warmth of the living tissue touching him, and every fibre of his being tingled with nauseous revulsion.

Speak then! One of you! She demanded again. *What happens now? You stare us to death, or what? I tell you again, we are not dead! We are alive and we're here to free you!*

You are His now, came a voice in their heads, *dead or not, you are one of us.*

Stephen looked the congregation over and saw no one step forward, no one gestured, no face became animated.

Who is speaking? Penny called, her voice loud and surging in Stephen's brain.

I, came the voice again, and this time the tones were not echoing all around the insides of their skulls, but rather the words were pressing upon the backs of their heads.

They turned together and saw the figure that was standing behind them, high on the altar, looking down.

Penny's father, Everett, smiled at them broadly from behind a clean white beard. His eyes glistened blue in the pale light, and his dark, flushed complexion told of a man who had enjoyed the outdoors. He was wearing a traditional black cassock and white collar, and his hands were politely folded against his chest. He looked every bit as real, alive and well as any living person.

Stephen held his young friend close, wrapping his fingers tightly through hers, as she stared agape at the thing on the altar.

You are not my father. She said in a voice that was so calmly threatening it took Stephen aback. *Stop taunting me with his form.*

Still smiling, the priest stepped down from the box and walked past them to the edge of the steps. Stephen glared at the side of his head. The neatly combed hair and the lines of his face, the pockmarks, the pores. The perfect, human detail of him. He looked alive.

The priest then raised a hand to his profane flock and they began to step backwards in unison, spacing themselves out, giving him room. He turned to face Penny with the ghosts at his back.

You've grown, Penelope. He observed, smiling fondly.

Stop it! Her composure was slipping. *Stop using his face and his voice! What are you, really? Name yourself!*

He raised his tufty white eyebrows and said *I do not mock you. I thought that this form would please you.*

Lies. This thing, whatever it was, knew it was the opposite and it revelled in it.

Who are you? Stephen said now, shoving his terror deep down and daring to look into the eyes of something that appeared harmless but was anything but. This wasn't a man with blue eyes and kind features. It was a vastness he couldn't comprehend.

As old as the stars.

Names do not matter here. They are empty things. The priest said. *I am but a part of a greater whole. I, in this hour, am a voice. His voice.*

Stephen threw a desperate glance at the thrumming impossibility of the portal, a tear in the flesh and a tear in time and space itself. He was half tempted, in a moment of insanity, to grab the priest and try to throw him in.

Whose voice? Penny said.

Our great father, the priest went on, his lips never moving over his rictus grin, *he keeps us, and in turn we keep him. He is fed and we serve. Our congregation grows ever greater. We are legion. And now, Penelope, Stephen, you too have joined our flock.*

You don't belong here. Penny said. *You never did, and you've fed enough. We're here to send you back. Let these souls go. Go back to whatever pit is meant for you.*

He laughed delicately. The same single laugh they'd heard in the earlier darkness.

I go where I please, I do as I wish, I take what delights me. He said. *Stop me? There is no such concept. How singular you are.*

He walked out among the spirits as he continued to speak, occasionally touching one of them gently, affectionately, on the shoulder. As he did so each one lowered their heads in a reverent bow.

As I consume I learn and I grow, he said, *each soul that I acquire strengthens me and widens my influence.*

He stopped at the bride, and smiled at her as if she was his own daughter. He reached to lift her veil.

Stephen had already had enough nightmares about what must be underneath that bridal shroud, and he tried to look away but just couldn't will himself to move.

She had large, pretty eyes, glassy and searching. Pleading eyes, and somehow perhaps even trusting. Innocent eyes that didn't understand what had happened to her. Everything below those eyes was in ruins. She had no bottom jaw whatsoever. It had completely melted away to a bloody nub, a few of her top teeth remained, and her top lip hung in semi-liquified tatters. Her nose was little more than two hollows.

Everett ran a loving finger down one side of her cheekbone before he turned back to Penny and Stephen. Standing among them he looked every bit the faithful minister among his parishioners. He raised both his arms and formed a cross of himself.

I am the way and the light, he said, *none can come to the father except through me.*

Wounds opened up in the palms of his hands, and blood began to flow.

The pair stared at this blasphemy, this profane stigmata. Penny raged in silence and wordlessly spoke in a tiny voice inside Stephen's head. *The portal is huge, but I don't think it always was.*

He glanced at it. *It's getting bigger?*

Yes. Slowly, but yes. I think that as this entity grows in power, the portal widens.

So... eventually...

Over enough time, yeah. She squeezed his hand. *We have to close it somehow. If we don't, it'll keep expanding forever.*

Come. The priest said. *Come and join your brothers and sisters. Come be part of the divine feast.* And with those words the ghosts began to step forwards again, passing Everett on all sides as he stood in his Christlike pose, pouring blood from his palms. A wound had opened in his right side too, and ran like wine from a cask.

The horde was approaching the steps in silence, the only sound their watery footsteps on the abominable floor. Their white eyes were wide and hungry. Their arms crooked, spindly, and reaching for them.

Penny pulled Stephen away from them, back up the slippery steps and towards the altar.

We're dead. That was all Stephen could think. We've walked into hell and there's no way out. How could I ever have imagined we had a chance? Me, of all people? Against this? I was right. I'm nothing. I'm weak. I should have left the moment I clapped eyes on this godforsaken town. I should never have come at all. I want to go home. I want a normal world, not this madness, this nightmare. I'm so scared. I'm so fucking scared. I want to see my mother. I want to see Ed. There's no hope, not against this.

Whitey! Penny was yelling at him. He just stared

blankly into space like someone drugged. His eyes half-lidded, his mouth contorted in horror. *Whitey!*

The first of the vast crowd stepped with dead, pale feet onto the first steps of the altar.

Perhaps I deserved this all along, Stephen thought, perhaps this is my punishment. Perhaps I was always destined for this, and this is my destiny coming true.

Penny had dragged him as far as was possible. Now they were pressed against the back wall of the sanctuary, beyond the altar itself. There were walls on all sides and the portal was unreachable.

The rotting spirits were at the top of the steps now, and were walking around the slab, their hands like talons and reaching hungrily.

Whitey! Penny screamed, and now she swung him around to face her, taking both of his hands now instead of one, and shaking him like a doll. *Stephen White! You listen to me! Right now!*

He blinked. His eyes sharpened and met hers.

If we lose our connection then this is over! She barked with unmoving lips and eyes on fire. *I know what to do, but if we lose one another, if they separate us, then we won't have the power to do it!*

Stephen reanimated as if electrocuted and he searched her face. *You know what to do? Are you serious? How?*

The portal is a wound, right? She said, and seeing his panic, *Hey, hey. It's okay Steve. It's okay. Just look at me, okay? Don't look at them. Just focus on me. The portal. A wound. Yeah?*

He nodded frantically.

We can make things happen here. We proved it. She said with a voice that shook. The two of them were consumed in shifting shadows now as the dead descended. *Just like this thing has power in our world, we have power in this one. We made light, Steve? Get it? We* made *light happen just by both wanting it. So think, what else could we make?*

Stephen stared, listening but lost. *So... so, what?*

How do you seal a wound, Whitey? She shook him again. *How do you knit a wound closed?*

But there was no more time for words.

The ghosts had them.

38

Conflagration

They were pushed to the warm, pulsing floor by the sheer weight of bodies.

There was no crying out, no screaming; neither of them could form the thought to do so. They were both on their backs, cheeks pressed hard against the revolting ground as hands as cold as ice fixed on them. Hands as dry as old leather, as sharp as knotted sticks, wrapped around their arms and wrists. Slimy fingers that stank of old mould wormed their way around their necks and squeezed. The weight of dead flesh as cold as snow pressed them into the floor, crushing them. All was dark.

The first collision alone had yanked one of Stephen's hands from hers, but the other one he still had, their two fists as one and clamped together so hard it could break bones.

Don't let go of me. Penny's voice was distant. He clung to it like a life raft in a storm. *Don't let them...*

Stephen kept his eyes screwed shut. He couldn't bear them touching him. Couldn't stand them so close. Their faces, their horrific faces were inches from his. Thin limbs and joints poking into him, crushing him.

Then suddenly he felt them starting to pull. He felt his arm yanked, and stretched out to its maximum. He shifted, dragged across the floor away from Penny.

Don't let go!

Cruel hands were grabbing at theirs now, trying to prize fingers apart, scratching at them, squirming their fingers into their closed fists.

Penny! Help me!

The weight grew greater. Whether this body of his was real or not, it felt like it was going to break. Bones splintering. His skull, collapsing. More fingers now, clawing at his arm and the hand that held hers, while the others tugged at them. Could his arm pull from its socket? Could they just pull his arm clean *off*, tearing it from the shoulder cuff?

Seal the wound! Penny's distant voice screamed. *Close the portal!*

I don't know how! He bellowed, finding his voice again. It resonated so high in his head and hers that it physically hurt.

Yes you do! How do you seal a wound?

Stitches? Bandages? I don't know Penny, I don't fucking know! I can't hold on, I can't...

Despite the crushing weight and the clawing hands, and the huge pressure of them being pulled from one another, somehow, Penny's fingers fastened harder around his.

You cauterize it! She yelled.

His eyes snapped open in the darkness. The figures writhed on top of him. Dusty old clothes, bloody wounds, cold flesh and the overwhelming stink of purification swarmed him.

But Stephen White was calm now. Even as the monstrous face of The Green Lady game grinning into view, with her bleached-white eyes and her elongated skull, and her black rotten tongue running along his jawbone. Even as their palms were separated, and only the interlacing of their fingertips kept them joined, Stephen was calm.

He found a quiet place within himself. A place where he was still, and solid. A place of certainty and faith. Faith in himself, faith in Penny, and even, to his surprise, faith in something far bigger than the both of them. Something greater than this hellish place and the entity that had created it. Something eternal. Something divine.

He drew a strength to himself that he didn't know he possessed, and it was no effort at all. He found his power and his worth. Stephen White fully realised himself. And in doing so he found that his connection to the divine had always been there, just like Penny had always said. And then Stephen spoke.

Let's burn this place to the fucking ground.

And together, with their fingers joined and their connection pulsing like an electrical current, they both visualised fire. A fire that burned hotter than the centre of a sun. A fire that could melt steel and rock, a fire that could liquefy bones, a fire that could sear flesh and cauterize wounds.

Something screamed.

The ghosts that swarmed and crushed upon the pair suddenly froze, and a moment later they started to shift. The weight loosened from Stephen's chest and from around his throat.

Penny started scrabbling against the sodden floor beside him, wrestling and writhing, her arm swinging and jolting his all around in turn. The ghosts were moving. The ghosts were lifting from them.

Stephen managed to lift his head, straining his neck to see where the scream had come from.

The spirits were standing up, climbing off them slowly but surely, and turning to face something that he couldn't see.

He kicked at them, sending some staggering into the others, thudding and falling. Some of them toppled on shinbones snapped in two as his boot struck them, and collapsed to the ground in a heap.

Using one arm to push, he scuffled into a sitting position with his back pressed against the wall. He turned left and saw his arm, scratched and sliced, and the fingers that were still tightly laced with hers. Penny stared back in wonder, never leaving his eyes as she pushed herself up against the wall too.

Together, they looked down the nave as another scream rang out. A scream that shook the very brains in their skulls. The inhuman scream of something never alive.

It was the priest.

He was ablaze.

The figure was consumed with fire. Waves of roaring flames rolled over the human form but it didn't move or thrash about on the floor. It just stood there, burning. The flames rose wild and high, licking and twisting up into the spired ceiling and spouting thick black smoke.

It was still standing bolt upright with its arms raised in the sign of the cross. Its cassock billowed and whipped in the intense heat. The blood that poured from its hands bubbled and hissed. Its head was flung back and burned like a great candle.

The ghosts were all crowded round the figure now, encircling the spectacle and staring dumbly with blank, lifeless faces. The flames danced in the whiteness of their eyes and illuminated their corrupted flesh.

Penny and Stephen, dumbstruck, exchanged a flash of a glance. A great understanding passed between them, and then in unison they climbed to their feet. She reached out to him, and now both of their hands were firmly locked again.

They stepped across the sanctuary together, coming down the steps. The heat was blistering, making the already hot space more of an oven, and they felt the cleansing fire almost catch their skin and clothes. And it was good, and it was right.

Then they turned to see the portal.

The impossible thing was rippling with flames too, but not in the same way as the priest. No smoke billowed from it, and the intense centre of the blaze, blindingly white and flashing like an electrical discharge, matched the centre of the portal's circle. The flames coming from it didn't whip upwards, they whipped inwards from all edges. It was as if the fire itself was burning through the portal to whatever lay on the other side.

It roared and crackled, spat and steamed, and now, like real flesh, it began to tremble and shake.

The room suddenly broke into spasms all around them, throwing the pair about. The ground shook like muscle violently contracting, and the walls of the unholy church tensed and swelled, just like a human body would. Then the air came, that horrible breath of a cosmic being beyond understanding, whooshing and spinning around them like a cyclone. The flames only grew stronger because of this, and they sparked and bellowed into further intensity.

Stephen and Penny fell to their knees, but would not let go.

The room was filling with acrid smoke, blacker than black and as searing as sulphur. It swirled in the great whirlwind of dying breath as the flames raged and the roar became deafening.

Penny pulled him close and held him. Her arms

wrapped around his middle, and his hands clasped the small of her back and the back of her head and he secured her to his chest.

Look! He heard her say, and he lifted his head from hers to watch.

The ghosts were levitating. The great crowd slowly but surely lifted from the fleshy shuddering floor as gracefully as swimmers in deep water. There went the faces they knew and the hundreds, if not thousands, of people they didn't, from ages past. Centuries of lost souls were rising in unison up into the swirling vortex of the flaming smoke.

And as they reached the black cyclone they joined with it. Each of them began to dissipate into the dense vapor, flaking into pieces and into dust, exploding into fragments and then crumbling into dark sand. And the dust and sand spun up into obscurity like a desert storm, lost to the smoke and the fire. The last of them went, and then the phantoms were gone.

The portal was simply a white, glowing sphere now. It hung in the air like a burning sun, so dazzling that they couldn't look at it. The church was bleeding. The arteries had burst open, and the veins released like sieves. The blood that spouted and sputtered was black, and when it met the intense heat it hissed and steamed and bubbled, giving off the powerful vapour of copper, sharp and gagging.

Penny spoke. Despite the chaos and the thundering of the flesh and the burning and the storm, Penny spoke in a quiet calm voice.

I bind you to your realm, she said, *I forbid you to return. I banish you. I cleanse this place. I cleanse our souls.*

The portal flashed. Just once. A great detonation of white light so brilliant that it consumed everything as easily as a silent, infinite explosion.

Penny and Stephen closed their eyes as the light touched them, and then the church was gone.

The burning priest was gone.

The portal was gone.

Stephen spoke one last time before the brilliant light died, and what he said both broke Penny's heart, and filled it with love.

I can... I can see my son... Penny! I think I can see...

39

Like Mist in the Rays of Morning

Penny was staring into the face of Ned Bailey.

She was standing upright in the medieval chapel, staring wide-eyed at the tall figure of Ned, whose nose looked broken. Blood had stained the entire lower section of his face and hair, and his nostrils were black with it. He was staring back at her with equally wild eyes and he was brandishing a pocketknife, raised high and poised.

Standing beside Ned, frozen in place just like him, was Dave, the young skinny lad carrying the golden crucifix. He stared at Penny, then looked at Ned with absolute bewilderment.

There was a groan and the two men turned. Sam was heaving his heavyset frame to its feet, purple-faced, with a hand to a great lump on the side of his head. He squinted and blinked, and looked from his position beside the front doors to his fellows. Their eyes met, and then they all turned and looked at Penny.

Ned realised he was holding the knife, gaped at it with horror, and dropped it as if it was scalding hot. Disorientated, he took a shaky step back away from her, his eyes darting about as if he'd been awoken from a dream he was sure had been real.

'I…' he croaked, '… I apologise… I don't quite know what I'm… you're Miss Black, aren't ye? Everett's lass?'

The girl was a mess. Her hair was soaked and muddy, her makeup washed away, her dress ripped and slashed, and she looked like she'd been rolling about in a field. She even had a couple of nasty scratches across her chest. She stared at them as if they were monsters.

'I...' Ned looked to his mates, '...do any of you lads know what we're doing here? What in god's name is this about?'

They shrugged and looked around, realising they were in the church.

'Bloody 'ell is this All Saint's?' Sam said from across the nave.

Before anyone could answer, Dave made a noise of exclamation and said 'who the heck's that down there?'

Penny had been too transfixed by these bizarre happenings to even look around. She was back in the church, all right. It was night, the rain was falling, and up until – what had been for Ned and his men – seconds ago, she and Stephen had been in a life-and-death fight with them. The astral journey had been instantaneous. The lights still buzzed in the twin candelabras hanging above them, and the church, made of stone and glass and tiles, was exactly as it'd been before. Though, not entirely.

She looked down to where Dave was gawking.

Stephen.

He was on his back beside the plinth with the cross and candles. One arm lay sprawled out. His fingers were frozen in a reach, his fingers still spread out. His eyes were closed.

She knelt, forcing herself to find the strength to look at him. His skin was as pale as stone, beaded with cold sweat, and his mouth was agape with a look of wonder.

'You,' she said, surprised by the sound of her own voice, real and loud and human, '*all* you boys. I think it'd be best if you left now, and never spoke about this again. Not to anyone else, not to each other.'

'Young Miss!' Ned said. 'Shouldn't we fetch the doctor or call for an ambulance? Whoever this man is, he needs help!'

'Is...' her voice broke and she hunched over, her back to them, '...is the warden still there?'

A pause as they looked around. 'Fled,' came Sam's voice.

'Then I'll call the ambulance myself.'

'Miss Black, I really think I want to know what's going on here! I mean... this is madness! What are we all doing here? Why can't I remember what..'

'I think you know.' She replied, her voice thick. 'I think, deep down, you know. And I think it's something you'll be glad to forget.'

Ned swallowed, looking down at himself, at his hands. The hands started to shake. He closed his eyes and in a small broken voice said 'oh... oh, dear lord in heaven.'

'You'll forget. Told you.' Penny said. 'Now go. You won't be seeing me again. There'll probably be a call from the police, though.'

After an uncertain pause, the men wordlessly moved. The scratching of shoes on a gravelly stone floor. The turn of a key in a lock and a heavy iron bolt screaming with rust when drawn back. The door swung open and paused there.

'Out!' Penny yelled, and it closed quietly.

The church was still. The silence hung heavy.

She fell to sobbing then.

A miracle in disguise had entered her life in the most unexpected way, and exited just as quickly. A man the opposite of her. Ying to her Yang. White to her Black.

A man she might well have hated when they first met. But the man that had now left had been a man she'd grown to love. Her best friend, really. A soulmate. A cosmic twin.

She rested her head against his chest and she held his hand.

'Oh, you silly old man.' She whispered. 'You broke your own heart.'

He might have seen himself as a nobody; a miserable alcoholic, unhappy in his work and his life, with a broken family and a lost son, but she saw through such trivialities. She saw through to his soul; compassionate, funny, gifted, and – right to the very end – brave.

She lifted his hand and put a black-smudge kiss upon it, and then upon his forehead.

Something caught her attention then. She couldn't have exactly said now, but some sense in her tingled. Pins and needles in her fingertips. The unmistakeable rush of cold on the back of her neck, washing down her arms and raising gooseflesh all over her.

She looked up.

Down the length of the gloomily-lit nave, where it became the transept, someone was standing.

The altar was behind the someone, but she could still see it. The shape was translucent and shimmering with a quiet light in the shadows of the sanctuary. Transparent. Not quite there. An outline, really. A man, standing in the centre of the tiled floor, and beside him there was a child. A little boy, standing at chest height.

She couldn't see faces, nothing so distinct, but she knew the shape of the man all too well. And, she suspected, she knew who the boy was too.

The tall man, fading in and out of sight like mist

evaporating in the sun, turned and looked at the child, and in turn the child, on tiptoes, looked up at him. The little boy raised a hand, and the man reached out and took it.

The two of them looked back at her now, far across the space, as she knelt beside the body of the apparition that now saw her.

Penny smiled wide through her flowing tears and her heart swelled to bursting.

She nodded at them with understanding, and then she blew them a kiss.

The ghosts just looked back at her and did nothing, but she could feel them. She could feel their love for one another, and maybe just a little for her, too.

But then, as the dawn began to dissolve the rainclouds outside to illuminate the cold stone with a wash of colours through stained glass, the little boy let go of the man's hand, and his little feet took a single step back.

Penny stared as the man knelt, and the two spirits took part in a wordless discourse that she could not hear. The boy stared up at his father, and the father, slowly and resignedly, nodded his head.

Then the two ghosts evaporated like mist in the rays of morning, and were gone.

Penny stood and dashed across the aisle to the door, where she picked up the phone and frantically dialled.

40

Everywhere is Haunted

The summer was one of the hottest the town had ever seen.

Helmsley market square was bustling. Crowds of holidaymakers and locals piled through the narrow walkways of the weekend market in sunglasses and shorts, while the stalls, full of fruit and vegetables, sweets and keepsakes, rang with the sound of sellers declaring their prices.

The sky was cloudless and the colour of sapphires, the high midday sun was harsh and unforgiving. It swarmed with birds, gliding in the rising hot air and swooping for the flies that gathered in clusters by the trees.

The bells of All Saint's chimed over the din of the market, declaring it to be noon. The spire of the church glistened in the radiant heat, poking up through the flourishing greenery of the churchyard trees. Bright flowers filled the graveyard now, with bees dancing between them, filling the air with a comforting drone.

The Black Swan was the busiest it had ever been. Since it had been taken over by a new landlord last month (the last one vanished overnight. Did a runner. The bailiffs never found him) it had never found itself empty once. The windows and doors were all open to alleviate the intense heat, and music drifted from the windows as drinks were poured and laugher rang.

The sunlight reached the ground nowadays. The air was light again. The shadows were now simply shadows and nothing more. The elderly that retired to the old town lived pleasant, peaceful lives. The weight of the place, the cold of it, was gone.

Nothing that had passed before was remembered by a soul. The locals still entertained their ghost stories, of course, it was good for bringing in the tourists, but no one remembered anything about the darkness that had soured the ground and swallowed up the town. Those local farmers, Ned and the rest? Arrested for grievous bodily harm. Apparently, they'd beaten a man so badly that it caused a heart attack. Bloody lucky they weren't send down for longer. But that was all passed now. Small towns like these didn't concern themselves with nasty things like that. They got off lightly, those men, and they moved away. Never returned to town again.

The castle was busy, too. The high peaks cast a deep shadow over the emerald grass below as white birds circled them. Schoolkids on their holidays ran in and out of the ruins with plastic swords and foam shields as parents picnicked in the shade of the old manor house. Apparently, someone once said that a poltergeist had actually scrawled words in the interior of the east tower. More fanciful local tales. Many searched for the supposed writings, but nothing was found.

Beside the lively square and the noisy pub the shutters of a large white removal van were dragged down, slamming shut with a metallic crash. The engine started, the driver wound down the window and called a few things to the people standing out front, and then the van trundled off, carefully making its way past the marketplace carpark and off out of town.

There was a girl left standing outside of the old Tudor house. It gleamed, dazzlingly white in the sunshine against the stark black of the painted timbers. The sun shone through the lead-latticed windows, creating dusty shafts of light in empty rooms. The wooden post that had been hammered into the grass beside the front gate bore a sign that read *sold*.

A young man with a neat side parting and a pressed suit approached the girl with a clipboard and pen. He gave them to her, and with a smile – albeit a rather melancholy one – she signed the paper, and the following two sheets below that one. The man thanked her, shook her hand, and left.

This young girl was certainly quite a sight, especially in the middle of a hot summer's day when anyone not wearing as little as possible must have looked quite mad. Her hair was as black as coal, her face was as pure a white as the house behind her, and her black eyes and lips made her look like she was more ready for Halloween than an August holiday. Her T-shirt and tight jeans were black, and her boots – huge uncomfortable things, they looked – shone like polished glass. She wore sunglasses, and above her head there rested a large black sunshade umbrella, which she twirled with black-nailed fingers. There was a large bag slung over her other shoulder which she adjusted, heaving it up to keep it steady as she turned back to look at the house.

The girl thought about her father and her mother, her sisters and her youth. She thought about magic and mysteries, about horrors, spirits, and the great unknown. Mostly she thought about the man that had helped save her, saved *all of these people*, from something unspeakable.

And then, turning away, she decided that she had had quite enough of all that. She needed to let the past go. All of it.

She had wasted quite enough of her life trying to right

these wrongs, and now that they were remedied, it was time to start her life over again. And what an exciting, beautiful thing that was.

A car pulled up beside her at the kerb, and politely beeped once.

She smiled at the man in the driver's seat.

He was wearing a fine pinstripe suit with an open collar. His hair, dark with silvery temples, wasn't as short as it used to be, and was no longer severely slicked back. There was stubble on his chin, and his eyes were bright and vivid in the bright sun. He smirked back. Beneath the fine white shirt he wore there was a thin scar that stretched from his breastbone down to the top of his abdomen. A reminder of a life left behind, and a new life promised.

'Coming?' Stephen said.

There were plenty more people in the world that might need the help of someone with talents like theirs. There were plenty more mysteries to uncover, plenty more places smothered by darkness, and troubled by the unnatural. After all, as Penny had put it:

The earth is a graveyard.

Everywhere is haunted.

The girl in black took one last look at the house, the square, the church and the castle, then she climbed into the car and with a grateful heart she pulled the door closed.

The house moved out of her sight, dashing away like a spectre, then the large sign for The Black Swan dashed after it. Then there were rows of old cottages and terraces, and then there were open green fields and a long road ahead.

The girl smiled along with the man at the passing countryside.

'Where to, Miss Black?' Stephen asked, pressing his foot down, swallowing up the rolling moorlands beneath them.

Penny paused to think before a wide grin lit up her pale face.

'I know just the place, Mr White.' She replied.

The car, followed by the van, disappeared over a tall hill and down into a steep valley. The sun blazed in the sky, and the world turned as it should.

ABOUT THE AUTHOR

Tom Newton

Tom Newton is an author from North Yorkshire, England. Finding inspiration in local lore and legend, he has been fascinated by the supernatural all his life, and pours his love of gothic horror and fantasy into his work.

Find him at

https://tomnewtonbooks.com

https://facebook.com/tomjnewtonauthor

https://twitter.com/tomnewtonauthor

https://instagram.com/tomnewtonauthor

BOOKS BY THIS AUTHOR

The Wolves Of Greenwold Hall

North Yorkshire, 1895.
A girl at odds with a cruel world.
A dying lord in a crumbling mansion.
A vast forest with a dark secret that binds them all.

The Wolves of Greenwold hall. A tale of transformation, of old magic, and of visceral horror.

A Bloody Kiss - The Tales Of The Revenants Book One

Alex Sinclair enjoyed a simple and safe life, until a chance meeting with a mysterious woman changed things forever. Gifted with immortallity and plunged into the complex world of the undead, Alex finds himself drawn into a centuries-old conflict, forcing him and his friends into a fight for survival.

Suspended In Dusk - The Tales Of The Revenants Book Two

Alex Sinclair, lost in mourning and desperate for redemption, embarks on a journey that leads him deep into forgotten occult arts. He must journey through hell to find what he seeks, but what he discovers will change the world of the revenants forever.

The sequel to 'A Bloody Kiss', Suspended in Dusk is an epic journey through the heart of purgatory, self-destruction and rebirth. Alliances will change, and the ancient truths of revenant origins will be revealed.

The Last Of The Elders - The Tales Of The Revenants Book Three

The revenants have enjoyed a time of peace, following the world-shaking events of previous years. But that will soon change. Now, the greatest horror the undead have ever faced emerges, threatening their very existence. Alex Sinclar must unravel the mysteries of the past if he and his companions are to save the future.
The third and final installment in The Tales of the Revenants, The Last of the Elders is a work of gothic horror you will never forget.

Printed in Great Britain
by Amazon